IRON WILL

KRIS NORRIS

OTHER BOOKS BY KRIS NORRIS

SINGLES

CENTERFOLD

KEEPING FAITH

IRON WILL

MY SOUL TO KEEP

RICOCHET

ROPE'S END

SERIES

'TIL DEATH

1 - DEADLY VISION

2 - DEADLY OBSESSION

3 - DEADLY DECEPTION

BROTHERHOOD PROTECTORS ~ Elle James

1 - MIDNIGHT RANGER

2 – CARVED IN ICE

3 - GOING IN BLIND

COLLATERAL DAMAGE

1 - FORCE OF NATURE

DARK PROPHECY

1 - SACRED TALISMAN

2 - TWICE BITTEN

3 - BLOOD OF THE WOLF

ENCHANTED LOVERS

1 - HEALING HANDS

FROM GRACE

1 - GABRIEL

2 – MICHAEL

THRESHOLD

1 - GRAVE MEASURES

COLLECTIONS

BLUE COLLAR COLLECTION

INTO THE SPIRIT, BOXED SET

IRON WILL

KRIS NORRIS

Iron Will

Copyright © year, Kris Norris

Edited by Chris Allen-Riley and Jessica Bimberg

Cover Art by Kris Norris

Published by Kris Norris

Released ~ August, 2017

To my cabin sisters, aka the Ladies of the Lake.
Thank you for endless laughs, amazing conversations and for being
part of legendary cautionary tales.

Love you bitches.

CHAPTER ONE

"What the Hell do you mean we lost two more men?"

Cullen James turned, ignoring the way his voice seemed to bounce off the walls of the sheriff's office as he grabbed his hat, clenching it in one hand as he scrubbed the other down his face. He hadn't been gone more than forty-eight hours, and somehow, they'd managed to suffer another setback, making his job that much harder.

He crushed the growl rumbling through his chest. This day was quickly taking a turn for the worse, and the sun hadn't even set, yet. That's when the liquor started talking, making otherwise calm men act like bullies with something to prove. And he couldn't afford to let a stupid fight over cards or a working girl at the saloon lead to more injuries.

He set his jaw, staring at the man off to his left, wishing his feelings for the guy didn't lessen some of the anger coursing through his veins, but it was pointless. Just looking at Lucas eased the tight feeling in his chest. Took the edge off the uncertainty gnawing at his gut. "I sent three men on horseback as guards. How did those idiots manage to get themselves shot?"

Lucas leaned against the wall just inside the doorway, arms crossed over his massive chest, one foot braced against the wood paneling. He gave Cullen an arch of one brow as he shrugged. "Dangerous times, Cullen. You know that. For every armed man we send out to stand watch, three more gunmen are waitin' in the trees, ready to attack whenever the situation looks promisin'. We should consider ourselves lucky. Could have lost the whole damn crew."

Cullen tilted back his head, fighting the urge to slam his fist into the wall, or drown his anger in a bottle of whiskey. Ten weeks. That was how long they had to finish the damn spur before the heavy mountain snow set in, and if the men weren't having shootouts in the saloon, the bloody gangs were raiding the town or ambushing crews on their way back from the rail.

He raked a hand through his hair, cursing under his breath when it flopped back into his eyes. "Any others get injured?"

"Not this time. I just happened to show up before those bandits had gotten off more than a couple of rounds each. Managed to convince the gunmen it was in their best interest to leave, but not before they'd helped themselves to some of our supplies. But it was just dumb luck I was headed back from the outpost. Otherwise, we'd be faced with a room full of patients with no one to treat them."

"What you mean is you're damn lucky you didn't get yourself killed."

Lucas grinned. "You almost sound as if you'd miss me."

"Fuck off. You know what you mean to me."

Lucas' gaze dropped to Cullen's crotch. "You keep promisin'—"

"And you keep turnin' me down...*mate*."

The other man's shoulders drooped, his smile fading into a thin line. "You know why."

"You still think we're missin' a piece of the puzzle."

"Not a piece...a third." He huffed at Cullen's glare. "Don't give me that look. I know you sense it, too. If you didn't, you would have pressed the subject far more than you have." He released a rough breath. "I'm not saying I'm not your mate. Trust me, my damn grizzly is feeling more than a bit possessive where you're concerned. It doesn't like waitin' any more than your Kodiak does. But... We both know we have another mate out there. And somehow, claimin' each other first... It doesn't sit well with either part of me."

Cullen sighed. Fuck, he hated when Lucas was right. And the man was definitely right. Cullen had known the moment they'd met he was bound to Lucas. His scent, his skin, his sheer presence affected Cullen in a way he'd never experienced before. But he also couldn't deny that he'd sensed something was off. Lucas hadn't been lying. The fact they'd been around each other for several months and hadn't yet given in to the fury involved with mating— that was proof enough. Though damn if the other man didn't make Cullen want to put that theory to the test. Slam Lucas against the wall and taste that cocky mouth of his. Feel the man's tongue tangle with his, the hard planes of his body firm against him.

Lucas grinned, the smug tilt only fueling Cullen's possessive feelings. "I know that look, too. And Hell yeah, I want all of that and more...just as soon as we find that missin' piece, as you put it."

Cullen fisted his hands, breathing deeply in the hopes of stemming the fire beneath his skin. Keep his other half from seizing control. A hint of claws scratched at his palms before he managed to pull the animal back—temper it with token promises. Ones he wasn't sure would ever come true. A hand landed on his shoulder, and he turned to gaze at Lucas.

His mate smiled. "I won't be able to fight the urge much longer, either. But until my damn bear decides it's done waitin'..."

Cullen nodded, giving the man a good-natured shove to help calm his beast. "So...do I have a couple of bodies out on the spur I need to tend to? Or did they manage to make it back before succumbing to their injuries?"

"I managed to drag their asses back on the wagons. Wounds weren't all that bad, but without any form of treatment...they bled out." Lucas shook his head as he paced to the other side of the room before turning, again. "We need a doctor, Cullen. A *real* one. Not some drunk barber who thinks bleedin' the men with leeches is the answer to every damn problem that stumbles through his doors. The jackass hasn't saved a single life since that holier-than-thou physician the company hired packed up his clinic and rode out of here three months ago. And we don't have the resources to keep replacin' these men."

Lucas walked over to him. "Word's getting 'round. Everyone knows Buford's gang is shootin' up everything within a hundred miles of Durango, and rail camps and lines are easy picking—gives them a steady supply of explosives and ammunition so they can hit the bigger towns. Maybe take down a bank. As long as we're here and vulnerable, Buford will keep sending men our way, especially when he knows we don't have the resources to protect the line against his numbers. It's getting harder and harder to find good people to fill these spots. This isn't a large-scale undertaking like some of our previous jobs. Being privately commissioned as we are means limited funds, which in turn means smaller crews, less support. We can't afford to lose any more men...not like this. Work's dangerous enough without worrying a trip to the clinic will kill ya."

"I'll send more guards. Ride out myself if I have to."

"And when one of those bastards clips you with a bullet?"

"Cold day in Hell, my friend. We both know that."

"Not if half your attention is focused on worrying about how far we got on the line instead of which scraggly bastard is hidin' behind the next hill."

"Even if that happened, I'll heal. We're not like the others, Lucas, you know that. And I'm far from an easy target."

"Being a shifter doesn't make you invincible." Lucas clasped Cullen's shoulder. "I suppose we could get a few more of our kind out here, seeing as they wouldn't really need medical support, but—"

"But that would end in bloodshed of another kind. If we were fully bonded, we could tolerate having other shifters cross over into our territory, but in our current situation..."

Lucas nodded. "I'll see to the crews. Find more men if we need to, but it won't mean much without a doctor."

"You think I haven't fucking tried?" He stomped across the room, kicking at a chair. It clattered to the floor, the loud sound soothing some of raw feelings burning in his gut. "I've requested a replacement every day for the past three months. No one wants the job, simple as that. Hell, they don't even get off the damn supply train, just stare at the makeshift town through the window and go right on back to Boston or New York or wherever the Hell else they came from. Face it, the kind of man that'd be willin' to come this far and work in these conditions quit after the war. And these new doctors simply don't want to make that kind of sacrifice. Not when they can find work in the big cities or established towns. The kind with money and shops and federal marshals."

"The war's been over for thirty years."

"Land's still tainted with blood. You don't clean that kind of horror away in a hundred years. The farther we go, the worse it gets." He scrubbed a hand through his hair, pushing the damp mass out of his eyes. "I'll send another telegram. Maybe if they believe the line's in jeopardy, they'll find someone who won't quit before they've stepped onto that platform."

"The line's always been in jeopardy."

Cullen scowled when the door squeaked open, the glare of the setting sun streaming through the open space. He raised his hand, shielding his eyes from the light as a dark figure walked through the doorway, a long shadow stretching across the floor.

"Bloody Hell." Cullen shoved his hat back on, adjusting it low over his forehead. "Shut the damn door before we all go blind and the room fills with dust."

The floor creaked, followed by the slamming of the door. Cullen blinked as the room dimmed, staring at the person standing just inside the doorway. Blue eyes held his gaze, tousled strands of brown hair fluttering around her face. She took a step forward, placing a couple of bags beside the door before removing a black Stetson and shaking out a mass of long hair across her shoulders. It disappeared down her back, the lazy curls bouncing as she settled her weight on one foot, the other tapping restlessly against the wooden floor. Her oilskin jacket covered her body, the open section in the front displaying a white shirt and tan trousers. He didn't miss the belt slung low over her waist, or the twin handles resting against her hips.

Cullen gave her body a long slow sweep, then focused on her face. "Can we help you?"

She glanced between the men then stepped over to him, the hollow echo of her footsteps ringing through the room. "They told me I could find a Mr. Cullen James in here."

Cullen smirked. "Guess that depends on whether you're here to help me or issue a duel."

Her lips quirked, a hint of a smile lifting one corner. "I try to avoid killin' people unless it's absolutely necessary." She rocked on her heels, seemingly uncertain before tilting her head. "Mr. Gilmore sent me. The name's Hollis Chambers."

Cullen glanced at Lucas, but the man merely shrugged. Shit. Cullen really didn't have time for journalists or whatever this woman had to offer. He motioned to his partner. "This is Lucas Quinn, the resident sheriff. Now, with all due respect, Miss Chambers, it's been one Hell of a day. Raidin' parties are attackin' my crews, and I've got a barber who thinks he can cure men by bleedin' them dry. I really don't have time for riddles."

Her expression never faltered. "Sounds like you have more than a few issues at Devil's Gate, so I'll get straight to the point. Mr. Gilmore hired me to fill that position you've had vacant for some time."

"Position?"

She reached into an inner pocket, removing a telegram. "I believe this will clear things up for you."

Cullen took the paper, unfolding it before holding it up. He read through the short sentences, his gaze rising to hers once he'd finished. He gave Lucas a sideways glance before crossing his arms over his chest, her telegram still clenched in one fist. "Are you serious?"

Those perfect lips quirked, again, as humor crinkled her eyes. "Do I look as if I'm jokin'?"

He snorted, handing the paper to Lucas, smiling when the man had a similar reaction. Cullen nodded at her. "So, you're telling me my boss hired you to be the resident doctor? *You?*"

Her eyes narrowed slightly, the line of her jaw firming. "Tell me, Mr. James, which part do you find incredulous? That Mr. Gilmore actually found someone to come out to this Hellhole, or that it's me?"

"Both."

"I see. Then, let me put your fears to rest. Yes, I really am a doctor. I graduated from Philadelphia four years ago, and I've been workin' in small towns and camps just like this one ever since. No, I didn't travel all this way on a ruse or a whim or to admire the scenery, and yes...I know how to use the guns strapped to my hips." She arched a brow. "Did I leave anything out?"

He resisted the chuckle that bubbled in his chest. "I admire your tenacity, Miss Chambers—"

"It's Dr. Chambers, or Hollis."

He glanced at Lucas, slowly releasing a harsh breath. "Dr. Chambers—"

"But?" She scoffed at him. "There was definitely a but coming, so..."

"While I'm not saying you aren't qualified, I'm not sure how well-received you'll be."

She smirked. "So, you're saying that the men in this camp would rather die at the hands of a barber pretendin' to be a doctor than be saved by a woman who really is one."

It wasn't a question, and he didn't miss the piercing tone.

He sighed, leaning back against a desk. "That's one way of putting it."

"Then, the men here have all spent far too much time in the hot sun." She pointed at the telegram. "None of which matters. I was hired, plain and simple." She leaned in closer, her breath rustling the edge of his shirt. "And just to make things clear, even I didn't want to come out this far. It's no secret how many men you lose on a daily basis, or the risks involved in merely taking the train to get here. There isn't anyone else willin' to apply for the job. As it is, Mr. Gilmore had to guarantee my wage for the next three months, regardless of whether I stay or not. Thinkin' it's in your best interest to show me to the clinic —put me to work." She straightened, plastering on a sweet smile. "Unless you'd rather have the barber continue on as he has. I know where you can get a whole jug full of leeches for next to nothing."

Lucas took a step forward, offering her the scrunched paper. "With all due respect, Doc... We can't force the townsfolk to accept you, regardless of your credentials. Afraid the men that work the rails aren't quite as forward thinkin' as other, more refined folks. They tend to think a woman has a certain place."

She hitched out one hip. "Let me guess. On their backs with their legs spread wide?"

He coughed, glancing at Cullen as if seeking help.

Cullen pushed to his feet. "Right or wrong, it's the way things are in a rail camp, being they're so transient. The women that travel with us up the spur are either wives or painted ladies. Maybe a teacher or a seamstress if we get lucky. Other than that..."

Hollis laughed, the tension easing from her body. "I see. Well then, I suppose I'll just head on over to the saloon. Bide my time until I can catch another train out of here. As I said...I've been paid either way."

She placed the telegram on the desk behind him, giving him one more long sweeping gaze. Then, she tipped her hat and spun, making it to the door before looking back at them. "Shame, though. The railroad can't afford to send you anyone else. Guess that means you'll need those leeches, after all. Good day, gentlemen."

She opened the door then picked up her bags, her silhouette melding into the blinding light of the setting sun before the door slammed shut again, nothing but a billow of dust in the air as proof she'd ever ventured inside.

Lucas moved in front of Cullen, glancing from the doorway back to him. "That was...unexpected."

"She was serious. Gilmore actually hired her and sent her out this way. What the Hell was the man thinkin'?"

"Maybe that we'd stop askin' for something he obviously can't give us? Hell if I know for sure, but we'll never get this spur built if we can't stop men from dyin' from a simple cut, or a case of dysentery. One outbreak of cholera, and we'll lose over half of the workers here."

"You say that like I don't already know. I'm just not sure what you want me to do. I've begged, repeatedly, and Hollis Chambers seems to be the company's solution."

Lucas turned, once again leaning against the wall. "She seemed..."

"Antagonistic?"

"Intelligent. Hell, at least she went to medical school, which is a far sight better than any other option we've come across. Pretty, too."

"I agree, but... You were right. We can't force anyone to accept her, even if she turned out to be a brilliant physician. And we both know if she stays—puts herself in a vulnerable situation—she's liable to get hurt."

"You mean raped."

Cullen growled at the thought, cursing when Lucas arched a brow. "What?"

"Haven't heard you growl over the thought of someone getting hurt since...well, since me." He straightened, staring at the closed door as his expression softened.

"Whoa, hold on. It doesn't mean what you're thinkin'. My other half simply doesn't like the idea of any woman getting hurt."

"Nor does mine, but that was more than idle concern."

"It's called being a decent human being. I'd like to think at least half of me fits that description. And you'd be the first to rip the throat out of any man who took advantage of a woman that way."

"Damn straight, but—"

"No buts. Besides, if she meant more to us, don't you think we both would have picked up on it? I knew you were my mate the moment I shook your hand, caught your scent."

"As did I, but need I point out we didn't touch her? Hell, I don't even recall getting a whiff of her. Too much dust in the air, and with her wearin' that coat—the oilskin must have masked her natural scent. Not to mention the fact I'm pretty much useless when you're this close. All I can focus on is *your* scent. Everything else just gets lost."

Cullen smiled at the thought. Though he didn't enjoy having to resist that part of him, knowing Lucas was equally affected—invested—made it slightly more bearable.

He grinned at the man. "Lucas...she's just a passin' stranger. Albeit an attractive one, even if she does her best to hide it. Though I suppose dressin' like a man helps with the image." He chuckled. "Can't say I'm not more than a bit curious to know if she really can handle those pistols on her hips."

"I know what I said, what's likely to be the outcome, but maybe we should give her a chance?"

"Not that I wouldn't love to do that, it's just not sensible. Between you spendin' every wakin' hour trying to police the town, keep these men alive, and me spendin' half my day scoutin' out the rest of the spur... We don't have time to babysit a doctor who might end up getting her fool head shot off because she can't seem to curb her tongue. It's safer for everyone if she just hops on the next train back to Boston."

Lucas sighed, giving Cullen a curt nod before heading for the door. He paused at the threshold, glancing back at his mate. "I'll go send out a few telegrams. See if I can round up another half a dozen men."

"We'll find a way to get this damn line finished. Promise. Then, maybe we should head north. My family still owns a few purchases in Alaska. It's new territory. Might be just what we need. Wouldn't have to hide what we are up there."

"Guess it's worth considerin', assumin' we're both still alive when this is over."

Cullen frowned as Lucas opened the door then left, the hollow thud of it closing resonating through Cullen's chest. One break. That's all they needed, and they could push the damn line through. Too bad there wasn't one in sight.

He glanced at the crumpled paper. The girl was right about something, he just wasn't sure if it was him who had been standing out in the sun too long. Who had lost touch with the cold reality of how bad the situation truly was. If he'd just sent his only chance at salvation on a one-way trip out of town.

CHAPTER TWO

"Of all the pig-headed, ignorant..."

Hollis Chambers muttered to herself as she strode across the dusty street, her displeasure mirrored in the gait. She should have known better than to trust Gilmore—believe the man when he'd assured her she'd be more than welcomed. While he hadn't been exaggerating about the camp's desperate need for a physician, he'd greatly overestimated her appeal. At least at the other camps she'd resided in, she'd been given a chance to pass or fail, even if that test seemed to be never-ending. Here... She hadn't gotten past the two men in charge.

She cursed, wishing she'd acted on her instincts and smacked the smug grins off both of their faces. Damn, those two boys were infuriating. Gilmore had shown her the telegrams Cullen had sent the man—how he'd practically begged for his boss to send someone, anyone— yet, Cullen had brushed her off without even bothering to see if she was worth taking a chance on. If twisting the arms of the men in the camp to accept her might be worth his while.

She shoved at the swinging doors to the saloon, heading straight for the bar. More than a few gazes followed her progress, their attention no doubt centered on the pistols on her hips. She hadn't been lying to Cullen. She knew how to shoot, how to fight—thanks to her father's unusual occupation. Not that she enjoyed killing people. But she'd discovered long ago that, regardless of her desire, she couldn't save every soul.

Hollis snorted. She'd read Cullen and Lucas' disbelief. Had sensed that they thought she'd merely been posturing. Exaggerating her abilities. Of course, being underestimated was one of her greatest attributes. Some might have seen her gender as limiting, but she saw it as a way of gaining the upper hand. Men expected her to be weak. Fragile. And she had no qualms about proving otherwise. Knowing she could treat most of the wounds she inflicted didn't hurt, either. Though even she realized that her medical skill could only go so far. That sometimes defending herself meant someone else would suffer.

The barkeep stopped in front of her, giving her a hard glare. "Can I help you?"

She placed a few coins on the bar. "Whiskey."

The man gave her the once over then poured her a glass. She tipped her hat, taking a seat at one of the tables closer to the wall. A spot where she could watch the other patrons interact without being too close. She'd never been fond of saloons or large gatherings, but under the circumstances, it seemed a better option than waiting for the next train somewhere else—like the sheriff's office.

Hollis took a sip of the alcohol, allowing the liquid to

burn away some of her tension. She didn't like being dismissed, especially by Cullen and his friend, Lucas. For some reason, their rejection had stung more than usual. Whether it'd been the knowing looks they'd given each other or the seeming ease with which they'd discounted her, she wasn't sure. All she knew was that she'd worked hard to appear unaffected as she'd spun on her heel and left.

Disappointment soured her stomach as more workers entered the saloon, the noise level rising with each new wave of men. She watched the steady flow of people for over an hour before venturing to the train platform. But the departure time came and went with nothing more than a shrug by the man at the station. He offhandedly mentioned the times for the following day then left.

Anger heated her skin as she returned to the tavern and ordered another drink and a bowl of stew, finally switching to something less potent as the sun sank below the horizon, dusk settling around the camp. Just her damn luck she'd get stuck at the end of a dead-end spur, with no other recourse but to wait it out.

She shoved her two bags beneath the small table, resting her feet on the edge while keeping her hat low over her face. She glanced at the barkeep, wondering if the man would let her stay the night, when the doors to the tavern crashed open. Three men stormed through the entrance, carrying a fourth, blood staining the man's shirt. They headed toward a table on the far side of the saloon, shouting out for someone named Henry.

The man in question rose from the table, knocking over his chair. It clattered onto the wood floor, cutting through the din of conversation. Henry's mouth gaped open as the other men cleared off the surface with a sweep of their arms, shattering glasses onto the hard planks below then draping their friend over the table, a muted groan lighting the air.

One of the men grabbed Henry's shirt, yanking him closer. "One of Buford's men clipped my brother in the shoulder. Fix him."

Henry pulled free, then crossed his arms over his chest. "The man's been shot. Bleedin' him ain't gonna fix nothing. The only place he's going is to the undertaker's."

"I know he's been shot. Why the Hell do you think we dragged him in here? You're always runnin' your mouth off about how skilled you are. How you're as good as any doctor the company ever sent out here. That means it's your job to fix him before I decide you're not worth keeping around."

Henry shoved at the man when he tried to grab him, tripping them both back a few steps when the swinging doors opened again, Lucas and Cullen barreling through. Lucas pushed his way through the crowd, grabbing the injured man's brother and pulling him off Henry. Cullen moved around to the opposite side, stepping between the others and Henry, motioning the surrounding men to stand down.

Lucas palmed his weapon. "Easy, boys. Everyone just take a step back." He shuffled closer to the brother. "Frank, you need to calm down before you get yourself shot."

Frank pointed at Henry. "I'll calm down just as soon that bastard takes care of Jack."

Henry lunged at Frank, held back by Cullen's arm. "No

one can save your brother, now, you fool. He's already dead."

Cullen pushed the man back. "Are you trying to get yourself killed? Just do everyone a favor and shut the Hell up." He cursed, shoving Henry, again, when he tried to move past him. "I mean it, Henry. There are more than a few men in here who would love to see you covered in your own damn leeches, so back away."

Henry sneered but stopped pushing against Cullen's hold, finally taking a couple of steps backwards. He mumbled something under his breath, looking as if he was considering making a run for the door.

Cullen gave the man a curt nod, glancing down at Jack splayed across the table. Though Hollis was too far away to see the full extent of Jack's injuries, she knew by the tight press of Cullen's mouth and the concerned look he gave Lucas that Cullen wasn't expecting the man to live.

Tension clenched Hollis' stomach, but she forced herself to remain in her seat. Allow the events to unfold without getting involved. It didn't matter that her skin crawled at the thought of sitting idly by as the man slowly bled to death. Of ignoring the incessant voice in her head begging her to uphold her oath. Both Cullen and Lucas had made their feelings regarding her presence crystal clear, and she knew she'd never gain anyone's respect unless they made the first move. An uneasy calm settled over her as she watched the two men exchange another look before Cullen sighed.

He raked his hand through his hair, nodding at Frank. "I hate to admit it, but your brother's lost a lot of blood. Even if Henry patches him up, he might not make it."

Frank sneered at Henry still standing behind Cullen. "He ain't dead, yet."

Cullen gave Frank a grim smile. "I realize that but…we all know this is way beyond Henry's ability to treat." He glared back at Henry. "In fact, everything is beyond his ability to treat."

Henry huffed. "I don't see you doing any better? If you're so disappointed with my skill, then why haven't you found us another doctor? Men around here are droppin' like flies, yet you keep telling us the same excuses. Maybe you're the one who needs to 'fix this'."

Cullen twisted toward the man, his sheer size making Henry take another hurried step back. Having interacted with Cullen and Lucas on their own, Hollis hadn't really noticed how much larger the two men were, standing several inches taller than any of the other men in the bar. But it wasn't just their height—their shoulders were broader, their bodies thicker. And she guessed, by the way their shirts bunched against their torsos, that well-formed muscles flexed beneath the fabric.

Heat swirled through her core, settling uncomfortably in her groin. She gave herself a mental shake. Despite the fact the men were ruggedly handsome—both sporting square jaw lines with high cheekbones and symmetrical features—their attitudes earlier had told her all she needed to know. And she'd be damned if she allowed herself to feel anything for either of them other than the anger still churning in her gut.

Cullen stared at Henry, his lips quirking slightly when the other man took another step back. "Don't you think I've tried?" He turned back to Frank. "I've asked. Hell, I've fucking begged, and all they've sent me was a wo—"

His voice cut off sharply as Lucas swatted him in the back, pointing toward Hollis when Cullen glared at the sheriff over his shoulder. Cullen frowned, following the man's motion. His gaze clashed with hers, disbelief widening his eyes. He held up his hand, silently telling the other men to wait before picking his way over to her table.

He stopped a foot away, giving her body a long, slow sweep, finally making eye contact, again. He nodded at her. "I thought you were headin' back?"

She shrugged. "Train never showed."

"I see…" He seemed to force himself to swallow before waving at Jack's body spread out on the table. "Seeing as you're still here…we could use your assistance."

"What?" Frank pushed his way across the room, barely held back by Cullen's arm across his chest once he'd reached them. "We need a doctor, James, not some tavern girl who makes a living spreadin' her legs."

Cullen fisted the man's shirt, tossing him backwards. "Goddamn it, Frank. Shut up before you guarantee your brother dies by sunrise." He released a harsh breath, looking at her, again. "Miss Chambers…" He cleared his throat at her arched brow. "Dr. Chambers—"

"Doctor?" Frank tried to push past Cullen, only to end up on his ass. "Women ain't no doctors."

Cullen growled this time, the sound far more animalistic than she thought possible. Something flashed in his eyes, but the hint of red she thought she'd glimpsed was gone before she could be certain it had ever been there.

"One more word and I'll have Lucas drag you out of here. See that you spend the next few days in jail." He turned to her. "Doctor, as you can see, we're in need of your... expertise."

Hollis thumbed the empty glass beside her hand. "I'd love to help out, Mr. James, but...as I recall, you and Sheriff Quinn didn't feel my services were welcome here."

Cullen's jaw clenched, jumping the muscle in his temple. "Obviously, that was a bit of a rash decision."

She glanced at the injured man. "Your barber was right about one thing. That kind of wound won't heal itself. Without treatment, that man will be dead within the hour."

"Which is why we could use your assistance."

"No fucking way she's touching my brother." Frank pushed upright, only to be held back by Lucas when the other man darted across the room.

Cullen shook a finger at him. "Shut. Up."

She smiled at him. "Again, I'd like to help, but..."

Cullen exhaled, fisting his hands at his side. "Fine. Consider yourself officially hired. Now, if you'd kindly take a peek..."

Hollis placed her feet on the floor, rocking onto her heels. She glanced at the surrounding men, noting the firm scowls gracing their faces. Damn, she knew those looks, and it generally meant she'd have to prove herself in more ways than one before the night was over.

She skimmed her palms over the handles of her guns before bending and grabbing one of her bags. Then, she made her way over to the other table, arching her brow. "Goddamn. Don't you men know even the basics about keeping someone alive? You need to put pressure on the wound. Stem the bleedin'. Christ, he looks like a bloody ghost."

She placed her bag beside Jack, reaching for the guy's shirt when a hand grabbed her shoulder and yanked her backwards. She managed to catch herself against another worker a moment before a fist connected with her jaw, tumbling her against a table then onto the floor. She hit hard, sending black dots swimming across her vision as the metallic taste of her own blood filled her senses. Shouts erupted around her, followed by the sounds of fighting.

Years of training took over, and Hollis rolled onto her hands and knees, quickly gaining her feet. Cullen and Lucas each had two guys by the shirt, doing their best to toss them toward the swinging doors as more men threw punches at each other. Frank appeared in front of her, arm cocked backwards as he readied his next strike. She gauged his attack, dodging the punch as she spun out of the way, then landing one of her own. Then, she kicked the back of his knee, dropping him hard to the ground. Another punch had him face down, blood trickling from his nose.

A hand landed on her shoulder, but she elbowed the guy firmly in the chest, following the strike with a hit beneath his jaw, snapping his head up and away. The movement broke his grip, giving her enough time to grab a chair and slam it against him, crashing both to the floor. She used the momentary distraction to draw her guns, cocking them then pointing them point blank at two more men as they closed in on her.

The men stopped, the sound of the hammers clicking into place spreading silence throughout the saloon. The shouting died away as all gazes focused on her.

Hollis blew the wisps of hair out of her face, endlessly

scanning the room as she glared at the surrounding men, sweat stinging the cut across her lip and forehead. "Enough! I swear to God, I'll shoot the next man who so much as looks at me the wrong way."

She kept surveying the crowd, searching for anyone who might challenge her, when a flicker of movement caught her attention near the bar. She cocked her head, firing a single shot when the barkeep raised a rifle in her direction. The bullet hit him in the hand, knocking the gun from his grasp. He howled and reeled backwards, grabbing his hand as blood seeped out between his fingers. A hushed gasp passed through the crowd, all focus returning to her.

She didn't flinch, keeping the weapons aimed at the men closest to her as she arched a brow. Her gaze clashed with Lucas', the amused tilt of his lips catching her off-guard. She didn't linger, fixing her attention on Frank as he staggered to his feet.

"Let's get a few things straight, gentlemen. I'm not here on some holier-than-thou mission from God to save your souls. If you want that kind of salvation, I suggest you see the preacher. And I don't appreciate it when men try to take advantage of me because they think I'm weak. I'm not."

She made a point of meeting each of their gazes. "So, in case there was any confusion... I'm not your mother. Or your sister. And I'm sure as Hell not some two-bit whore you can manhandle whenever the feeling strikes you. I took an oath to help those I could, but if you ever challenge me again, I'll just as soon kill you as save you. Now, as I see it, you all have two choices. You can sit the Hell down and let me treat this man before he bleeds to death, or I can send a few of you to the undertaker, because I promise you my next shot won't be an injury I can fix."

She focused on Frank. "Well, Frank? Are you going to join your brother in a pine box or plant your ass on that chair so I can try and help him?"

Frank sneered at her, falling onto his backside when Lucas grabbed him by the shoulders and shoved him onto a seat.

The sheriff shook his head, moving over to her. He grinned, nodding at her pistols. "Guess that answers our question as to whether you know how to use those Colts of yours. That was one Hell of a shot, if I do say so. Haven't known many lawmen who have that kind of accuracy. And you don't have to worry. The next person who tries to challenge you will have to deal with me."

"I don't need your protection, Sheriff. I can take care of myself."

"Didn't say you did, darlin'. Just making sure everyone in here understands my position." He nodded at Jack. "Now, if you're done making more work for yourself..."

She ignored the slight flutter in her gut at his use of the word, "darlin'", scanning of the room before easing back on the hammers and lowering her weapons. She holstered them then moved over to the table. The bloody patch on Jack's shirt had increased, the bright color openly mocking her.

"Damn." She ripped the sides apart, cursing at the puckered hole on his upper chest. "Did you even think to clean his wound?"

Jack groaned as she rolled him enough to see the back of his shoulder, sighing at the unblemished skin.

"Bullet's still inside, which means he'll die of infection if I don't remove it, though there's a fair chance that'll happen, anyway." She gazed around the room. "I don't suppose there's any chance of moving him into the clinic? This place... It's not close to being sterile let alone clean."

Frank hissed out a breath. "You say you're a doctor, so fix him. Here. Where we can all see you."

Lucas swatted the man in the back of the head. "Shut up. If she says she needs to move him—"

"It's fine. He's probably too damn weak to move, anyway, seeing as his brother wasted too much time fightin' when he should have been helping." Hollis leaned toward Lucas. "Can you get me some whiskey, please? Strong."

Lucas arched a brow but strode away, the clinking of glass filling the air. Hollis opened her bag, placing a cloth on the wood before laying out some instruments.

She nodded at Cullen. "I need another table beside this one for his legs. So he's flat."

Cullen didn't question her, just did as she asked, helping her arrange Jack on the surface. Once he was positioned, she poured some liquid onto a cloth, handing it to Cullen.

He turned his head, scrunching up his nose. "What the Hell is that?"

"Chloroform." She whistled. "Using ether in here might just blow up the entire saloon. And the chloroform will knock him out until I'm done. I'll need you to hold it loosely over his mouth and nose until I tell you to stop. Okay?"

Cullen frowned but nodded, placing it on Jack's face. The man groaned again, then went limp.

Lucas returned with the whiskey, handing her the bottle. She offered her thanks, pouring a healthy dose over Jack's wound, thankful she'd already knocked him out. Last thing she needed was the man screaming in pain. His body tensed, but his eyes remained closed. She bit back a curse. This wasn't how she preferred to disinfect wounds, but the circumstances had left her with few options. And she didn't have the necessary supplies in her personal bag.

She motioned to Frank. "Your canteen."

The man mumbled something under his breath but handed it to her. She nodded, pouring some of the water over her hands before giving it back to him. Then, she grabbed a scalpel. She drizzled a bit more whiskey over the blade, then set to work.

No one spoke as she opened the wound slightly, dabbing at the blood before finally digging out the lead slug. She placed it in a bowl, gently probing the open laceration, again, as she searched for any fragments. She'd removed several pieces before she felt confident she'd gotten all of them. She motioned for Lucas to give her the whiskey again, pouring another healthy amount over Jack's shoulder, hoping the alcohol would combat against infection, or her efforts would be wasted. Then, she readied a needle, meticulously stitching up the various layers until she'd closed the wound.

Hollis straightened, surveying her work. Though Jack was still deathly pale, the bleeding had stopped, and the wound no longer looked as red around the edges. She motioned for Cullen to remove the cloth from the man's face, then turned back to her bag, grabbing another jar.

Lucas cursed once she'd opened it, twisting his head away. "That smells even worse than the chloroform."

She resisted the grin tugging at her lips. "It's a salve that helps prevent infection. Seeing as Jack's buddies decided to drag him through every damn mud hole on the trip over here, I need to do everything I can to guard against a fever."

Lucas shook his head. "It smells terrible. Where did you get it?"

"It's made from various plants. I was shown how to make it from a shaman at my last post. And I promise you the benefits outweigh the smell."

Frank sprang to his feet, crowding closer. "You're trustin' my brother's life to some native remedy? I thought you were a doctor?"

Lucas fisted Frank's shirt, shoving him back into the chair. "Already warned you about disrespectin' the lady."

Hollis rolled her eyes. Hadn't she already told the good sheriff she didn't need protecting? And where had this sudden concern for her wellbeing been when Frank had punched her in the jaw? "A wise person doesn't limit their resources. We could learn a lot from the people who called these lands home long before we can along. This salve has saved more than a few lives. If you're lucky, it might just save your brother."

She smeared on the ointment, covering the area with a clean bandage, before taking a step back. "I assume, now that I'm done, I won't face any resistance on having the man taken to your clinic? He needs to be monitored for a fever for the next day or two. He'll need the bandages changed, as well. But if all goes as hoped, he should be back on his feet inside of a week."

Frank stood again, waiting until Lucas gave him a nod before moving over to his brother. He ran his gaze the length of the other man, avoiding eye contact with Hollis as he motioned for his friends. They each took a limb, hoisting up the injured man.

"Gently." Hollis released a forced breath. "I'd rather not have to re-stitch his shoulder. Especially since he can't afford to lose any more blood. Now, take him to the clinic and place him on one of the cots." She glanced at Cullen. "I assume you have cots in there. Or was everything cleaned out?"

Cullen crossed his arms over his chest. "There are cots. A room in the back you can stay in, as well. It doesn't have much, but it's a place to sleep and store your belongings until we can find you something else, if you'd prefer."

"I'm sure it's fine. I don't need much."

"I don't know what supplies are there. You can take stock tomorrow and let me know. I'll have what you think you need shipped in."

She waved at the men, cringing at the way they haphazardly carried the man. "Christ, I'll be happy if they don't drop the poor bugger."

Lucas cupped her shoulder, giving her an odd arch of his brow before removing his hand and stepping back. He stared at her as if he hadn't met her earlier, his gaze finally straying to Cullen then back. "Well, I'll be damned."

She frowned. "You'll be damned about what, Sheriff Quinn?"

CHAPTER THREE

Lucas Quinn stared at Hollis—their missing piece—and wasn't sure whether to laugh or curse. Her display in the tavern had been nothing short of awe-inspiring. The way she'd handled herself with the men. Christ, he'd wanted to kiss her when she'd cracked one of them over the back with the chair, giving herself enough time to draw her pistols. And her marksmanship—he hadn't been lying. He didn't know many lawmen, Hell, gunslingers, who could have shot the rifle out of the barman's hand. But what had truly amazed him had been her skill with a scalpel. She'd cut into Jack's shoulder without hesitation, methodically cleaning out the wound then stitching him back up. And all while a few dozen people watched. Not even their previous doctor had been that calm under pressure. The woman was like a bat out of Hell. He just wasn't sure if her feisty nature would work for them, or against them.

Hollis snorted, snapping her fingers in front of his face. "Sheriff Quinn?"

He smiled, wishing he could take her hand in his, hold

it against his chest as he drew her close, breathing in her scent. It matched her personality—fiery with a hint of sweetness. He hadn't picked up on it until he'd cupped her shoulder a few moments ago, finally sifting through all the other aromas until he'd pinpointed hers. Now, he couldn't focus on anything else.

Cullen gave him a swat on the back, shaking him from his thoughts. His partner raised a brow, opening his mouth when he stopped. Cullen tipped his head back slightly, nostrils flaring before his gaze landed on Hollis. His eyes widened, the hazel color darkening to a burnished bronze.

Cullen clenched his jaw, looking pointedly at Lucas before taking a healthy step back. "I'll see to it Frank doesn't drop your patient. And make sure the clinic's in decent shape while you clean up here." His gaze shifted to Lucas, again, before he spun and followed the other men out.

Hollis spared Lucas a quick look, shaking her head as she watched Cullen leave. "Are the men in town like this all the time?"

Lucas chuckled. "Not really. Sometimes, they get nasty and violent."

She lifted one side of her mouth. "Then, I'll be sure to keep my guns fully loaded."

"From the way you handled them, you might make more work for yourself."

"Beats the alternative. You didn't answer my question. What are you damned about?"

He gave her an easy smile. "You. You're definitely more than we bargained for."

"I'll take that as a compliment." She spun, crossing her

arms as she stared at the barkeep. "I'll stitch that hand if you'd like."

The man cradled it against his chest, eyes wide, the white in them impossible to miss.

She sighed. "Damn. Sheriff Qui—"

"It's Lucas."

"Fine. Lucas, then. Would you be so kind as to get the barkeep and have him plant his ass in this chair? I can tell from here he's not fairin' well."

"Perhaps it's because you shot him."

"The man was aimin' a rifle at me. I'm not much help to others if I'm the patient. Besides, I don't like being shot at."

"That would imply some people do."

He smirked at her as he made his way to the bar, strong-arming the other man back over to the table. Lucas shoved him into a chair. "Behave, Caleb, or I'll be the one taking the next shot."

"I already told you. I don't need your protection. Not to mention the fact your sudden show of support is more than a bit late."

Lucas bit back any reply. She wasn't wrong.

Hollis grabbed a clean cloth, sitting in the opposite chair as she reached toward the barkeep. "Your hand."

The man glared at her.

Lucas sighed. "Just give the lady your hand before she gets upset and lets you bleed to death."

Caleb huffed, begrudgingly placing his hand on the table.

She dabbed at it. "It's not that bad. Bullet went all the way through. If you think you can stand the pain, it'd be best if I stitch it." She reached for the whiskey, holding his wrist tight when he tried to pull his hand back. But instead of pouring it on the wound, she handed it to him. "Take a few swigs of that. It should help."

Caleb downed several gulps, finally handing her back the bottle. She smiled then poured some on the wound, ignoring the way he cursed.

He sneered at her. "You did that on purpose."

"If you don't like my bedside manner, then perhaps you should avoid being my patient, again, in the future." She readied another needle. "This will go much faster if you try not to move."

Lucas grasped the man's shoulders, holding him firmly in the chair as she quickly closed the wounds, wrapping his hand in a clean bandage.

She sat back, finally releasing his wrist. "Try to keep that clean and change the dressin' if you get it dirty or wet. I'll cut those stitches in about a week."

Caleb mumbled a curse as he walked away, not bothering to thank her, not that Lucas had expected it. Hollis snorted, humming to herself as she gathered up her supplies. He took a moment to study her. Admire the soft lines of her face and the way her beautiful blue eyes seemed to continually scan the room, as if she wasn't convinced she wouldn't have to defend herself, again.

He growled at the thought. While watching her best the other men had made him smile, another part of him had wanted to rip their throats out for daring to touch her. And that was before he'd realized who she was—what she was to them. Now—now, his inner bear wanted to stalk down the street to the clinic and strangle Frank's scraggly neck for hitting her.

Lucas frowned at the split along her lip, the cut across

her forehead. He moved in closer, nudging her arm. "You've got a cut along your temple. And your lip looks swollen."

She shrugged. "Neither feels that serious. I'll clean them before I go to sleep."

"Shouldn't you clean them now? What if that cut gets infected?"

The smile she flashed him dropped his damn stomach. "I'll be fine."

He merely nodded as she wrapped the leather strap around her bag. "You're the doctor." Though he secretly wondered if her refusal to clean her wounds stemmed from something deeper. That to do so might make her appear weak. The thought made his other half huff. She was anything but weak.

He mentally told the beast to back down as he motioned to the doorway. "If you're ready, I'll see you safely to the clinic."

She scoffed at him, lifting her medical kit then heading back to other table to collect her suitcase. "I don't need an escort. Just tell me where it is, and I'll make my way over."

He tsked when she tried to grab her other bag, taking it in one hand as he turned to face her. "It would be best if I accompanied you there."

"Are you afraid I'll lose my way, being such a delicate flower in this harsh land?"

He couldn't quite stop his smile from lifting his lips. "I'm more concerned you might get waylaid in the street and kill a few of our men. We really don't have any to spare."

She hitched out her hip, cursing when he started

toward the door. She darted forward, nearly jogging to keep up with his long strides. "I told you before. I prefer not to kill people if I can manage it."

"Yet, you just stitched up the man you shot. And need I remind you that you also said you'd just as soon kill anyone who challenged you as save them?"

"I won't apologize for protectin' myself, Sheriff. Qui—"

"Lucas. And I didn't say it was wrong. Just pointed out that I'd rather you not be put in that position, again. Despite what you said, I get the feeling you don't enjoy hurtin' people. I assume it goes against your nature."

Her eyes narrowed, the cockiness fading from her expression. She glanced back at the swinging doors, a rough sigh fluttering the wisps of hair around her face. "If I've learned anything working this far west, it's that I can't save people who don't want to be saved. Who don't value anyone's life but their own." She tilted her head to the side. "But while we're on the subject, since when do you and Mr. James give a damn about my feelings?"

Lucas stopped short. He closed the distance between them, leaning in until his breath rustled her collar. "His name is Cullen, and who said we didn't care?"

"Actions speak louder than words."

"So, askin' you to treat Jack? Having your back in there?"

"Damage control at best." She tsked. "Please. Did you think I didn't hear your friend back in the saloon? He was about to say that he'd asked for a doctor and all they'd sent him was a woman. Then, there's that part where neither of you wanted to honor Mr. Gilmore's offer of employment. I believe you were worried that I wouldn't be welcome. Or was it my skills you thought were lackin'?"

Lucas sighed. God, he hated that she was right. On all accounts. He lifted his chin, not sure which to apologize for, first, when a voice sounded behind him.

"I'd say we're sorry, but something tells me that might not be enough for you."

Hollis spun, watching as Cullen closed in on them. Lucas didn't miss the way her gaze ran the length of his mate, or how her breathing sped up when the other man stopped an arm's length away. Lucas inhaled, rewarded with a hint of earthy musk that mimicked her usual scent. Just thinking that their presence aroused her, even if it was more of an unconscious reaction on her part, eased the tight feeling in his chest he hadn't realized had taken root. It meant they still had a chance to change her perception of them.

The woman slid her glance toward Lucas, seemingly measuring them both up before grinning. "It's a start."

"Then, we're sorry for jumpin' to conclusions."

A tentative smile teased her lips before she shifted her focus up the street. "I reckon that building at the end is the clinic. If you gentlemen will excuse me, it's been a long day. And I still have work to do before I can rest."

Cullen stepped aside but then fell into place beside her. "We'll just see that you get settled."

She laughed. "What is it with you boys and worryin' about my safety? I think I've proven that I can handle myself. Besides, if I get myself killed, Mr. Gilmore won't have to pay me, and you might get yourself a new doctor." She paused for a moment then arched a brow at Cullen. "Maybe even a *male* one."

Cullen took a quick stride forward, crowding into her personal space. "Don't joke about getting yourself killed. Neither Lucas nor I find it at all amusing. And I already tried to apologize for my shortsightedness."

Her expression softened. "The West is a dangerous place, Mr. Jam—"

"Cullen."

She took a deep breath, glancing at Lucas before making eye contact with Cullen, again. "Cullen. I'm intimately aware of all the ways one can die after crossing the Mississippi River. If it's not the natives raidin' the town, it's outlaws and gunslingers shootin' it up. When that fails, there's disease and infection. As I see it, survival out here is like a card game—equal parts skill and dumb luck. I do all I can to up the ante in the skill department, but luck... That's beyond my control. No use worryin' about what you have no control over." She cracked a smile. "And I believe I said your apology would be a start. But it takes more than token words to prove sincerity."

"Then, perhaps you'll do us the courtesy of stayin' alive long enough for us to earn that sincerity. Which means seeing you reach the clinic without having to challenge half the men in this camp. It'd be a shame to lose you so soon after finally finding you."

"Finding me?" Hollis furrowed her brow, obviously puzzled by Cullen's odd statement. She opened her mouth then shut it, looking as if she wasn't quite certain how to continue. "What—"

Lucas tugged on her arm, urging them all forward. "What Cullen means is...you not only proved you can handle yourself with the townsfolk, you also gave us a glimpse at how skilled you truly are as a physician. Not sure we've had a doctor in our ranks, yet, that has displayed that level of grace under pressure. And seeing as it took us a few months of beggin' to get you here..."

She nodded, though her expression suggested that she wasn't quite convinced of his reasoning. Cullen darted ahead to grab the door for her, ushering her in. He'd already lit the oil lamps hanging from some of the posts, the warm light chasing away the shadows. Lucas smiled as she did a slow circle, taking everything in.

A genuine smile lit up her face as she turned to them. "I'll be honest. I was expectin' little more than a tent with an old wooden table in the center. This... It surpasses any rail camp I've worked in yet. Some of the small towns, too. I can't imagine why the previous doctor left."

Lucas shrugged. "Something to do with the caliber of patients. And there was that time someone fired a few shots his way."

"I don't scare easily. And I've been shot at before."

A low rumble vibrated the air. Lucas cursed inwardly as he glanced at Cullen. The last thing they needed was to have Hollis wondering why they were behaving oddly. Hell, she already thought they were.

Hollis stared at Cullen, cocking her head to the side. She looked as if she was going to say something then seemed to change her mind. Instead, she nodded toward where Jack was asleep in one of the cots. "I'm surprised Frank isn't hoverin' over him. Or threatening to kill me if his brother doesn't make it."

Cullen took a step toward her, and Lucas noticed the hint of claws on Cullen's hands before he tucked them in his pockets. His partner was obviously more agitated than Lucas had first thought. Though, he was certain the dried blood on Hollis' forehead wasn't helping. And knowing Frank had struck her probably angered Cullen far more than usual, now that they'd realized what she meant to them.

Cullen gave her a wry smile. "I had a...chat with Frank. If he's got any sense at all, he won't bother you."

"I see. Then, I'll just check on Jack, clean myself up, and get some sleep." She turned then looked back at them across her shoulder. "Unless there's something else you need?"

Lucas palmed Cullen's shoulder, stopping the man from answering. "Nothing. We'll see you in the morning. Good night."

She tipped her hat, heading over to the cot. Lucas didn't miss the way she smiled as she touched Jack's forehead, obviously pleased with whatever she found. There was a distinct change in her mannerisms. Where she'd been tough and somewhat indifferent in the saloon, she now seemed far gentler, genuine concern shaping her features. She wet a cloth, softly dabbing it on the man's face as she sat on the edge of the bed.

Lucas gave Cullen a shake, motioning with his head toward the door. Cullen spun, taking one last glance at Hollis before walking out, his stride firm and steady. He stopped just outside the door, crossing his arms over his chest.

A frown tipped the corners of his mouth down as he huffed out a slow breath. "Any particular reason you rushed us out of there?"

Lucas matched his mate's grim expression as he shut the door behind him. "You mean besides the fact you're barely in control? Please, I saw your hands. And you growled. Twice."

"Did you miss the cut across her forehead? Her swollen lip? Or maybe it was the part where she confessed she gets shot at on a regular basis."

"She didn't say that."

"It was implied. As was the part where she's basically resigned herself to an early grave."

Lucas sighed. Cullen was definitely more intense than Lucas was, though part of it probably stemmed from them fighting their natural instincts to claim each other as mates. That, or it was simply that Kodiaks were more highly strung than other grizzlies. Either way, it meant his partner would have a Hell of a time remaining distant until they could figure out a way to court the new doctor. Convince her they were worth getting to know beyond friends.

He groaned inwardly. After tempering their urge to mate for months, he wasn't sure how long either of them would be able to remain distant now that they'd found their missing piece. Just thinking about having to spend the next few months trying to win over Hollis—it made Lucas' inner bear claw at his control.

Cullen snorted. "Looks like I'm not the only one fightin' to keep their skin."

"I didn't say I was unaffected. I'm just not sprouting fangs and claws, yet."

"I wouldn't either, except, shit, Lucas. She's human. Fully human. Which means simply telling her she's our mate isn't going to work. Hell, the fact there's two of us…"

Lucas cupped Cullen's forearm. "Pretty sure she

wouldn't be the other half of us if she didn't feel an equal pull. We just need to convince her three's the perfect number."

"Right, because every girl grows up dreamin' of being married to two men. And we don't even care about the marriage part. Shifters don't need vows."

"Thinkin' few girls grow up dreamin' of becoming doctors, either, but there she is. Something tells me the woman isn't that concerned about venturin' outside the social norm."

"Still. Wanting to help people and loving two men aren't exactly on the same level. That's assumin' she could ever fall for us. She thinks we're jackasses. And she's right. We dismissed her without a second thought." Cullen kicked at the dirt, before glancing at Lucas. "*I* dismissed her. I seem to recall you suggestin' we give her a shot."

"It was a mutual decision. I didn't want to see her get hurt, either. Though, with the way she handled herself..." Lucas sighed. "Doesn't matter. We can't change the past. Gotta move forward. So, we have to grovel a bit. Pretty sure we can swallow our damn pride long enough to apologize. However many times it takes." He nudged Cullen. "What, exactly, did you say to Frank?"

Cullen's jaw tensed, the muscle in his temple flexing. "It was more along the lines of actions speakin' louder than words."

"Shit. Please tell me you didn't threaten the man."

"I simply made it clear any unwanted advances toward the good doctor would be taken personally."

"So, you did threaten him." He pushed out a rough

breath. "Was that before or after you tossed his ass out onto the street?"

Cullen cracked a smug grin. "Before."

"Christ." Lucas carded his hand through his hair. "How good did it feel?"

"Far better than it should have. We've only known Hollis for what? A day? And that's being real generous because she was only around us for five or ten minutes. But damn it... Already my bear is pacin' back and forth inside my head—demanding I stake my claim. And not just with her." Cullen gave Lucas a hard look. "It wants you just as fiercely. Not sure how long I can fight this. Already been far too long where you're concerned."

"You think I'm any different? I'm feeling more than a bit possessive. But if we go too far, too fast..."

"I know. I just hope I can keep my other half contained. Though, that does bring up another issue. At some point, we'll have to tell Hollis what we are. What she means to us. Doesn't seem right mating without her knowing exactly what she's getting herself into."

Lucas lifted one brow. "You worried she'll run screamin' in the other direction?"

"Aren't you?"

He snorted. "Of course I am. But then, the girl just took on a room full of men. I can only hope that means she was telling the truth and that she doesn't scare easily." He gave Cullen a pat on the back. "Let's just let her get settled. Then, we'll see what we can do to bridge the distance. In the meantime, we'll keep an eye on her. Make sure she's safe."

"Speakin' of which...why don't you head on in? I'll hang out for a while."

"If anyone's going to stand guard at her door, it's me." Lucas held up his hand, cutting Cullen off from replying. "I'm the sheriff. Besides, you have to see that the crews get up and out on time. And I know you'll be riding the line shortly after sunrise. Go. Sleep. I'll stay for a couple of hours then get some sleep."

Cullen growled. "If anyone comes lookin' for her…"

"I'll yell, promise. Not that you won't sense it if she's in trouble, anyway. Now, go get some sleep. You can check in on her in the morning."

Cullen cursed under his breath as he looked at the closed door to the clinic one more time before spinning on his heel and marching purposely down the street. Lucas sighed as he watched the man pause, again, at his office before heading inside.

He glanced at the clinic. One slab of wood. That's all that separated him from his other mate. All he had to do was figure out a way to actually open it to the point she'd be theirs.

CHAPTER FOUR

"She's sleeping. Finally."

Cullen turned, sighing as Lucas stepped out from the shadows lining the short walkway beside the clinic. Cullen leaned against the wall, crossing his arms over his chest. "I thought you were going to get some rest?"

Lucas pursed his lips, glancing at the closed door. "I tried to leave a couple of hours ago, but…" He huffed, punching Cullen in the shoulder. "Gloat if you must."

"You think I've slept? If I'd paced that room any longer, I'd have worn a damn groove in the floor. I can't get her off my mind. Her scent, the shape of her face, those eyes." Cullen shook his head. "And it's not just her. My damn bear is having a real hard time remembering all of those reasons we've stayed distant." He locked his gaze on Lucas. "In fact, I can't seem to recall a single one. Which isn't helping with my control. My skin feels as if it's going to split apart. There's an incessant growlin' inside my head. And if I got any harder…"

Lucas glanced at Cullen's crotch. "I'd joke, but I'm not

fairin' any better. You think my shirt's hangin' low because I was too damn lazy to tuck it in? My bear hates this as much as yours does. I'm just not sure how to fix it. We just met her. Hell, she doesn't even like us."

"Have I told you how annoying it is when you're always right?" Cullen scrubbed his hand down his face. "She can't be completely unaffected, can she? I mean... we're mates. There's got to be some measure of attraction, doesn't there?"

"I sure as Hell hope so."

Cullen arched a brow. "Whatever happened to three being the perfect number, mate?"

"It *is* the perfect number. I just didn't count on feeling this...obsessive. I thought the pull would stay the same, just split between both of you, but... It's so much more. Like a damn fire I can't put out."

"I've never had a problem letting you do whatever had to be done. Put your life at risk. Maybe it's because I know you have your grizzly to back you up if things go wrong, but with her—can't think past the next time she's going to challenge some cowboy because he thinks he can best her. All the ways that encounter could turn ugly."

"Nothing's going to happen to her. We won't let it."

Cullen merely nodded, deciding not to push the subject further—not when he didn't have a clue how to fix it.

Lucas glanced at the closed door. "Not sure if it's a glimmer of hope or not, but I'm pretty sure I caught a whiff of arousal last night when all three of us were together. Of course, having her body react to us on a primal level doesn't mean shit when she's not a shifter.

Women are stubborn enough. I have a feeling our feisty doctor is so much more."

"Then, she's not the only one. We can be just as hardheaded. Just as determined."

"Of course, we can. I'm just not sure she'll find those qualities endearin'."

Cullen chuckled. "Probably not. You think she'll open fire if I take a peek inside? Assure myself she's okay?"

"Door doesn't squeak. And seeing as she's been up most of the night with Jack…"

"You've checked, haven't you?"

"Spent the last twenty minutes watching her sleep. Had to drag myself away. Didn't want you to think I was obsessed."

"Or have her wake up and catch you inside."

Lucas grinned. "That, too. Girl's got a Hell of a shot. Makes me wonder who taught her how to handle those pistols."

"I'll just be happy if she doesn't aim one my way. Not exactly how I envision revealing the other side of me."

"Not sure there's a good way to do that."

"We'd best find one if we ever want her to be our mate."

"And just when I thought you were going to be the positive one in this undertakin'."

Cullen sighed. He wanted to be positive. To tell Lucas it was only a matter of time before Hollis succumbed to their charms. But damn if a part of him wasn't worried that they'd done irreparable damage yesterday. That their cavalier attitude had ruined any chance of ever gaining her love.

Love.

He'd settle for her not thinking they were jackasses.

He gave Lucas a pat on the shoulder as he moved to the doorway. The handle turned easily within his grip as he slowly opened the door, revealing the clinic in a wedge of dull light. A single oil lamp flickered at the rear of the room, dancing shadows across the floor. Cullen scanned the area, stopping on the silhouette slouched over in a chair. Her hair hung in a cascade of brown around her shoulders, the gentle waves softening the firm line of her jaw. Long lashes rested against pale skin, her full, pink lips pursed into a small smile.

He took an involuntary step forward before he caught himself. The last thing he needed was to startle her awake and give her another reason not to trust them. Even if his motivations were simply to assure himself she was okay, he doubted it would seem that way. Hell, who was he kidding? Honor wasn't the reason he was there. Raw, burning need had brought him through the door. And if the tumbling sensation in his gut was any indication, that feeling wasn't going to change any time soon. A hand landed on his shoulder, and he glanced back at Lucas. Heat burned in the man's eyes, the fine lines around his mouth deepening.

Lucas sighed, leaning in close. "Woman doesn't know when to quit."

The words barely reached Cullen, but there was no mistaking the intensity behind them.

Cullen quirked his mouth, keeping his voice low. "Part of her charm." He nodded at the door. "Reckon we should let her get whatever rest she can, seeing as she seems determined to put Jack's health above her own."

He headed out again, taking one last glance at her

before closing the door. His bear growled, clawing at his control. It didn't like leaving its mate, not when their future was uncertain. When there was still a chance she'd reject them.

He cursed. Hadn't she already done that?

Lucas gave him a gentle shove. "Stop overthinkin' everything. We just met the girl. Surely, we can get through a few days without our damn bears going rogue. Besides, we still have a spur to finish. Weren't you on your way north? Surveying that bridge site?"

"After what happened, I thought it might be best to ride out with you today."

Lucas grinned. "You know I can handle a few wayward outlaws."

"Of course you can. But the last thing we need is you going all claws and fur if more of those outlaws show up." He tsked at Lucas' glare. "You think I don't feel how restless you are? Means your other half is far worse. And now that we've found..." He motioned at the door. "I know you're just as antsy as I am. One wrong word, a stray punch or bullet—let's just say this town will develop a sudden and severe grizzly problem. And the last thing we need are men like Frank forming a bear-huntin' posse."

Lucas pursed his mouth then sighed. "And you cursed me for always being right. You're no better." His mate closed his eyes, taking what looked like a fortifying breath before nodding. "In view of the current circumstances, it probably is best if we stay together for a bit." He stared at Cullen, his eyes darkening. "If anything were to happen to you out there while I was babysittin' a crew thirty miles off..."

Cullen took a quick glance around the deserted street before grabbing Lucas and shoving him against the wall, hiding them in one of the long shadows gathered across the clinic's walkway. He stepped into the man, trapping him against the rough wood. The scent of leather and gun oil filled his senses, a hint of sweetness from beyond the closed door weaving through the other aromas.

He leaned in, forcing Lucas to palm his chest to prevent Cullen from crushing his weight against him. "Nothing is going to happen. To any of us. Period. I won't let it, not when I've waited this damn long to find her. To finally taste you." His gaze dropped to the other man's mouth. "Mine."

He closed the distance, taking Lucas' lips with a firm press of his mouth. He didn't wait for Lucas to join in, twisting the other man's lips open then delving inside. Cullen's bear growled in agreement, surging forward enough to sink his claws into the wall as he devoured his mate, refusing to ease up until the incessant pounding in his head had lessened.

Lucas snarled at him the moment their lips parted. Red flashed in the shifter's eyes a second before he moved, somehow reversing their positions in the space of a heartbeat. Cullen slammed into the wall as Lucas crowded against his chest, sinking his fingers in Cullen's hair as he slanted his mouth over Cullen's.

His mate's taste wove deeper this time, curling around every nerve until it had infused Cullen's own scent. Became a part of him. Lucas moaned, the throaty vibration spiking Cullen's shaft against his pants. He snaked one arm around Lucas' back, pulling him hard against his erection. A tremor worked through Lucas' body before he finally eased away, nipping at Cullen's lower lip then taking a healthy step back.

He held up his palm when Cullen moved to grab him. "You touch me, again, and the only place we'll be going is to your damn bed. And we won't be leavin' there for a week if my bear has anything to say about it." His gaze slid to the door behind Cullen. Another tremor shook the man as he cursed and lowered his head "Christ. I need..."

Cullen ignored the man's warning, fisting his hand in the sheriff's shirt then yanking him against him. "You're not alone in this. Tasting you while scenting Hollis behind this fucking door..." He hissed out his next breath. "You're right. I'll back off...for now. But consider you and your bear on very short notice. I won't let you stay distant for long." He glanced at the door behind him. "Either of you."

"She'll join us." Lucas flashed him a cocky grin. "No way she can resist this much charm."

Cullen chuckled, appreciating the way his mate eased the tension with nothing more than a few words. Lucas was definitely more even-tempered than Cullen was, always finding a way to calm the situation.

Cullen rolled his shoulders, finally releasing his hold on Lucas. "I'll go pack some supplies then round up the men. We'll head out after a quick breakfast. See how far we can get. Who knows, maybe we'll make some actual headway."

"We're still down a few men, but—with both of us keeping watch and the crew working instead of worrying about getting shot—that might not slow progress too much. Just remember what I said yesterday. You can't keep your ass in one piece and worry about the line at the same time. If I think for one second you're putting your life in jeopardy to do just that..." His smile was feral this time. "Let's just say that ass won't know what hit it."

"Careful, mate. We both know my grizzly is far less tame than yours."

"Really? Care to put that to the test...*mate?*"

Cullen stilled. While Lucas had never denied their connection, Cullen hadn't missed the way the other man had avoided using the term to directly address him. Hearing it roll off Lucas' mouth in those gravelly undertones damn near took Cullen to his knees.

He drew a few ragged breaths, desperately trying to gather even a hint of control, when the door opened and Hollis came bustling out. Cullen turned, catching her around the shoulders when she barreled into him, her gasp of surprise sounding loud in the early morning gray.

She reacted, catching Cullen across the jaw as her foot swept behind his feet, tripping him down the stairs and effectively dumping him on his ass. Dirt and dust billowed into the air, gathering in a cloud around them before dissipating with a gust of wind. The telltale click of hammers cocking into place lit the air, and Cullen looked up to find Hollis a few feet back, guns aimed at them, eyes more white than blue. Her beautiful hair sat in a tousled mess about her shoulders, streaks of gold visible amidst the brown.

Her chest heaved, her raspy breathing drawing his attention. Her eyes widened as recognition dawned in the blue depths. "Jesus. You two scared me half to death. What on Earth are you doing out here?"

Cullen huffed. "Making sure you're okay."

"Well, you damn near got yourselves shot." She

furrowed her brow, glancing from Lucas back to him as she holstered her weapons, some of the tension easing from her shoulders. "And it's only sunrise. Don't you boys ever sleep?"

"That's rich coming from someone who spent all night in a chair beside Jack's bed."

"How..." She narrowed her eyes, studying them as if she could see through them. Uncover any secret they'd kept hidden inside. Mixed emotions crossed her features before she sighed, leaning against the door as if needing the support. "He was starting to burn up. With him being as weak as he was, I didn't want it to get worse, so...I stayed up to keep him cool. Get him to drink some tea that helps lower fevers."

Lucas extended his hand to Cullen, his amused grin not helping matters any. He helped Cullen up, seemingly oblivious to the glare Cullen flashed him. "Did it work?"

She nodded, not seeming to care when a few curls fell across her face. "His fever broke an hour ago. While he's not out of the woods, yet, it's a good sign. I'm optimist he'll make a full recovery. I was just off to see if I could get some coffee at the saloon. Something to help me stay awake. I keep driftin' off." She snorted. "If Caleb doesn't shoot me on sight, that is."

"I've got the stove lit in my office. And a drip pot ready to go if you'd like. Won't take long to make you some."

Her gaze swept between them, again. She glanced over his shoulder toward the main street before finally sighing. "I guess this is my fault. I did say it would take more than nice words to sway my opinion of you two. Thank you, Sheriff...Lucas. I'd appreciate the coffee, especially if I don't have to dodge any bullets to get it. If you have the time," she added.

"Cullen and I were just finishin' up our morning sweep of the town. It'll be a good twenty minutes before the crew gets up. Another thirty before we head out for the day. I'd say we have plenty of time."

"Fine, then. I'll just check Jack's condition, again." She turned then looked back at them across her shoulder. "I noticed a stream just south of the camp. I reckon I'll clean up a bit before I make my way over. I won't be long."

"Stream?" Cullen closed the distance between them. "Did you just say you were headin' off to the stream? Alone? With dawn barely breakin'?"

Amusement crinkled the fine lines around her eyes. "Is there a problem?"

"You mean besides it being damn near freezing outside? And the water's even colder. All the rivers up here are glacier fed. They never truly get warm."

"I won't be in it long enough to freeze. Just need to wash off the grime."

"Regardless, it's not safe to be alone outside of the camp. Hell, it's barely safe enough inside the camp."

"I'd think the best time to sneak a dip in the water is before there are people around to watch. It's not far. I'll be fine."

"Damn straight you will because I'll be accompanying you."

Her brow arched as defiance gleamed in her eyes. "I think I've proven that I'm more than capable of handlin' myself, should something arise."

Cullen inched closer. He could be just as damn stubborn as Hollis. "Did you miss the part where Lucas said we were doing a sweep of the town? Or how on your first day here, you had to treat a gunshot wound, not to mention draw your own weapons? Or that two men died out on the rail yesterday from similar injuries?"

"This isn't my first rail camp, nor would it be the first time there's been risks." She smiled, and his damn stomach dropped into his boots then jumped up into his throat. "I plan on bathing nude—"

"Which will make it insanely hard to draw your Colts should you get in trouble." He quirked his lips. "Or do you take them into the water with you?"

The muscle in her temple jumped as she clenched her jaw.

He breathed out a calming sigh. "I can arrange for a bath for you in my quarters."

"I don't need anything that fancy. Besides, it'd take too long, and you have other responsibilities. A quick dip in the river..." She held up her hand, stopping him from interrupting her. "Cold beats dirty, Cullen. I'm used to making do. I grew up on a small parcel of land outside of town. We didn't have that much, so..."

"Then, I'll be sure to turn my back while you disrobe. But I'm going with you."

"Are all the men here this stubborn, or just the two of you?"

He gave her a wide smile. "Wouldn't have gotten to where we are if we accepted defeat easily. Now, gather what you need. Lucas can warm up the office and get that coffee made while you attempt to freeze yourself."

She laughed, the light, lilting tone wrapping around his cock then squeezing tight. If he wasn't careful, she'd be the death of him long before he got a chance to get close.

Hollis disappeared into the clinic, reappearing a minute later. She nodded at Lucas when he headed for the office then walked over to Cullen. "I'm ready."

He turned, making his way between the buildings then down the small hill. Streaks of pale pink brightened the sky off in the distance, the first hint of the sun edging above the horizon. He moved slowly, reminding himself she couldn't see as well as he did in the dark as he wove down the narrow trail to the stream. The constant rush of water against the banks broke the silence, the occasional flash of white shining in the dawning light.

He stopped next to the river, spinning to face her. "Current's not too bad close in. It gets pretty strong in the middle."

She laughed, again, this time making his chest squeeze tight. "Been swimmin' since before I could walk. But I just need a quick dip to rinse off all those miles I traveled. I won't venture into the rough section."

He nodded, watching as she placed a few items on the grass before shucking out of her jacket. She placed her holster on top, then flicked at the first few buttons before swinging her gaze over to him. She cleared her throat, making him jump.

He took a few steps away, putting his back to her. "Sorry."

She murmured something under her breath before everything fell silent. He tried to busy himself by working through scenarios for the workday ahead, until the soft rustle of clothes falling onto the grass jarred him from his thoughts. Not that it'd been loud, but with his senses so acute...

Footsteps padded the ground behind him, followed by a gasp as she waded into the water. Cullen fisted his hands, letting his claws scratch his palms to keep himself rooted to the spot, despite the clamoring of his other half. His Kodiak didn't seem to care that gawking at her while she bathed would only earn him a slap on the face or a round from one of her revolvers. All it knew was its mate was close—not to mention naked—and Cullen wasn't doing a damn thing to claim her.

Water splashed behind him, each sound drawing a mental image of her progression. How she moved away from shore, paused for a while, then headed back. He knew the instant she'd gotten out of the water. A fresh, earthy musk wove through his senses, the warm womanly essence in it impossible to miss.

He tilted his head slightly without looking at her. "You're shiverin'."

The rustling behind him stopped. "How the Hell can you tell that?"

"I can hear your teeth chattering from here. Bet your fingers are numb. Going to be mighty hard to button that shirt."

He heard the whoosh of air a moment before something hit his shoulder. He glanced down, chuckling at the bar of soap. "Now, now, Doc. Temper." He picked up the bar. "I bet you're stickin' your tongue out at me, too."

"Has anyone told you that you're quite infuriating?"

"All the time, sweetheart."

Her breath hitched at the endearment, and he did his

best to just let it slide. He hadn't meant to let something like that slip, but... Not turning around, striding over to her and kissing her until she melted against him was taking most of his restraint, so calling her sweetheart seemed fairly benign in comparison.

He reined in his bear, again, promising the damn animal that he'd find a way to get closer to Hollis, when the faint crack of a stick prickled his senses. He froze, working out the location in his head when another limb snapped. Hollis must have heard it, as well, the slight rustle of her behind him stilling.

Cullen reacted, spinning quickly then racing toward her. She barely had time to gasp before he'd wrapped his arms around her and taken her to the ground, covering her small body with his. He quieted his breathing, listening for more movement as Hollis squirmed beneath him.

She swatted at his shoulders. "I know you heard something, but damn it, Cullen, I don't need you to shield me. So, move."

Though she'd kept her voice low, he didn't want to risk that it'd carried across the water.

He glanced around, bending down until his mouth hovered above hers, every inch of their bodies touching. "I'll move when I know you won't get your head shot off and not a moment before."

Irritation creased her brow. "I'm armed. And I'm a pretty good shot."

"Your guns are still beside your boots, which are more than a few feet away."

"And whose fault is that? If you hadn't bowled me to the ground."

He snorted, scanning the other side of the riverbank. "I hardly bowled you over." He frowned when he realized she was still shivering. "Shit. You're still naked and lying on the wet grass."

"Again, wh-whose fault i-is that?"

"And now, you're stutterin' from it." He weighed his options, sliding off to one side when words carried across the water. He didn't need to see the people to know they were part of Buford's gang. He'd recognize the younger brother's voice anywhere.

He kept his arm over Hollis' chest, motioning her to stay as he shrugged out of his jacket. He handed it to her, mouthing for her to put it on, then drew his gun, crawling toward the river, careful to stay amidst the tall grass. Men rustled the reeds on the other side, a few hushed curses reaching Cullen. He scented the air, allowing his other half as much freedom as possible without actually shifting. The noises around him sharpened, the distinctive aroma of three men hanging in the air.

He lined up where his bear suspected the gang was hiding, waiting to see if they'd pop out, when the sounds faded, nothing but the echo of horses clopping away reaching him.

He stayed there, his gun at the ready, until he was sure it was clear before twisting to face Hollis. She'd slipped on his jacket, her guns shaking in her grasp as she copied his approach, constantly scanning the other side of the bank. There was no missing the pale cast of her skin or how her teeth chattered.

He took one last look then stood, helping her to her feet. "Christ, you're damn near blue."

She shrugged, trying to holster her weapons, only to miss.

He tsked, taking them from her and jamming them in the leather pouches. "Come on. Let's get you back to the office and warmed up." He gathered her clothes before she could argue. "You can dress there."

"B-but I-I'm…"

He merely smiled before he picked her up, ignoring her startled gasp. Her hands instinctively went around his neck as he hurried back along the trail, then onto the street, holding her close in the hopes of sharing some of his body heat.

She snorted against his neck, the soft caress of air sending a rash of goosebumps along his arms. "I c-can w-walk."

"You can barely talk." He shook his head. "No arguing. Yes, I know your near frozen state is partly my fault, but… safety, first. Modesty and pride second. Besides, we're almost there."

He jogged down the road, hoping he didn't drop any of her things as he neared the sheriff's building. As if on cue, Lucas opened the door, frowning when he took them both in. His gaze rose to Cullen's, before he motioned them inside, closing the door behind them.

Cullen walked straight over to the stove, placing Hollis on her feet in front. She swayed for a moment then let go, tugging his jacket tighter around her. He grabbed a chair and dragged it across the floor, laying her belongings across the seat, and her boots and guns beneath it.

He backed up a few feet. "We'll step outside for a minute and give you some privacy. But you're not going anywhere until some color returns to your cheeks and you're no longer shiverin'." He headed for the door, taking Lucas with him. "And we're going to have a chat about putting yourself at risk once we get back, so get everything straight inside that pretty head of yours before we return."

CHAPTER FIVE

"Of all the…"

Hollis stuck out her tongue at the closed door. While she realized it was a somewhat childish act, it eased the fluttering sensations in her stomach that felt like a thousand butterflies taking flight. And all because of the two men standing on the other side of the door.

She groaned, tugging Cullen's coat a bit tighter. The rich scent of worn leather and spicy man wrapped around her, and she wondered if he'd let her put the damn thing back on once she'd dressed.

The thought caught her by surprise, and she shrugged out of the heavy garment, stepping clear of it once it hit the floor. She needed to remember both men had yet to fully apologize for dismissing her. And after all she'd done in the saloon, they should be the last ones to lecture her on safety. She'd proven she could handle herself and more.

She reached for her clothes, wiggling into her pants. Her damp skin caught on the rough fabric, making it hard to tug over her hips. She left them hanging open as she slipped on her chemise, tucking the end into her trousers. Her hands shook as tightened the laces as best as she could, then pulled on her shirt, cursing when the buttons refused to slide through the holes.

The door creaked, making her jump. She glanced at the opening, her breath catching when both men appeared in the sliver of space. They gave her a quick once-over then strode inside, a gust of cold air prickling her skin as shivers racked her body.

Lucas tsked, quickly walking over to her and tugging her against his body. "Christ, you're still a dozen shades of blue."

Her hands hit his chest, the firm flex of muscles beneath her palms making the room feel as if it were spinning slightly. She'd never met men as large as him and Cullen, with strength to match their frames. Cullen had carried her as if it'd barely taken any effort, and she was certain Lucas could do the same.

Hollis thought about shoving the sheriff away when Cullen moved in behind her, trapping her between them. Two sets of hands rubbed the length of her arms and torso, obviously trying to generate some much-needed warmth into her body.

Cullen's breath tickled her nape as he leaned in close. "You're still barefooted."

"I w-was getting t-there." She groaned at the stuttered reply, knowing it'd only fuel their side of the argument more.

Lucas chuckled. "You are a stubborn soul. Come on, let's get you all the way dressed."

He picked her up then turned, placing her in his lap before wrapping his arms around her, again. Heat seeped through her clothes as the scent of gun oil filled her senses, and she couldn't resist from resting her head on his shoulder for a moment. The bone-deep chill from the water and grass finally ebbed, a soothing warmth spreading through her.

A throaty hum vibrated Lucas' chest. The low sound spiked another round of butterflies in her stomach as a needy ache settled in her groin. She wasn't sure why she reacted to both men on such an intrinsic level, but her inability to control her body's arousal was more than frustrating.

Hands landed on her feet, and she snapped her head around, staring into Cullen's hazel eyes. He held up a sock, a bemused smile curving his lips before he smoothed it over her foot and up her calf. The soft glide of his fingers against her skin sent a rash of goosebumps beading down her arms.

Cullen sighed. "This is supposed to warm you up, not make you colder."

Hollis dampened her lips, cursing when Cullen's gaze fell to her mouth then back to her eyes. "Have you stopped to consider it tickles?"

He laughed. "You shouldn't tell me that when there's another foot to go."

She glared at him, despite the grin that lifted the corners of her mouth. "You did see the shot I made last night, didn't you? Might be wise not to upset me."

Cullen arched a brow, glancing at the floor. "Pistols are still by your boots, sweetheart. Thinkin' I'll risk it." He held up the other sock. "Ready?"

She pursed her lips at the endearment. Having him call her sweetheart shouldn't feel as right as it did. Similar to how her heart had kicked up when Lucas had called her "darlin'" the previous night, though she'd played her response off to the adrenaline rush from the fight. But now...now, it didn't feel quite so innocent.

Cullen cupped her heel, holding her still as he eased the fabric over her toes then up her leg. His touch was firmer this time, the sensuous caress increasing the needy sensation in her core. She forced herself to swallow past the tight feeling in her chest, her gaze never leaving Cullen's.

The man eased back, then grabbed her boots, helping her into both before standing. He offered her his hand, practically yanking her into his chest as Lucas set her on her feet.

He leaned in from behind. "Cullen can button your shirt and trousers while I get you some coffee. Maybe it will finally drive away the chill."

She wanted to say that she felt strangely hot, not cold, but the words got lost as Cullen gripped the sides of her shirt, holding them together as he meticulously closed her top.

Unexpected disappointment settled in her gut when Cullen secured the last button on her pants then stepped back, reaching for her pistols. She glanced down at her torso when he strapped them around her waist, suddenly wishing he'd gather her in close, again. Only this time, she wanted to him to remove her clothes.

Hollis gave herself a mental shake. Obviously, the fatigue was catching up with her. That was the reason her thoughts were so scattered. All she needed was some sleep, and she'd go back to wanting to knock the men on their asses.

"Here you go, darlin'."

A mug appeared in front of her, the steam blurring Lucas' face as he smiled at her, his fingers brushing against hers when she accepted the cup. The brief contact quickened her pulse, and it was all she could do to manage a raspy, "Thanks," past her clenched lips.

Cullen sighed. "You'd best drink all of that before just holdin' it cools it down."

"I'm not that cold. In fact, I feel much better already."

Cullen arched a brow. "Then, why are your lips still blue?" He moved before she could reply, bending low to grab his jacket. Then, he shifted behind her, draping the coat over her shoulders. "You can wear that until you're warm enough."

His scent infused her senses, again, mingling with the hint of Lucas' that seemed to have rubbed off onto her shirt while she'd been curled up in his lap. The aromas wove together, creating a new one that eased the restless feeling still churning her stomach. The one she didn't want to investigate too closely, right now.

She took a sip of the coffee, moaning as the rich flavor burst along her tongue. A low chuckle drew her gaze to Lucas.

He smiled, reigniting the butterflies in her stomach. "I'll assume by that noise you approve of my brewing techniques."

She laughed. "I wasn't expectin' it to be this sweet. All the coffee I've had at other rail camps is quite bitter."

"The secret's in not boiling the beans directly in the water. Of course, adding sugar helps. Perhaps this can be our atonement. A steady supply of good coffee. Might save you getting shot at by Caleb, to boot."

"Not getting shot is definitely an added bonus, but the coffee's good enough, I'd except your offer on its merit, alone."

Cullen moved in beside Lucas. "Does that imply we're forgiven?"

She lifted the cup, hiding her grin. "As long as the sheriff can keep his end of the bargain, I'll agree not to threaten to shoot you both on sight."

"That's not exactly the agreement we were lookin' for, but I reckon it's a start. Now, about your tendency to find trouble…"

Hollis took another swig, cradling the mug in her hands for warmth as she faced the men. "I don't go lookin' for trouble. It just sometimes finds me."

"Maybe that's because you make rash decisions. Rush headlong into a situation without any concern for your well-being."

"I don't consider wanting to wash off the filth from travelin'—from this camp—a rash decision. And I heard those men. I would have taken appropriate measures to ensure my safety."

"Was that before or after I had to pry your guns from your shaking hands because you were so damn cold?"

"So, you would have preferred I stay dirty? Risk spreadin' infection to my patients?"

Cullen took a step forward. "I seem to recall offerin' to draw you a bath in my quarters."

Hollis sighed. Damn she hated being wrong. She glanced up at the man, noting that Lucas had moved forward, too. Like a unified wall of male muscle standing in front of her. "Perhaps choosin' to bathe in the river wasn't one of my better ideas. I didn't realize how cold the water got around here."

Cullen cracked a slight grin. "Is that your roundabout way of admittin' you were wrong?"

"I wasn't wrong. You were simply more right. Regardless, I don't believe I thanked you for making sure I was safe, or carryin' me back here. So, thank you. Though, I still contest that if you hadn't bowled me to the ground while I was naked, I wouldn't have gotten as cold as I did."

Both men looked at each other then laughed, shaking their heads as they stared at her.

Hollis frowned. "I'm not sure what you find so funny."

Lucas did his best to school his features. "It's you, darlin'. You are, without a doubt, the most unique woman we've ever met. Feisty, stubborn, but with enough skill to back up your reckless nature. I have a feeling you're going to be quite the force to be reckoned with, and a constant test of our sanity."

"I won't apologize for the choices I've made, even the questionable ones, or I never would have had the courage to go to medical school in the first place." She smiled. "My mother always did say I have too much of my father in me."

"We wouldn't want you to change, Hollis. Just try to keep it from getting you into dangerous situations."

She sauntered closer, placing her hand on Lucas' arm. "I'm a female doctor trying to make a life for herself out west. Just doing my job is dangerous. Men like Frank are the norm out here, which means every new case I get is another test I have to pass or risk getting fired." She looked them both in the eyes. "Or worse." She backed away, cradling the cup in both hands, again. "It's like I said last night. I've done all I can to tip the cards in my favor." She shrugged "The rest..."

"The rest is to realize when to let others give you a hand." Lucas motioned to Cullen. "Even if the men in question are a bit late with their support. Though, once we give it...we don't back down. I meant what I said in the tavern last night. If anyone lays a finger on you, they'll have to answer to me and Cullen. Period. And I can promise you it won't end well for them."

"Careful, Sheriff. You might not want to put all your faith in me just yet. There's still a lot about me you don't know. It could turn out that I'm the dishonorable one."

"Guess that's a risk we're willing to take. We're a pretty good judge of character. More coffee?"

She held up her hand. "While I'd love some, sounds like the rest of the camp is wakin' up. You both have work to do, and I probably shouldn't leave Jack alone for too long. Just my luck his brother will be waitin' for me, and I'll have to explain why I thought it was all right to leave Jack's side, even for a few minutes."

"I already have more made. I'll pour you another cup, and you can take it with you."

"Won't you need your mug?"

"Not while I'm out with the crew." Lucas winked at her. "It'll give me an excuse to drop by the clinic later."

Cullen stepped forward. "As for Frank...he won't bother you if he knows what's good for him."

A warm feeling spread through her chest. "Dear Lord, you threatened the man, didn't you? Last night. After the fight."

Cullen's expression changed, and she swore another

flash of red glinted in his eyes, then vanished. "Any man who'd hit a woman deserves far more than me tossin' him on his ass with a few words of warning. The fact he hit *you*..."

Hollis frowned when he didn't continue. "Why would hitting me be worse?"

Cullen glanced at Lucas, giving the other man an arch of his brow.

Lucas sighed as his gaze found hers. "Cullen just meant that Frank was lucky you were still willin' to treat his brother after hurting you like that."

Despite the fact Lucas had sounded sincere, Hollis couldn't quite shake the feeling that there were other reasons behind Cullen's statement. Ones they obviously didn't want to divulge.

"Doesn't seem right to fault a man for his brother's actions. Though, I could have done without the split lip." She grazed her fingers over her bruised flesh. "Damn thing still stings."

Lucas frowned then stepped forward, gently cupping her chin. He tilted her head slightly, looking at her mouth in the dawning light. "Shit. I can't believe we didn't notice it was still swollen. Or see that light bruising on your forehead."

"It was dark—"

"Not that dark." He skimmed his thumb along her lip. "It's just been so hard to focus on anything other than your scent."

"My scent?"

Cullen cleared his throat. "He meant your perfume."

Hollis furrowed her brow. "I just went for a dip in the river. I'm not wearing any perfume."

"Must be the fragrance from the soap, then. It's very... pleasing, but distracting. Guess we're not used to being close to anyone who doesn't smell like sweat or liquor around here."

"I guess, but—"

"How about I get you that coffee?" Lucas eased the cup out of her fingers then strode toward the stove.

She released a weary exhale. Maybe she was far more fatigued than she'd first thought. She nodded when he returned, placing the steaming mug in her hands. "Thank you, again."

"Our pleasure." He waved at the door. "We'll walk you back to the clinic."

"You don't have—"

"We're headed that way. Might as well walk together."

She opened her mouth to comment, then closed it as they ushered her to the door. Streaks of yellow and orange filled the sky, most of the night's shadows chased away by the muted light. Cullen moved to her left side while Lucas stayed on her right, their large forms making her feel small.

She swallowed past the thick feeling in her throat then struck off toward the clinic, noting the way they fell into perfect step beside her. They didn't speak, just walked along, each scanning the road as if they expected to find something dangerous between every building. It wasn't until they'd arrived at her door that they seemed to relax.

She turned to face them. "Thank you for walkin' me back. And for the coffee."

Lucas tipped his hat. "As I said. Our pleasure."

She gave them a smile, grabbing the handle when she realized she was still wearing Cullen's coat. "Damn, your jacket." She shrugged it off her shoulders, instantly missing the comforting weight of it. She held it out to him. "You should have reminded me. I nearly walked into the clinic with it still on."

Cullen shrugged. "You needed it more than I did. You're welcome to hold on to it if you're still cold."

She shivered as if on cue, though she wasn't sure it had anything to do with the temperature. "I'll be fine. There's a small stove in the back room. There wasn't any fuel to start it up last night, but I'll gather some coal so I'll be prepared tonight. The days are still warm enough."

"I'll have one of the crewmen bring you some before we head out."

"Cullen, I don't need to be waited on."

"No, but you don't need to get yourself dirty, again, when you'll likely have more patients. We already saw how well your first bath faired."

She swatted his arm. "I did get clean, so in that respect, it was a shining success." She sighed in defeat. "Fine. I appreciate it." She paused with one foot inside the door, looking at them over her shoulder. "Are you gentlemen going to be this...accommodatin' all the time?"

Cullen quirked his lips. "Is that a problem?"

"I suppose not. It's just... I'm not used to people being supportive of me. Honestly, I half expected you to dump my ass on the first train back to Boston today, seeing as I've already dealt with Jack."

Lucas stepped forward. "We misjudged you once already. We don't plan on making that same mistake, again."

"Fair enough. Then, I suppose I'll see you both later."

She stepped inside, closing the door behind her. She

leaned against it, curbing the urge to move to the window —watch them walk away. She didn't like the restless flutter of her pulse or the nervous roll of her stomach when she realized she wouldn't see either of the men, again, before sunset. It wasn't like her to let her guard down this quickly, especially when she really didn't know them. Maybe they were being nice so she wouldn't suspect their real motivations. Wouldn't see it coming when they changed their minds and sent her packing.

She groaned inwardly. This had nothing to do with being fired and everything to do with the riot of emotions churning inside her since Cullen had tackled her down by the river. Having his body over hers shouldn't have felt that...exciting. That right. It was the same feeling she'd gotten when Lucas had tugged her against his chest, then gathered her in his lap.

Get ahold of yourself.

They were most likely just doing their job. And the fact there was two of them—what was she thinking? She couldn't be attracted to both men at the same time. And not shoving her on a train didn't mean either of them felt anything other than idle responsibility for her. After all, Lucas was the sheriff, and Cullen had his job riding on the success or failure of the spur. It was only natural they'd look out for anyone in town, especially if she could help keep the men working—keep the line moving forward.

She straightened. Now wasn't the time to let her heart rule her behavior. She'd come here to play her role as camp doctor, and nothing was going to interfere with that. The sooner she made peace with the fact she'd most likely spend her life alone—that the chance of having any man embrace her profession was a long shot at best—the easier it would be to work in the camps without getting distracted by any romantic notions. After all, this was only a stop. A temporary place to stay until it shut down for the harsh winter months. Then, she'd be off to another camp—another test of her skills. Getting attached...

Hollis moved over to the cot, checking Jack's temperature. This was what she knew. What she was good at. Cullen and Lucas—they were just wishful thinking for a life she knew she couldn't have.

CHAPTER SIX

Lucas paced the length of the newly laid line, watching the workers prepare the next section for the narrow-gauge rail. The sounds of metal against metal echoed around them, making it extremely hard to listen for possible threats. He removed his hat, wiping the sweat from his brow before flopping the Stetson back in place. The weather couldn't seem to make up its mind. Freezing temperatures at night, hotter than normal days. Just their luck the winter snow would come early this year and shorten their timeframe even more.

He glanced at Cullen, drawn to the way his muscles flexed as he swung a pickaxe, obviously trying to get through the last bit of rock and clay. His mate had taken off his shirt hours ago, and the smooth expanse of sun-kissed skin mixed with the hint of hair along his chest was slowly driving Lucas crazy. But it wasn't just Cullen.

It had been five weeks since Hollis had stumbled into their lives, and Lucas hadn't had a moment's peace since. Between fighting his attraction for both his mates and trying to keep the crews safe—he hadn't found a spare minute to fully act on the blistering arousal consuming him. While that was probably a good thing where Hollis was concerned, Cullen—he was a different story.

They'd both worked hard to try and maintain their distance—wait until Hollis was part of their coupling—but they were failing miserably. Lucas had lost track of the number of times they'd slammed each other into a handy surface, each vying for possession of the other's mouth. The word "mine" had been playing over and over inside his head, to the point he'd finally fallen to his knees last night, determined to claim just a piece of Cullen by sucking the other man dry, only to get interrupted when shouts had risen from the saloon.

Lucas cursed. Men like Frank were going to drive Lucas past the breaking point. It was bad enough Hollis had already had to deal with what felt like an endless series of work-related injuries. Having to consistently patch up the crew because they lost their temper over a card game was pushing her to the edge, too. He wasn't sure if she'd gotten more than a few hours of sleep each night since arriving there, and the noticeable smudges beneath her eyes were like knives to his and Cullen's souls. They should be courting her—finding ways to win her heart, not spending what little time they could manage together just ensuring she ate. That she was strong enough to hold her own when one of the men thought they could best her.

A growl rumbled through his chest. He'd already tossed half a dozen men in jail for a night for trying to take advantage of her, and he suspected it was just the beginning. It was getting to the point he was considering shooting a few, himself, as a deterrent. Though that would only make more work for Hollis. And Lord knew she already had her hands full. Thankfully, between him and Cullen, she hadn't had to do more than punch the odd cowboy in the jaw before they'd had the problem corralled.

His cock jerked painfully against the confines of his trousers. The damn thing had been in a constant state of arousal since meeting Hollis, and all the limited contact and interruptions with Cullen had only made the situation worse. Another few days and his bear might simply break free and ruin everything.

His grizzly huffed, pacing back and forth inside his head. The animal was restless and not just because of Cullen and Hollis. The endless attacks on the line were testing both his and his bear's patience. While the injuries hadn't taken another life, yet—largely due to Hollis' skill and determination—Lucas' inability to prevent adding to her workload was irritating the Hell out of him. But it was nearly impossible to cover every angle when the men were currently out in the open, with endless trees and boulders to hide behind on either side of the line. Even with Cullen devoting half his time to security, there just weren't enough eyes. And with the amount of blasting they were doing to help get through the unrelenting rock, the explosives made a worthwhile prize for any of Buford's gang, and reason, enough, to keep targeting the rail.

His bear snarled this time. It didn't like feeling helpless. He'd given the poor animal as much freedom as he could without sprouting fur, but with all the other noises, Cullen's scent hanging in the air and hints of Hollis' lingering on his shirt or jacket—wherever she'd innocently touched him—it made it next to impossible to unearth other dangers. Lucas was quickly becoming more of a liability than an asset. And if he didn't find a way to stake his claim with his mates soon, going rogue might be the least of his concerns. He could end up missing something and getting someone killed. Someone like Hollis.

He barely contained the growl that rumbled through his chest. Cold day in Hell before he allowed anyone to harm his mates. He'd camp outside Hollis' clinic if he had to. His animal snorted. Christ, who was he kidding? He and Cullen already spent every night watching the building. Slowly losing their sanity.

Footsteps sounded nearby, and Lucas looked back toward the line. Cullen strode toward him, scanning the woods behind Lucas as he went. Rippling muscles glistened in the late afternoon sun, the thick bands across his chest and abdomen creating shadows along his torso.

Cullen missed a step as their gazes clashed, catching himself before moving in close. Red flashed in his eyes, a hint of claws showing on his fingers before he stuffed them in his pocket. "You keep starin' at me that way, and I'm liable to fuck you right here, right now."

Lucas let the growl he'd crushed surface. "You'll have to wait your turn, mate, because I'm not really in the mood to be submissive. And seeing as you're already half naked…"

Cullen's eyes darkened at the term, mate. Lucas had gone to great lengths not to use it in that way while they'd been waiting to find their missing piece. Now that they'd found her… The word rolled off his tongue as if it had a mind of its own. He only wished he could say it to Hollis. Hear her use it when referring to them.

Cullen's jaw clenched, pulsing the muscle in his temple. He inhaled, though based on the repeated clench of his jaw, the simple act hadn't helped calm him down. "We can't keep dancin' around Hollis like this. If my damn bear rides me any harder, I won't be able to stop from waltzin' into the clinic, scooping her up and carryin' her away. With you beside me."

"You think I don't know that? I can't focus on the damn railway when all I can think about is touching you. Tastin' her. Hell, I hadn't even realized one of the men had cut themselves until you'd sent him back to town on your horse. I should have smelled the blood, but..." He lifted his hands, watching the way they shook as he tried to hold them steady. "I'm consumed with this need that's got me so tied in knots, I'm compromisin' everyone's safety. Including yours."

Cullen laid a hand on Lucas' shoulder. "It's not just you. I'm drownin' right along with you. We need to talk to Hollis. Do something to soothe our other halves before we ruin any chance at a future with her by doing something rash."

"Well, if you've got an idea on how to sweep the girl off her feet, I'm listenin'."

Cullen kicked at the dirt. "You mean besides taking her in our arms and kissing her until she surrenders? Not really."

"The problem is that, every time we finally get her alone, an emergency pops up and either she has to leave or we do. We need to go someplace private. Where we can't be interrupted. Maybe she'd agree to ride out to survey that bridge site with us. Stay the night in a tent. Even if it's just her inside and us outside, it might be enough to get our bears to back off. Give us the time we need to properly court her. Show her for certain that we want to be more than a couple of men she has coffee with."

"And when we come back to discover Buford's gang has raided the camp while we were gone?"

"Can't have it both ways, Cullen. Either we make peace with the fact Hollis is unattainable while we're focusin' on finishing this spur, or we take a leap of faith. Pray the town can survive a night without us. There're some decent marksmen amidst the crew. I can make up a rotation. I'm sure they can manage to hold the fort for twenty-four hours."

"You think she'll agree to go?"

Lucas shrugged. "Only one way to find out."

"She doesn't seem to stray far from the clinic."

"Maybe because no one's ever asked her."

Cullen frowned. "Even if she does, I doubt we can gain her affections in the space of a single night."

"We've already had five weeks' worth of single nights, and we're on the verge of going rogue at every turn. We need more than coffee or a warmed up dinner to truly court her. Especially when we're interrupted more often than not. Hell, we haven't even come out and told her we're interested. Not in plain terms. This could be a start toward something more. Give us a chance to voice our intentions without the entire camp listenin' in. Might make carryin' on in camp for the next month feasible."

"I really hate when you're right. Fine, we'll go see her once we're done for the day. See if we can convince her to accompany us on an adventure. Now, we just have to make it through the rest of the day without giving her another patient to treat, or she'll never leave the clinic."

Lucas nodded, scanning the tree line. "Even with my enhanced senses, it's impossible to cover every angle out here. And it's only going to get worse. There's a narrow passage between us and that bridge. Bandits will be able to hide on both sides and have the advantage. I'll have to post sentry guards until we're through."

Cullen raked his hand through his hair. "We knew this line wouldn't be easy, not when it wasn't part of the main branch. The gangs know we're vulnerable, that our supplies are easy pickings, and our progress is sufferin' because of it."

"I've been thinkin'… We might need to take matters into our own hands. Go after Buford and his men. God knows there're bounties out for all of those boys."

"I'd hoped we could hold out until the snow stopped us—let the few months of hiatus cool things down—but you could be right. But if we do go after that gang, we'd best 'round them all up because the retaliation against the camp will be ten-fold if we don't."

"Agreed. We'll keep it in mind. Maybe we'll get lucky and they'll decide to move onto a more profitable line."

Cullen chuckled. "Right. 'Cause we've had nothing but luck on this project."

"We found Hollis."

"Which won't mean much if we can't earn her love." He groaned when the back end of a wagon collapsed, dropping the next load of ties and spikes on the ground and narrowly missing crushing two men in the process.

"Bloody Hell. We don't need Buford's men to kill anyone. The crew's going to do it all by themselves."

Cullen struck off, yelling at the men as he went. Lucas sighed, wiping away the sweat, again, when shots rang out from farther up the line. He dropped his hat then drew his weapons. Several horsemen raced toward the gathering of men, puffs of smoke rising from their pistols as they fired at the crew.

Lucas lined up the closest men, downing three then clipping another bandit's arm as he bore down on the crew. The force knocked him sideways, but he managed to remain on his mount as he raised his other hand. Flames flickered above his fingers before he tossed a shadowed object at a collection of boxes.

"Shit." Lucas raced across the open grass, his next shot hitting home this time. "Dynamite! Everyone get down!"

The outlaw fell off his horse, landing in a heap on the ground. Cullen ran over to the man, retrieving his weapons then shooting at the other bandits galloping away on the far side of the rail. Lucas headed for his mate, knocking into him from the side and tackling him to the ground just as the dynamite exploded, setting off their supplies in the process. Fire erupted around them, launching debris into the air as smoke billowed outwards, clogging the air with thick plumes.

The men landed hard, pain radiating down through Lucas' shoulder and into his chest, stealing what breath he had. Black dots danced at the edges of his vision, the telltale tingling of an impending shift working its way along his nerves.

"Lucas. Goddamn it." Cullen's face appeared above him, flecks of blood splattered across his chest.

Lucas frowned. "You're bleeding."

"Not my blood. It's yours." Cullen's jaw tensed, his expression a mix of pain and fear. "You caught one of those spikes in your shoulder. Looks bad." He held Lucas down. "Don't move. I need to put pressure on it. Let me grab my shirt. It doesn't look like it was ruined in the explosion."

"Damn it, Cullen, you know I don't need you to tend my wounds." Another tremor shook his limbs. "Just pull the fucking thing out, haul my ass over to the trees, and let me shift."

More shots rang out, the last few drowned out by the thunder of hooves. Cullen returned fire, covering Lucas' body when a box of gun powder ignited. His mate stared down at him, huffing out his next breath before grabbing the spike and yanking it free. Lucas growled, arching his back as his grizzly surged forward, tearing at his control.

Cullen leaned in close, his breath washing over Lucas' face. "Hold it together, mate. Just for a bit longer. Buford's men are still shootin' up the area, and there're too many people to shift here without being seen."

"The...trees..."

"You mean the ones behind us where I see three more of Buford's gang pokin' their heads out from between the branches? You're strong but not enough to take on armed men, even outfitted with claws and fangs."

Lucas locked his fingers around Cullen's forearm, holding him close. "Can't hold off...the pain..."

Cullen growled then bent low, biting Lucas' good shoulder hard enough to scratch the skin but not puncture it. The firm pressure pulled his animal back slightly.

"Stay with me. We need to get somewhere safe, first, so I can take care of the rest of the gang. Once they're gone, I'll help you to the woods." He shuffled him onto his shoulder then ran toward the piles of railway ties and boxes the dynamite hadn't reached.

The crew huddled within the odd stacks, armed with only shovels and axes. Two more horsemen rode past, raining bullets into the crates and logs. Cullen placed Lucas near the edge, using his body to shield Lucas from most of the workers. Even if he managed to stave off his impending shift until it was safe, he'd never be able to explain how he healed so quickly if the men saw the extent of his wound. Groans and whimpers sounded around them, the metallic stench of blood saturating the air.

Cullen reloaded his gun, firing enough to keep the outlaws from getting too close, before focusing on Lucas. He balled up some cloth, pressing it on the wound as he nodded at the men behind them. "Shit. This is worse than I thought it'd be. We'll run out of ammunition if we stay here. Not to mention you're nearly out of time. I'll make a distraction, then you see if you can make it to the trees. We'll just have to hope I draw all those men away and no one sees you change. That you aren't challenged the second you shift."

Lucas glanced at the tree line. "While it kills me to say this…I'm not sure I can make it that far."

Cullen's gaze dropped to his shoulder. Lucas didn't need to see the cloth to know it was already drenched with his blood. A desperate snort sounded in his head, followed by another violent tremor.

Cullen lowered his head. "Damn it. Fine, we'll go

together. I'll cover us. Just...don't you dare fucking die on me, you hear?"

"I'll do my best not to." Lucas wrapped his arm around Cullen's shoulders when shots rang out from the other direction. He inhaled sharply as he glanced at Cullen. "Please tell me I'm imagining that."

Cullen grunted. "You mean the part where Hollis just showed up and is positioned beside the locomotive, firing that rifle at Buford's gang? The woman's downright crazy. She's going to get her fool head shot off."

Men charged toward her from up the line, the thunder of horses making the ground shake. Lucas tried to draw his gun, but his fingers couldn't seem to grip the handle. Hollis never flinched as she aimed her rifle then fired again, hitting the closest bandit off his horse. She reloaded, spinning to catch another as the man raced past where the crew was gathered. The man's foot caught in the saddle as he toppled to the side, and his horse raced off, dragging him behind.

Cullen muttered continuously under his breath, trying to gently shuffle Lucas off him, when Hollis picked up two bags then darted over to the men, immediately working her way through the casualties. She caught their gazes, her eyes widening as her focus dropped to Lucas' shirt. The color drained from her face, and she pushed through the last of the uninjured men then stopped in front of them.

Cullen glared at her. "Do you have a death wish? What the Hell do you think you're doing?"

"Trying to prevent a massacre." She stared at Lucas then opened her bag. "You're hurt. Take off your shirt and let me have a look."

Lucas pushed off Cullen, praying he didn't fall on his face as he did his best to draw himself up. "It's only a graze. You'd best tend to the others while I go have a quick scout around."

"Graze? You've bled through that cloth. That's more than a graze."

She reached for him, but Cullen stepped in front.

"There are men hurt far worse than Lucas. Trust me, he'll be okay."

"I realize that. But it's my job to assess *all* the crew so I can prioritize my time. I've already looked at everyone else—got some of the men helping me deal with the worst injuries as we speak. I need to see how bad Lucas' wound is so I know how long he can wait."

"He's fine." Cullen held up his hand. "Please, Hollis. Tend to the other men. We'll be back before you know it."

"Back? He's in no shape to go anywhere. Cullen…"

Her voice faded as Cullen snagged Lucas' arm, making it look as if he was leading Lucas over to the trees, all the while supporting half his weight. They managed to trip their way to a thicker part of the woods before Cullen turned and helped Lucas undress. Then, he backed away, checking the area one more time before nodding.

Lucas let his shoulders droop as he released his hold on his bear. The animal growled in response, surging forward. There was a moment of disconnectedness before his grizzly took control, and Lucas fell forward onto all fours. The feel of the ground beneath him changed, the thick padding of his bear's paws softening the rough bite of dirt and rocks. Odors and images sharpened, the din of distant voices making his ears twitch.

A hand landed on his back, and he turned, staring into

Cullen's hazel eyes. A soft green aura hung around him like a mist, the wispy essence a visual extension of his mate's scent. Lucas took a lumbering step forward, knocking Cullen with his head as he tried to rub against him, imprint on him as best as he could until he could leave a permanent mark on Cullen's skin.

Cullen chuckled, giving Lucas a playful shove. "You already know I'm yours. You don't have to dump me on my ass to prove it." A smile spread across his face. "Damn, I'd forgotten how impressive your bear is. Makes me think we've neglected this side of ourselves for too long. Can't remember the last time we ran together as our other halves."

Lucas snorted, twisting to glance back the way they'd come. He sniffed, shifting through the various odors until he honed in on Hollis' sweet essence. A light blue trail wove through the trees, disappearing into the clearing beyond. Lucas managed to shuffle sideways before Cullen stepped in front.

His mate barred his way, moving with Lucas when he attempted to limp around him. "I know what you're thinkin', what your bear wants, but you can't go after Hollis. Not like this."

He snarled, knocking at Cullen, again.

Cullen growled in response. "Don't take that attitude with me. You're not the only one who's unhappy about the situation. But if you go charging over there dressed in fur and fangs, the girl will probably shoot you. At best, you'll destroy any chance we have of gaining her love. We'll figure it out. But right now, you need to heal."

Cullen gave Lucas another shove. "Come on. I'll see you safely to the river just over that rise, then I'll go and make sure Hollis is okay." He cocked his head to the side when Lucas simply stood there, staring in Hollis' direction. "You need to trust me to protect her until you're well enough to shift back. Now, let's go before Buford's men return. As good a shot as she is, I'd rather she not scare another ten years off of my life."

Lucas inhaled again, looking at the trail one more time before lowering his head and slowly turning around. Cullen's hand landed on his shoulder as he limped toward the river. His mate was right about one thing. She'd scared more than a few years off Lucas' life, too—a fact they'd definitely be discussing once his bear had healed the worst of the damage.

CHAPTER SEVEN

Cullen leaned against the side of the sheriff's office, watching the oil lamps flicker in the clinic just down the street. His stomach clenched every time Hollis passed in front of the window, her lithe form darting off toward the back of the building, only to reappear, again, a few moments later. She hadn't stopped working since she'd returned, despite the fact it was well after midnight.

A mixture of anger and frustration burned beneath his skin. While he respected her dedication to her profession, if she didn't start taking better care of herself, she'd be her next patient. That, or she'd get herself killed.

His bear growled this time, scratching at Cullen's control, as if it wasn't already frayed. Between Lucas getting injured and Hollis showing up amidst a blaze of gunfire, both sides of Cullen were strung tight. One more incident, and Devil's Gate would have more than just the Buford gang to deal with. They'd have his and Lucas' bears trotting down the main road with every intention of claiming their mate.

Cullen raked a hand through his hair, tugging on some of the strands in an effort to calm his other half. If he'd learned anything about Hollis over the past month, it was that they needed to tread carefully. He'd witnessed more than a few casual conversations end up with her drawing her weapons when one of the men tried to strong arm her, and just because Cullen and Lucas were her mates didn't mean she wouldn't take the same stance with them. She didn't have the luxury of an inner animal telling her she was destined to be with them. And God knew they hadn't had many chances to show her, themselves.

Of course, if he wasn't currently avoiding her, he could have gone inside the clinic—offered to help. But until Lucas shifted back, Cullen couldn't risk venturing too close to her. Not when he knew Hollis would corner him, again, regarding Lucas' condition. He'd managed to avoid answering any of her questions thus far, and as much as he disliked staying distant, they needed the time apart to account for the fact Lucas' shoulder would be healed. That he wouldn't have more than a faint line where the spike had impaled his flesh. It hadn't taken Cullen's increased senses as Hollis' mate to know she hadn't believed them when they'd told her Lucas' injury had been nothing more than a graze.

The thought had Cullen digging his nails into his palms to stay in control. He'd spent the day shuttling back and forth between his mates. After he'd left Lucas at the river, he'd circled the crew, checking for more bandits before helping her load the injured onto wagons. Unfortunately, the one platform car they'd brought along had still been loaded with rail ties and other supplies, and Hollis hadn't wanted to waste the time it would have taken to unload them all. Something about how much blood some of the men were losing.

Cullen had ridden alongside the convoy until the camp had wavered into view in the distance before turning around and heading back to his other mate. While he had no doubt Lucas could fend for himself, they couldn't afford to draw attention to themselves. Not to mention the fact Lucas' other half wasn't really fit to go up against a gang of outlaws.

They'd waited until the sun had set, nothing but a blanket of stars in the sky, before returning to the camp. Cullen had ensured the street was deserted before marshaling Lucas' bear into his office, then on to his quarters in the back. His mate's grizzly had been more than a bit antsy being this close to Hollis, but Cullen had eventually been able to settle the animal. Now, all he could do was wait.

The door to the office creaked open, the soft press of boots on the wooden planks drawing his attention. He glanced over, grinning as Lucas emerged from the building, his shadow stretching out toward Cullen as the moon rose higher in the sky behind his mate. Lucas's gaze swung to his, a flash of red noticeable even in the darkness.

Cullen straightened, ready to move in front of the other man if he made a dash for the clinic. Instead, the sheriff marched over to him, grabbing Cullen by the shoulders and shoving him against the wall, their bodies blending into the black pockets lining the walkway. His mate didn't talk, just trapped Cullen with his arms, inhaling as he leaned in close.

A low growl vibrated between them, followed the firm

scrape of Lucas' teeth across Cullen's shoulder. Even through the fabric, he felt the sharp scratch of canines—a clear sign his partner was teetering on the edge.

Lucas grazed a path to Cullen's neck, his breath hot against Cullen's skin. "Mine."

Cullen fisted Lucas' shirt, holding him close as he nipped at the man's earlobe. "I know how raw you feel right now, especially after shifting. It increases all those urges boiling your blood. As I see it, we have two choices. Claim each other, first, or keep fightin' it until we can have a serious chat with Hollis. But know this... Once I get you naked, I won't be able to stop. Hell, I would have taken you in the damn forest today if you hadn't been on the verge of dyin'."

Lucas closed his eyes, the muscle in his jaw clenching. "If we're going to talk, first, we need to do it soon. I never expected it to be this hard to push aside. The need... God, it's like a fire inside my veins I can't put out."

"You and me both, partner. Let's just allow her to get through this emergency. I'm sure everything will settle by tomorrow. Then, once she's rested, we'll ask her to go survey the bridge with us. Thinkin' it'd be best if she couldn't simply dart into the street and start screamin' that we're shifters."

Lucas chuckled. "We both know she wouldn't run. She'd just shoot us, herself."

"I'll make a note to wait until after she's unclipped her holsters before we spring the news on her. Just to be safe."

Lucas nodded, still pinning Cullen to the wall when a wedge of light appeared up the street. They both glanced at the glow, frowning when two silhouettes exited the clinic, pausing on the walkway. The glare from the room dissolved them into nothing more than dark shadows, but he knew one was Hollis by the shape of her body. The way she tilted her head. The pair stopped near the short set of steps leading up to the building, standing far too close for Cullen's liking. The low din of voices carried to them as Hollis nodded at the guy, his hand lifting to rest on her shoulder. A menacing growl echoed in Cullen's head as Lucas tensed, releasing Cullen then heading down the street.

Cullen cursed, darting after his mate in an effort to calm the man down. With Lucas' senses heightened from the shift, just seeing Hollis with another man—regardless of the circumstances—might be enough to push his mate over the edge. Have his animal go rogue once Lucas got close enough to catch the foreign scent on her clothes.

Cullen snagged Lucas' elbow, pulling him to a halt before rounding in front of him. "Easy, mate. I know what your bear's thinkin', but...if you jump to conclusions and shift on me, we'll never win her over."

Lucas snarled, his gaze focused on the man standing off to Hollis' side, his head bent slightly in conversation. "Don't care why he's touching her. She's ours."

"Yes, she is. And it's not as if it's the first time one of the crew has touched her. She's a doctor. It happens. I'm sure it means nothing."

Red flashed, again, in Lucas' eyes. "It was a mistake not to tear those other cowboys to shreds. One I won't make, again."

Cullen tightened his hold, growling at Lucas in challenge. "Do you really want to go a few rounds with me? Pull back."

His mate's jaw clenched, the obvious strain creasing his brow. Cullen hedged his bet by dragging Lucas closer, doing his best to obscure everything else from view. Lucas finally managed to focus on Cullen, but there was no mistaking how close the man was to holding true to his threat, regardless of the consequences.

Cullen nodded. "Perhaps you should go back to your quarters. Let that hammerin' inside your head lessen. I'll figure out what's going on."

"Cullen?"

Cullen froze as Hollis' voice washed over him, the soft tone igniting every nerve. God, all it took was a single word, a passing glance, and he fell a bit harder. Needed her a bit more. And all without her knowing the effect she had on him. On them.

She jogged down the steps, heading toward him. He gave Lucas a hard glare then released him, turning to face their mate, doing his best to block Lucas from view. She stopped a few feet away, her gaze darting to where Lucas stood behind Cullen. The fine lines around her eyes looked deeper, from lack of sleep, no doubt. She'd piled her hair into bun on top of her head, a few errant strands curling around her jaw as they fluttered in the light breeze. Blood stained the apron she'd slipped over her other clothes, though her regular garments were still covered from tending the men on site.

She scrunched her nose, creasing the skin between her eyebrows. "So, that is Lucas with you. I've been more than a bit worried not knowing what happened to him. You two should have stopped by the clinic as soon as you got back."

Cullen cringed. This conversation was definitely going in the wrong direction. "Hollis—"

She focused on Lucas, her expression guarded. "I need to see your shoulder."

Cullen moved with her when she stepped to her left. "It's late. I'm actually surprised you haven't turned in, yet."

Hollis narrowed her eyes, grunting when he blocked her next attempt. "I'll sleep when I'm done." She glared at how he kept her at arm's length. "What's wrong with you? I need..." She paused when the man behind her wished her a goodnight, disappearing into the darkness. She acknowledged him with a small wave then turned back to them. "I'm not going anywhere until I take a look at Lucas' wound."

A growl lit the air, the menacing sound loud in the stillness.

Hollis frowned, staring at them as if they'd lost their minds. "Did one of you just growl?"

Lucas sidestepped, revealing half of his body from behind Cullen. "Was that the reverend?"

Cullen groaned inwardly at the accusing tone of Lucas' voice, knowing there was no hope that Hollis had missed it for what it was. A challenge. She took a step back, glancing at the empty street before focusing on them, again.

"Yes. I needed some help treating the more serious injuries. It gets hard to hold a man down and stitch him up at the same time. Reverend Miller said he'd assisted that kind of work before, so he offered to stand in. But that's hardly what's important right now."

Lucas pushed against Cullen's back. "So, why was he touching you? Standin' so close?"

"Touching me?"

Cullen twisted to look at Lucas, mentally telling his mate to back off. Lucas glanced at him, another flash of red in his eyes his only answer. Cullen answered in kind then faced Hollis, again.

He nodded at the clinic. "What Lucas meant was it's late. And you look exhausted. Thinkin' you should turn in, now that you're done."

Hollis furrowed her brow, obviously confused by the distinct change in subject. "Not until I check Lucas' shoulder."

Lucas tensed, his muscles flexing against Cullen. "That's not necessary."

Hollis huffed and crossed her arms over her chest. "Are you going to play me for the fool, again?"

"Of course not. But...as you can see by the fact I'm standing here, I'm fine."

"So, all that blood I saw on your shirt? On that cloth Cullen used to stem the bleedin? I've been doing this long enough to know when something is much more than a 'graze'. I was too busy to push the subject before, but now that I've tended to everyone else, there's no reason to avoid examinin' your wound."

Cullen raked his hand through his hair, trying to think of something—anything—to get her to go back to her quarters without discovering the truth. "It wasn't just Lucas' blood. He didn't get anything more than a scratch."

She arched a brow. "Then, he shouldn't mind showing me the laceration."

"Hollis...you're about to fall down you're so tired. You

can look at Lucas' shoulder tomorrow. Once you're rested."

"How about I make you boys a deal? I won't tell you or Lucas how to run the camp, build the railroad or keep the townspeople safe, and you won't tell me how to keep your crew alive as best I can."

"Of course." He blocked her from getting to Lucas, again. "And that deal can start first thing in the morning. As soon as you've gotten some rest. After we've all gotten some rest."

"Damn it, Cullen. Minor or not, any wound can become infected if it isn't treated properly. Which is why you spent the last three months beggin' the company for a real doctor."

"I realize that, but... Lucas doesn't need your kind of help." He sighed. "Just trust us. This once. Please."

"My kind of help? What's that supposed to mean?"

"Nothing. It came out wrong."

"So, he'll let me examine his shoulder, then?"

"It's not a matter of letting, and more the fact that you can't help him."

"I can't help..." She glanced at Lucas, a volley of emotions shaping her features, before focusing on Cullen, again. Tears gathered in her eyes as her chin quivered before she clenched her jaw and took a couple of steps back. Color rose high in her cheeks as she drew herself up. "Is this your way of informing me you don't consider me to be a *real* doctor? Like the *male* one you asked for? Like that first night when you said all they'd sent you was a woman? Is that why neither of you want me to look at Lucas' shoulder?"

Cullen frowned. "No. That's not what I said."

"You didn't have to say the words. The truth is written all over your face." She turned, marching toward the clinic.

Cullen growled then darted after her, Lucas on his heels. "What? Wait. Hollis."

She ignored them, increasing her pace.

Cullen moved to her left as Lucas flanked right. "Why would we go to the trouble of defendin' you with the crew if we thought you weren't worthy of it?"

She shoved at her hair when it bounced free of the bun, falling in a tousled mess about her head. "What better way to get me to play by your rules than to pretend to support me. Christ, I can't believe I was so foolish. Thought you actually cared."

"Pretend? We weren't pretendin', and we do care." Cullen huffed, hooking her elbow and spinning her around. "Would you stop running and just talk to us?"

Hollis tugged her arm free, another quiver trembling her chin as she seemed to swallow with effort. "There's nothing to say. I should have guessed you changed your minds too quickly. Should have realized all the coffee and the time we spent together was merely for appearances. Get your crew to stop houndin' you for something you obviously can't provide. It doesn't matter whether you think I'm capable of doing my job, as long as you convince the rest of the camp to play nice. After all, compared to the damn barber, I'm a *fucking* miracle worker!" She snorted. "Sorry, didn't mean to offend you with such strong language. But then, perhaps you don't really know me at all."

She spun, tripping her way up the stairs and into the clinic. The door rattled as she slammed it shut, the loud bang echoing down the deserted street. Cullen stared at the wooden slab, wondering what in the Hell had just happened. How it had all fallen apart so quickly. He turned, marching back to the sheriff's office, using every trick he knew to keep from shifting.

Lucas followed behind him, moving to stand in front of him once they'd shut the door behind them. "Shit!"

Cullen tipped back his head, wondering if the past five weeks had just been part of some elaborate joke. "I know this looks bad—"

"Looks bad? She just accused us of lyin' to her. She thinks we don't give a damn. That we don't respect what she does. That's far worse than lookin' bad."

"You think I don't know that? But what the Hell was I supposed to do? We both know she never would have believed you'd simply *healed* in less than twenty-four hours. And I didn't have time to come up with some other explanation, not that she would have believed one, anyway."

Lucas kicked at the floor. "Maybe we should just show her. Put it all out in the open."

"Right, because the truth is so much more realistic. You know how this goes, Lucas. We can't risk tellin' her if there's a chance she's going to turn on us. Especially here. If Frank and the others get even an inkling we're 'different', it won't just be our lives on the line. Hollis could get caught in the crossfire. I don't know about you, but I'm not strong enough to be responsible for her getting hurt. Dyin'."

Lucas glanced at the window, his gaze no doubt lingering on the lighted window down the street. "We're already dyin' here without her."

Cullen nodded, ambling over then kicking out a chair. He fell onto the seat, wishing he could turn back the clock. Think of something else to say that wouldn't end with her shutting them out.

Lucas' hand landed on his shoulder. "Not your fault. It's mine. If I hadn't gotten hit today—"

"Then, that spike would have hit me in the chest. You think I don't know that? Christ, I haven't even thanked you for savin' my damn life."

"Letting you get hurt wasn't an option—for the man or the bear."

Cullen sighed. "This thing with Hollis goes far deeper than just today. We're on the edge without a clue of how to reach her without simply fallin'. I guess I never expected it to be this difficult."

Lucas nudged him. "She's a woman and a doctor. I'd say that makes her ten times more difficult than regular women."

"Well, we'd better find a way to fix this, or we'll have to leave before our bears go rogue. And I'd rather not die in this Hellhole if it's all the same to you."

Lucas glanced at the window, again. "No one's going to die. But Hollis is going to give us a chance to explain. That, I promise you."

"God, I hope you're right because..." He glanced at his hands, noting the claws extending past his fingers. "I'm going to end up exposin' myself, one way or another."

"Get some sleep. I'll make a few rounds then come back and wake you when it's time." Lucas held up his hand. "I'm fine. Got plenty of rest while healing. And Hollis' reaction just scared my bear enough it's pulled back. But you'll never be able to keep your Kodiak in check if you're using half your strength to keep your eyes open. Not fall off your damn horse. Reckon we'll head back out and survey the damage once the sun rises."

"I'll head out. I want you to stay here...keep an eye on her."

"You're the one who'll be in danger."

"We weren't the only ones to suffer loses today. Between us and Hollis, they're down a few men, as well. Betting they'll be lickin' their wounds for a while before they decide to challenge us, again."

"And when they do?"

Cullen shook his head. "It'll be twice as bad. So, we'll need to be ready. But for now...I'd feel a whole lot better if you were watching out for our stubborn mate. The girl has a penchant for pissin' off the crew. And after the number of injuries... We never know who might blame her for the ones she couldn't save today."

"I hadn't thought about it like that. Fine, I'll stick around tomorrow. But we need to move ahead with our plan, even if that means exposin' ourselves here, instead of somewhere safer."

Cullen could only nod, before heading back to Lucas' quarters. While Cullen's were close, he needed to soothe his other half, and lying on Lucas' bed, surrounded by the man's scent, was enough to ease the tight feeling beneath Cullen's skin. Make it feel as if it fit better. Noises drifted in the background as he faded in and out of sleep until a hand landed on his shoulder. He bolted awake, nearly knocking into Lucas as he stood next to the bed.

"Easy, Cullen. It's only me."

Cullen grunted, scrubbing a hand down his face then swinging his feet to the floor. The scenery tilted a few times before he'd blinked enough to bring it all into focus. He glanced at his mate, smiling at the scruff on Lucas' jaw. God, what Cullen wouldn't give to feel that light beard scratch across his skin as Lucas explored every inch of Cullen's body. Let Cullen do the same in return.

He forced himself to swallow, bracing his weight on his elbows and knees. "Right. Just the one man I want to pounce on. Can't imagine why I'm antsy."

Lucas crowded the bed. "Might be best if you didn't use the term 'pounce' when you're still sitting on *my* bed."

Cullen shifted his view. Christ, he was damn near level with Lucas' groin, and just the thought that he could reach out, take the other man in his hand—his mouth— made his skin burn. Lucas speared his fingers through Cullen's hair, all but inviting him to act on the images playing inside his head. Cullen leaned forward, mouthing Lucas' cock through the fabric. The thick length hardened against his lips, the heady scent of the man's skin clouding his vision with a red haze. Cullen reached for the buttons, slipping the first one free when footsteps sounded on the wooden walkway outside the sheriff's office. A sweet, feminine aroma tickled his senses, the fragrance impossible to misplace.

Lucas tensed, staring down at Cullen before stepping back. He headed for the main office just as the door creaked open, a strong gust of wind swirling the familiar essence throughout the building. Cullen pushed off the bed, shoving his hands through his hair in an attempt to get the unruly locks under control as he marched into the other room, stopping dead. Hollis stood in front of the closed door, her gaze alternating between them as she fisted a paper in her hands. She seemed somewhat reluctant to speak as she shifted her weight from foot to foot, either unwilling or unable to remain still. The tension in the office escalated until it felt hard to breathe.

He glanced at Lucas, cursing at the flush staining his mate's cheeks and the noticeable bulge in the man's pants, similar to the one pushing against Cullen's trousers. Lucas must have felt him staring. He yanked the ends of his shirt out, leaving them to cover his erection before leaning back against his desk as he fisted his hands together in his lap.

The simple action shook Hollis out of whatever daze she was in. She straightened, looking as if she wanted to anywhere but there. "This is for you."

Cullen's stomach dropped as she took a few steps forward, offering him the sheet still clenched between her fingers. Christ, if that was a formal letter of resignation, he wasn't sure how he or Lucas would react, let alone their other halves. How could they bridge the distance between them if she left?

Cullen plastered on a fake smile. "What is it?"

She pursed her mouth, uncertainty furrowing her brow before she returned a small smile just as forced as his. "A list. I realize I've already asked for supplies, and that the railroad doesn't have money to spare, especially with the gangs stealing or destroying various shipments, but with the rash of injuries, I'm nearly out of those."

She tucked some hair behind her ear, the slight tremble in her hand like a knife to his soul. It killed a part of him to know that he was responsible for putting the wariness in her eyes. He nodded as he took the sheet, making a point of reading the items she'd written down.

Hollis glanced at Lucas, her gaze falling to his shoulder

before she backed up until she hit the door. "If it's too much, I can use some of what Mr. Gilmore paid me—"

"It's fine. After three months without a doctor, there're some funds already allocated that haven't been used. And you really aren't askin' for much. Are you sure this is enough?"

The handle behind her rattled as she clamped her fingers around it. "That should last the next five or six weeks—or until you have to stop for the winter."

"I'll have them ordered right away. Might take a couple of days to arrive, though."

"I'll make do with what I have. I just didn't want another incident like yesterday to happen and have to compromise on your men's safety." She twisted the handle, opening the door slightly. "If one of the crew can stack them on the platform when they arrive, I'll transport them back to the clinic."

"Lucas and I can deliver them for you."

Another shiver, though if it weren't for his increased senses, he might not have picked up on it. She opened the door wider. "No need. I'm more than capable of carryin' a few supplies."

Cullen took a few steps toward her. "Hollis. Let me explain about last night."

Tears glistened in her eyes before she turned away, looking back slightly over her shoulder. "No need. I made a deal with Mr. Gilmore to stay until you close for the winter. I'll keep that agreement. I'm sure he can find someone more to your standards to fulfill the position for your next project."

"You are to our standards. I never meant to imply otherwise."

"I have patients that need tendin' to before they can go back to their quarters. If you gentlemen will excuse me."

She walked out, shutting the door loudly behind her. Cullen pushed his hand through his hair then down his neck. He was going to lose control. He just wished he cared enough to fight against the telltale tingling beneath his flesh.

Lucas grabbed his shirt, yanking him in close and pulling him back from the edge. Red flashed in his mate's eyes, the tips of his canines poking beneath his upper lip. "This ends. Now." He turned, marching to the door then out into the street.

"Fuck!"

Cullen raced out, catching up with Lucas halfway down the road, just as Hollis disappeared into the clinic. The door banged behind her, hitting hard enough it bounced open slightly, leaving it hanging slightly ajar.

He grabbed Lucas' arm, yanking him to a halt. "Lucas, wait. You can't—"

The report of a gun drowned out the rest of his words, the loud noise followed by panicked voices from inside the clinic. Something crashed to the floor, a moment before two of Hollis' patients rushed out of the building and stumbled their way down the steps, a collection of bandages covering their bodies.

Cullen released Lucas and raced for the stairs when another man tumbled out of the open doorway. He hit hard, rolling backward down the short stairway then landing in a heap on the ground. Dust billowed upwards, temporarily blanketing the front of the clinic in a thick haze. Footsteps rang out, Hollis' silhouette blurring into view as the cloud started to dissipate. Red welts marred the left side of her face, her lip once again split. Blood dripped from a cut over her eye, the upper lid already starting to swell.

She staggered to the top of the stairs, pointing both pistols at the man lying in the dirt. She glared at the guy, cocking her weapons. "You stupid son of a bitch. Did you really think I wouldn't fight back? That lyin' in wait would give you the upper hand? Last damn mistake you'll ever make."

"Hollis!" Lucas moved forward, hands palms up by his shoulders. "Easy, darlin'. You don't want to do something you'll regret later."

Her gaze slowly slid to his, her anger rolling off her in waves. "I warned your men I'd kill the next person who challenged me."

"That you did. But you're the one who'll have to live with the guilt."

"I can't save souls that are already lost, Sheriff. Don't even want to try."

The man glanced at Lucas, then rolled, obviously trying to escape. Another gunshot echoed through the town, dropping the man back to the ground. He cupped his face, blood seeping out from between his fingers.

Hollis didn't even flinch as she stood there, tendrils of smoke rising from her pistol. She arched a brow. "I don't believe I told you to move. The next bullet's going clear through your skull, so I reckon you should stay down."

The guy eased his hand away, exposing a long, ragged gash the length of his cheek. "You shot my face."

Lucas reached for the man, pulling him to his feet by the scruff of his shirt. "You're lucky she didn't aim a lot lower, or you'd be cryin' over losing a different part of your body." He glanced at Hollis. "Can I toss his ass in jail or do you just want to kill him?"

The guy's eye's bulged wide. "What? You can't let her shoot me. I—"

Lucas head-butted the man, knocking him back a few steps. The guy swayed then fell as his shirt pulled free of Lucas' hold, once more landing in a heap on the ground.

Lucas nodded at Hollis. "Well, darlin'? Your choice. No one here is going to stop you if you want to finish him off. As I see it, he issued you a duel, and you're just following through."

Her gaze darted to the man unconscious in the dirt then back to Lucas. Her bravado faltered slightly before she relaxed, holstering her guns. "He isn't worth the bullet. But if he ever comes near me, again—"

"He'll be on the next train to Durango...after he wakes up, and I have a long chat with him. He won't bother you, again, if he wants to keep breathin'." He bent down then stopped, looking at her. "If that's enough for you?"

"I don't really care what you do with him as long as he disappears." She stumbled backwards, hitting the wall before catching her balance. "That wound of his will get infected if someone doesn't clean it. Perhaps Henry has a few leeches he can spare."

She turned, tripping her way back inside before slamming shut the door. Cullen went to dart up the steps when Lucas grabbed his arm.

His mate shook his head. "Best let her be for a bit."

"Did you see her face? The bastard hit her. There was a bloody gunshot. What if she got clipped?"

"Of course, I saw her face. Couldn't stop lookin' at the damn welts blossoming on her cheek. But my bear didn't smell that much of her blood. Thinkin' maybe the bastard's gun jammed or he missed. Either way, she's far too upset to listen to anything we might say, no matter how badly we need to say it."

"I just want make sure she's okay."

"And we will...once she calms down." He sighed at Cullen's huff of disapproval. "She's a doctor. Reckon she knows how to treat herself. I'll check in on her every hour. Promise. Now, help me get this idiot to the jail cell until he wakes up and I can plant his ass on the first train out. Folks will think it's strange if I pick him up on my own, even though I could. And we'll talk to Hollis. Tonight."

Cullen growled, taking one of the man's arms and wrapping it around his shoulder. "You really think I'll be able to focus on the line?"

"We still have a job to do. And after all that's happened, I just want to finish the damn spur so we can leave here—with Hollis. If the snow hits before we're done, we might lose her for good. I trusted you to see to her safety yesterday. You need to grant me that same privilege today."

"Not fair."

"Didn't say it was. But you were right. If I'd gone in the way I was, I'd have ruined everything. Rushin' in, trying to force this, will only push her further away. We have a lot to make up for. Let's try to get it right this time."

Cullen cursed under his breath as they headed back to the jail, images of Hollis' marred flesh lingering in his mind. He didn't want to toss the guy in jail. He wanted to rip out his damn throat. Then, he wanted to march into the clinic and hold Hollis until his bear was convinced she was all right.

Of course, neither was likely to happen. All he could do was trust Lucas as he'd asked his mate to do yesterday. And pray Hollis would eventually give them the opportunity to atone.

CHAPTER EIGHT

Hollis leaned against the small dresser as she removed the cold cloth from her face. Shades of blue and purple stared back at her from the mirror, the hazy reflection making her wince. The upper part of her eyebrow was swollen, along with part of her cheekbone. Christ, she looked even worse than she'd thought she would after several hours, even knowing how quickly facial bruising appeared.

She probed at the laceration she'd had to stitch closed, grunting as even her gentle pressure sent throbs of pain pounding through her skull. Though she'd been involved in her fair share of brawls, she'd never been hit quite as hard as she had today. Even Frank hadn't punched her with the same amount of force that first night in the bar when his brother's life had been on the line. Thankfully, that was one patient she hadn't lost.

Unlike yesterday.

As if not saving two of the men hadn't burned deep enough. Made her question her own worth as a doctor. Getting attacked had only increased the uneasy feeling she'd had since her conversation with Cullen in the street —the one she'd been reliving over and over, and the reason she'd been distracted. Which explained why the guy in her clinic had gotten the jump on her—attacking her from behind the moment she'd stepped through the door. He'd muttered something about her not saving his friends, his words slurring together. There had been no missing the stench of whiskey on his breath as he'd spun her around, punching her in the cheek and knocking her into a small table before she'd had time to react. She'd used the surface to catch her balance, only to topple to the floor with the table when he'd hit her a second time with the handle of his revolver.

The force of that impact had discharged the weapon into the ceiling, which, in retrospect, had probably saved her life. Being only a single-action pistol, he'd either lacked the dexterity or the sense to cock his weapon, again, before she'd swung an iron candlestick holder she'd grabbed off the floor against his knee. The strike had dropped him onto his other knee, giving her enough time to sit up and hit him square in the chest, tumbling him onto his ass. He'd only just regained his balance when she'd kicked his groin then used the iron rod to send him careening out the open door.

The sound of him rolling down the stairs into a crumpled heap on the ground still echoed through her head. And she hated the part of her that cringed at the memory. What she'd told Lucas was right. She couldn't save every soul, despite the fact even the lost ones gnawed at her conscience.

Her chin quivered as her mind once again returned to Cullen's conversation the previous night. Though she'd been criticized and dismissed by more than her fair share of men, nothing had stung—had gutted her—as much as realizing they'd been playing her all along. That while she'd slowly been letting down her guard—had been falling for them, despite her better judgment and her determination not to—they'd been saying what they knew it would take to keep her complacent.

And she'd acquiesced.

Had bent to their wishes. Hell, she'd allowed Cullen to draw her a bath every other day since her mishap at the river. She'd also stopped going to the saloon, preferring to eat and drink with them either in Lucas' or Cullen's office. She'd even started to come to terms with the fact that they both seemed equally invested in their growing interaction—that they might even want to court her together—only to discover the attraction had all been one-sided. Hers.

Images of them from this morning slammed into her. Lucas had looked more than flustered when he'd marched out of his quarters, a flush coloring his cheeks, his cock pressing incessantly against his pants. If Cullen hadn't followed out behind him, a similar expression on his face, Hollis would have thought she'd interrupted Lucas with one of the saloon women. Learning that it might well have been him and Cullen she'd interrupted...

Her pussy clenched emptily at the thought, the slick slide of her juices along her cleft making her shift uncomfortably. Picturing two men touching each other shouldn't excite her half as much as it did. Especially when she wanted to be much more than just a spectator. She'd spent most of the past few nights imagining the three of them together, their hands discovering every inch of her body. It had seemed perfectly natural in her dreams that the men also interacted. But discovering it might be a reality... She'd been restless since.

She bit back the tears that clogged her throat. It didn't matter whether they were a couple. Whether she could have come to terms with being part of something unconventional. Any attraction they might have shown for her had all been part of the ruse, and the deeper down she shoved any residual feelings for them, the quicker she'd be back to her old self. The one who had made peace with the fact she'd spend her life alone.

She glanced at her reflection, again. What she wouldn't give to simply lie down and sleep for a while. Get a slight reprieve from the ever-present pounding in her head, not to mention the hollow feeling in her chest. But every time she tried, her stomach knotted as snippets of the attack played in her mind. She'd thought about asking Reverend Miller to stay in the other room while she rested for a few hours—pretend it was all about her patients—but she'd quickly dismissed the notion. There were only two men she would have trusted to stand watch, and they weren't an option anymore.

A shadow passed by the window of the clinic. She spun, guns already in her hands as she waited to see if anyone would enter. The clock ticked in the distance as she stood there, heart racing, hands shaking slightly. When nothing happened, she eased up on the hammers then holstered the weapons. It had most likely been Lucas.

She snorted. He'd walked past her window a few dozen times since she'd staggered back inside, though she wasn't sure why. Perhaps he and Cullen wanted to keep up appearances for the rest of the camp. Prevent an uprising from within if the crew discovered the truth. Either way, his constant presence, however distant, only added to the pain already strumming through her body. Only she was pretty sure the medicine she had wouldn't touch it.

Her head throbbed as if in agreement. She sighed, then headed for the door. Maybe a few shots of whiskey and some soup would calm her nerves enough she'd be able to sleep, even for just a couple of hours.

She moved through the clinic, checking the men still recovering on the cots. While those capable of walking had left during the showdown, a few had slept through the entire ordeal, and she couldn't let her own injuries prevent her from doing her job. She made the rounds, taking stock of their condition until she was confident none of them had developed a fever while she'd been tending to her wounds. Chances were, they'd be able to return to their quarters once they woke up, which meant she might actually get some peace and quiet…if the rest of the men managed to avoid getting hurt or throwing a few punches later.

She sighed at the thought then headed for the door, slipping out into the street. Dull gray clouds hung over the camp, making it look more like twilight than early afternoon. The rain had started shortly after she'd locked herself away, the heavy droplets falling in a steady sheet— turning the dusty streets into muddy ruts and puddles.

Hollis turned up her collar as she descended the stairs, nearly tripping down the last one. She caught herself on the small railing, bracing her weight until the scenery stabilized. More pain pulsed through her temples, and she stood still for a few moments, allowing the cold water to drive some of the hazy feeling from her head.

Once she thought she'd be able to make it all the way to the saloon without falling face-first in the rutted street, she struck off, weaving a bit before finding her stride. Each step sent a resonating throb through her temples, but she managed to make it to the tavern steps without looking as if she'd already had too much to drink. Two men stood on either side of the swinging doors as she carefully climbed the short staircase, frowning when the one on the left stepped in front of her, barring her way.

He grimaced as his gaze lingered on her left cheek before settling on her eyes. He nodded at her. "Dr. Chambers."

God, she hated that they all knew her name while she'd barely learned more than a few of theirs. Not that any of the men besides Lucas and Cullen had been forthcoming with that information.

She glanced at the other guy, then returned the first man's nod. "Gentlemen."

He moved with her when she tried to sidestep him.

She arched a brow. "Is there a problem?"

"No, ma'am, except..." He motioned to her hips. "You'll have to check your guns with us if you want to go inside."

"Cold day in Hell before I go anywhere in this town unarmed. Not when every other man is."

"It's not just you. Sheriff Quinn passed this rule for everyone."

"Since when?"

He glanced at the other man, who hadn't moved, yet.

"About a week ago. Something about the men getting too liquored up and shooting each other."

She pursed her lips, wondering why Lucas hadn't mentioned anything to her before shoving the thought aside. Obviously, the man had hoped to keep more of the men healthy to work the rail. It didn't mean he was trying to lessen her load.

The guard motioned to her weapons, again. "Afraid I have to ask for your Colts."

Hollis snorted, backed up a step, then drew, leveling the barrels at both their heads. She cocked the hammers, then gave them a smile. "How about I make you boys a deal? I'll gladly leave my weapons with you once the men in this town stop swinging their fists at me. But until then, they stay where I can reach them. Now, you can either get the Hell out of my way, or I can shoot you. Your choice. But I'm heading inside *with* my guns."

The color drained from their faces before they raised their hands and slowly moved out of her way.

She waved the pistols at them. "Farther. And if either of you even think of jumpin' me from behind, I'll be sure it takes a few rounds to actually kill you."

They swallowed hard, taking four more healthy steps away. She nodded her thanks, spinning as she moved through the swinging doors so she could watch both sides of the entrance. The guy on the left muttered something about getting the sheriff, bolting down the steps once she'd entered the saloon. Hollis shrugged, taking a few heavy steps inside. The din of conversation stopped as folks stared at her, their gazes locked on her pistols.

She arched a brow, twirling the revolvers around a few

times before holstering them. "Anyone else in here got a problem with me being armed?"

A few of the men shook their heads, no one voicing any objection.

"Good." She made her way to the bar, sliding onto one of the wooden stools.

Caleb stopped in front of her, a cloth slung over one shoulder. His lips quirked as he glanced at her face, his gaze lingering for a few moments before shifting back to her eyes. "What can I get you, Doc?"

Hollis gaped at him. "Doc? Since when do you call me anything that...nice?"

The muscle in his jaw jumped. "You're a doctor, ain't ya?"

"Same one who shot you that first night."

He rubbed the hand in question, then shrugged. "Let's just say Sheriff Quinn's been pretty vocal about what he'll do to folks if they disrespect you. Getting shot once was enough. So, what can I get you?"

She groaned inwardly at his words. She didn't need Lucas or anyone else fighting her battles for her, especially when she knew it wasn't because he actually believed what he was preaching. "Whiskey. And some soup if you have any."

Caleb frowned. "A bit early for you to be drinkin', ain't it?"

She glanced around the tavern. "Doesn't seem too early for your other patrons."

"They're not workin' today. What if one of the men gets hurt?"

"I doubt a shot of whiskey is going to impair my ability

to stitch a man up. Though it might help with the pounding in my head."

He glanced at her left side, again, then sighed. "I'll see what Marla has cookin' in the back."

"Much obliged."

She stared down at the bar, lost in thought, when a glass and a bowl full of dark broth appeared in front of her. She thanked the man, downing the whiskey in one gulp. The liquid burned a path through her chest, the instant punch of alcohol finally easing the incessant hammering in her skull. She raised the small glass, indicating to Caleb she'd like another as she took a cautious spoonful of the soup. A warm mix of vegetables and beef burst on her tongue, the heady flavor drawing a throaty moan from her. She hadn't eaten since the cornbread she'd shared with Lucas and Cullen yesterday morning, and the warm offering finally settled the uncomfortable feeling in her stomach.

She thanked Caleb when he set another drink beside her hand, then ate in silence, paying just enough attention to her surroundings she wouldn't get caught off-guard. She'd almost finished the bowl when the swinging doors opened, hushed footsteps padding across the room. The background of voices silenced as the person drew closer to her. She sighed, not needing to look around to know Lucas was standing behind her, the knot in her stomach twisting to life, again. She hated that she reacted to him and Cullen. Hated that her breathing and heart rate kicked up, or that her nipples tightened into hard little buds beneath her shirt and camisole. Or how a jumpy feeling coiled tight in her core as arousal coated her cleft.

She did her best to latch onto the anger still seething

beneath the surface as Lucas took the seat next to her, his strong arms resting on the bar. His broad fingers laced together as he turned to face her, his hat tilted back just enough the light reflected off the blue in his eyes. She slid him a quick glance, frowning when she thought she saw a flash of red amidst the blue before it quickly vanished. Lucas released a weary breath, twisting and shifting his gaze to the rest of the crowd.

"If you're here to scold me for not leavin' my pistols with your watchdogs outside, you can save your breath. I'll tell you what I told him." She turned to fully face him. "I won't go anywhere unarmed until the men in this camp stop swinging their fists at me, not to mention their guns."

Lucas inhaled sharply, his gaze fixating on her cheek. He reached for her before he seemed to think better of it, allowing his arm to return to the top of the bar. A red flush colored his cheekbones as he clenched his jaw. "I didn't come here to scold you."

She returned to her food, not that she wanted it anymore. Everything she'd eaten felt as if it'd turned to stone in her gut, making her wish she'd just stayed in her damn room—faced her demons alone like she always had.

He nudged her gently with his shoulder. "You okay?"

She snorted, glancing at him, again. "Do I look okay?"

His nostrils flared, and his body tensed. "You look angry, and hurt, and like you're liable to fall down any second."

"See. You didn't need to ask, after all."

"Hollis…"

"Even I need to eat from time to time. And the whiskey's good for dullin' the pain."

"There isn't enough liquor in this saloon to dull the pain I suspect you're feeling."

Her chest tightened at his words, and she couldn't help but wonder if he was talking about her face or her heart. Not that it mattered. He was right. While the initial spike had tamed the pain a bit, there was no denying it had returned, stronger than ever.

She turned away, closed her eyes, and pressed one hand to her temple, tempted to simply bang her head against the bar until the pounding stopped. A throaty growl rumbled close by before Lucas cupped her shoulder. She clenched her jaw against the rush of heat from the gentle touch, praying it wasn't the last straw that pushed her over the edge, when his breath feathered across her neck.

He'd leaned in close, his body skimming her right side, his mouth a mere inch from her ear. "Let me take you back to the clinic. I'll tuck you in your bed—let you get the rest you need."

She swallowed to keep from moaning a raspy, "Yes," in reply, grazing her hand across swollen cheek in order to snap herself back. The pain hit her hard, and she found herself scrambling off the stool, bracing most of her weight against the counter as she distanced herself from him. He huffed out his irritation, but she didn't care. Not when she feared she might pass out before she even made it past the swinging doors.

Hollis drew herself up as best she could then faced Lucas, pushing down the resulting guilt at the hurt in his eyes. The pain creased along his forehead. She reached into her jacket pocket and fished out some money, leaving it on the bar.

Lucas glanced at it then frowned. "Did you even bother to count it? That's more than you need."

She shrugged, steadying herself as she fought to stay upright. "Can't really see well enough to care. Now, if you'll excuse me, I'll save everyone the worry of me being in here against the rules and see myself out."

Hollis struck off, mentally placing each footfall as she walked across the saloon, then out the door. Somehow, she managed to make it down the stairs without falling then headed up the street toward the clinic. Nightmares or not, she needed to get some sleep, or she wouldn't be able to stand let alone treat anyone.

Footsteps splashed behind her. "Damn it, Hollis, are you trying to hurt yourself more?"

Lucas fell into step beside her, his mouth sculpted into a frown, his hands fisted at his sides. He caught her shoulders when she teetered after stepping in a puddle, cursing under his breath when she tugged free of his hold, nearly falling in the other direction.

He grabbed her arm this time, cupping her elbow as he stopped her halfway to the clinic. Rain pelted her skin, but she barely registered it above the heat of his touch. The resulting pang of longing tightening her chest before settling hot and needy in her groin.

He moved in close, his large frame blocking out everything but the hint of gray beyond his shoulders. "I know you're angry with me. With Cullen. But please don't let that dictate your actions. I'm sure you haven't survived this long in these kinds of camps by putting your life in danger when it doesn't have to be." He tucked some wet strands of hair behind her ear. "I promise you can kick my ass as soon as you're better, just let me help you."

Her chin quivered at the pleading tone in his voice, and she had to sink her nails into her palms to keep from closing the last bit of distance and falling into his embrace. Rest her head in the crook of his shoulder and allow herself to feel safe, if only for a moment.

His thumb brushed the length of her jaw, staying clear of her injuries. "Darlin', please."

She pried open her eyes, taking a healthy step back as she attempted a reassuring smile, even though the simple action sent another jolt of pain through her cheek. "Thank you for your concern, but I can see myself back. And I'd already planned on lyin' down for a bit."

"If you'd been keen on lookin' after yourself, you would have gone to bed as soon as you'd tended to your wounds."

More images of the attack played in her head, but she'd be damned if she admitted to him that a part of her was too scared to sleep. That just thinking of being vulnerable and alone made her stomach heave in protest—brought back too many unwanted memories from before she ventured off to medical school.

Hollis turned, deciding to let his statement go unchallenged. She took two steps then swayed sharply to her left when her vision dimmed and blurred, making the ground tilt beneath her feet. Hands snaked around her torso before she hit the mud, lifting her against a wall of male muscle. The familiar scent of leather and gun oil filled her senses as her head lolled against his shoulder, his arms holding her in close. She tried to blink open her eyes, but they felt too heavy to move.

Lucas growled. "Christ, I knew you were pushin' too hard. You should have laid down hours ago."

"Couldn't. Kept seeing his face inside my head."

"The bastard won't touch you, again. That I can promise you. No one will, if Cullen and I have any say about it. And we want to have a say, I assure you." He gathered her closer, the sway of his body suggesting he was walking. "You could have asked someone to stand watch. Keep you safe while you healed a bit. I'm sure the good *reverend* would have. He seemed quite taken with you last night."

Had she imagined the tightness in this voice? The hint of anger?

She shook her head without opening her eyes. "I'm not interested in him. Besides, there're only two men I'd trust to keep me safe, but I couldn't bring myself to ask. Not after everything that happened."

Lucas sighed. "Not sure how we managed to fuck up to this degree but...rest. We'll straighten everything out once you've got your strength back. But know this... We're done letting you run from us. So, sleep well, darlin'. You're in for one Hell of a ride once you wake up."

CHAPTER NINE

Lucas cursed under his breath as Hollis tensed in his arms then went slack, her breath already deepening. He held her tight, jogging up the short steps to his office before wedging open the door then marching inside. While he knew she'd probably assumed he'd take her to her quarters, he'd just instinctively brought her to his.

His bear snorted at the thought. She was unconscious in his arms—had barely made it out of the tavern under her own steam. She hadn't been thinking much of anything, other than probably not falling flat on her face. Which she would have if he hadn't been close enough to catch her before she'd collapsed. He huffed as he headed for the bed. The girl needed a stern talking-to regarding her hardheadedness. And he was more than up for the job.

Hollis groaned as he placed her on the mattress, her body still supported against his chest. He tried not to jostle her too much as he worked her jacket over her shoulders, tossing it on the floor. Then, he unclipped her holsters, finally allowing her to settle on the bed. Her lips twitched into a grimace as her head lolled to one side, a patchwork of bruises glaring up at him. He reached out and traced the line of swelling, careful to stay just above her skin. But even an inch away, he swore he felt the heat from the wound. Sensed the throbbing pain that seemed to pulse with every beat of her heart. But it was the touch of fear coloring her scent that burned the blood pumping through his veins.

Despite her bravado, her continued reassurances that she could handle herself, the recent attack had obviously broken through her defenses. While he didn't think she was actually afraid of him, or Cullen, just knowing she'd been sitting in her tiny room in the back of the clinic, scared another bastard might try to hurt her, ate at Lucas' soul. Gnawed at his sanity until he thought his grizzly would just break free. Hunt down the man in Durango, or wherever he'd gotten to by now, and kill him.

There're only two men I'd trust to keep me safe, but I couldn't bring myself to ask.

Her words replayed inside his head, the harsh truth in them souring his gut. If they hadn't managed to alienate her the previous night, she wouldn't have had to suffer in silence. He could have been holding her for hours instead of shuffling past her room, hoping to get a glimpse of her inside. Hell, chances were, she never would have been alone in the clinic to begin with, and they could avoided the entire incident.

Lucas sighed as he sat on the edge of the bed, brushing back her hair from her face. Moisture cooled his fingertips, but he wasn't sure if the drops were from the rain or if some tears had slipped free while she'd been nestled in his arms. Either way, he longed to warm her skin. Hold her close until nothing remained but blazing desire.

That was the only thing stopping him from shifting. Despite the awkward distance between them, she'd still reacted to him physically when he'd sat beside her in the saloon—her sweet earthy musk wafting around him like a soothing mist. It'd increased when he'd cupped her elbow in the street before she'd collapsed on him. Even now, the fragrant aroma wove around him, weak but there.

Thoughts and questions tumbled through his head, but he did his best to let them slide. Hollis was safe. Hurt, but still safe. And she'd stay that way. He'd meant what he'd said. He was done keeping secrets from her. If he and Cullen had any hope of gaining her love, they needed to trust her enough to put their lives on the line.

Lucas mumbled under his breath as he shuffled sideways and removed her boots, placing them next to the bed. He reached over her and dragged a quilt across her body. She stirred a bit then settled, again. He tucked the blanket around her shoulders then straightened, gazing down at her. Damn, she looked good in his bed. Looked right. The only thing that would have completed the picture would have been to have Cullen snugged up against her, his scent merging with hers. He longed to see how their skin contrasted with hers, feel her body mold to theirs.

Lucas tamped down the desire hardening his shaft then headed for the door. While he didn't want to leave her alone, he needed to ensure her patients were taken care of, or she'd bolt the moment she woke. He checked the clinic then made his way to Reverend Miller's makeshift church. The man seemed more than a bit surprised when Lucas walked in, straightening his clothes as if he sensed Lucas' barely contained anger. Lucas' grizzly still pictured the man touching Hollis' shoulder. It didn't matter that Hollis had said she wasn't interested, or that the act had most likely been innocent, all his animal knew was that Hollis' scent still lingered on the man's clothes.

Lucas kept the meeting short, explaining the situation before walking the man back to the clinic. He didn't miss the nervous dart of the reverend's eyes as he watched Lucas grab some of Hollis' belongings, stuffing them in one of her bags before returning to the doorway. He heard the reverend sigh as he closed the door, heading to the saloon next.

The men at the door nodded at him, their eyes widening when he informed them he'd take it personally if anyone got injured tonight and he had to rouse Hollis from some much-needed sleep. Of course, the growl from his other half that followed the statement probably carried more weight than anything he'd said, but it didn't matter. As long as Hollis got the time she needed to heal, he'd use whatever means worked.

Worry weighed heavy on his shoulders as he returned to his quarters, dropping her bag next to the bed. She hadn't moved in the small measure of time he'd been gone, and he smiled, again, at the sight of her hair tousled across his pillow. His bear huffed, reminding him she hadn't agreed to be their mate, yet, as he lit an oil lamp then scraped a chair closer to the bed.

The seat creaked as he settled in it, crossing one ankle over his other knee in the hopes of relaxing. Cullen wouldn't be back for another few hours, at best, which hopefully meant relative peace in the camp. Especially after yesterday. If Cullen was right, Buford would be too busy replacing the men he'd lost and tending to his gang's injuries to mount another attack. Though Lucas knew it was only a matter of time before the outlaw sent a substantial force their way.

His grizzly snarled, pacing restlessly inside his head. Lucas couldn't deny its need to protect its mates, which meant he'd be hard pressed to leave Hollis' side, again, until Cullen returned. Not that his bear would want to leave, then, either. But at least he'd be assured of Hollis' safety with Cullen standing watch.

Fatigue strained his muscles, and he rubbed the back of his neck, hoping to relieve the ache that had taken root. Hollis snuffled in her sleep, the sound easing the tight feeling between his shoulder blades. He leaned back in the chair, content to watch her sleep. The odd flicker of lightning flashed beyond the window, the accompanying thunder rattling the panes.

The steady clatter of rain against the roof eased the rush of adrenaline that had kept him moving—the sleepless nights finally catching up with him. He closed his eyes, listening to the soft whisper of her breath. The room faded as he allowed himself to drift, confident his other half would rouse him if needed. Sounds chirped in the background, nothing concrete until his bear snorted.

Lucas blinked, his head still fuzzy, when the door to the building creaked open. A gust of cold air swirled around him, a familiar scent wafting through the room. He gave himself a shake, then turned to glance at the door just as Cullen walked through. His mate stopped, his gaze focused on the bed, his mouth hinging open. Red flashed in his eyes as he slowly shifted his focus to Lucas. Uncertainty furrowed his brow before he looked back, the lines in his forehead deepening.

"Shit." Lucas stood, darting between Cullen and the bed as his partner stalked forward, hands fisted at his side, his canines poking out beneath his upper lip. He palmed Cullen's chest, holding his mate back. "Easy, Cullen."

A throaty growl resonated through the air. "Easy? Have you seen her face?"

Lucas moved with the man when he took a quick sidestep. "Trust me, I've been fightin' the urge to track down the bastard, myself. Probably a good thing he left on the train before I saw the extent of the bruising, otherwise, he'd be dead, and I'd be a few miles away wearin' fur." He pushed harder against Cullen's chest. "She's already scared. Hurt. You losin' control isn't going to help the situation. So, pull back. She's here. Granted, not quite in the capacity we'd like...but it's a start."

Cullen's head bowed forward, some of the tension easing from his muscles. "How did you get her through the door, let alone convince her to stay?"

Lucas chuckled. "I wouldn't exactly say she volunteered to come here. More like she passed out in my arms, and I made the decision for her. But that doesn't matter. Once she wakes up, we're going to have a long chat with her. It's time we laid it all on the line. Stopped dancin' around the real issues."

The muscle in Cullen's jaw jumped. "If she says no..."

"Then, at least we'll know. We can...adapt."

"Adapt? Are you seriously telling me you'd simply walk away?"

Lucas sighed. "Probably not, but...perhaps our damn bears would stop stonewalling *our* relationship. Despite the fact I want nothing more than to shove you against that wall and swallow your release before fucking you into submission, my damn grizzly keeps insistin' I wait." He grunted as a punch of lust nearly doubled him over, the strong spicy scent of male musk filling his senses. He stared into Cullen's eyes. "Christ, what I want to do to you."

Cullen fisted Lucas' shirt, yanking him against his chest. "You can tell your damn bear to shut the fuck up, because regardless of what Hollis says, I'm done waiting. You're mine."

The man's lips crushed down hard on Lucas', his taste spreading across Lucas' tongue. He moaned, threading one hand through Cullen's hair as the other splayed out across his chest, Cullen's heartbeat thrumming beneath his fingers. The frantic rhythm matched his, soothing the burning need coiling in his groin.

Cullen nipped at Lucas' lower lip once they'd parted, laving the slight hurt before kissing a path along Lucas' neck. The man nudged his way beneath Lucas' shirt, mouthing his shoulder. The slight scrape of teeth across his flesh sent a shiver down his spine, and he arched into the firm caress, mentally telling his mate to stake his claim.

Cullen smiled against his skin, repeating the hard bite but not breaking the surface. "Soon. But I want you wrapped around me when I finish this. I want your bear to know who it belongs to." He made another pass. "Me."

Lucas yanked on Cullen's hair, needing something far rougher to calm his beast. "Then, show me. Prove it."

"Dangerous, mate. We both know I'm far too gone for you to challenge me. Which means it's time we finally..."

"No!"

Lucas froze, twisting to look at Hollis as her voice echoed through the room. She thrashed on the bed, screaming the word, again, before bolting upright, clawing at the blanket as it tangled around her.

He released Cullen then darted to the bed. He grabbed her shoulders, trying to calm her without hurting her as Cullen joined him, stopping her from vaulting to her feet. Her gaze swept the room before settling on his face, the usual blue barely visible amidst the white.

Her chest heaved against his forearm as he held her steady, her increased breath rasping around them. She blinked a few times, frowning when she finally seemed to focus. Her chin quivered as tears pooled in her eyes.

Lucas smiled, tucking some hair behind her ear. "Easy, darlin'. It was just a dream. You're safe."

The skin over her nose crinkled as she glanced from him to Cullen then back. A few of the tears slipped free, and she cringed as they tracked down her cheeks. "Where..."

She groaned, palming her head as she swayed. Cullen moved in closer, gently drawing her against his chest. She stiffened, looking as if she might pull free before relaxing against him, her head nestled in the crook of his shoulder. Pain shadowed her expression, the bruising around her eye and along her cheek more prominent.

"My room. You passed out in the street, remember?" Lucas brushed his thumb along one side of her jaw at her obvious uncertainty. "I'm sure it's all confusing to you. But that's because you need to rest. Heal."

She swallowed with effort, another groan slipping free. "Can't. Patients—"

"Are taken care of. I sent Reverend Miller to the clinic to watch over them. He said you'd mentioned they could go back to their quarters once they'd woken and eaten something. Cullen just got back from the line, and there's nothing new in need of your attention. While I'm sure you haven't eaten much, either, I think it's obvious you need to rest more. Which means you're going to lie back down and sleep until you can look at me without seeing double."

"How do you know—"

"Because I've had enough cracks to the head to have a reasonable guess at how bad you're feeling. So, lie back down and sleep."

More tears glistened in her eyes before spilling onto her cheeks as she turned her head away, shame hunching her shoulders. But it was the instant punch of fear in her scent that dropped his stomach.

He glanced at Cullen, then gently tilted her chin until she made eye contact, again. "Hollis? I know you're angry with us, but...you don't think we'd ever hurt you, do you?"

She furrowed her brow, grimacing when the simple movement must have aggravated the pain in her cheek. "Why would you say that?"

"Please. We can smell your fear. And it's not the first time I've scented it today."

The lines deepened above her nose. "Smell my fear?"

Cullen cleared his throat. "What Lucas means is...it's

obvious by the way you're breakin' eye contact and shakin' that something's scaring you."

She glanced at him. "Some cowboy just tried to kill me. Inside my own clinic." She winced, again, rubbing her temple before lowering her voice. "While I've had to deal with men like Frank more times than I can count, that... that I didn't anticipate. It's been a long time since I haven't felt safe in my own space, so I'm understandably upset. I just need a day or so to shake it off."

"When else did you..." Cullen's voice trailed off into a low growl before he exhaled. "Never mind. That's not important right now. We just wanted to make sure you weren't afraid of us."

She sighed, looking between them. "I'm not sure how I feel about you two, but...I'm not afraid of you." A hint of a smile teased one corner of her mouth. "Though, I do wish I was feeling well enough to knock you both on your asses."

Cullen chuckled. "We'll see what we can arrange once you're healed. But for now, rest."

The fear in her eyes returned before she looked away, again. "I think it would just be best if I went back to the clinic. I'll make sure I nap—"

"Nap?" Cullen's voice rose above the steady patter of rain. "You need to sleep, not sit in some chair and doze. You're hurt." He shook his head when she tried to interrupt him. "No more excuses. Even doctors need to take their own advice from time to time."

Lucas skimmed his thumb along her cheek. "You told me before that you couldn't sleep because you kept seeing his face. Is that what this is all about?"

Her gaze snapped to his. "When did I..."

"While I was carryin' you back here."

She groaned, leaning more fully against Cullen. "I don't know why it's botherin' me so much. I'm not usually—"

"What? Human?"

"This weak."

He brushed a few tears off her skin. "Darlin', being cautious doesn't make you weak. It makes you smart. You've already proven you can handle everything that comes your way. And need I remind you that you actually won that little challenge, despite the bruises. So, stop worryin' and rest."

She sucked her bottom lip between her teeth, holding it captive before finally releasing it. "What's the point? The nightmare will just come back."

"What if we lie down with you?"

Her eyes widened as she chanced a quick glance at Cullen. "But…"

Cullen smiled. "No buts. We'll just sleep. I know it's barely seven, but believe me, we're all exhausted."

She seemed to war with the decision before nodding. "This doesn't change anything. I'm still angry with you."

"We'll only consider it a temporary truce. Until you're healed."

The tension bled from her muscles, and she moved with Lucas as he eased her up, allowing Cullen to kick off his boots and toss his jacket on the floor before positioning himself behind her. She grunted as she shifted over on the bed, her obvious pain like a punch to Lucas' gut. He managed to hold in the snarl that rumbled through his chest, watching as she settled against Cullen, her head resting on one of his arms as his other cupped her hip. Their combined scent calmed the riotous thrash of Lucas' heart, and he smiled as he rose to close the door then joined them, lying on his back. Hollis inched toward him, placing one small hand on his chest, each finger like a brand upon his skin.

He placed his hand over hers, giving her a squeeze. "Sleep. We'll talk once you're feeling better."

She nodded, and he swore she was gone in the space of a heartbeat. He glanced over her shoulder at Cullen, but the man had his eyes closed, an easy smile shaping his lips.

Lucas closed his eyes. While he realized they were still a long way from gaining her love, having her trust them enough to stay spoke volumes. And he vowed he wouldn't stop until they'd proven that trust wasn't misplaced. Until she realized exactly what she was to them.

CHAPTER TEN

"No."

Cullen jolted awake, grunting when Hollis elbowed him in the ribs as she twitched beside him. Her rapid breathing sounded loud in the still room as she mumbled in her sleep, most of the other words undecipherable. He reached for her, gently easing her back against his chest. She continued to groan for a few more moments before sighing. Her muscles relaxed, her body molding against his. He brushed back her hair from her face, careful to avoid the patchwork of bruises on her skin. The purple color glared at him, openly mocking his failure as her mate to protect her.

"You didn't fail her."

Cullen looked across Hollis' shoulder, his gaze clashing with Lucas'. "You reading my thoughts?"

Lucas chuckled quietly. "Can't help it if you're yellin' them inside my head. Besides, we both knew the connection would only get stronger."

"*After* we've completed the bond. Not while I'm lyin'

here, still having to deny it. And I did fail her. She never should have been put in the position she was. If I hadn't stopped you, we both would have been in that clinic." He sighed. "My other half hates not knowing what she faced. What haunts her dreams."

"You can ask her once she wakes up."

"As if she'll confide in me. In us. Despite the fact she's here, it'd be foolish to assume it's due to anything other than desperation on her part. You heard her. This doesn't change anything."

"That's because we haven't explained anything, yet."

"I'm not sure grovelin' at her feet will repair what we've done."

Lucas sighed. "The truth might."

"You know, if you boys are going to talk about me, you might want to wait until I leave."

Cullen inhaled, looking down. Brilliant blue eyes stared up at him, an amused smile tilting one side of her mouth. He lifted his hand, softly tracing her right cheek before tucking some of her hair behind her ear.

He swallowed around the lump that had suddenly formed in his throat. "Christ, you're beautiful."

Her eyes widened, a light blush slowly coloring her skin. She glanced between him and Lucas then focused on him, again. "And what truth are you two talking about?"

Cullen sighed. Though he agreed with Lucas—that they'd never gain her love without risking theirs— somehow simply saying, "Oh, nothing much, sweetheart, we're just bear shifters," didn't sound like a viable plan. Not when her body still touched his, her heartbeat echoing inside his head.

He mustered a smile, skimming his fingers along her arm. "It's...complicated."

The skin over her nose creased. "Then, use a few more words to explain it. I'm fairly certain I'll be able to follow along."

"That's not what I meant." He looked desperately at Lucas, silently asking his mate to help him out.

Lucas snorted. "Like I know what to say." He pushed himself up then gained his feet, pacing away a bit before turning around. "What Cullen means is...we're not sure how you're going to react."

"React to what?" Hollis followed Lucas off the bed, swaying a bit before catching her balance on the headboard. She steadied herself, making her way over to the wall then leaning against it. Uncertainty flashed in her eyes as she shifted her gaze between them.

"Enough dancin' around the truth. There's been something off about you two since I met you. And it's more than the way you seem to communicate without talking. Or your odd behavior." She drew herself up, still teetering a bit on her feet. "First, you dismiss me. Then, you act as if you're afraid to leave me alone. You put on this show for the crew, but when one of you needs my attention, you say I'm incapable of helping you."

"We don't think you're incapable. That's not what Cullen meant, as we've tried to explain."

"You haven't explained anything."

"And you haven't been in the mood to listen. You've been avoiding us at every turn."

"Fair enough. But I'm here, now, and you're both still talking in riddles and sullen glances at each other. Hell, you act as if me simply being near you hurts you, somehow." She released a weary breath, pushing her hair back from her face. "I thought…"

Cullen waited for her to finish, but she simply stood there, lips twitching, gaze wary. He allowed his bear a bit more freedom, searching for any hint of what she might be thinking when images of them entwined on the bed flickered in his head. He glanced at Lucas, noting the man's wide eyes before focusing on Hollis, again, though he wasn't sure what surprised him more. That the thoughts had been hers, or that he'd picked up on them without completing the bond.

He scrambled off the bed, closing the distance between them. He didn't miss the tremble in her fingers as he took one of her hands in his. "You thought what, sweetheart?"

She shook her head, her hair bouncing wildly about her shoulders. "Doesn't matter."

"Of course it matters." He took a fortifying breath. "You matter. More than you know."

She frowned, glancing at Lucas before slipping her hand free. She moved over, as if needing the distance, before huffing. "I swear, sometimes, I wonder if you're both speakin' another language, and that's why I always feel so damn lost around you two. If I matter so much, then why did you shut me out when Lucas got hurt? Why mock the one thing you know defines me?"

Cullen cursed the tears that gathered in her eyes, glistening in the wavering light. He looked at Lucas, reading the man's thoughts without trying. Fear prickled the edge of Cullen's consciousness, but he knew it was time.

"You're right. We did shut you out, but not for the reason you're thinkin'." He waved at Lucas. "You might as well show her. I have a feeling nothing short of cold, hard proof will convince her."

"Show me what? And why would you need to convince me of something?"

"Just...do us a favor and don't run out of here screamin'."

She furrowed her brow, looking utterly lost. "Okay."

Lucas glanced at the door, as if he was considering barricading it, before sighing. He moved over to Hollis. "Are you sure you want to do this?"

"Do what? I don't know what you boys are talking about, only that I'm not supposed to scream." She glanced at Cullen. "I don't make a habit of screamin', if you must know."

God, Cullen hoped that wasn't true. There was nothing his bear wanted more than to hear his name rattle the walls as she orgasmed against his mouth or around his cock. Hell, he wanted to hear Lucas' voice do the same.

Lucas glanced at him. "Might be best if you concentrate on something else for right now."

"See?" Hollis crossed her arms over her chest. "Why does it always feel as if I'm missin' half the conversation?"

"Because you are." Lucas shushed her. "One piece at a time. You wanted to know why I didn't let you treat me."

The wariness returned to her eyes, and there was no mistaking the defensive line of her back. "You two said I couldn't help you."

"Cullen said that because he knew you'd never believe the truth."

She shifted on her feet, looking uncharacteristically uncertain. "Which is?"

Lucas glanced at Cullen one last time before fisting the hem of his shirt. He focused on Hollis then yanked his shirt over his head, revealing sun-kissed skin over firm muscles. The mix of planes and angles created shadowed pockets across his torso, a scattering of hair covering his chest.

Cullen's shaft jerked at the sight, and it took all the restraint he had not to step forward—run his fingers across his mate's flesh. He wanted to feel the strength coiled in Lucas' muscles. Taste the man's skin as he traced his tongue across every band. Leave his mark on Lucas' shoulder. Instead, he fisted his hands at his side as he waited for Hollis' reaction.

Hollis swallowed with effort, her lips twitching until her gaze landed on his shoulder. Disbelief shaped her features, and she lifted her hand, skimming her fingers across the patch of skin where the spike had torn through Lucas' flesh. A nervous silence stretched between them as she glanced at Cullen then back to Lucas. Confusion marred her brow, her sharp inhale breaking the oppressive quiet.

She shook her head, still running her fingers over his shoulder. "This can't be. There isn't a mark on your skin."

Lucas sighed and placed his hand over hers, holding it tight to his flesh. "I know—"

"How is it healed?" She looked between them, color rising on her cheekbones. "I know what I saw. Your shirt was soaked with blood. Several of the men told me they thought you got hit with a spike. Christ, you looked as if you were about to pass out from the blood loss. My damn heart stopped when Cullen helped you walk away. I honestly wasn't sure I'd ever see you, again."

Lucas held firm when she tried to yank her hand away. "Hollis."

"No." She took a stumbling step back when she finally managed to pull free. "You should have a gaping hole in your shoulder. Even if it wasn't as bad as I suspected... There's not even a scar. A hint that you were ever injured. How..."

Lucas moved forward, his hands palms up. "I promise we'll explain everything. But now, you know why we couldn't let you treat me. It had nothing to do with our faith in you. There was simply nothing left for you to treat. All you would have seen was a jagged line. And the middle of the damn street wasn't the place for this conversation."

"What conversation could ever explain that?" She pointed at his shoulder. "That shouldn't be possible."

Lucas glanced at him, cringing a bit despite Cullen's nod. "Have you ever heard of the term shape shifter?"

She frowned. "Excuse me?"

"Shape shifter. Do you know what it means?"

She rolled her shoulders, looking between them, again. "If I remember correctly, some native tribes believe a person can alter their form between a human and an animal. Something to do with it being their spiritual guide. So?"

"I know this is going to sound crazy, but it's true. Shifters are real."

To her credit, she didn't react more than a slight twitch of her mouth at his statement. "Shifters are...real?"

"Very much so."

The muscle in her temple jumped. She took several deep breaths, visibly relaxing her posture. "Okay. Let's say, for a moment, I believe you. What has that got to do with you healing from a potentially fatal wound in the span of a few hours?"

Cullen stepped forward. "One of the benefits of being a shifter is accelerated healing. Changing into our animal form speeds up our recovery."

She blinked a few times then arched a brow. "You said that as if *you're* one of these shifters."

Cullen looked at Lucas, then back to her.

Hollis frowned. "Cullen?"

"That's why Lucas had to leave. A wound that severe... It was only a matter of time before his animal forced him to change. And mine needed to make sure he was safe before I could see to the rest of the crew."

"Your animals..."

Cullen nodded, watching as she stood there, staring at them. He glanced at Lucas, but his mate didn't seem to know what to do, either. Minutes ticked by before Cullen finally lost his patience. "Hollis? Aren't you going to say something?"

She dampened her lips, opening and closing her mouth a few times before focusing on Lucas' shoulder, again. "I..."

"You what?"

She huffed, leaning against the wall. "I'm not sure what you want me to say. Obviously, something unusual is going on, but... You can't honestly expect me to believe that you two are...shifters."

"We said we'd tell you the truth. We didn't say you'd like it or believe us."

She frowned. "You're serious? You're standin' here

telling me you two can change your form. That you both become animals."

"Bears, to be specific."

"Bears?" She shook her head, drawing herself up. "You know, you could simply tell me you don't believe in my skill as a doctor. You don't have to make up this elaborate lie to spare my feelings. You aren't the first men to question my ability, even if, for some reason, your lack of faith in me hurts more than usual."

"We're not lyin'. And we have complete faith in you. But you said it yourself. There's been something off about us from the start. All that odd behavior..."

Her expression sobered as she stared at each of them as if seeing them for the first time. "All those times I thought I saw your eyes flash red—that wasn't just a trick of the light?"

"That was our other halves pushing at our control." Cullen sighed. "There are certain situations that set us off. Makes it hard to hold that part of us back."

"So, the growlin', the way you seem to scent the air? All the weird things you've said, like saying you could smell my fear?"

Lucas moved in closer. "All part of our animal side. Just because we aren't currently wearing fur doesn't mean we still aren't part grizzly."

Her mouth gaped open before she snorted, pushing her way past them. She paced over to the bed then spun. "This is crazy. I..."

Cullen sighed. Somehow, he'd always known it would come down to physically proving it to her. He nudged Lucas. "Might as well show the lady that, too, partner. We both know nothing short of changing is going to sway her."

Lucas growled, his canines already poking beneath his lip. "You know shifting increases the need."

"And you can take that all out on me. I told you before. I'm done fightin' this. Regardless of what Hollis' answer is."

"My answer to what? What need?" Her eyes widened. "You two are a couple, aren't you?"

"It's not quite that simple." Cullen held up his hand. "Just...hold off until after Lucas shows you. And remember. You promised not to run out of here screamin'."

She gave him a curt nod, though he sensed her doubt. Cullen turned to face Lucas, silently asking him if he was okay.

Lucas grunted. "Ask me after I've changed."

"I can shift if you'd prefer."

"Right, because your damn Kodiak is much calmer than my grizzly." He gave Cullen a shove. "No way you'd be able to hold anything back if you shift in here. Not with my bear just as raw, and Hollis' scent saturating the air."

Hollis cleared her throat. "My scent is saturating the air?"

Lucas glanced at her. "Like I said. Just because we're both men right now, doesn't mean we don't retain a heightened sense of smell, albeit not as good as when we're in our animal form. But enough to smell that you're nervous." A hint of a smile lifted his lips. "And oddly, a bit aroused."

Color flamed along her cheeks and down her neck

before she released a slow breath. "I never said you boys weren't handsome. And seeing you standing there, without your shirt... I'm still a woman beneath the clothes."

"Let's hope you still feel that way once you see that we're more than just men beneath ours."

Hollis' eyes widened, but she remained quiet. Lucas groaned then stripped off the rest of his clothes, handing them to Cullen. Cullen placed them on a chair then took a moment to appreciate Lucas' body. The firm flex of muscles under smooth skin. The dusting of hair along his chest, though it was the narrow patch leading down to his cock that held his attention. There was no mistaking the state of his mate's arousal, the plum-shaped head swollen with need—the thin slit shiny with fluid. His bear growled in agreement, and Cullen wanted nothing more than to go to his knees. Take Lucas' shaft in his mouth until the man spilled along his tongue.

A hand connected with his chest, knocking him back slightly. "Would you stop thinkin' about that, or I won't have any control left after, either."

"Doing the best I can, mate."

A strangled moan sounded off to his right, and Cullen glanced at Hollis. Her lips were pursed tight as she dragged her gaze up from Lucas' groin. The blush on her cheeks deepened, the blue of her eyes nearly engulfed by the black. Cullen inhaled, rewarded with the sweet, earthy musk of her desire. She could distance herself all she wanted, but she couldn't hide that they affected her physically.

Hollis arched her brow. "He's your mate? That's like being married, right?" She muttered under her breath when he held up his hand. "Fine. Questions after…" she waved at Lucas, "…he shifts."

Cullen didn't miss the hesitation in her voice, not that he could blame her. If their positions were reversed, he doubted he'd believe in shifters without concrete proof. He just prayed she'd hold true to her promise and not run off as soon as Lucas changed.

Lucas sighed then focused Hollis. "Ready?"

She nodded.

"I'll try to slow it down a bit, otherwise you won't really see anything at all."

She stared at him, mouth pinched tight, then gave him another guarded nod.

Lucas took a deep breath then closed his eyes as his head bowed to his chest. There was a moment of utter silence before pops and creaks filled the void. The man shook, his limbs jerking at his sides as a ripple undulated down his body, distorting the perfect symmetry. Fur erupted along his skin, cascading outwards as he fell forward onto all fours. Paws hit the wooden floor in place of his hands, thick claws clicking against the slats. He shook his head, revealing a long snout and whiskers. The thin hairs twitched as he scented the air, a low growl vibrating around them.

His grizzly took a step forward, stopping when Cullen moved in front, blocking his way. The animal knocked him with his head, nearly sending Cullen onto his ass.

"Damn it, Lucas. How is it you manage to forget how strong you are every time you shift? I swear your bear has a twisted sense of humor."

He gave the grizzly a shove, scratching behind his ears before turning to look at Hollis. Pupils blown wide, she stared at the creature, the back of her hand pressed to her mouth. She didn't speak, just kept her gaze fixed on the bear.

"Hollis? You okay?"

She blinked a few times, finally managing to spare him a quick glance. Her chest heaved against her shirt, the ragged sound of her breath spurring him into action.

He crossed over to her, gently cupping her elbow. "Try to slow your breathing, sweetheart, or you're going to pass out on us."

She frowned, staring at Lucas, again. "I...I... Dear God."

Cullen caught her as her legs buckled, easing her onto the bed. She tensed as Lucas lumbered over to them, his massive head level with hers.

"Shit." Cullen shoved at the bear. "You might want to give her some space, mate. I'm pretty damn sure she's never been this close to a grizzly, let alone the likes of you."

Lucas' bear tilted its head, looking as if it didn't quite understand.

Cullen chuckled. "You're not exactly small, and the last thing we need is to scare her."

The animal snorted then turned.

"Wait." Her voice barely rose above a whisper, but Cullen felt the weight of the single word hit him in the gut.

Hollis swallowed as Lucas swung back to face her, his snout dangerously close to her. She moistened her lips, tentatively reaching toward the animal. Cullen sighed at the noticeable shake of her hand before she glanced at him, finally stroking Lucas' neck when Cullen nodded at her.

She gasped, allowing her fingers to fist around the fur. "The undercoat is so soft."

Cullen nudged her. "What were you expectin'?"

"I...I..." She exhaled. "I don't know. Not this. Lucas falling onto his knees, maybe crawlin' around grunting, but definitely not this. I..."

Cullen palmed her back, smiling when she didn't shy away from him. "I know it's a lot to take in—"

"A lot to take in?" She scoffed at him. "I'm touching a bear that's also a man. They lock people up for believing in this kind of stuff." She released her grip on Lucas and pushed to her feet. "I need a moment. Some air, I..."

Cullen stood beside her, stopping her from attempting to dart past Lucas. "You promised you wouldn't run."

"I'm not running. I just... Christ, I just need some air. To process..." she waved at them again, "...this." She looked at Lucas. "I'll come back."

She edged past the animal, as if she wasn't quite sure how it'd react, then slipped out the door. The exterior one creaked then banged shut, the hollow echo of it followed by a swirl of cold air.

"Damn it!" Cullen raked his fingers through his hair, resisting the urge to throw any handy object across the room at the door.

A throaty growl sounded next to him as Lucas' bear pawed at the floor. Cullen cursed, again, doing his best to move in front of his mate. The animal snorted, rising up on its hind legs as it sniffed the air. It roared this time, obviously angered at the diminishing strength of Hollis' scent.

Cullen raised his hands in the hopes of calming the bear. "You're not the only one who's upset, but the last thing we need is to wake up the camp. It's the middle of the night. Another roar, and Hollis' reaction will be the least of our troubles. We'll have a dozen armed men in here, looking to bag themselves a bear. So, you'd best shift back before your grizzly decides it doesn't care."

The animal snarled, falling back to its front feet before pacing away, despite the fact there wasn't enough room for it to take more than a couple of steps. The small side table tipped over as it knocked into it, the loud bang resonating through the air.

"Lucas! I'm right here. Not going anywhere. But you can't claim me wearing fur."

The animal whimpered, the mournful sound tightening Cullen's chest. His mate sounded lost, hurt, and Cullen wasn't sure if he'd be enough to lessen the pain. To keep the human part of his mate whole. God knew he was barely holding on. Chances were, they'd have to leave. Escape before either of them did something foolish and exposed their other halves to real danger.

More pops echoed through the room, and Cullen watched as Lucas misted into view, the bear simply fading into the man. His mate grunted, his muscles flexing from the obvious strain before he raised his head, his gaze locking on Cullen's.

Cullen caught him when he sprang to his feet, looking as if he intended to run out the door after Hollis. "Easy."

Lucas growled, though it wasn't quite as deep or as menacing as his bear's. "She left."

Pain stole Cullen's breath as the words hit him full

force. "I know, but...you're not in any shape to go after her."

"Why the Hell not?"

"For starters, you're naked."

Lucas frowned then leaned against Cullen, allowing him to bridge most of his weight. "I knew it wouldn't be easy to see that side of us, but... Shit! I didn't think she'd leave. Not really."

Cullen tugged the man against him, hoping the gesture would ease the pain lacing Lucas' words. Cullen hadn't thought she'd leave, either. Though, they'd probably just been fooling themselves into believing she'd want to get involved with a couple of men who obviously didn't fit in.

"I didn't leave."

They spun as Hollis' voice sounded behind them. She stood in the doorway, hands fidgeting at her sides, her eyes wary. But it was the lack of obvious fear that grabbed his attention.

"I said, I needed some air. Leaving implies I wasn't coming back." She stepped inside the room, closing the door behind her.

Cullen snagged Lucas' pants off the chair, shoving them at him. Lucas grunted but yanked them up, his focus still centered on Hollis. Cullen waited until his mate was halfway decent before looking at their girl. *Their girl*. That shouldn't be his first thought. While the fact she'd returned gave him and his bear a glimmer of hope, they weren't close to marking her as their mate.

Lucas moved past Cullen, padding his way across the room before stopping in front of her. Hollis looked up in order to maintain eye contact, and it didn't take much for

Cullen to picture Lucas' hand cradling the back of her head, his mouth molded to hers.

Lucas glanced back at him then faced Hollis. "Hollis—"

"Wait." She held up one hand. "You said I could ask you questions once I'd watched you..." She swallowed noisily then shook her head. "I think it's time you told me the whole story, including how I seem to fit into it."

CHAPTER ELEVEN

Hollis stared at Lucas, praying she'd composed herself enough that neither he nor Cullen would sense the nervous roll of her stomach. See the slight shake of her hands as she crossed her arms over her chest. But after everything she'd witnessed, she had little hope that they'd miss any reaction, regardless of how small it was.

Lucas frowned. "Are you okay?"

She nearly laughed at the thought. "Considerin' what just happened, I'd say I'm handlin' it all pretty well."

"You're scared."

"Of course, I'm scared, Lucas." She groaned then leaned against the door. "But it's not what you think. I'm not afraid of you—that you'll hurt me—it's just... You're a...shifter." She shook her head. "I can't believe I'm even saying that. Until five minutes ago, I didn't believe they actually existed. And it's not as if you turn into something small, like a coyote. You're a grizzly bear."

Lucas' mouth quirked. "You think I'm large, wait until you see Cullen's Kodiak. He's twice the size of my bear."

Cullen grunted, walking over to give Lucas a swat on his shoulder. "You're supposed to be putting her at ease, not making it worse."

Hollis let her head fall back against the wood. "It's fine. I just think I'm allowed to be nervous when I'm only beginning to understand. I came back. That should count for something."

Lucas smiled. "It means more than you know."

She gave him a small smile, grimacing when the simple movement sent a pulse of pain through her head. While interacting with them had pushed it into the background, now that the immediate tension had lessened, the steady throb in her cheek and lip had returned.

Lucas frowned and leaned in close, his upper body skimming hers. His gaze slid to her left side then back. "You're in pain."

The heat from his torso bled through her shirt to warm her skin, and she had to resist arching into him— running her hands along his chest, finally tasting his lips.

Lucas exhaled, fluttering the hair tangled around her face. "Be careful what you wish for, darlin'. Cullen and I aren't exactly in full control, right now. You have no idea how hard it is not to kiss you."

"What I'd like is for my head to stop pounding. My lip not to sting. Not to feel as if I've lost my... Wait. How did you know I was thinkin' about kissing you?" She inhaled sharply. "Can you two read my mind?"

She groaned inwardly. If they were capable of knowing her thoughts, she had a lot more to be embarrassed about than wanting to kiss them. And if she started thinking about all the other things she'd like to do to them—had already pictured doing to them while they were in the same room—her body would betray her in other ways. Ways they'd already said they could sense.

"Damn." Hollis let the door support more of her weight as her legs buckled slightly.

Lucas tsked her then bent low, scooping her up. He snorted at her irritated huff. "Please, we don't need our enhanced senses to see you're on the verge of passing out. And that was before you learned the truth." He set her on the bed. "Do you still want to talk, or do I just tuck you under the sheets?"

"Talk. Definitely talk." She palmed her head. "Though, I wouldn't say no to a shot or two of whiskey if you have any. Might ease my head a bit."

Lucas frowned, glancing at her left side before heading for the door. He slipped into the darkness beyond, returning a few moments later with a bottle and three glasses. He dragged a chair close to the bed as Cullen sat down beside her, the mattress dipping against his weight. The glasses clinked together as Lucas poured them each a drink, handing them out. Hollis whispered her thanks, swallowing the offering in a single gulp. The liquid burned a path down her throat, warming her chest. She relaxed, smiling when he refilled the glass.

Lucas took a swig of his, arching his brow at her. "Better?"

She nodded. "Now that I'm calmer, we can get back to the part where you seem to be able to read my mind. And where you two are mates."

Cullen chuckled. "Glad you're starting with the simple questions."

"I have a feeling nothing is simple where you two

gentlemen are concerned. Least of all why I have this unexplained...pull toward you. The fact there're two of you should have be enough for me to keep my distance, but I just can't seem to get either of you off my mind, which makes even less sense now that I know you're involved."

Both men smiled as the obvious tension in the room eased, though she wasn't quite sure why. Lord knew her heart still felt as if it was thrashing against her ribs. Though, she wasn't convinced it was from apprehension, not with Lucas' chest still bare, his muscles flexing with every small movement. She dampened her lips, wondering when it had gotten warmer in the small room, when Cullen nudged her.

"You're not the only one who wants to run your hands all over his body, but we promised we'd answer your questions. To start, no, we can't read your mind in the way you're probably thinkin'. It's more sensing your feelings, though, sometimes, it's like hearing you scream your ideas at us. But, for now, that's only when we're close."

"For now?"

The muscle in his jaw clenched. "Under the right circumstances, the ability strengthens over time."

"Are you saying you'll be able to sense everyone's thoughts from farther away?"

Cullen glanced at Lucas, again, then sighed. "Not everyone's. The connection is primarily between mates, though we can pick up on another shifter's thoughts if they're unable to shield them."

Hollis furrowed her brow. "But...how are you able to

read mine, then? I'm not a shifter, and you've already said that Lucas is your mate."

Cullen reached for her, taking one of her hands in his. "Lucas is my mate, but he's not my only one."

She frowned, wondering what he was hinting at, when the answer clicked into place. She inhaled, staring from Lucas back to Cullen. She opened her mouth, then closed it. Heat billowed up from her legs, and for a moment, she thought she might pass out.

Cullen tightened his hold on her hand, using his other to cup her shoulder. "Easy, sweetheart. Try to breathe."

She snapped her head toward him, ignoring the slight tilt of the scenery before drawing in a few choppy breaths. "Breathe?" She pulled her hand free then stood, pacing a few shaky steps away before turning. "This is crazy. Obviously, I must have passed out in the street, and this is all a dream."

Both men stood, though judging by the way their muscles strained, she knew they were working hard not to march over to her and shake some sense into her. Not that a part of her would mind. Just thinking about them touching her, running their hands along her body…

She grunted, giving herself a mental shake. Now wasn't the time to be drifting into those kinds of thoughts. Not when part of the frantic beating of her heart was from just trying to get a grasp on what, exactly, was happening, and how she was going to deal with it.

Lucas tilted his head, his lips quirking. "We realize we've thrown a lot at you, all at once—"

"A lot? I've spent the past few weeks trying to figure out why I feel the way I do, only to believe you were both just lyin' to me. Now, you're standing here telling me I'm your mate. That we're all mates. There're three of us, or do you have more mates that I'm unaware of?"

"It's not like that." He raked his hand through his hair. "Shifters are different when it comes to love. We can have sex with anyone we choose, but our hearts are drawn to certain people. Sometimes, there's only one, but often, there're two. Whether it's to help reduce the number of people that know about our secret or just the nature of our kind, I don't know. All I know is that I recognized Cullen was mine the moment I shook the man's hand. But as sure as we were, we also knew there was a part missing. *Someone* missing. Then, we met you, and everything changed."

"Then, why did you dismiss me that first day? Wasn't I good enough for you? Is it because I'm not a shifter?"

Lucas darted forward, followed closely by Cullen. "No. We're the ones who don't measure up, and we don't care that you're not a shifter."

"So, you weren't immediately attracted to me, then. Like you were with each other."

"What?" He groaned. "That first meeting...your damn oilskin jacket hid your scent, and we never got a chance to actually touch you. We had no idea who you were to us until the saloon." He winked at her. "Other than a very beautiful woman."

She hitched out one hip. "That's because you were too busy telling me to get my ass back on the train."

The man chuckled. "Christ, you never back down, do you? And trust me, it's an oversight we won't make, again."

She sighed, knowing there wasn't really any use in

arguing over the past. "So, where does that leave us, now?"

"We know where we'd like it to lead."

She swallowed against the nervous flutter in her stomach. "But aren't you two..." she waved her hand between them, "...together already?"

Lucas grinned as Cullen moved in behind her, lightly pressing his chest to her back. Her breath hitched, the fluttery feeling in her gut increasing as his hands landed on her hips. She glanced at him, noting the flash of red in his eyes as his gaze dropped to her shoulder then back up. She opened her mouth to question him, when Lucas cupped her chin, drawing her focus back to him. Their gazes clashed, a similar flicker of red in his eyes coloring the usual blue depths.

He stroked her cheek with his thumb, the intimate gesture coiling desire low in her groin. "We've been fightin' the need for months. Guess our bears were waitin' for you. But now that we've found you..." He inhaled, humming to himself. "It's taken all our restraint to try to move slowly. Get you to notice the men, not the animals. Then, I got hurt, and we ended up pushing you away." He released a weary breath. "Let's just say our other halves are having a hard time understandin' why we haven't charmed you into our bed, yet. Hell, Cullen and I haven't even had a chance to claim each other. Just doesn't feel right without you."

Her chin quivered at his words. Despite her tough bravado, she'd never been intimate with a man, let alone two.

Cullen nuzzled her shoulder, dropping a soft kiss on neck. "We'd never force anything on you, Hollis. Never take what you didn't want to give. Mating is about love. Trust. Not us exerting ownership." He winked at her. "Even if the word 'mine' plays over and over inside our heads."

She moistened her lips, again, noting the way he followed the path of her tongue. "Which means?"

"Which means that as much as we want to take you in our arms and love you until there's no doubt that this is exactly where you need to be, the decision's yours. We realize you don't have the luxury of a bear telling you we're the men you're supposed to spend the rest of your life with. That, despite our rocky beginning, we'll stand by you until the day we die. So, if you need more time, we'll give it to you, even if that means we have to distance ourselves for a while. Prevent our animals from going rogue, because I assure you, they have no doubts what they want. Neither do we."

Lucas thumbed her cheek, again. "Come on. Let's get you tucked back into bed. You can think up more questions for us after you've gotten some rest. Allowed that pounding in your head to ease, and from more than everything we've just confessed. Your face is still ten shades of blue."

"But—"

"Not taking no for an answer. You're still healing." Lucas' gaze softened. "Please, darlin'."

She relented, allowing them to lead her over to the bed.

Cullen pointed at her clothes. "We can step out if you'd like to get more comfortable. I need to grab another chair, anyway."

She snagged his arm when he started to turn. "Aren't

you going to sleep in the bed with me? Like we were before all of this happened?"

Cullen's eyes narrowed, his expression far more feral than it had been moments earlier. "That was before you knew what you were to us. We don't want you to think we're trying to pressure you if you're not ready. Hell, we don't even know, for sure, if you like us."

"I know you're not pressurin' me, and I think the fact I'm still standin' here is proof that my feelings for you two are...complicated." She sighed. "I'll be honest. I've been too busy training to be a doctor then trying to find work to focus on any emotional or physical ties. But I'd be lyin' if I said I wasn't attracted to you. A fact you've already told me you can sense. So, if you and your other halves can handle it, I'd like to spend the rest of the night here." She cleared her throat. "With you. The past few hours have been the first good sleep I've had in longer than I can remember. Unless you'd rather not."

Cullen's lips lifted into a smile. "Can't think of a better way to spend the night than with you in our arms. Though, don't think we missed the part where you just admitted you haven't been taking good care of yourself."

She smiled, snagging her bottom lip between her teeth when Cullen removed his shirt, tossing it on the floor behind him.

He glanced at her, his gaze running the length of her body. "Thinkin' you might be more comfortable if you undressed a bit. As I recall, you usually wear a camisole beneath your other clothes, don't you?"

"I do, but..." She inhaled when Cullen set about undoing her shirt as Lucas worked the buttons on her pants. Christ, if just having two men undress her felt this arousing, she wasn't sure she'd survive having them both touch her.

Cullen smiled when her outer clothes joined his on the floor. "Much better. Now, you can actually sleep."

Her stomach fluttered as he crawled across the bed, extending his hand to her. His muscles twitched beneath the wide expanse of skin, and she longed to run her fingers across his chest. Feel the hidden strength creating bands beneath his flesh.

Her nipples hardened from the images playing in her head, and she crossed her arms over her chest to hide her reaction. Twin growls sounded around her, and she knew they were more than aware of their effect on her.

Lucas drew her hair back from her shoulder, his breath washing across her neck. "We know that, despite your obvious desire, you're uncertain. Confused. The fact you're still here—still willin' to spend the night with us— is more than we'd hoped for. While we won't lie and say that we don't want to taste every inch of you more than we want to breathe right now, we can wait. Holding you... It's enough to ease the tight feeling inside us. Pacify our bears. So, stop worryin' and climb in beside Cullen. We'll see you get a proper sleep."

His words eased the panicky feeling in her chest. She followed Cullen onto the bed, smiling when he wrapped his arm around her waist and gently pulled her back into his torso, her head resting on his arm. Lucas extinguished the lamp then climbed in beside her, once again allowing her to lay her hand on his chest. His heart thrummed beneath her palm, the steady beat chasing away any doubts. And she knew it was only a matter of time before she took the next step. Finally gave in to the heat simmering beneath her skin, slicking her cleft with moisture.

"Stop thinkin' and sleep." Lucas inched closer. "Your head will be easier to understand once it's not pounding."

She stuck her tongue out at him, grinning at his chuckle. "Thank you."

"For what?"

"Telling me the truth. Trustin' me with it. I know it probably isn't something you share often."

"There's a first time for everything, darlin'."

"First time?" She glanced back at Cullen then over to Lucas. "You've never told anyone before?"

He shrugged. "Haven't had to. It's not something we'd ever share with strangers, and Cullen's a shifter so...once we realized we were mates, there wasn't a reason to mask our identity from each other. You, on the other hand. You've had us tied in knots for weeks." He gave her hand a squeeze. "And we should be thanking you for not runnin' off on us."

"Guess you boys were lucky my Colts were on the chair so I didn't put your healing theories to the test."

Lucas laughed. "Guess we were. Now, go to sleep before you change your mind."

CHAPTER TWELVE

Lucas studied Hollis' face as she smiled at him, then closed her eyes. She burrowed into Cullen, drawing Lucas closer to her with nothing more than a gentle pull of her hand on his chest. She rested her head on both his and Cullen's arms, her breath softly caressing Lucas' skin as she quickly gave herself over to sleep. He lifted his hand, skimming his fingers along her arm, grinning at the line of goosebumps that beaded her flesh from his touch. Her warm, sweet essence surrounded him, the feminine aroma mixing with the spicy musk he knew was Cullen's.

His bear snorted then settled, the incessant scratching beneath his skin finally easing. While Hollis hadn't outright agreed to be their mate, having her in their arms —allowing them to tend to her needs, even for just a few hours—was enough to calm his other half.

Cullen sighed, drawing his attention. "Should we be worried our bears seem to have a soft spot for our feisty mate? Because my Kodiak's never been this accommodatin' where you're concerned, yet..." He sighed.

"One bat of her eyes, one touch of her hand, and my damn bear rolls over and is more than content to let her lead."

Lucas chuckled. "You're not the only one. I've been fightin' my grizzly ever since she walked into our lives. Hell, I was about to go rogue when I thought she'd walked out on us. And now...now, all my bear wants is to cherish her. Prove to her we can be the men she needs us to be. That we'll keep her safe. That no matter how long it takes, whether she'll ever want more from us than this, we'll still be there. To hold her. Protect her."

"You know, if she hears you talking like that, she's liable to shoot you in the ass."

"The girl's welcome to try. Thinkin' it won't turn out quite the way she imagines."

"You might not want to put that to the test, seeing as your grizzly is so smitten with her."

"Yours isn't any better, mate."

Cullen smiled. "Damn, I like the sound of that. Especially, when I have both of your scents surrounding me." He brushed some of her hair back from her face. "It's just past midnight. Reckon we should all get some sleep while the camp's quiet. Damn miracle we've been left alone this long."

Lucas nodded, smiling as he watched Cullen settle behind her, one hand on her hip, his fingers grazing Lucas' waist. Cullen stared at Hollis for a while until his eyelids drifted shut, his body easing. Lucas listened to him breathe, the even rhythm making Lucas smile. While he wouldn't deny he wanted to run his hands and lips all over Hollis and Cullen's bodies, watching them sleep soothed another side of him. And he knew he could spend a lifetime with them and never tire of being this close. Of holding them in any way he could.

Images played inside his head as he closed his eyes, allowing himself to drift. The room faded until a soft creak of the floor roused him. He blinked open his eyes, glancing toward the door, only to inhale sharply. Hollis leaned against the door as she slipped on a pair of boots, her silhouette outlined by the splash of moonlight filtering in through the windows. She had Cullen's jacket covering her camisole, her hair hanging in a loose mass around her. She didn't seem to notice him as she stood, reaching for the handle.

"Hollis?"

She jumped, knocking against the door as she spun around, her hand clutching at her chest. Her hair bounced across her shoulders, and she used one hand to shove it back from her face. "Damn it, Lucas, you scared me half to death."

He pushed onto his elbows, aware Cullen had woken behind him. "You're the one sneakin' out in the middle of the night."

"I'm not sneakin' out."

"So, you're putting on your boots and grabbing the handle because..."

She glared at him, tapping one foot on the floor. "Because I need to relieve myself. I'll be right back."

"I can go with you."

"The Hell you will. I've been taking care of that all by myself since I was two. Thinkin' I got it figured out by now."

He pursed his lips, hating the restless feeling that fluttered his stomach as she opened the door and slipped out. He hadn't meant it the way it had sounded. He knew she'd come back—that she didn't need his help. Unfortunately, all his bear saw was their mate walking out the door. He mentally told the animal to shut up, swinging his legs over the edge of the bed as he waited for her to return. Cullen followed suit, moving over to the chair as a clock ticked away in the background. Minutes passed before the outer door opened, her scent preceding her into the room on a swirl of gusting air.

She stopped at the doorway, glancing between them before making her way to the small pitcher and bowl beside his bed. She rinsed her hands in a splash of water, then turned to face them. Amusement tilted her lips, and she crossed her arms over her chest as she stared at them. "Do I want to know why you two are lookin' at me as if I'm crazy?"

Cullen exhaled, holding up her gun belt. "You didn't take your pistols with you."

She chuckled. "That's because I was coming right back."

"What if you'd needed them?"

"In the outhouse?"

He huffed. "Outlaws don't care where you're going."

"It's just on the other side of the building. I figured you two would hear me if I needed to scream for help. Besides, they get in the way."

"Still." He placed them behind him on the chair. "We just don't want you to get hurt, again."

"While I appreciate the sentiment, are you sure that's what this is really about?"

Cullen glanced at Lucas but didn't answer her.

Hollis' expression softened. "Surely, you both didn't

think I was runnin' out on you. Not after all that's happened."

"We're well aware that the situation was unconventional when you thought two men were interested in you. Knowing we're something else, entirely, that we're interested in far more than making you a notch on our bedposts..." Cullen sighed. "We wouldn't blame you if this was simply too much to commit to. And for the record, our other halves aren't nearly as reasonable as we are. All they see is our unclaimed mate walking away or standin' apart from us. They don't care why."

A hint of a smile tugged at her mouth. "Unclaimed?"

Lucas stood. "What Cullen meant was, our bears are just antsy. Patience isn't one of their virtues, not where their mates are concerned. And we've been fightin' this for weeks." He held up his hand to stop her from speaking. "Which, we realize isn't that long in normal terms. In fact, it's barely enough to properly begin courtin' a lady. Doesn't make us want you any less, though."

Any trace of humor vanished. "I see. And you're sure?"

Lucas frowned. "Sure about what?"

"That I really am your mate. That your bears haven't lost their minds in pairing you with..." she waved her hand the length of her body, "...me."

"Why would you even ask that?"

She threw up her hands as she stalked back to the door, once again leaning on it. "Maybe because I'm not a shifter. Hell, most people don't even see me as a woman because of what I do. What I am. Cullen just chastised me for *not* taking my weapons with me to the outhouse. How many women have you met that even carry guns?" She toed at the floor. "Face it. I'm an outcast, at best, and I'm sure you could both do far better where a mate's concerned. One that will actually be accepted by the towns you work in. One your bears don't find frustrating. Maybe that's why you didn't initially know what I was to you. Maybe you and your bears are wrong."

Lucas grinned. Damn but she was far more than they deserved. He nodded at Cullen, picking his way over to her. "Trust me. When it comes to being outcasts, we have you beat. Hands down. Do you know what the townsfolk would do if they ever discovered we weren't what they thought we were? Not sure simply being asked to leave would be enough. And we'd be lucky to love someone half as deserving as you are. Christ, you stitch people back together. Sacrifice so much to try and save them. You're incredible, darlin'. Inside and out." He thumbed her jaw, grinning at her when she met his gaze. "Though you're right about one thing. You're more than a bit frustrating."

She frowned, swatting him in the shoulder. "You two aren't any better. I swear I want to pull my hair out sometimes."

"Or you could just let us pull it for you."

Her breath hitched as the blue in her eyes darkened. She glanced between them then reached behind her, sliding the bolt over. The hollow sound echoed through the room, the sheer weight of the statement stealing Lucas' breath.

He motioned to the door. "Do we want to know why you just locked the door?"

She wet her lips, looking more than a bit uncertain, before visibly drawing herself up. "I just thought that if we're all going to get naked, it might be best if no one could simply walk in on us."

His jaw dropped open before he managed to close it. He gazed at Cullen, noting the man's wide eyes. "Hollis. That wasn't intended to pressure you. We'd never force—"

She cut him off with a finger against his lips. "I know. But you two aren't the only ones who have been fightin' this." She closed her eyes for a minute, the sweet scent of her desire wafting around them. "I feel as if I'm dyin' inside. There's an ache that just won't go away. I'm not saying I don't have reservations. That I'm not scared this isn't more than a passin' fancy for you, despite what you say, but..." She sighed. "I also know that I don't want to go another minute without feeling your skin against mine. Making all these images in my head more than just wishful thinkin'—convention and propriety be damned. So, if you're sure..."

Lucas reached for her, snaking his arm around her waist and tugging her in close. Then, he turned, backing her against Cullen's chest. Cullen's knuckles brushed against Lucas' waist as the man grasped Hollis' hips, nuzzling her hair aside as he dropped a kiss on her neck. Hollis hummed, tilting her head to the side, moaning this time when Cullen licked his way up to her earlobe. She shivered as he nipped at the flesh, her eyelids fluttering a few times before she gazed at Lucas.

He smiled, once again tracing her jaw with his thumb. "We realize you only have our assurances that we're sincere, but if there's one thing we're certain about, it's that you're our mate. No mistakes. No regrets. And it's about time we proved that." He brushed his thumb over where she'd split her lip. "Is this going to hurt you?"

"Only way to know for sure is to try."

He leaned in, skimming his lips over hers, tasting her anticipation. "Mine."

He closed the last breath of distance, gently pressing his mouth to hers. Soft flesh molded against his, and he traced the seam of her lips in silent invitation. She moaned, opening enough he could sweep his tongue inside, dancing it over hers. A sweet tang infused his senses, the essence matching her scent. He smoothed his hand back, cupping her head as he tilted it against Cullen's chest, using the position to thoroughly possess her mouth. Her small fingers threaded through his hair, holding him close when he finally released her. A contented huff sounded in his head, the antsy feeling inside him easing.

"You okay?"

"Only if you do that, again."

He dropped another soft kiss on her mouth, smiling down at her. "Just as wild and sweet as I'd imagined. I bet Cullen would like to see for himself."

She inhaled a shaky breath as Cullen's hand joined Lucas' in her hair, gently turning her head toward him. Lucas moved just enough to allow the other man to twist her slightly, granting him better access. He smiled at Hollis then slanted his mouth over hers, all but lifting her off her feet with the intensity of the kiss. She looked doe-eyed when he finally eased back, keeping her trapped between them.

Cullen glanced at him, his focus dropping to Lucas' lips. Lucas didn't need further encouragement before leaning in and tasting the man's mouth. Spicy musk mixed with a sweet zest, the combined flavor burning into his senses. He growled as he pulled back, wanting nothing more than to rip off all their clothes and stake his claim.

Cullen chuckled. "We're getting there." He looked at Hollis, the lines over his nose creasing. "Sweetheart? You okay?"

Her lips were slightly parted as she swung her gaze between them.

Lucas frowned. "Hollis? Are we scaring you?"

A slow smile lifted her mouth. "I just never expected seeing two men kiss to be that arousing. Don't suppose you'll do it, again, for me."

Cullen grinned then struck, making his last kiss appear tame in comparison. The way he ate at Lucas' mouth, tasting every inch before ending with a nip, made the room feel suddenly hot. Lucas grunted when his mate finally released him, knowing he'd come inside his damn pants if he didn't get a taste of one of them soon.

"You're not the only one, mate. And I know exactly what I'm in the mood for." Cullen focused on Hollis. "You smell good enough to eat."

Cullen stepped back, taking Hollis' jacket with him. It fell heavily to the floor, the dull thud sparking a chain reaction. Lucas scooped up their mate, allowing Cullen to remove her boots and socks before carrying her over to the bed. He placed her on her feet, letting her catch her balance before fisting the edge of her camisole.

He leaned in close. "Are you sure? Not that we wouldn't stop if you asked but..." He blew out a shaky breath. "We're so close to the edge..."

She silenced him with a soft kiss. "I'm giving you boys far more than just my body. I'm giving you my trust. My heart."

"We won't let you down. Promise, despite our previous shortcomings. And you already have our trust. Our love."

Her eyes widened at his last word, and she opened her mouth, but he shook his head, silencing her with a gentle touch. "You don't have to say anything. Not yet. Wait until everything's not such a jumbled mess. We'll love you enough for all of us. But if you're ready..." He tugged on the material gathered in his hands. "This has got to go."

Hollis snagged her bottom lip then smiled, raising her arms. "Try not to rip any of the seams. I like this one."

Lucas growled, again, waiting for Cullen to undo the ties holding the bodice close to her body, before lifting the garment over her head. It fell in a flutter of beige to the floor, puddling beside him. He swept his gaze the length of her body, mesmerized by the expanse of creamy skin. A few scars marred the sheer perfection of it, and he made a mental note to uncover every detail behind them. Learn every story that had brought her into their lives.

But for now, he focused on how soft her flesh felt as he trailed his fingers through the valley of her breasts and along her ribs. Lean muscles flexed beneath his touch, random patches of goosebumps erupting across her skin. He stopped at her hip, drinking in the increased scent of her arousal, knowing he'd need to lick her cleft before his bear would quiet enough he'd be able to savor the rest of her.

He forced his gaze up to her face, smiling at the deep flush staining her neck and cheeks. "God, you're stunning."

Her breath hitched as he brushed his knuckles across one distended nipple, noting the way the tight bud hardened further. Cullen's hands appeared beneath her breasts, slowly sliding up to cup each side. Her chest rose and fell within the man's grip, a shattered cry sounding when he used his thumb and fingers to lightly pinch each nub.

Lucas moaned. "Damn. Not sure I'll get my mouth on you before I explode." He nudged her nose with his. "Tell us. Have you experienced any of this before?"

Her focus darted toward Cullen then back to him, the flush on her cheeks deepening. "Is that your subtle way of asking if I'm a virgin?"

"Thinkin' it wasn't too subtle."

Her chin quivered slightly. "Does it matter?"

"Of course not. Nothing you tell us will change how we feel about you. It's just...the first time can be a bit uncomfortable, especially if we just barrel ahead, assuming you're not new to this. We've messed things up enough, as it is. We don't need to add to that list by being insensitive."

"So, this isn't your other halves hoping to be the first? To have a part of me I've never shared before?"

Cullen growled this time, lifting one hand to twist her head toward him. "Do we want to be your first? Your only lovers? Hell, yes. And that's not just the animal side of us talking, sweetheart. Imagining anyone else touching you..." He released a raspy breath. "It tests the human part of us, too. But we'd be foolish to think other men haven't had the sense to court you. Charm you into their beds. Despite your best efforts, you can't hide how beautiful you are. The kind of soul you have. Like Lucas said...we'll love you either way."

Indecision flashed in her eyes. "I assume you've both been with other women. Men."

Cullen sighed. "A few women, though they were empty encounters, at best. But I've never wanted another man until Lucas came along. He'll be my first and only in that way."

She shifted her gaze to Lucas.

He nodded. "Same for me. A handful of women over the last several years, but Cullen definitely caught me by surprise, not that I'm complainin'. The man's got more honor than ten men. And I can't wait to run my tongue all over his body."

A small smile lifted her lips. "Then, I suppose you'll both be getting two firsts, because other than some token kisses, no man has given me so much as a second look since I went to medical school, five years ago, when I was sixteen. I suppose between the clothes and the pistols, no one's wanted to take that much of a risk. Not until both of you."

A dull roar sounded in Lucas' head, and he had to rest his forehead on hers in order to stay on his feet. Just thinking they'd be her only lovers... As primitive as it might have been, he couldn't deny the satisfied huff of his bear, or the way the damn thing puffed up its chest. He was surprised the animal didn't force him to shift so it could strut around the room, gloating.

Her finger landed on his jaw, drawing him back. "I'll assume by your reaction, you cared more than you thought."

He chuckled. "Happy? Yes. But we meant it. It wouldn't have mattered. Though, it also means we need to ensure we do everything we can not to cause you any additional discomfort. The bruising on your face is more than you deserve."

"Pretty sure any trace of pain will be worth the pleasure. So, stop worryin' about deflowering me, and stake your claim."

CHAPTER THIRTEEN

Cullen swallowed around the tight feeling in his throat and chest. Despite all the ways they'd let Hollis down since she'd first walked into his office, she was still there. Still willing to give them a chance. It had been nothing short of a miracle that she hadn't run off after Lucas had shown her the truth about what they were. That she'd had the courage to stay. Now, she was standing between them, naked, her unwavering acceptance smiling back at him, when she turned to stare into his eyes.

He shook his head, reminding himself to spend the next eighty years proving to her it hadn't been a colossal mistake to trust them, before palming her jaw and drawing her lips to his. A contented hum sounded between them as he slanted his mouth over hers, her soft flesh spiking his need. His bear roared, but there was no denying the sense of peace that soothed the scratching feeling beneath his skin. The way his other half settled for the first time since he'd shaken Lucas' hand all those months ago.

Hollis' eyelids fluttered a few times once he'd eased back, giving him fleeting glimpses of blue before she fully opened them, looking up at him as if he was the answer to whatever questions were rattling around inside her head. He smiled, fully aware she and Lucas were the answer to his. Cullen glanced at the man and immediately wanted to smack the smug grin off his mate's face.

Lucas chuckled. "I feel the same. And while I don't mind a bit of rough foreplay, I think your efforts would be better spent showing Hollis just how thankful we are she didn't shoot us when she had the chance."

Hollis grinned. "Colts are still handy if you two continue to keep me waitin'."

"Wouldn't dream of it, darlin'. Why don't you help Cullen get more comfortable, then join him on the bed?"

She grinned at Cullen, flicking at the first button on his pants as she glanced at Lucas over her shoulder. "Can't wait to get you both naked. But I was thinkin' I could start this night off on my knees."

Cullen groaned, looking at Lucas when the man had a similar reaction. His mate tucked some of Hollis' hair behind her ear as he leaned in close, his breath rustling some stray strands.

He dropped a kiss on her earlobe, grinning as her raspy breath. "While I love the thought of you wrapping your lips around my shaft, this first time is about you."

Hollis popped open the second button. "If you're both determined to please me, then you'll start by letting me make a few of my fantasies come true. While I might not have actually been with a man, it doesn't mean I haven't dreamed of what I'd like to do a thousand times over, especially where you boys are concerned. I've been picturing all sorts of things since we met." She glanced downwards. "And there's nothing I'd like more than to watch both of you give yourselves over to me. Paint your releases across my chest."

Lucas swallowed with apparent effort. "Hollis—"

"Are you suggesting neither of you would recover enough to make love to me after? I'd have thought with your bears' healing abilities, stamina wouldn't be an issue."

Cullen chuckled, drawing her face back to his. "Not even five minutes since we managed to charm you into our bed, and you're already challenging us. Damn, you're something else."

"Haven't quite made it to the bed. Which makes kneelin' on the floor a logical starting place."

Cullen wrapped his hands around her wrists, stopping her from opening the next button. "How about I make you a counter-offer?" He nodded toward Lucas. "You get Lucas naked, then we'll both concentrate on making him finish. You're not the only one who wants to taste him."

Her eyes widened. "I like your negotiation skills. You've got yourself a deal." She spun toward Lucas, her hands landing on his chest.

Lucas clenched his jaw as she skimmed her fingers along his ribs to the edge of his breeches. "Don't I get a say in this?"

She laughed, and Cullen knew by the way Lucas sighed the man was helpless to deny her anything. "Indulge us this time, and you can have full control over the next phase."

"You drive a hard bargain, darlin'. But seeing as I have my mind set on buryin' my face between your legs until you come all over my tongue, I'll concede this first round." He snagged her wrists when she started opening his trousers. "Just remember. You can only tease me so much before I pounce."

"Have I told you boys how much I love pushin' boundaries? Figure now's a good a time as any to see just where yours lie."

Lucas grinned, releasing his hold. Hollis opened the rest of the buttons then paused. She lifted one hand, thumbing Lucas' jaw before tiptoeing up and taking the man's lips with hers. Lucas wrapped one arm around her waist, pulling her tight against his body as he dominated the kiss, tilting her head back until it rested against Cullen. Cullen brushed her hair off her shoulder, mouthing her skin as Lucas finally eased back.

Lucas focused on the twin marks that appeared on her flesh as Cullen released her shoulder. He hadn't used enough pressure to break the skin, but it was definitely a show of ownership. Lucas growled, drawing an answering snarl from Cullen's bear.

Cullen waited until Lucas' gaze clashed with his, shifting his focus from Hollis' shoulder back to mate's face. Cullen arched a brow, gathering Hollis closer as he threaded his fingers through her hair, keeping her head tilted to the side. Lucas dampened his lips, watching Hollis as he leaned in, licking at the small divots just beginning to disappear. She trembled then moaned, pushing her head into Cullen's hold.

Lucas repeated the caress then mouthed her skin, scraping his canines across the surface. She rasped his name, threading one of her hands through his hair before pulling him harder against her. He growled, again, in warning, making another pass, but still not breaking the skin.

She huffed, tugging on his hair this time as she pushed against his mouth. "Do it."

Lucas retreated, cupping her face until she finally met his gaze. He thumbed her lip, careful to avoid the blemish, only to curse when she sucked at the pad of his finger. "Do you know what you're askin' me—askin' us —to do?"

She blinked a few times then nodded. "Even if the image wasn't playing over and over inside my head, somehow, I know animals often like to mark each other. I'm assumin' your bears are no different."

"And do you understand the ramifications if we bite you?" He glanced at Cullen. "We'll all be bound. Until death."

Her eyes widened as she looked at Cullen across her shoulder before focusing on Lucas, again. "Are you two having second thoughts?"

"Us? Darlin', if we'd had our way, we would have bitten you that first night. But we're trying to ease you into this. Give you the proof you need that we're sincere. After all, you did confess you weren't convinced this wasn't just a passin' fancy for us."

"Thinkin' there's no better proof than this."

"And if you have second thoughts in the morning?"

"Lucas, in all the years I've been learning about medicine then practicin' it, I've never had any man stand up for me. Ever. Pretty sure I could search the Earth and never find two men who believe in me the way you boys do, even if I did have to practically beat it out of you. There won't be any regrets. And if it feels half as good as you just scrapin' my skin did..." She lifted her chin defiantly. "I said to stake your claim. And I meant it."

Lucas speared his fingers through her hair, layering them over Cullen's. "God forbid I don't accept a challenge." He leaned in, testing the patch of skin he intended to mark. "Mine."

He struck. Hollis stiffened between them, a throaty moan sounding in the air as she melted into Cullen, her heart thrashing wildly against his palm as he shifted his hold in an effort to keep her upright. Lucas didn't rush, seemingly drawing the act out until Hollis whispered his name. His mate eased back, looking down at Hollis before locking his gaze on Cullen. There was no mistaking the pure need darkening his eyes as he stared at the same patch of skin on Cullen's shoulder.

Cullen mentally told the man he'd have to wait as he bent over Hollis, sliding his tongue along the marks Lucas had left. Hollis moaned, tiptoeing up in an obvious attempt to increase the pressure. Cullen smiled against her skin, making a few more feathery passes with his lips before sealing his mouth to her flesh. She yelled his name when his teeth sank deep into the muscle, the warm taste of her blood increasing his desire until his damn pulse throbbed inside his head. His cock hardened against her ass, and he had to mentally tell his bear to release her shoulder when the damn thing lingered longer than Lucas had.

Hollis sagged in his arms, the simple motion sending a flash of cold across his flesh. It beaded with bumps as fear dropped his stomach. If he'd hurt her...

He moved back, sinking onto the bed, Hollis cradled in his arms. She didn't resist as her head rolled against his shoulder, her breath caressing his skin. Her eyes seemed out of focus as he drew her hair back, tucking it behind her ear.

"Hollis?" He brushed his fingers across her cheek. "Are you okay?"

Her mouth opened and closed a few times before she groaned, the hint of pain impossible to miss.

Lucas kneeled in front of her. "Darlin'. Tell us what's wrong."

Creases bunched the bridge of her nose as her gaze cleared. "Nothing's wrong, I'm just…" She groaned, again. "God, I'm hungry."

Lucas frowned, glancing at the locked door. "I might have some smoked meat—"

"Not that kind of hungry. I need…" She slipped off Cullen's lap, snaking her arms around Lucas' neck. "Mine."

She captured his mouth, looking every bit as wild as Cullen felt. He followed the couple to the floor, smoothing his hands down her sides then along her thighs, stopping with his fingers brushing the insides of her knees. He waited until she'd released Lucas before curling over her, pressing every inch he could against her.

He ran his thumbs along her skin, smiling at her sharp intake of breath. "I know you want to taste him, sweetheart. But I need you to open your legs. Show him how desperate he makes you feel. Give him a glimpse of what he'll get once he comes all over your chest."

Hollis looked back at him. "Christ, Cullen."

She moved easily when he applied pressure against her knees, splaying her thighs apart. Her warm, earthy essence saturated the air, and he couldn't stop from mouthing her other shoulder and scraping his canines along her flesh.

She pressed into him, even as her fingers returned to the band of Lucas' pants. The man waited until she'd fisted the material in her hands before shifting to his feet. Hollis kept ahold of the waistband, dragging the rough cotton over his hips as he stood, freeing his cock the moment he was upright. The heavy length bobbed down toward them before springing back up, the head shiny with fluid.

Hollis purred her satisfaction, skimming her fingers up his thighs and across his groin, scratching a path along the base of his cock. "Damn, but you're large. If Cullen is equally big, I might have spoken a bit too soon."

Cullen chuckled. "I'm fairly certain we'll fit. Now, are you going to taste him, first, or should I?"

Her breathy gasp made him smile. She slid him a quick glance then wrapped her tiny fingers around Lucas' shaft. The man reached for her, gathering her hair in one hand as he stared down at his mates, the blue in his eyes nothing but a small ring around the black. Hollis grinned then angled his cock toward her, slowly leaning in until her lips hovered just shy of touching his skin. She waited until Lucas released a hushed growl before slowly licking the fluid off the tip.

The man's head tilted back, the muscles in his neck cording. "Fuck, Hollis."

She merely hummed, making another pass before sinking down the length. Cullen clenched his jaw as he watched Hollis work Lucas to the brink, only to ease back as she dropped kisses along his groin, dipping down to nuzzle his sac. Lucas mumbled something about pushing him too far, but Hollis either didn't hear, or didn't seem to care as she continued to explore and taste at her own pace. It wasn't until the hand in her hair flexed, Lucas' knuckles connecting with Cullen's shoulder, that she glanced up at him. Lucas arched his brow, but Hollis only sighed, thumbing the tip of the man's cock.

She glanced back at Cullen, snagging her lower lip before offering Lucas' shaft to him. Cullen growled, leaning forward to lick the man's swollen flesh. Lucas' musky flavor filled Cullen's senses, and he knew he wouldn't be satisfied until his mate had fully surrendered and painted his release across Hollis' skin.

Cullen reached for Lucas, wrapping his hand over top of Hollis' on the man's shaft before slipping his lips around Lucas' wide crown and taking the man deep to the back of his throat. Smooth skin glided across Cullen's tongue, the hard length stretching his mouth. He savored the full feeling, rubbing the underside as he eased the man's shaft free, smiling at the sight of it covered in his saliva.

Hollis moaned beside him, her scent even stronger than before. "Please tell me you'll do that, again, because…" Her words trailed off into a breathy moan.

Cullen chuckled, repeating the deep pass before devouring Hollis' mouth then offering her a turn. She bobbed along Lucas' length, her eyes squeezed shut, her body shaking against Cullen's. He kept one hand wrapped around Lucas then dropped the other to her thigh, smoothing his fingers along her creamy skin. Her motion faltered when he reached the soft vee of her groin, her flesh already slick with arousal.

He pressed his chest harder against her back as he

dragged his finger through her drenched slit. "Damn, sweetheart. You're dripping."

She moaned around Lucas, still moving up and down his length. Cullen repeated the intimate caress, gathering some of her essence on his finger before sucking it clean. Her gaze snapped to his, the flush on her neck and chest deepening.

"So damn sweet. Lucas might end up having to share your first release."

"Fuck that." Lucas grunted as Hollis paused with his shaft lodged deep. "Christ, I won't last long. And she already promised I could have control of the next round. Which means you're both mine."

"Greedy bastard. Fine. Come for us, and you can lick her dry."

Lucas glanced at him then allowed his chin to bow toward his chest. His muscles rippled from the obvious strain, the bands across his abdomen casting box-like shadows on his skin. His hips jerked then started moving as he began a steady rhythm of pushing deep then retreating. Hollis held firm, angling his cock so it glided in and out of her mouth, the thick head wedging her lips apart. Cullen continued to tease her cleft, slipping just the tip of his finger inside her before focusing on another part of her body. She moaned around Lucas' shaft, glancing at Cullen before seemingly renewing her efforts to take their mate over the edge.

He leaned in close, rubbing his arousal-damp fingers along Lucas' length. "Soon, sweetheart, we'll make you fly apart, but first...finish him. I want to see his release all over your skin."

Her eyes rolled back slightly, and he didn't miss the way her muscles tensed.

Lucas grunted, upping his pace. "Damn it, Cullen. I won't last another minute if you keep touching me and talking like that."

Cullen grinned. "Then, perhaps I should put my mouth to better use."

He bent even closer, nodding when Hollis popped off, offering up Lucas' cock. Cullen devoured the other man, making several passes before handing him off to Hollis, again. She mimicked Cullen's technique, hollowing her cheeks as she moved then presenting Lucas back to Cullen.

Lucas mumbled above them, burying his other hand in Cullen's hair and anchoring both his mates to him as they took turns plunging deep then watching. His grip tightened, the telltale flexing of his muscles preceding a firm yank on Cullen's hair. He glanced up, smiling at the tight press of Lucas' jaw as the lines in his neck corded. His mate's eyes rolled back before his head bent forward in seeming defeat.

"Going to come. Can't..." Lucas' voice rasped into a throaty version of their names as his hips jerked frantically.

Hollis eased his shaft free of her mouth, still pumping the length as Cullen helped her angle the tip toward her chest. Their hands slid along the slick flesh, each pass drawing a muted moan from Lucas. The man had managed to hold off his release for several strokes before the head flared, and he came, painting ropey white fluid across Hollis' upper chest.

Hollis gasped, sealing her mouth around the tip after

the third pulse. Lucas shouted her name, the sound of her swallowing the next spurt spiking Cullen's cock against his stomach.

"That's it, sweetheart. Swallow everything he has left." Cullen drew her head toward him once she'd finally released Lucas, claiming her mouth in a long, wet kiss. He nipped at her lips when they parted. "Damn, he tastes good on you."

He glanced at her chest, inhaling the heady aroma of Lucas' release mixed with the sweet essence of Hollis' skin before twisting her enough he could mouth her flesh. Cullen struck, sinking his canines into her flesh. The combined flavor of her blood and Lucas' seed drowned his senses, and Cullen knew he'd need to taste them both for himself.

Lucas growled, using his hold on Cullen's hair to gain his attention. The man shook his head, a flash of red coloring his eyes. "While I love the thought of that, you'll have to wait your turn. You two made a deal, and I intend on capitalizing on it. So, get your asses on the bed, and I might consider sharing a taste of her." His gaze drifted to Hollis. "Then again…"

CHAPTER FOURTEEN

Hollis inhaled at the predatory gleam in Lucas' eyes. There was no denying that the wild side of the man lurked just below the surface, the continual flashes of red amidst the blue proof enough. She allowed Cullen to help her to her feet, but instead of moving directly to the bed, she stepped against Lucas as she wrapped one arm around his neck. He didn't wait for her to lean in, possessing her mouth in a frenzied mix of lips and tongues. Cullen pressed against her back, the heat from his body intensifying every sensation. She didn't know if the unrelenting ache was from watching Lucas surrender to them or the combined bites, but she was determined to finally have the men ease the constant fluttering of her stomach. The empty clench between her legs.

Lucas stared at her once they'd parted, his gaze traveling the length of her body as Cullen backed her toward the bed. He didn't stop once they'd reached it, merely helping her scoot across the mattress until he was braced against the wall with her trapped between his thighs. His cock felt like a brand against her lower back as he wrapped his arms around her, the firm flex of his muscles making her smile. She loved that they seemed as equally affected as she was—equally invested.

Cullen tsked behind her. "Are you still questioning our devotion, sweetheart? Means we're not doing this right."

She glanced at him across her shoulder. "That wasn't quite what I was thinkin'."

"Wasn't it?" Cullen dragged his teeth along her collarbone, and she couldn't stop from angling her head to the side—giving him better access.

He chuckled. "You seem surprised that we can't get enough of you. That our damn blood is boiling just thinkin' about touching you. Tastin' you. And that equates to the same thing. Thought we'd made it clear we plan on spending the rest of our lives loving you. Ensure your stubborn side doesn't get that pretty head of yours into trouble."

"You mean like getting involved with two men who clearly aren't the least bit tame?"

He smiled against her skin. "Exactly like that. And speakin' of tame..." He motioned to Lucas as the man stood at the side of the bed, a cloth dangling from one hand. "He looks like he's about to sprout fur you've got him so worked up."

"I don't think it's just me he wants."

Lucas grunted as he crawled onto the bed. "Already told you I intended to have both of you. But first..."

He brushed the cloth along her chest, removing any remaining evidence of his release from her skin. "As much as I love seeing my claim painted on your flesh, you won't be truly comfortable with your skin all sticky, especially when we've only just begun."

Goosebumps erupted along her torso, the cool brush of the cloth a direct contrast to the burning sensation beneath her flesh. She reached for Lucas, dragging him to her before he'd had a chance to dispose of the cloth. But she didn't care about being clean. All she wanted was his lips on hers as Cullen traced his hands down her side then along her thighs, once again settling them near her knees. She moaned into Lucas' mouth when Cullen slid his fingers along her inner thighs, tracing a line through her slick folds.

The man hummed. "Damn, I think you're even wetter."

She glanced at him as he raised his finger to his mouth, sucking off her arousal. The sight made her pussy clench, again, and she swore her entire cleft felt ready to burst.

Cullen grinned. "So fucking sweet. Open wide, sweetheart, and show Lucas how badly you want to come all over his face."

"God, Cullen. When you talk like that…"

He chuckled this time. "Makes you feel even more desperate for his tongue on you, doesn't it."

It wasn't posed as a question, though she nodded anyway as he applied pressure to her thighs, finally lifting them up and over his. She tensed as the new position completely bared her to their gazes, feeling more than a little exposed. She focused on Lucas, quivering at the intensity in his eyes. No one had ever looked at her like that, as if she somehow held his life in her hands.

He smiled, bending forward and nipping at her lip

before kissing a path along her shoulder. "You do hold my life in your hands. Cullen's, too. You're what makes us whole." He licked his way down her body, flicking his tongue over one distended nipple. "God, Hollis. What you do to me. To us. I can hear Cullen's thoughts, and it's all he can do to keep true to his promise." He raised his gaze to hers, shifting to Cullen then back. "I might have to give the man a taste, after all. Appease his bear just a bit."

Her stomach flip-flopped as he returned to her breast, drawing on the tight nub until she thought she'd scream. She lifted her hands to force him where she needed him, only to gasp as Cullen snagged her wrists.

He pulled them down to her legs, holding them tight. "You promised Lucas he was in control. Wouldn't want you to go back on your word, Doc."

She huffed, letting her head loll against his shoulder. "But...yes!"

She hissed out the word as Lucas slid two fingers along her cleft, pushing them slowly inside her. The thick penetration pinched slightly, but it quickly burned into red-hot need. He didn't rush, giving her plenty of time to adjust to the new sensation before easing back and rubbing the moisture around her clit. Dots flickered at the edge of her vision as heat gathered low in her core. Pleasure whipped along her nerves, coiling tight in her abdomen.

Lucas eased back, dropping his gaze. He seemed focused on the way his fingers moved in and out of her in a slow, steady rhythm. "So beautiful. All warm and wet and waitin' for me." He dragged his attention up to her face. "I really hope you were joking before when you told us you weren't the screamin' type. Because there's nothing I want more than to hear my and Cullen's names vibrate the walls as you come all over me."

Hollis snagged her bottom lip, using the slight hurt to keep her from simply flying apart at his words. Did they have any idea what they did to her? How desperate they'd made her? Lucas chuckled as if he'd heard her, and she resisted sticking her tongue out at him. Instead, she tried to reach for his hair, only to huff when Cullen maintained his hold on her, tsking in her ear, again.

"Promises, sweetheart. Now, stop pouting and let us make you feel so damn good."

Cullen moved both of her hands into one of his, snugging them against her left hip as he skimmed his free hand up her ribs to her breast. Rough calluses prickled her skin as he cupped the mounded flesh, using his thumb and forefinger to tease her nipple.

She pressed her head into his shoulder, watching Lucas through heavy-lidded eyes as he stared at Cullen's hand then settled fully between her legs. He wet his lips then darted his tongue forward, licking a path along her cleft. The coil in her groin tightened, making it hard to breathe.

Lucas hummed, dipping in for another pass before brushing his finger over her clit. "You taste just as sweet as I thought you would." He removed his fingers from within her grasping channel, offering them to Cullen. "So, your bear doesn't pout."

Cullen leaned forward, sucking Lucas' fingers into his mouth. The gravely moan that rumbled through his chest and into hers only spiked her desire higher—made the quivering feeling inside her intensify. "More."

Lucas grinned but plunged back inside, once again

offering his fingers to Cullen before taking the man's lips in a brutal kiss.

"Dear God." Hollis pushed out a few rough breaths, snagging Lucas' gaze once he'd moved back. A hint of moisture glistened on his skin, but she wasn't sure if it was hers or from Cullen's kiss. "Lucas…"

Her voice faded into a low rasp as Lucas possessed her mouth, the tangy flavor of her essence mixing with the spicy taste of him and Cullen. Lucas dropped another quick kiss on her nose then worked his way down her body, pausing to lick and nip every sensitive inch. She grunted when he bypassed her groin, kissing his way to the soft spot behind her knee. Shivers worked through her, the heat beneath her skin threatening to ignite.

She clenched her jaw, still tugging against Cullen's hold, when Lucas moved back up and buried his face in between her thighs, dragging his tongue the length of her slit. "Yes, right there."

The man chuckled against her flesh, nipping at her folds before returning to her clit. Colored dots exploded across her vision as he sucked at the small nub, tugging on it as he eased his fingers back inside her.

Cullen moaned behind her, his breath caressing her neck. "God, Hollis. If only you could see yourself. Your skin flushed a pretty pink. Your muscles clenching as you fight not to finish. Just watching Lucas devour you— hearing him fuck you with his other hand—it's better than I ever imagined." He scraped his teeth along her skin. "Come for us. I want to see you give yourself to him. Flood his mouth."

She shouted Lucas' name as he increased the pressure, swirling his tongue around her clit as he added another finger. She arched into his touch, needing one more thing to push her over. Cullen growled against her shoulder then struck, sinking his teeth into her flesh as Lucas plunged deep. The combined sensations shattered her control, and she came with another shout of their names. Heat rolled across her body, stealing her strength. She collapsed against Cullen, no longer pulling against his hold on her.

Cullen kissed the spot he'd bitten, slowly working his way up her neck to her ear. "So beautiful. And the way you shouted our names..." He kissed her jaw. "Breathe for us, sweetheart."

She managed to roll her head to the side so she could glance at him, wishing she had the strength to smack the smug smile off his face.

He shook his head. "Still challenging us. Guess that means we have more work to do. But first..."

He reached for Lucas, spearing his fingers through the man's hair then yanking him in for a hard kiss. Cullen licked his lips after they'd parted, his attention returning to her. "Make no mistake. You'll come like that for me next time. But for now...move with us."

She gasped as he released her hands then wrapped his arm around her waist, effectively lifting her up and shuffling her into Lucas' arms. Her mate drew her in close, nuzzling her nose before taking her lips in a slow, searing kiss. She held on tight, certain she'd simply melt into a puddle on the bed when he eased back.

Lucas smiled. "We'll see you get plenty of sleep once we've staked our claim. Now, I believe Cullen's been more than patient, especially when his bear is far less tame than mine."

She laughed at the thought, remembering the sheer size of Lucas' grizzly when he'd shifted. If he considered that tame, she could only imagine what Cullen must look like in his alternate form.

The idea rolled around her head as Lucas positioned her on top of Cullen, her legs straddled around his. "Wait. Why didn't you show me your bear?"

Cullen arched a brow. "You just drowned Lucas with your climax. I'm seconds away from making love to you, and you're thinkin' about my other half? That doesn't speak highly about our mastery between the sheets, sweetheart."

"You two are more than skilled. You're lucky I'm not passed out on the bed from the pleasure. But...don't I get to see all of you? Feel how soft your fur is? Show your bear I'm not afraid of any part of you?"

His gaze softened, and he reached for her, drawing her to him with a finger beneath her chin. "God, I love you. And you can see whatever part of me or Lucas you wish. Though, I'm hoping it can wait until morning, now that I've finally got you where I need you."

He rolled his hips, accentuating his statement with the press of his cock against her cleft as he sank the first inch inside her. The intense pressure purged any other thoughts from her mind except the thick, firm length slowly entering her. Lucas eased her upright against him, holding her close when her head fell into the crook of his shoulder as Cullen withdrew slightly then pushed back in, regaining the lost inches and gaining a few more. Her walls spasmed around the intrusion, somewhat fighting his possession until he thrust up and buried himself completely inside her.

A throaty growl sounded around them as Cullen's hands flexed around her thighs. "God, Hollis. So tight. Hot. It's all I can do not to finish on the first stroke." His thumbs made small circles across her skin. "Are you okay?"

Her fingers fisted against his shoulders as the pinching sensation eased, leaving her feeling raw. Hungry. She forced herself to meet his gaze, noting the worried furrow of his brow.

She nodded, moaning when Lucas lifted her up slightly, then lowered her, sending a jolt of pleasure coursing through her body. "Damn, Lucas. When you do that..."

Lucas chuckled. "Makes you want Cullen to pound into you, doesn't it? Make you come all over him."

She glanced over her shoulder at him then focused on Cullen. "Yes, God, yes. Cullen, I need..."

Cullen eased back a bit, then forward, taking her slow and steady. "Soon. But I don't want to hurt you. We'll take it easy until you're accustomed to me. Then..." He growled, again. "Then, sweetheart, I'm going to make you come so hard you won't know whether to scream or cry." He pressed out then in, again. "Mine."

The single word tightened her chest as warmth spread through her core. Lucas wrapped his arms around her, sliding up and down with her as Cullen pushed into her from below. She lost track of time, of the wavering shadows across the wall, the patter of rain against the window. Cullen kept true to his word, his slow maddening pace pushing her to her limits. But whenever she tried to move faster, Lucas shifted his grip, stopping her.

The man nuzzled her ear, nipping at the lobe. "Cullen's pace, darlin'."

"But—"

"No buts. Do you know how long he's waited to love you like this? It already isn't going to be long enough. Indulge him, this one time."

She closed her eyes at the honesty in his voice, giving him a small nod. She still wasn't sure why they were so taken with her. What their bears thought made her worthy to be their mate when no other man had so much as given her a second glance. Between Cullen and Lucas' rugged good looks and gut-wrenching charm, she had no doubts they could have their pick of any available woman.

Cullen paused, his groin pressed into hers. He waited until she opened her eyes, then sighed, lifting one hand to cup her chin. "You really don't know how special you are, do you?"

Tears gathered behind her eyes as she stared at him, unable to do more than breathe.

He smiled, motioning to Lucas before starting up the same slow pace. "Do you know why men look the other way? It's not because you aren't beautiful. Hell, you're stunning. It's because you intimidate them. But make no mistake, we aren't the least bit intimidated. We love that you're smart, and tough, and strong. That you can handle yourself against cowboys twice your size. We don't want you to change."

Lucas grinned against her ear. "Well, maybe the stubborn part, just a bit." He coughed when she elbowed him. "Fine. Be stubborn. But you have two mates who are equally hardheaded. So, stop worrying about why we love you, and let us show you how much we do."

He lifted her, giving Cullen room to move freely beneath her. He levered his hips, going deeper than he had before. The coil in her stomach gathered strength, again, sending waves of pleasure cascading along her nerves. She wanted to meet his thrusts, but Lucas simply held firm, lowering one hand until his palm cupped her mound with his fingers vee'd around Cullen's shaft.

"Damn, Hollis. He's got you stretched so tight. I bet he's just as desperate as you are to go faster. Stay exactly like this."

Lucas dipped behind her, his other hand skimming down her back then across her ass, settling around Cullen's cock from behind. He eased the man free, the wet sounds of him taking Cullen into his mouth making her eyes roll slightly. She tried to turn to watch him, but he tapped her ass.

"Stay. Still."

There was no missing the commanding tone to Lucas' voice as he helped press Cullen inside her, again, encouraging her to ride him before stopping her a second time. Lucas repeated his possession, humming as he tasted Cullen then watching her take him deep.

Cullen growled, threading one hand through her hair then pulling her down to him. He took her lips in his, tracing every inch of her mouth as Lucas kept alternating between them until Cullen paused, the muscles beneath her flingers clenching.

He pulled away enough to glance beyond her shoulder. "Lucas. Mate. I need..."

Their mate shifted, again, reclaiming his position behind Hollis. He eased his hand between them, urging her upright as his other settled on Cullen's torso. Lucas licked at her ear, nipping the lobe. "He can't hold off any longer, darlin'. Though, I don't think you can, either. Try to relax your muscles and just let him take you over."

His hand slid to her groin, pressing against her clit as Cullen started moving, his pace noticeably quicker. He didn't pause between thrusts, making her entire body shimmy as his slammed into hers, each punishing stroke whipping the coil tighter in her core. She clamped her fingers around his shoulders, allowing Lucas to bear some of her weight as her vision dimmed. The warm feeling beneath her skin expands outwards, stealing her breath for a few frantic moments before pushing her headlong into release.

She broke, her ragged cry sounding around them as pleasure flooded her body, making it feel as if she was shattering into a thousand pieces. Cullen grunted below her, still pushing into her grasping channel before stiffening. Her name filled the room, the gravelly quality only adding to the sensations coursing through her. He jerked upward, locking his mouth around her shoulder as he emptied into her. The firm bite coupled with the hot, wet evidence of his release stole the last of her strength, and she sagged against Lucas once Cullen collapsed on the bed, aware she'd join him if Lucas let go.

His contented hum broke through the murky haze. "Oh, Hollis. God, you're beautiful when you fly apart. Your skin's all flushed. Your body's like liquid in my arms. And hearing you climax... Damn, I nearly came listening to your voice crack like that. You've exhausted Cullen. But something tells me that as satisfied as you are, you still want more. *Need* more."

Hollis managed to pry her eyelids apart, twisting to

look back at Lucas across her shoulder. His lips were pressed together, the skin over his cheekbones taut. But it was the hunger in his eyes—the same way he'd looked at her when she'd gone to her knees—that held her attention.

He arched against her, his long, hard erection renewing the desire she thought she'd quenched. She moistened her lips, knowing she wouldn't truly be content until he'd staked his claim, as well.

Lucas smiled. "Thought so. Now, be a good girl and give Cullen a kiss."

CHAPTER FIFTEEN

Lucas inhaled, holding his breath as Hollis sank into Cullen's embrace, allowing the man to possess her mouth. If he were honest with himself, he'd been worried that his pleasure would be tainted by a hint of jealousy while watching his mates interact. But seeing the way Hollis fluttered her eyelids as she opened them, gazing at Cullen with the same love-dazed look she'd given Lucas just moments before, made his damn chest ache with need. And he knew he'd go to any lengths to ensure nothing and no one ever threatened them, again.

Cullen locked his focus on Lucas, arching a brow. "Do I need to worry where your thoughts are drifting, mate? Because I can assure you, my bear doesn't like the tone. You already took a spike to the shoulder for me. I'll be damned if you put your life at risk, again. Not that now is the time to be discussing this, anyway." He grazed his finger along her cheek. "Our girl needs you."

Lucas looked at Hollis, smiling at the way her breath caught when their gazes clashed, or how her lips parted slightly, as if she were waiting for him to kiss her. The thought had him moving, and she opened willingly when he slanted his mouth over hers, licking his way inside. She tasted warm and sweet, and he threaded his fingers through her hair to deepen the kiss.

Hollis moaned, allowing him to tilt her head against Cullen's shoulder without turning her. Lucas took his time, wanting to savor every nuance. Her contented hum as she gave herself over fully to the kiss. The heady scent of her and Cullen's release. The soft play of her skin as it brushed over his.

He eased back, holding Hollis' head as he stared at her and Cullen. While Lucas realized this was only the beginning of their time together, he wanted to be able to look back and remember each moment. Burn it into his mind until he could picture Hollis and Cullen staring at him exactly as they were right now. Hungry. Entranced.

Hollis smiled, and Lucas' heart skipped.

He leaned forward, dropping a kiss on her nose. "And you wonder why we love you."

She furrowed her brow, obviously puzzled by the random comment. Though he had no doubts she'd learn to read their thoughts in record time. She opened her mouth, laughing when he simply claimed it, again, tracing every contour before releasing her.

He thumbed her cheek. "Are you sure you're not too sore? Tired? Despite what I said, how much I want to love you, I can wait—"

It was her turn to cut him off with a soul-searing kiss. "Then, love me."

"With pleasure. Why don't you give Cullen another kiss while he helps me get you positioned?"

She snagged her lip, glancing between them before following Cullen's lead. Lucas watched as Cullen settled her above him, again, knees on either side of his hips. He traced his hands along her thighs then up her back, drawing small circles on her skin. He tangled one hand in her hair, fisting the brown mass around his fingers as he dragged her down to him. Any tension in her muscles eased as Cullen took her mouth.

Lucas smiled, dividing his attention between his mates and the steady progression of his hand as he smoothed it down her spine, lightly scratching her skin. Goosebumps prickled her flesh as he skimmed his finger along her crease, pausing to brush the tip across her ass. He circled the opening, waiting to see if she'd tense. Hollis glanced back at him, watching his face for several heartbeats before closing her eyes and dropping her head to rest on Cullen's chest.

His bear roared its approval, growling when Lucas gathered some of her arousal on his finger before slowly easing it past the tight ring of muscles. Her low, throaty moan spiked his cock against his stomach as he pushed into her channel, feeling her walls give around his penetration. He paused for a few moments then eased back, teasing the surface, again.

"God, Hollis. You've got the perfect ass. Watching you take my finger..." He hummed. "I can't wait until you take me and Cullen this way. But not unless it's what you want." He leaned forward. "I know Cullen wants me to fuck his."

"And you want me to take yours, mate. But not this time. Tonight's about making Hollis realize how much she means to us." Cullen's expression intensified. "Though, next time…"

Lucas growled at the images that flashed in his head. Hollis beneath him, his cock deep inside her while Cullen rode Lucas' ass, his mate's large form covering both of them. Knowing they'd get to explore their love in more than a few ways made Lucas' head spin. After all the months of fighting his desire, it seemed surreal that he was there, Hollis and Cullen sharing his bed.

Cullen nudged him with his foot, motioning to Hollis. Lucas smiled, hissing out a breath when she pressed back against him, mentally begging him to love her already.

He chuckled, giving her ass a light smack before settling between her legs, her body snugged against his. "God, your skin is so soft. I'll never tire of touching you." He dragged his cock through her drenched folds. "Are you ready, darlin'?"

Her reply was a raspy whisper of his name. He nodded, making another pass through her cleft before nudging her opening and sinking just the tip inside her. Hot fluid bathed his crown, and he couldn't stop from thrusting forward—claiming her sheath in one smooth motion.

"Yes!"

The word hissed free as Hollis clenched around his intrusion, her walls rippling from the firm penetration. Lucas paused with his shaft lodged deep, savoring the tight clasp of her channel before slowly easing back. The shiny evidence of her desire coated his skin, gleaming in the flickering light. He swallowed hard, half wishing Cullen would lick him clean before thrusting back into her warm, wet heat.

Cullen grunted, drawing Lucas' attention. There was

no mistaking the fire raging in his mate's eyes, and Lucas knew the other man had heard his thoughts. Cullen grinned and mouthed the word *soon*, then dragged Hollis forward for another punishing kiss.

Lucas moaned as the sight sent a punch of lust through his gut. He increased his pace slightly, needing the steady motion to calm the burning sensation beneath his skin. Seeing his mates interact, feeling Hollis give around his shaft—he'd never imagined it would be this intense. That the actual act would pale in comparison to the volley of emotions tightening his chest. The knowledge that he got to spend the rest of his life showing his mates how invested he was. How deep his love ran.

The stark truth unhinged his control, and he squeezed Hollis' hips as he let himself go. Her ass shimmied with each forceful stroke, the wet echoes of his penetration sounding around them. She chanted his name, pushing into each thrust, as Cullen held her close, kissing any available inch as he moved his fingers along her back until they covered Lucas' hands.

The added connection set him off, and he knew he wouldn't be able to last much longer. He clenched his jaw, willing himself not to finish, yet, when Hollis gasped, arching upwards as her pussy contracted around his cock, squeezing the length with rhythmic pulses.

He bowed his head, wedging one hand free of Cullen's grasp before skimming it up her spine and locking it in her hair. He pulled her upright until her head fell against his shoulder, Cullen's hand shifting to support her from below before he levered up, trapping her between them.

Lucas tilted her head to the side, scraping his teeth

along her skin as his release burned a path down his spine and into his shaft. He managed several more strokes before the fire shot forward, emptying him in a series of spurts. He let his mouth settle on her muscle, before sinking his canines into her flesh, sending her into another climax.

He held tight, riding through the spasming waves of her orgasm before slowly lifting his mouth. He stared at the twin puncture marks then gazed at Cullen. His focus dropped to the man's shoulder, the unmarked skin glaring back at him. Lucas eased Hollis to the side just enough to pull Cullen closer. His mate smiled, his canines showing beneath his upper lip before Lucas captured his mouth. He traced along the pointed ends, wondering if it'd feel half as good as he'd imagined, before releasing Cullen and moving to his shoulder. Lucas didn't wait, just licked a path along Cullen's skin, then struck.

Cullen's taste filled Lucas' mouth, the spicy essence tempered by a hint of sweet. He lingered, enjoying the play of the man's muscle beneath his lips, as his grizzly paced inside his head. And he knew he'd need to claim his mate in every way before his bear would truly be satisfied. A throaty moan brought him back from his senses, and he eased away, smiling at the small wounds. "Mine."

Cullen's fingers speared through Lucas' hair, fisting around the strands before yanking his head to one side. Cullen growled then latched onto Lucas' shoulder, marking him with the same hard bite. Pleasure tore through his body, hardening his shaft just starting to weaken within Hollis' body, and for a moment, Lucas thought he might climax, again.

A hot lick across his flesh eased the sensation as

Cullen drew back, nodding at his handiwork. "That was long overdue, mate. Which means I'll have to mark you several more times before it comes close to mollifying my bear. But it'll do, for now."

"Are you two sure you don't need to love each other right now? Because I could stay awake for that." Hollis tightened around Lucas' cock. "Lord knows you 'feel' ready for another round."

Lucas snapped his attention to Hollis as she sagged in his embrace. He smiled at the deep flush of her skin. The hint of moisture coating her brow and how her hair sat in a tangled mess around her head and shoulders. Christ, she was beautiful.

He pressed hard against her, rewarded with a flutter of her eyelids. "Naughty. And while I'd like nothing more than to pound into Cullen…we all need to get some sleep. My bear can hold off, for a bit. But make no mistake, when we do claim each other, you won't be sitting idly by."

"Never said I only wanted to watch. Though I do— want to watch you two." She stifled a yawn, blinking several times as if trying to keep her eyes open.

"I'm sure we'll find a way to satisfy both of your desires."

He withdrew, loving the small huffing sound she made, as if she didn't want him to leave, then helped her snuggle against Cullen. The other man whispered in her ear, drawing a contented laugh as Lucas climbed off the bed. He grabbed a couple of cloths, dunking them both in the water before rinsing himself off. He turned, tossing one cloth to Cullen before returning to the bed. Hollis watched him as he eased her thighs apart then gently cleaned her groin, doing his best not to roar at the combined scent of their releases.

A flash of red caught his attention. He unfolded the fabric, staring at the blood smeared across the surface. A knot formed in his stomach, and he glanced at Cullen before focusing on Hollis.

Cullen frowned. "What?"

Lucas swore under his breath, holding the cloth up.

"Shit." Cullen juggled Hollis in his arms until they were both upright, again. "You should have told us we were going too rough."

Hollis arched a brow. "You weren't too rough."

Cullen's lips pressed tight before he took the cloth from Lucas and held it out to her. "Then, why is there blood?"

She sighed, barely giving the cloth a glance. "Because I'd never been with a man before, and neither of you are exactly small." She shook her head as she grabbed the fabric then tossed it on the side table. "Cullen. It's not unusual to have proof of that afterwards. Besides, that's nothing. A few drops."

Lucas huffed. "That looked like more than a few drops."

"Trust me. Doctor, remember? I'm fine." She yawned, again, gazing at them with half-lidded eyes. "Stop worryin' and come to bed. If you're determined to feel guilty over nothing, you can make it up to me by loving me, again, in the morning."

"You need to heal before we—"

"What I need, is for you to hold me while I sleep. Then, make me scream, again, once I wake up." She shushed them. "Now, whose chest am I using as a pillow?"

Cullen snorted. "I'd almost forgotten how damn stubborn you are." He smiled at her glare, dropping a kiss on her nose. "We just don't want to be the reason you feel pain. We've already done that enough."

"All I seem to recall is an immense amount of pleasure. Promise. But either way, you're forgiven."

"Fine." He gathered her close, again. "I think Lucas is dyin' to have you snuggle against him. Sleep. We'll see how you feel in the morning. If you're up for an adventure."

"An adventure?"

"We'll talk about that once you're gotten some rest. See how your head's feeling."

She gave them a stunning smile. "It feels fine as long as you're both touching me."

"Still dangerous." Cullen helped her settle against Lucas once he'd climbed under the blankets. Cullen leaned in close, dropping a lingering kiss on her lips. "Not sure we can thank you enough for giving us a chance. Now, rest. No more nightmares for you tonight."

Her eyelids fluttered as she burrowed against Lucas' chest. Cullen smiled, shifting enough he could taste Lucas' mouth one more time before relaxing behind Hollis, one arm draped over her hip, his hand resting on Lucas' abdomen. Soothing warmth spread through Lucas' body, the echoed beat of Hollis and Cullen's hearts easing any remaining tension.

This was where he belonged. Where he needed to be. He glanced at Hollis. Her breathing had already deepened. Damn, she must be exhausted, especially after they'd pounced on her just when she was starting to get some quality rest.

"We didn't pounce. And she'll sleep even better, now."

Lucas gazed over at Cullen. "I didn't say it was a bad thing. In fact, I still can't believe she didn't run when she had the chance and have the townsfolk string us up."

Cullen chuckled. "Girl's got too much grit for that. Though not shooting us was a pleasant surprise."

Lucas smiled, but it faded. "You convinced we weren't too rough?"

"I know you let your bear search her feelings as much as I did. I didn't sense any deception. In fact, if she wasn't so damn tired, she might have *pounced* on us, this time. Her desire is more than real."

"I just don't want to cause her more pain. In all the excitement, I kind of pushed aside the fact her face is still ten shades of purple."

"Mating will hopefully help with that. If what I've heard is true, it'll give her a bit of a kick in the healing department. Either way, she's safe, now."

"Let's just make sure she stays that way."

Cullen arched a brow. "We back to discussing those thoughts I picked up on earlier? Because my grizzly is more than up for the challenge. Especially since I haven't been able to fully bond with you, yet."

Lucas sighed, relaxing his head into the pillow. "Nothing to discuss. You're equally as determined to keep us safe, so...no sense wasting time puffing up our chests. And for the record, my bear wants you with the same burning need. Best we follow our own advice and get some sleep." He glanced at Cullen, again. "Because I don't see us getting much for the next couple of nights. Not if Hollis agrees to come with us."

"She will. I just hope she's up to it."

"We'll see that she doesn't push herself too hard."

Cullen merely nodded, settling, again, as he closed his eyes. Lucas watched his mate fight against his exhaustion before finally drifting off. The room grew quiet, with only the occasional patter of rain sounding beyond the windows. The thunder had stopped while they were making love, and if Lucas' senses were right, the worst of the storm had passed. Which hopefully meant they'd be able to avoid getting soaked on their journey tomorrow.

The thought sent a mix of emotions coursing through him. While he longed for some alone time with his mates —without having to worry about anyone walking in or disturbing them—knowing they'd be possible targets for Buford's gang along the way didn't sit well with his other half. Not that his mates couldn't handle themselves. He simply didn't want to put any of them in the position they'd have to.

He reran Hollis' previous words. She was right. The West was a dangerous place, and all he could do was try to minimize the risks. And now that he and Cullen didn't have to hide what they were from Hollis, they'd be able to use their other abilities to help keep her safe.

Safe. That was a hard to promise to keep with men like Buford roaming the hills. But Lucas meant what he'd thought earlier. He'd sacrifice anything to keep Hollis and Cullen safe. No hesitation. No regrets.

CHAPTER SIXTEEN

Cullen glanced at the gray clouds blanketing the sky, the thick layer obscuring the usually colorful sunrise, before turning up the collar on his jacket. He hadn't wanted to venture out of the warm bed—leave his mates—but he needed to organize the men if he and Lucas were going to steal Hollis away for a couple of days to scout the last section of the line. While Cullen doubted any of his crew would argue over having their resident doctor leave for a while, he didn't want Hollis to face any backlash from them in case he was wrong. Especially when she was still fighting to fit in. And he didn't need anyone giving her a reason to decline their offer. To put her oath above their need to complete the mating. Not with their bond so new. Even now, his bear scratched at his hold, doing everything it could to make him turn around—step back inside the sheriff's office and reassert his claim.

The thought had him stepping off the landing and into the street. Mud splattered across the bottom of his pants as he made his way to the saloon. Marla provided breakfast for the crew, and he'd likely find everyone he needed to talk to in one place. The swinging doors creaked as he walked into the tavern, scanning the crowd before narrowing in on a group of men. He marched over to the table, leaning down so he could address them at the same time, before outlining their schedule for the next few days. A couple of the men frowned but nodded, pushing their chairs back then moving off to relay the news to the rest of the crew.

The other workers watched Cullen as he headed for the doors, again, their expressions clearly conveying their confusion. Not that he hadn't ventured up the line before, but he'd only once taken Lucas with him, and never overnight. Though, Cullen realized the crew was probably more concerned with the possibility of the camp getting waylaid by bandits than why the three of them were leaving.

Cullen shoved the twinge of guilt aside. There was still a day's worth of cleanup on the line, if not two. Chances were, the men wouldn't get more than a few hundred yards of track laid before he returned, not with all the mud and colder temperatures hampering their every move. And it wasn't as if he was leaving them unprotected. Lucas had already arranged for half a dozen men to accompany the crew as guards, and even more to watch over the town during the night. Surely, Devil's Gate could last long enough for Cullen to confirm the final stretch of tracks and have some quality time with his mates before the workers made the last push to finish the spur.

He sighed. Regardless of the lingering doubt, it was a chance they'd have to take. He needed to see the grade one more time before they boxed themselves in inside the canyons, and whether he wanted to acknowledge it or not, he needed to quench the restless ache burning beneath his skin. While bonding with Lucas and Hollis had mollified his bear last night, the damn thing was far from satisfied. And if he didn't get another taste of their skin soon, the animal might yet go rogue—an act which would put Hollis' life in even more jeopardy than it already was by being part of the camp.

His Kodiak snorted. Cold day in Hell before he'd let anyone threaten his mates, not after finally laying claim to them—even if it still felt incomplete where Lucas was concerned. His mate's thoughts from the previous night played in his head. The man had harbored similar ideas, not that Cullen was surprised. Lucas had always been protective, even if he'd gone to great lengths to disguise it —pretend he hadn't worried all the times Cullen had ridden off alone. But now that Hollis was part of the equation—there was no denying how far Lucas would go to keep both of them safe.

The thought sobered Cullen, and he tried not to run down the street as he did a quick scan of the town then made his way back to the sheriff's office. They'd done their notifying in shifts, not wanting to leave Hollis alone, not that they'd admit that to her. The girl was more than a little stubborn, and he had no doubts she'd get her hackles up if she thought they were babying her.

He smiled at the idea, picturing her with her arms crossed, cheeks tinged red. She'd have a series of creases across the bridge of her nose as she glared at them, one foot tapping the floor—marking her agitation. While he wouldn't go out of his way to anger her, there was no denying a part of him loved seeing the feisty side of her—the one that never backed down. That challenged anyone in her path, even if it was him and Lucas.

A warm feeling spread through Cullen's chest as he climbed the few steps to the building, coming to an abrupt halt as soon as the door had closed behind him. Lucas looked over to him from where he leaned against the desk, arms crossed over his chest, his shirt hanging open. Red tinged the man's cheeks, as the muscle in his jaw repeatedly jumped. Another man stood in front of Cullen, feet braced apart, long jacket covering his clothes. The guy turned, revealing a furrowed brow and dark eyes from beneath the brim of his hat, the white square at his collar practically glowing in the dull light.

Cullen cursed under his breath before nodding at the man. "Reverend Miller."

The preacher kicked at the floor, glancing between the two men. "Mr. James."

Cullen groaned inwardly at the harsh tone, guessing the man wasn't here to wish them a safe journey, then crossed the room, standing off to the right in front of the bedroom door. "Don't take this wrong, Reverend, but is there something we can help you with? We've got a line to scout, and I'd rather we get in as many miles as we can before more rain sets in."

The man's mouth twitched at Cullen's words, the flush in his cheeks deepening. He fisted his hands at his sides for a few moments before stuffing them in his pockets. "That's exactly what I've been discussing with the sheriff."

Cullen focused on Lucas, trying to ignore the swath of skin visible between the sides of his shirt. Christ, what he wanted to do to that flesh. Bathe it with his tongue, run his fingers across the muscular bands. If only the collar was open more, Cullen would be able to see exactly where he planned on marking his mate, again.

Lucas cleared his throat, looking far too smug when Cullen finally dragged his gaze up to the man's face. "It seems the good reverend is concerned about us taking Dr. Chambers along with us. He feels it's inappropriate without a proper chaperone. And of course, he's volunteered to join us so he can ensure her moral safety."

Heat burned along Cullen's skin, and he had to physically restrain his bear from breaking his hold. It didn't take his enhanced senses to detect the way the man's eyes darkened at the mention of Hollis' name. Or how his breathing kicked up as his gaze darted to the door behind Cullen for a few seconds before focusing on him, again.

A hand landed on Cullen's shoulder a moment before Lucas stepped in front of him, giving him a knowing smile that eased the tingling beneath his flesh. Damn, all the man had to do was look at him or touch him, and Cullen was lost.

Lucas spun to face the pastor, keeping his back pressed lightly against Cullen's chest. "I was just explaining how that wasn't logistically possible and assuring the man that Hollis was more than safe with us—morally or otherwise."

Miller pinched his mouth tight before giving them both a grim smile. "With all due respect, Sheriff Quinn, while it's your job to protect the lives of the folks who call this camp home, it's mine to protect their souls. It's bad enough she's already spent the night here. God only knows what people are saying."

"I hardly think God is wasting His time worryin' about where I slept last night."

Hollis' voice had them spinning to face her, her lithe form backlit by the gray light from the windows in Lucas' chambers. Her gaze ran the length of them before she moved forward, smiling when he and Lucas parted just enough she could squeeze through. Cullen frowned at the patchwork of bruises laced along her face, her one eye slightly swollen. While it was definitely better than it had been several hours ago, just knowing she was still in pain burned a hole in his gut. He never should have stopped Lucas. Never should have let her go into the clinic alone.

Hollis paused for a moment, glancing at him with a furrowed brow, before sighing. She reached for him, brushing her hand along his chest, before stepping forward and stopping with her back just shy of touching them, and far closer than Cullen thought she would. Not if she wanted to keep their intimate relationship a secret. Though, if the reverend had been able to see her touch him, it was probably a moot point.

The preacher gasped, pointing at her cheek. "Dear Lord. Is that from the other day?"

"Getting hit does tend to leave a mark. But, I'm fine. Is there a problem, Reverend?"

Miller huffed, staring at their loose-knit triangle before nodding at Hollis. "In a manner of speakin'." The man shuffled restlessly then straightened. "I was just explaining to Sheriff Quinn that having both of you accompany Mr. James on his scoutin' mission is ill-conceived."

Cullen groaned inwardly. They hadn't even had a chance to discuss the trip with Hollis—other than the suggestion of an adventure the previous night—though they'd hedged their bet and made arrangements on the hope that she needed to spend time with them as much as they did with her. But if the good reverend pleaded his case, he might sway her to stay.

"Trip?" Hollis glanced at them, giving them an arch of her brow before facing Miller. "Right. Scoutin' the line."

"The town's already being put at risk by losing our sheriff for a few days. Taking our only doctor, as well, seems like a foolhardy decision." The preacher gave Lucas and Cullen a pointed look. "The men need you here."

"The men in this camp barely tolerate me." She touched her cheek, though Cullen didn't think it was a conscious move. "If it weren't for Lucas, I'd have passed out in the street. And he and Cullen were more than gracious on insisting to treat my wounds, especially when I've been less than kind towards them lately. I can't imagine either man got much sleep last night."

Cullen managed to bite back the growl that rumbled through his chest. Just hearing her mention last night had his bear scratching at his control, again. Whether it was the fact another man was obviously interested in his mate or that her scent had woven around him, mixing with Lucas' until the combined essence seemed infused in his head, he wasn't sure. But he knew if Miller so much as tried to touch her, he might lose his internal battle.

The reverend glanced at him then crossed his arms over his chest, smiling at Hollis. "I could have tended your injuries if you'd asked."

"Never was much good at askin', which is probably

why Lucas brought me here in the first place. I tend to be quite stubborn at times. Though, I couldn't be more grateful." She took a single step forward. "As for the trip, I actually asked them if I could tag along."

The man's mouth gaped open for a moment before he cleared his throat. "You asked them? But why? We all know that Buford and his men will likely launch another attack against us. Or at the very least, the crew. With Sheriff Quinn gone, we're vulnerable. What if one of the men gets shot or cut out on the line today?"

"This last attack used up most of the medicine I'd first ordered. I gave Cullen a list, but it could take up to a week before anything arrives. In the meantime, I can replace some of them with natural remedies, *if* I can acquire the correct ingredients. Thankfully, many of the plants grow around here. As you can imagine, neither Lucas nor Cullen were keen on me going on my own, so...I suggested I accompany them. I should be able to harvest what I need to make the salves without slowing them down. It's only for a day or two. And this is better for the men in the long run."

Miller pursed his lips into a thin line, absently kicking at the floor. "I see. Then, it seems only reasonable that I accompany you."

The line of Hollis' back stiffened. "While I appreciate the gesture, I was hoping you'd fill in for me while I was gone. You did a great job helping me the other night."

The color drained from the man's face. "I'm not a doctor."

"But you don't shy away from the sight of blood. And you learned how to put pressure on a wound. Clean one if necessary. That could be enough until I get back."

"But…" He glanced at Lucas and Cullen. "I'm… concerned about you being alone with two men. It might cause a scandal."

Her easy laughter filled the room. "You do recall I shot Caleb that first night, don't you? I'm hardly worried about what the townsfolk say about me, when they're already gossiping."

"I'm talking about more than how skilled you are with a gun. I'm talking about your immortal soul."

"Reverend Miller—"

"You can call me Joseph."

The growl Cullen had suppressed resurfaced, echoing through the room. He took a measured step forward, stopping when Hollis shifted in front of him, pushing her back into his chest. Her hand landed briefly on his thigh, giving his leg a quick squeeze before letting go.

Joseph frowned, glancing around the room. "Did you hear that?"

"It was probably a dog outside. I've seen a few strays in town. Now, in terms of my soul—"

"I assume you would prefer not to go to Hell."

"Wasn't planning on it. But…" She held up her hand to prevent him from interrupting, again. "I hardly think travelin' with Lucas and Cullen will result in that. I trust them. In fact, they have more honor than most men I've met."

"This isn't a question of honor. It's about appearances."

"Then, I have nothing to worry about. The people in this camp had their minds made up about me before I left the saloon to tend Jack's injuries. Now, how about you head over to the clinic, and I'll meet you there in a minute. Show you where the supplies are should you need to bandage a cut. I just want to go over a few details with the sheriff."

Joseph glowered but nodded, tipping his hat to her before turning and marching to the door. The thing banged shut behind him, his footsteps quickly fading.

Hollis turned, palming her hips as she stared at them. "When, exactly, were you going to tell me about this trip?"

Lucas smiled, trailing his finger along her arm before allowing it to drop to his side. "I recall Cullen mentioning an adventure last night."

"Which I thought meant going for a ride together, not leaving the camp unattended for days. And despite what I told Joseph, he's right. I don't think a day has gone by without at least one person droppin' by my clinic. Which I realize is foreign to both of you since neither of you need doctors."

Cullen growled, again, stepping into Hollis as he cupped her hip, tugging her tight against him. "Are we back to you thinkin' we don't need you because we can heal ourselves?"

"All I meant was that being a doctor means I get called to work at all hours. Especially in small rail towns like this one, where pride and alcohol seem to overrule rational thought."

"This has nothing to do with him worryin' about the men, or whether you'll be around to treat a fistfight over a game of cards, and everything to do with the fact he wants you."

Her smile made his chest tighten as she leaned against him, resting one small hand on his chest. "I hardly think the resident preacher wants to court a gun-toting doctor."

"You weren't in the room when he all but drooled at the mere mention of your name."

Her expression softened as she lifted her other hand to trace the line of his jaw. "Are you jealous? Because I'd think after all we shared last night, you wouldn't question my devotion. In fact, I'm certain both of you can sense exactly how I feel."

Cullen cursed under his breath at the punch of emotion that rocked through him. While she might not have expressed her feelings in the way he realized he needed to hear—despite what he'd told her the previous night—she definitely cared for them.

"It's not your devotion I'm antsy about. With everything so new, my bear's feeling more than a bit territorial where you and Lucas are concerned. I'm just worried that if the man gets too friendly with you, he might end up facing an irate Kodiak."

"Make that two grizzlies." Lucas moved in behind her, trapping her between them. "Mine didn't like the way his scent changed when you walked in. Cullen's right. He wants you, darlin'."

"Then, I suppose I'll just have to disappoint him, seeing as I've already given my heart to two men. Now, about leaving…"

Cullen groaned. "I know. It probably goes against some oath, but…" He dropped his forehead to rest on hers. "We really do need some time alone. And it's obvious we won't get much of that here. Even if we toss propriety out the window and don't hide that we're all involved, there seems to be a steady stream of people in and out of all of our doors. Yours included." He gave her a squeeze. "Just one night, then you can come back and deal with anything that might have cropped up. If it helps, the men are mostly cleanin' up on the line today. Nothing risky."

"Simply breathing seems to be risky in this town." Hollis sighed, placing a soft kiss on his lips. "Though, I suppose the camp has survived without me for a few months. A couple of days shouldn't hurt that much, not if your thoughts on Buford and his men are correct. And as I pointed out the other day, I'm out of most of my salves. Wouldn't hurt to collect some of the plants along the way, if you boys don't mind. At least, I'll have something to treat any wounds while we wait for that shipment to arrive."

"If it means you'll spend the next couple of days with us, I'll clear the entire forest for you."

She laughed, the sound morphing into a moan when Lucas mouthed her neck, slowly working his way beneath the fabric and along her shoulder. "That won't be necessary... Christ, Lucas. Do you know what that does to me?"

He answered with a growl as he wedged his hands between them in order to cup her breasts. "We have to give you a reason to come, or you might change your mind and let duty rule."

She inhaled, allowing her head to fall back against him, and Cullen knew his mate was tweaking her nipples.

Cullen nuzzled the other side, moaning at the sweet taste of her skin against his tongue. "Damn, you're addicting. Just one lick, and I want you to unravel against me. Have you grind your pussy on my face before you cream my tongue."

"God, Cullen. I need..."

Hollis trailed off as he dragged his canines along her flesh, applying just enough pressure to ease the pounding inside his head without marking her.

She pushed up against him. "Stop teasing me, and bite me already."

He paused over the spot, wanting nothing more than to sink his teeth into her muscle—leave a visible mark of his claim over her. But he'd never be able to stop from shoving her pants over her hips and shafting her while Lucas held her suspended between them. And he had a feeling Lucas would need to do the same, only while Cullen fucked the other man's ass.

Lucas grunted then lowered his hand. His knuckles brushed against Cullen's cock as his mate cupped Hollis' mound, no doubt stroking it through her pants. "I swear, mate. You keep thinkin' along those lines, and we won't get anywhere today but back into bed."

Cullen glanced up, locking his gaze on Lucas' as red flashed in his mate's eyes. "Just say the word..."

Lucas clenched his jaw, closing his eyes before releasing an audible breath. He frowned then eased back, dragging Hollis with him until she was standing on her own. "As much as I want that... We really do need privacy for what I have in mind. And we'll never get that here, so..." He drew another ragged breath. "We'll put this on hold until we set up camp for the night. But once that happens..."

Cullen nodded, willing his cock to stand down, though he swore the damn thing had a mind and a pulse all its own. Even now, it throbbed in longing, pressing against his breaches until he thought it'd just burst free.

Hollis mumbled something under her breath before crossing her arms over her chest. "Don't I get a say in any of this?"

Lucas moved in closer, again, then palmed her hips. "I can hear your thoughts, as I'm sure Cullen can. But I think you'll agree that stickin' to the plan will pay off in the long run."

"So, I'm just supposed to spend the day like this? Wet? Wanting? My body constantly perched on the edge with no relief in sight?"

Lucas' eyes closed, again, and Cullen felt the man fighting for control. "Hollis."

She sighed, giving his hands a pat before stepping free of his hold. "Fine. I'll wait. But don't think I won't have my revenge later tonight." She straightened her clothes, smoothing her hands along her shirt as if she wasn't sure what to do with them.

Cullen frowned, closing the distance. "Are you okay, sweetheart?"

She snorted. "Other than feeling like my skin's on fire, I'm fine."

He glanced at Lucas, noting the concern in his eyes. "Mating can have a few side effects. Until we all adjust to being bonded, it's best if we don't stray too far from each other. Which is why this is so important." He trailed his fingers through her hair. "If you're in pain..."

She brushed his hand aside, drawing herself up. "Nothing I can't handle. And at least my face doesn't hurt as much. Even the bruising looks better."

"Better would be if there wasn't any, at all."

"And I thought I was stubborn. Now, if you'll excuse

me, I'll go show the good reverend where all the supplies are and grab my medical bag. Just in case."

Cullen snagged her elbow before she could turn around. "Take Lucas with you." He held up his other hand. "Humor me, please. We're all strung tight, and one stray caress on the reverend's part could push us over the edge."

A wicked smile curved her lips before she stepped into him, cupping his shaft through his pants. "You mean like this?"

He growled in warning. "Dangerous, sweetheart."

She laughed then moved back. "I know. But isn't that part of the reason your bears are drawn to me? Speaking of which...you promised I could meet your other half. I intend to hold you to that."

"You come along with us, and you can see whatever side of me you want. Lucas, too."

"Sounds fair." She motioned to Lucas. "All right, Sheriff. Let's go pretend we don't want to rip each other's clothes off while I gather my supplies. Just...no growlin'. And you have to play nice with Reverend Miller."

Lucas scowled. "You mean the man who wants you to call him Joseph?"

"It's his name, Lucas."

"Right. Which is why everyone calls him that."

"I promise to keep my guns handy, just in case he crosses a line."

"See that you do." He nodded toward Cullen. "I'll be right behind you."

Hollis gave them a stunning smile then headed toward the door and out into the street.

Lucas turned to Cullen, eyeing him suspiciously. "You okay?"

"Fine, why?"

"Mated, Cullen. I know when you're antsy, and this feels like more than just idle interest from the local preacher."

Cullen huffed. "I knew this connection would end up bitin' me in the ass."

"It goes both ways, mate." Lucas studied him. "You're upset because she hasn't said she loves us, yet."

Cullen glanced at the door. "And you're not?"

"Need I remind you that *you* were the one who told her not to declare her undyin' love for us until her emotions weren't a jumbled mess? And that happened just a few hours ago?"

Cullen frowned, kicking at the wooden floor.

Lucas palmed his shoulder. "She took some pretty huge leaps of faith for us last night. The bond's already strengthening, and I know you feel it, too. She's ours. Hell, she's willing to come with us—I think that speaks louder than anything else. Besides, her body is still adjustin' to being mates. If it's this hard for us to get our feelings under control, imagine what it's like for her. We have her trust and her heart, Cullen. Give her some time, and she'll say the words."

Cullen snorted, giving Lucas a good-natured shove. "Have I told you I hate it when you're logical?"

"You just hate that I'm right."

"That, too. Now, go get Hollis before something else crops up, and there's not a chance in Hell we'll be able to steal her away."

CHAPTER SEVENTEEN

"Do I want to know why there's a cabin in the middle of nowhere?" Hollis stood in the doorway, watching as Cullen and Lucas placed their supplies by a wood stove. "Doesn't anyone live here?"

Cullen glanced at her over his shoulder as he opened the stove door, adding some wood to the grill. "Not anymore. When the railway decided to build the spur, they relocated anyone who already had homesteads along the intended line. But since it's not directly in the path, they haven't torn it down, yet." He grinned. "Lucky for us. Beats spendin' the night in a tent, which is what we'd planned. And I can scout the last bit of the line from here tomorrow."

Lucas nudged him. "*We'll* scout the last of the line. Don't think I didn't notice that band of riders a few hours ago. With this place being so remote, I'll bet my ass they're Buford's men. Thankfully, they didn't see us, but that means no one's going anywhere alone."

Cullen swept his gaze the length of the man. "You

might not want to mention your ass until we have a fire going and some food in our bellies." He motioned at the far wall. "Looks like there's a pump at the sink, which means we probably don't have to venture to the river to get water. We'll warm some up so we can all freshen up a bit while we're waitin' on the soup to cook."

Hollis nodded, placing the bags of roots and leaves she'd collected on a small counter. With the men's help, she'd been able to gather enough material to make three different salves, each of which would come in handy. She just needed a few of the leaves to dry then she could grind up the ingredients, add some oil and flour to make it a paste, and she'd be set.

A set of hands settled around her hips, tugging her against a wall of male muscle. She inhaled, knowing it was Lucas by the hint of gun oil in his scent. She closed her eyes, humming as he kissed a path down her neck, lightly nipping at her skin. She pushed her shoulders back, helping him remove her jacket before he reclaimed his previous position.

Lucas licked at the shell of her ear, sending a rash of goosebumps across her flesh. "You've been strangely quiet the last couple of hours. Everything okay?"

"Fine. I just didn't want to distract either of you. I noticed the change in your demeanor the moment we spotted those men, and Cullen needed to double check that all the grading measurements were correct. It just seemed better if I let you do your jobs."

"I didn't mean to be distant. I just don't know what I'd do if I lost either of you because I missed something."

"You weren't distant. You were focused. I'm sure I get the same way when I'm dealin' with a patient. You wouldn't be good at your job if you let your feelings dictate your actions. Though, now that we've arrived safely..."

He sighed. "Hold that thought, darlin'. I just want to do a quick perimeter check before we all get comfortable for the night. My bear isn't quite satisfied that we're safe, yet."

Her breath caught, and she spun in his arms, watching as he took a few steps back. Even through his shirt, his muscles flexed against the fabric, giving her a ghosted image of the torso she knew hid behind the cotton. Though, she hadn't had nearly enough time to thoroughly inspect his or Cullen's body. Not the way she wanted to— to touch and lick every inch with more than wavering candlelight as her guide.

She glanced at Cullen, trying to imagine him as a bear. She wasn't sure if it was the bond or curiosity, but she definitely wanted to watch them change, again, especially if they both got naked first.

Lucas chuckled. "I'm not sure whether to be excited or concerned that the thought of us shifting has you so damn excited I can smell your need from here."

"Are you reading my mind, again?" She arched her brow at his smug smile. "Then, you won't be surprised that I didn't get to fully appreciate your other half that first time. And I haven't even seen Cullen's bear."

Cullen moved in beside Lucas. "There's a reason we don't go wandering around in fur, other than the usual risks."

"You mentioned something about it increasing the need."

She glanced at his crotch then back up, forcing herself

to swallow, only to end up coughing when she imagined talking Cullen's cock in her mouth. Playing with Lucas had only succeeded in increasing her desire to have both men surrender to her. Only this time, she wanted to have more than just a taste of either of them. She wanted to devour them. Wanted to know she could take both of them over the edge. Make them as wild and helpless in their need for her as they made her with nothing more than a smile or a touch.

Cullen growled, the tips of his canines showing beneath his upper lip. "Careful, sweetheart. Or I might forget you haven't eaten in a while and that this room isn't near warm enough to strip you down."

She grinned, leaning against the counter. "Pretty sure you two can keep me warm, and who said I was hungry for food?"

Lucas grabbed Cullen's elbow when the man took a step forward. "Perimeter check, first. Then, we can play. Besides, you did promise our girl she could see your other half. And I could use your bear's senses out there to ensure no one followed us."

Hollis snagged her lower lip between her teeth, worrying it for a few moments before letting it slip free. "So, you're both going to...shift? Here? Now?"

"Isn't that what you wanted? To see our animals?"

"Of course, I just... You're not the only ones feeling needy. Once you get naked..." She moistened her lips. "Not sure you'll make it out the door, after all."

Lucas clenched his jaw. "Damn, Hollis." He blew out a few shaky breaths. "Though, you have a point. Neither Cullen nor I have a lot of control left where you're concerned, not to mention each other." He tightened his grip on Cullen when the man tried to move toward her, again. "As much as I want to jump right in...safety, first. Cullen will wait until we've got a bit of distance between us before he shifts. But I promise we'll both put on a show once I'm certain we can play without worryin' about you getting hurt."

A hint of disappointment settled in her gut. While she commended their integrity, waiting even a minute longer to touch them seemed more like torture than concern.

Cullen smiled smugly, making her wish she could take the thought back. "We'll make it up to you. Promise. But Lucas is right. Your safety means more to us than anything else. And our bears won't truly relax until they've searched the area. But once we're back..." He let his gaze travel the length of her. "I suggest you grab a snack while we're out because you're going to be very busy."

He turned, marching purposefully toward the door, only to stop halfway out. He glanced back at her. "If anyone other than us comes through this door..."

She hitched out one hip as she crossed her arms over her chest. "I didn't suddenly forget how to fend for myself."

His mouth twitched as his gaze dipped to her belt then up to the bruising on her face. "Keep those Colts handy, sweetheart."

She smiled sweetly at them. "Just don't keep me waitin' or I might put those healing capabilities of yours to the test."

Cullen laughed then headed out.

Lucas shook his head. "Be patient with us, darlin'. We know you're tougher than nails, but...this is all new to us, too. And we're protective by nature. But where you're concerned..." He whistled. "You're a whole other level."

Warmth blossomed in her chest. "Must you always know what to say to gain the upper hand? Go. I'll be fine."

He nodded, looking as if he didn't want to take the last few steps out of the cabin, before grunting and striding off. The door rattled closed, the sudden silence a bit unnerving. While she'd spent the majority of the last four years alone, this felt different. As if she'd just shut out a piece of herself.

Hollis groaned inwardly. If she'd known mating with the men would make her this emotional, she might have simply shot them, instead. She smiled at the thought then turned her attention to readying the cabin. But even after lighting the oil lamps, fixing the bed, and using some lukewarm water to clean herself up, the boys hadn't returned.

An unsettling feeling coiled low in her core as she tugged her camisole back over her head and wrapped herself in a blanket, relaxing into one of the few chairs scattered around the room. She'd been experiencing sporadic cramps since the men had left, and the new position seemed to help ease the jarring ache. She glanced at her pistols resting beside her on a small table but resisted drawing one out and laying it across her lap. Just because Lucas and Cullen weren't back yet didn't mean there was any reason to worry.

She clenched her fists, watching the light start to fade beyond the window, before succumbing to the nervous roil through her stomach and palming one of her Colts. She'd give the men another ten minutes before changing into her clothes, again, and going in search of them. Just because they were shifters didn't mean they couldn't be killed. And she'd never forgive herself if she'd simply sat there, waiting, when she could have been helping.

Time seemed to drag by, nothing but crickets sounding through the cabin. Hollis fidgeted in the seat until the voice in her head started shouting at her. She pushed to her feet, letting the blanket fall in a puddle around her. She grabbed her clothes, quickly dressing then tugging on her boots. She'd just clipped on her belt when muffled voices sounded outside.

Hollis drew her gun, leveling it toward the doorway. A horse whinnied beyond the closed slab, followed by loud footsteps on the wooden veranda surrounding the cabin. The handle rattled then twisted, Lucas nearly tumbling through as he balanced Cullen against his shoulder. Blood covered Cullen's shirt, the soaked fabric leaving a trail on the floor.

Fear stopped her cold for two agonizing heartbeats, before her training kicked in. She holstered her gun then rushed over to the table, sweeping everything off it as she motioned to Lucas. The man trudged forward, placing Cullen's back on the hardwood surface, then working his way down his mate's body until Cullen was lying flat across the top. Cullen groaned, his head lolling to one side, his eyes never opening. She turned and retrieved her bag, thankful she'd restocked it with what few supplies she'd had left before they'd ventured out.

Lucas caught her by the shoulders when she spun around, waiting until she made eye contact. "Easy, darlin'. It's not nearly as bad as it looks."

She scoffed. "So, he's not unconscious and bleedin' out as we speak? Because it sure as Hell looks like that."

She shook her head, pushing past Lucas until she reached Cullen. Half his shirt was torn into frayed lines, the rest soaked through. She opened the sides and stared at two puckered holes in his shoulder and upper chest, both still oozing blood.

"Damn it." She glanced up at Lucas when the man stopped on the opposite side. "I don't understand. I thought you said you boys shift when you get hurt, like you did when you got hit with that spike."

Lucas released a weary breath. "Usually, yes. But the bullets are still lodged somewhere inside. If he shifts..."

She cursed, focusing on Cullen, again. "They'll be trapped. They could interfere with his mobility or cause chronic infection or even lead poisoning."

"Even we have limitations. He's undergone a few partial shifts to keep the bleeding manageable—as you probably noticed by the rips in his shirt—but he needs those bullets removed. Then, his bear can take over...heal the wounds."

Hollis didn't miss the strained tone of Lucas' voice or the tight press of the man's lips. He was scared, even if he tried not to show it. But it wasn't just fear she sensed. Every twitch of his muscles confirmed that he blamed himself for allowing Cullen to get shot.

"I'll see what I can do. Please remove the rest of his shirt while I get everything ready."

She dragged the small table over as Lucas juggled Cullen's weight, gently shifting him around until he'd removed the rest of the ruined cloth. Then, he pulled off the man's boots and unclipped his belt."

She smiled her thanks, placing her instruments and a bowl of water on the table. She wet a length of cloth, softly cleaning Cullen's wounds. "You two were gone a long time. I was just about to come lookin' for you. What happened?"

Lucas clenched his jaw. "We were only going to check the perimeter, but then, Cullen picked up on a scent. His damn Kodiak kept pushin' him, taking him farther away. We'd gone halfway back to where we saw those men before his bear finally stopped, even though the trail had gone cold for a few miles. Took me ten minutes to convince his grizzly to shift. I thought we were in the clear, but just as we mounted up to return, that group of men appeared over a rise, shootin'. Cullen got clipped before I could do more than fire off a few rounds."

Hollis nodded, probing at the holes. "Is that your way of telling me we might have visitors?"

Lucas' expression hardened, his lips nothing more than a thin pink line. "You don't have to worry about that. No one's going to hurt you or Cullen. Not again."

Hollis readied a cloth with some chloroform, holding it over Cullen's mouth and nose as she met Lucas' firm gaze. She didn't need any enhanced senses to guess what had happened. "You killed them, didn't you? All of them."

Lucas didn't speak, merely stared down at Cullen.

"This wasn't your fault, Lucas."

"Right. Not my fault."

Hollis sighed, motioning to the cloth. "Can you hold this for me while I remove the bullets?"

He moved to Cullen's head, taking the cloth from her then mimicking her position. It wasn't until she'd disinfected the instruments as best she could, Lucas broke the uneasy silence between them.

"I'm sure you think I'm a monster for killin'—"

"No. I don't." She lifted her gaze to his. "They were outlaws. Men like that don't have any honor. Any respect for anyone other than themselves. They simply take what they want, regardless of who gets hurt." She focused on Cullen's shoulder, again. "There's no loyalty. You're just unwanted baggage. A responsibility they drag around with them until it's no longer worth their while. Then, they leave and never look back."

Lucas touched her arm. "Are you okay?"

She pushed the unwanted memories out of her mind, nodding at Cullen. "You don't have to apologize for protectin' the people you love. And you're the farthest thing from a monster I've ever met." She cleared her throat. "Please hold that still until I'm done."

Lucas frowned but did as she asked, remaining silent as she worked on Cullen's injuries. Thankfully, the bullets hadn't ricocheted too much, though the one in his upper chest was deeper than she'd hoped. She went slowly, meticulously removing all the fragments then stitching up the various layers of muscle and tissue. Shadows danced across the floor, all semblance of light gone beyond the windows when she finally straightened. She stared down at the slashes of black thread against his skin, finally covering the wound with a square of white gauze.

She tried to ignore the way her hands shook as she secured the final bandage in place. "That's all I can do, other than watch him for signs of a fever and give him medicine for the pain once he wakes up. But I have a feeling you'll say he doesn't need any of that. I probably didn't even need to stitch him, but I couldn't leave..."

Lucas removed the cloth, joining her on the other side before wrapping his arms around her and holding her tight to his chest. "You did great. And you can ask him once he wakes up. Okay?"

She nodded, aware that if she tried to answer him, it would most likely come out as incoherent sobs. In all the time since she'd struck out on her own as a doctor, she'd never had to treat anyone she was intimately connected with. And just seeing him lying there—skin pale, eyes shut, his blood staining her hands—left her feeling hollow. As if she'd removed a part of herself along with the bullets. Another shiver raked through her, forcing her to clench her jaw in order to keep from screaming.

Lucas tightened his hold, brushing his lips along her neck. "He's going to be fine, thanks to you. Promise."

She swallowed past the thick ball of emotion in her throat, pulling free of his hold before making her way to the sink. She pumped in more water, washing Cullen's blood off her hands before finally daring to meet Lucas' gaze across her shoulder. "It won't be my skills that save him. Most men would die of infection from having me open them up like that. His bear is what will save him."

Lucas frowned. "Hollis. Do you have any idea what it is you really do? How much respect we have for you?"

"Respect doesn't mean much if I can't save him." She waved her hand, cutting off any reply. "Let's just move him into the bedroom. I put down some blankets earlier. He should be more comfortable until he wakes up."

"Right, and we have fifteen hundred pounds of pissed off Kodiak on our hands."

Her mouth gaped open. "Fifteen hundred pounds?"

Lucas flashed her a wicked smile. "I did mention he was larger than my grizzly."

"I thought you were joking after seeing your animal. Didn't think a bear could get any larger."

"Don't worry. He's still Cullen beneath the fur."

She nodded, not sure what else to say. Lucas shuffled Cullen into his arms, lifting him off the table then moving him across the room and into the adjoining space. She'd thought about offering to help, but if Lucas found the feat difficult, he didn't show it—carrying Cullen as easily as the man had carried her up from the river.

Cullen groaned as Lucas positioned him on the bed, the skin across his brow creasing. Lucas bent low, dropping a kiss on his forehead then drawing his finger across Cullen's jaw before stepping back. He waved Hollis forward, smiling at her when she eased onto the edge of the bed. She brushed back Cullen's hair from his face, still fighting against the sick feeling in her stomach. If anything happened to him...

Lucas sat behind her, enfolding her in his arms. "Nothing's going to happen to him."

"What if I didn't do enough? Or too much? I've never had to cut that deep before. What if I did more damage than the bullets? Or I missed some of the shrapnel?" She let her head bow to her chest. "Christ, what if you hadn't been able to make it back here in time?"

"Then, his bear would have seized control when it had no other choice, regardless of the consequences." He tucked some of her hair behind her ear, smoothing his lips along her skin. "But it knew you'd fix them both. That's why it hasn't broken free, yet. It trusts you. And you've done more than enough. But something tells me this isn't just about Cullen. That it goes deeper."

She shrugged, choosing just to sit there, wrapped in

Lucas' arms. She didn't want to think about why she'd pushed herself to become a doctor. Why she couldn't fail the one time her mates might actually need her help. She just wanted Lucas to hold her. Tell her everything would be okay, whether he believed it or not.

"Hollis."

She relaxed against him, suddenly tired. This wasn't the homecoming she'd pictured. She waved at Cullen. "Shouldn't we strip him down? So, it's easier for his bear to make the transition?"

Lucas chuckled. "I'd be worried you were going to pounce on him if it weren't for the restlessness I sense. The jumbled images inside my head I know aren't mine. There's something you're not telling us. What you said before you tended his wounds... Made it sound as if you have some personal experience." He sighed when she tensed. "But I'll let it go, for now. Don't think we're done discussing this, though." He released his hold. "Now, help me get our mate naked."

Hollis smiled her thanks, wishing it was sex they were getting ready for. But every shift of Cullen's body dragged a throaty groan from him, reminding her they could still lose him. That she could still fail like she had so long ago.

Lucas glanced at her, arching his brow as he lifted Cullen. She didn't speak as she removed his pants, watching as Lucas eased him back down, then tucked the blanket around him before straightening. An uneasy silence stretched between them as Hollis went into the other room, cleaning up as best she could before fetching a small basin of water. Lucas moved aside when she returned, allowing her access so she could gently dab

Cullen's face. Despite the pale cast of his skin, there was no denying the heat burning beneath his flesh.

She moistened her lips. "He's warm."

"It's just temporary."

"If it were anyone else, I'd call it what it is. A fever. Which you know as well as I do is the first sign of infection. What if me operating on him did something to his bear? What if he can't shift?"

"Hollis. Darlin'. Breathe. You did great. Shifters sometimes get fevers when they're having trouble mergin' with their animal, which is most likely a side effect of the chloroform. In fact, I expect he'll open his eyes any moment now and tell us both to bugger off. He'll be fine."

She stood, tapping her finger against Lucas' chest. "You don't know that. Don't make promises you can't keep."

Lucas frowned, huffing when she moved over to the far side of the room. "I'm not. You removed the bullets. And seeing as he didn't outright die during the procedure, I think it's safe to assume he's going to be okay. He just needs a bit of time to wake up enough to make the transformation."

She crossed her arms over her chest. "Really? Well, forgive me for not having the blind faith you seem to have. Because *he* promised we'd always be safe. That he'd always protect us. But he wasn't there. He didn't have to watch her die, all the while trying to stop the bleedin'. Trying to fix her. So, don't stand there and tell me Cullen's going to be fine when all I can do is sit here and feel him burn up beneath my touch."

The bed creaked. "Fix who?"

She snapped her head around, staring at Cullen as he

levered himself up enough to lean against the headboard, his eyes not quite focused, but open. Relief washed through her, and she stumbled over to him, sinking against his right side when he lifted that arm. She held on tight, mindful not to touch him close to his wounds, as she let his scent slowly surround her. Purge the doubts she'd allowed to fester inside her.

Tears burned her eyes, and she couldn't stop them from spilling over, dampening Cullen's chest. He dropped a kiss on her hair, whispering soothing words. The bed dipped behind her, Lucas' hand joining Cullen's on her back. She didn't speak, just sat there, breathing them in until she'd gathered back a modicum of control.

She pursed her lips, feeling incredibly vulnerable as she eased out of his hold. She glanced at Lucas, noting the tight press of his lips as he watched her. More tears threatened, but she snagged her lip to keep them at bay. She motioned to Cullen, praying she hadn't hurt him by wrapping her arms around him. Christ, she was the one who should be comforting him. "I'm sorry. You need to shift, not coddle me."

Cullen brushed his thumb over her chin. "I'm not coddlin' you, and seeing as you patched me up already, my bear can wait another couple of minutes. Who were you talking about? Who did you try to fix?"

She shook her head, pulling free of their embrace then heading for the far wall. "Nothing. No one."

The bed frame squeaked, and she spun, cursing when Cullen swayed to his feet.

"Damn it, Cullen." She darted back over and grabbed one of his arms, wondering how she'd keep them both upright if he lost his balance. "You shouldn't be awake, let alone trying to stand. In fact, you should shift, so your bear can finish the job. But either way, sit down before you fall and pull out those stitches. You really can't afford to lose more blood, shifter or not."

His hazel eyes burned into a burnished gold. "You mean the ones you put in there to save my life?"

"I merely removed what was preventin' your other half from doing that. So, let your bear make the real healing happen. Please."

"Seems my Kodiak is just as stubborn as you are. It won't make an appearance until you answer the questions. Who did you try to fix?"

"None of that matters."

"But I think it does. In fact, I think it's the reason you became a doctor. Why you're able to shoot better than anyone I've ever met." His eyes closed for a second, and she didn't miss how he leaned more of his weight on Lucas when the man shouldered up beside him.

She focused on Lucas. "He's about to take us all to the floor. Get him to sit his ass down. Or make him shift."

"Guess you're not the only one who doesn't always listen." Lucas arched a brow. "But I'll try to sway his decision if you answer the questions. Who taught you how to shoot? How to fight?"

She closed her eyes against the rush of memories, wishing she could run but aware she'd never be able to go far enough to put that part of her life behind her. Hide from the truth. A hand snaked around her before she was dragged against Cullen's bare chest, Lucas somehow holding them both up. They didn't talk, simply stood there as she listened to Cullen's heartbeat. Allowed the steady thrum of it beneath her fingers and inside her head to calm the erratic rhythm of hers.

Cullen dropped a kiss on her head as they eased away. "Please, sweetheart. Talk to us."

She wrapped her arms around herself as a chill beaded along her skin. "Sit down, and I'll talk."

Cullen narrowed his eyes but allowed Lucas to help ease him down onto the bed. She nodded her thanks then paced to the other side of the room, again, needing the distance to pull herself together. What had she been thinking? There was a reason she'd shoved those memories deep down. Why she never talked about her past. Yet, she'd blurted out enough she knew they wouldn't let the subject drop.

Cullen tsked. "I might not be fully coherent, but I know stallin' when I see it."

She sighed, leaning against the wall when her legs threatened to give out.

Lucas padded across the room, stopping next to her but not touching. "You mentioned before that you grew up on a small parcel of land away from town. Has that got anything to do with this? Why you left home at sixteen to pursue medicine?"

"I haven't had a real home in a long time." She broke eye contact, staring at a patch of floor. "My childhood wasn't exactly typical."

"Not sure such a thing exists, but...we're listenin'."

She toed at the wood, wishing she was anywhere but there. "Remember when I told you that you shouldn't put all your faith in me? That maybe I was the dishonorable one?"

"Hollis—"

"Just...let me finish." She took a few deep breaths, wishing she'd just kept her fears to herself. Buried her past like she thought she'd buried her heart. "I don't talk about my past because my father was...is...a gunslinger."

Lucas arched a brow. "I've been a sheriff for several years, now, and I've never heard of any outlaws with Chambers as their last name."

"Chambers is my mother's name. My father didn't want anyone to know who I was. To make the connection back to him." She tried to stop her chin from quivering before drawing herself up. "The truth is, my father is Brett McCalister."

Lucas inhaled roughly. "Brett McCalister?" He took a few heavy steps away before spinning. "The man's a legend. Has somehow managed to evade capture for damn near thirty years. From what I've heard, he had one Hell of a streak going—stage coaches, trains, banks, not to mention winning every duel he'd ever fought—then he disappeared for a while. Folks thought he was dead until he reappeared about ten years ago. Started up where he'd left off, only mostly with gangs this time. There has to be a dozen warrants out for his arrest, but no one's managed to corner the man, yet."

She gave him a weak smile. "He's exceptionally good at what he does."

Lucas merely nodded. "I assume you and your mother were the reason he stopped?"

"He'd promised her he wouldn't put us at risk. That he was done with that part of his life. He bought some land and became a rancher on the outskirts of some small town that had never heard of the name McCalister."

"But something changed that."

"He'd gone to acquire another horse. He wanted to breed this new stock. He wasn't there when a group of men like Buford rode up to the house. I guess they were outlaws he'd known before, because my mother recognized them. I knew something was wrong when she told me to run to the barn and get my father's rifle. She'd never so much as let me touch one of his guns before then. I ran out the backdoor, but when I got to the barn, I couldn't reach the rafter where he kept it. By the time I stacked some boxes high enough to touch the barrel, I heard gunshots. I managed to finally wedge it free and run back to the house, but...I was too late."

She swallowed the scream that tried to claw its way out. "She was on the floor—shot. Bleedin'. I didn't know what to do. We didn't have a doctor in town, just a midwife. My mother begged me not to leave her, and I wasn't strong enough to drag her to the wagon. So, I just sat there, pushing down on her side, waitin'. Screamin' for someone to help us." She brushed at the tears that escaped. "That's how he found us."

Lucas inched closer, the heat from his body making her want to curl into him. "How old were you?"

She forced herself to meet his gaze. "Ten."

He cursed under his breath, the pained look on his face nearly unhinging her. "What happened next?"

"He spent hours on the floor with her cradled in his lap, talking to her as if she wasn't dead, before he snapped. Started rantin' about how he never should have settled down. That anyone who couldn't shoot or fight didn't deserve to live. That we'd been nothing but a burden all along."

Lucas' eyes widened then softened. "Oh, darlin'."

She shook her head. "He loved her. I know he did. Up until that day, he'd doted on her as if the sun rose and set because of her. He'd given up everything for *her*. But you can't really bury the past." She shrugged. "He changed that day. Something inside him died along with her. That's when he started teachin' me how to shoot. How to fight. I think it was his way of justifying not leaving me behind. The man was relentless, always pushin'. Even when I could draw faster than him—take a punch and keep fighting—he didn't stop."

"Is that where you got that scattering of scars on your body? From training with him?"

Her lips quirked. "It took me a while to become proficient."

Lucas growled but motioned her to continue.

"Afraid it doesn't get any better. As I got older, he started taking me with him on jobs, instead of just leaving me alone for days at a time. I was the scout or his backup. Never directly in the line of fire, but there—armed and ready to defend him—just the same. Then, one day I woke up and all that was left was a pile of money and a note saying that I should find my own gang to run with. That he wasn't coming back. But that wasn't the life I'd ever wanted. Watching my mother die—that day I promised myself I'd never feel that helpless, again. So, I made my way east, and I never looked back."

Lucas cupped her chin, waiting until she looked up at him. "Hollis."

"Don't." She pulled away, stumbling halfway back to the bed. "I don't want your pity. Bad things happen. I understand that. And I've done all right for myself. Tried to make up for any wrongs I committed when I was runnin' with him. And I've made peace with the fact that I can't save everyone, no matter how hard I try. But then, you two came along, and everything changed. *I* changed."

"You don't have to change, darlin'. We love you the way you are. We don't care who your father is."

"That's not what I meant." She tilted her head back, knowing she couldn't deny her feelings any longer. That they'd be there, coloring how she saw the world, whether she said the words out loud or not. "All these years, I never really understood why losing my mother affected him that way—until now." She gave them a small smile. "How you could love someone so completely your entire world depends on their happiness. And that losing them cuts deeper than any knife ever could."

She focused on Cullen. "When I saw your shirt, your blood everywhere… All I could think about was that I'd failed. The one time I needed to put my skills to the test, and I'd failed you." She held up her hand when he surged to his feet as Lucas moved in behind her. "I know it's silly. That you don't even need my help. That whether you live or die is in the hands of a gift far greater than what I have, but…"

Her chin quivered, again, as she took a deep breath, twisting so she could look them both in the eyes. "It made me realize I'm very much my father's daughter. That falling in love with both of you has made me vulnerable. That I could end up like him if I ever lost you boys."

"You could never fail us. You…" Cullen trailed off, his eyes widening before he closed the last bit of distance, letting his forehead rest on hers. He clenched his jaw, his fingers landing on her waist. "Did you just say that—"

"I love you? Both of you? So much it frightens me?"

He waited, furrowing his brow when she just stood there, staring at them. "Did you?"

She released a slow breath, feeling the weight of her denial drift away. "Is the blood loss affectin' your brain? Because I'm pretty sure Lucas heard me just fine. Yes, I love you and Lucas. Though, it's tied right now with my desire to smack you up the side of the head for scaring me." She shoved at him when he went to tug her closer. "We already got you naked, so heal yourself, first. Then, you can love me back."

Lucas snaked his arms around her waist, pulling her close. He smiled against her neck before kissing it then lifting his head. "Girl's got a point, mate. As much as I'm enjoyin' the view, you look like you're about to fall over. You'd best get that Kodiak of yours to finish the wonderful job our girl did, then we'll show her that we need her far more than she realizes."

CHAPTER EIGHTEEN

Lucas stood there, watching Cullen stare at Hollis as if he'd never seen her before, and he knew his mate was mesmerized by the truth of Hollis' confession gleaming in her eyes. Not that Lucas needed to see her to feel her love. It radiated out from her, warming his chest until it was all he could do just to breathe, and he realized Cullen hadn't been the only one waiting to hear those words. Who might have been harboring a few lingering doubts. Cullen shifted his gaze to Lucas.

He laughed. "I love you, too, you ornery bastard. You know that. So, stop worryin' and get on with it."

Cullen stumbled forward, smiling when they both caught him before he fell.

Hollis huffed, moving to Cullen's right as Lucas took his left. "Damn it, Cullen. If you pull out those stitches, even your bear will have a hard time fixing you."

"I don't need my bear when I have you, Doc."

Her breath caught. She glanced at Lucas, wide eyed,

before shaking her head as she tsked Cullen. "Charmer. And you do need your bear. Trust me, those wounds…"

He frowned at the tears that pooled in her eyes then fell, leaving dots of moisture along her cheek. "I'm not going to die, sweetheart. Not today, anyway."

"Of course you're not. I spent too much time stitchin' you up."

"And you did a great job. I dare say my bear's a bit jealous." He thumbed her chin. "You're sure you're okay?"

"I'll be better once I know you're not going to pass out on me, or worse. Besides, while this isn't the way I envisioned meeting your other half, you did promise you'd show me that side of you. So, shift, already."

"You do know what shifting does, right? Once I change back…"

Hollis gave them a wicked smile. "You won't be the only one who's naked."

"Good to know. Now, you might want to move back a bit."

"Right. Fifteen hundred pounds probably takes up a bit of space."

Cullen held on when she went to pull away. "I'd never hurt you. Regardless of which form I take. You know that, don't you?"

"I'm standin' here, aren't I? And I promise I won't need to get any air this time."

"Fair enough."

He nodded his thanks when Lucas eased Hollis back, still holding her close. Hollis trembled in his arms, her muscles tense against his. He glanced at Cullen, knowing he'd sensed Hollis' uneasiness by the way he tilted his head, gazing at Lucas then back to their mate.

Hollis grunted, giving them both a pointed look. "I know you two can tell I'm on edge, but it's not because Cullen's about to shift. Ignoring the fact I just confessed my life story to you—including the part where I basically ran as a shotgun messenger for my gunslingin' father— I'm scared Cullen's going to drop dead on me if he doesn't do something about the gaping holes in his shoulder I had to stitch closed." She pointed at Cullen. "So, stop worryin' I'm going to bolt or get hysterical and shift."

He chuckled. "Wounds aren't gaping any longer, thanks to you. But you have a point."

Cullen winked at them then lowered his head. Lucas knew the moment he'd given over control to his animal. The man's thoughts changed, becoming more primal in nature, as his bear surged forward. The air thickened, raising the hairs on Lucas' arms when Cullen's body twitched, sending a cascade of fur down his limbs. The man jerked forward, landing on padded paws, his claws clicking against the wooden floor as his bear scratched its way free. He shook his head, finally relaxing as his form settled, the last few echoed creaks fading.

Hollis inhaled, glancing at Lucas over her shoulder. She worried her bottom lip then broke into a wide smile, gently easing out of his arms. Lucas smiled as she moved closer to Cullen, one hand stretched toward his bear. Cullen's Kodiak scented the air, snorting as Hollis tunneled her fingers though its fur, lightly scratching his neck.

"I...God, I don't know what to say." She ran her hands along his back before wrapping her arms around him. "You're magnificent."

The bear nudged her with his snout, snorting, again, when she stumbled against Lucas.

He caught her, chuckling when she glared at Cullen. "And Cullen says my bear forgets how big and strong it is. His damn Kodiak is worse. Thinks we all want to play with it."

Hollis steadied herself then crossed her arms over her chest. "Not funny."

Cullen's bear stepped forward, rubbing his head against her torso.

She sighed. "Fine, you're forgiven."

Lucas watched them interact, humbled by how easily she'd accepted them. Accepted what they were. The way she scratched behind Cullen's ears, holding him as if she never wanted to let go. Lucas hadn't realized how badly he'd needed her to love this side of them. While he'd understood her apprehension when he'd shown her his grizzly, he'd always worried that maybe it had been more than shock. That despite everything, she'd never truly trust them in their alternate form. Seeing her enthralled by Cullen's bear made it all very real. That they'd gotten far more than they deserved.

Hollis looked back at him, her small hand connecting with his shoulder. "Of course, I love both sides of you and Cullen."

Lucas arched a brow. "Did you just read my thoughts?"

"Hard not to when you're practically screamin' them inside my head." Her expression softened. "I know I reacted poorly when you shifted—"

"You didn't. It was a lot to take in. I understand that."

"Maybe. But I also know you're both still worried I could only ever love half of you. Which is crazy, because…" She shook her head. "Look at you. At Cullen. How your bears are a reflection of the men. The way Cullen's fur is lighter, with the same golden highlights as he has in his hair. Or how your bear's eyes are just as blue as yours are, right now."

She seemed to swallow with effort, more tears building behind her beautiful eyes. "You boys… You're amazing. And knowing your bears can heal you in a way I never could…" Her voice thickened before she let it trail off.

Lucas tucked some of her hair behind her ear then drew her into his embrace. "You're the one who's incredible. Your courage. Your strength. Especially after all you've endured. But why does it still sound as if you think we don't need the doctor side of you?"

"Maybe because you don't."

"Hollis. Darlin'." He spun her to face him. "Why do you think his bear held off this long? If you hadn't come into our lives, if it didn't trust you with its life, it would have seized control, risks or not. Left Cullen with a screwed up shoulder and lifelong worries. Our bears act on instinct, and his went against every one. To chance dyin' because it believed you'd ultimately save them both."

She glanced at Cullen, more tears spilling free. "How am I supposed to stay mad at you two for putting your lives in danger when you know exactly what to say to make me love you even more?"

His bear huffed, once again rubbing his head against her. She laughed, tsking as she removed the bandage hanging loose around his shoulder before moving over to the bed. Lucas motioned to the mattress, but she shook her head, sitting on the floor with her back braced against the frame. She beckoned Lucas to her with a crook of her finger, snuggling against his shoulder as he draped one arm around her, his palm resting on her waist.

Cullen padded over, his bear uncharacteristically gentle as he nuzzled them. Seemed the man's Kodiak had more than a soft spot for their feisty mate. Calm spread through Lucas' chest, their twin heartbeats echoing inside his head. Cullen pawed at the floor then eased down, resting his head on their laps, his injured side up. Hollis stroked his neck then settled her hand behind his front leg. She drew easy patterns through his fur as her eyes drifted shut. Lucas gave his mate an arch of his brow, mentally telling him to sleep. Cullen glanced at Hollis.

"She's fine, Cullen. I'm fine. She loves you. I love you. Sleep, so we can move on to other, far more pleasurable things than sitting on the floor. We both know our mate won't truly rest until there's not so much as a scar left on your shoulder."

"I'm sitting right here."

Lucas grinned when she peeked at him with one eye. "I know."

Cullen snorted then relaxed his head on his mates, again. Lucas sighed. Though he talked a good game, he knew Cullen sensed his overwhelming relief. That he'd detected the hint of fear that had tainted Lucas' scent since he'd lifted Cullen onto his horse and dragged his ass back to their small cabin. He'd been more than a little scared, though he'd never openly admit it.

Cullen placed his paw over Lucas' leg, mentally telling him it wasn't his fault. Lucas gave the animal a scratch, once again instructing him to sleep. If he was honest, he hadn't been convinced Cullen would shift after Hollis' confession. That he'd insist on letting their mate treat the wounds until they healed, naturally, just to prove their point. That they loved and needed every side of her, as well. And Lucas had no doubts that Hollis would have made herself sick watching Cullen around the clock.

Uncertainty weighed on Lucas' mind as he stared at the wall, rerunning the attack. He should have sensed the men long before they'd crested the hill. But between the fatigue, the miles of nothing but empty forest, and the aching need from bonding—he'd been too preoccupied with Cullen. On all the ways he wanted to touch the other man. Love him. How they'd make sure Hollis was a part of every encounter. That she never questioned their devotion.

And he'd somehow missed the tremble of horse's hooves. The faint echo of voices and the stench of sweat and liquor. He hadn't drawn fast enough to prevent Cullen from being hit. After that—Lucas didn't remember much, his actions clouded in the red haze of his bear.

He'd lost control. Emptied his guns then shifted, challenging the last few men still standing as his grizzly. And he hadn't stopped until the threat had been eliminated. Until their blood had stained the mud, and he knew Cullen couldn't sustain further injuries. That he wouldn't put Hollis at risk by returning to the cabin.

Lucas ran his fingers through Cullen's fur. Obviously, Cullen was equally worried, which was why his bear had shifted, now. Why it couldn't risk proving their faith to Hollis in the one way they longed to do. Cullen couldn't afford the week or two it would take to heal by his own means, even with Hollis' salves and medicine. And after the attack, Lucas doubted Buford would stay distant for long—not with the number of casualties he and Cullen had left behind. They needed to be ready for when the gang decided it was worth the risk to raid the camp.

Cullen nudged him, and Lucas knew his mate had picked up on his thoughts. He gave Cullen a light shove, chuckling when Cullen mentally told him to follow his own damn advice and get some sleep. Lucas nodded, allowing himself to fade. Images played in his head, visions that felt familiar, yet he knew weren't his. He watched as a girl ran across a dirt yard, a rifle clenched in her small hands as she headed for a figure lying in the middle of a wooden porch. She'd almost reached the short staircase when Hollis twitched within his arms, shaking him free of the dream.

He woke, watching Cullen roll onto all fours as Hollis jerked in Lucas' grasp, opening her eyes as a harsh sob sounded in the silent room. She fought against his hold until recognition softened her expression, and she fell against him, trembling.

Cullen rubbed his snout against her shoulder, rewarded with a teary-eyed smile and a soft brush of her fingers along his jaw. But when she glanced at Lucas, there was no mistaking the urgency in her eyes, the worry still creasing her brow. She needed her mates—whole. Human.

Cullen's bear whimpered a moment before he bowed his head. The air prickled Lucas' flesh, again, then Cullen was crouched before them, skin gleaming in the dull lamplight. Hollis inhaled as her hand fell to Cullen's chest when their mate straightened. She blinked a few times then focused on his shoulder, her beautiful mouth pursing.

She lifted her hand and skimmed it over his wound. "What are you doing? You're not fully healed. Not like Lucas was." She huffed then shook her head. "Christ, that means there was far more internal damage, doesn't it."

It wasn't a question. Lucas glanced at Cullen's shoulder, noting the red line on his skin surrounded by a scattering of bruises, the flesh puckered where the stitches held it closed. Not quite the flawless outcome it could have been if he'd stayed in his bear form for a few more hours, but so much better than when he'd gone to sleep.

Cullen smiled at her. "Hollis."

"I can remove the stitches if they're hamperin' your bear, but what if I missed something? There could be shards deeper in the tissue. Or maybe you got hit a third time, and it ricocheted, so none of us noticed. I should—"

He silenced her with a finger over her lips. "Sweetheart. You did great. I feel fine. You didn't miss anything." He pressed a bit harder when it looked as if she was going to talk around him. "It's nothing that won't be fixed."

"Then, why did you shift back? It's barely midnight. You need to sleep. Heal for as long as you can. We'll still be here in the morning."

"Afraid my bear doesn't agree. It thinks you need the man a bit more, right now. And I have to say, after seeing those images that just played in your head and sensing the mix of emotions still churning inside you, I have to agree."

Her chin quivered as she glanced at Lucas then back to him. "It was just a dream, Cullen. Nothing in comparison to your well-being."

"It's far more. It's what drives you. The reason you've always chosen to be alone, not that we're upset we're your first, and last. But...it's our job to slay your demons. Show you there's nothing to be afraid of."

She furrowed her brow, looking at both of them before scrambling to her feet then pacing to the other side of the room. She took a few deep breaths then turned. "Thinkin' I should be strong enough to put my own ghosts to rest. And you're wrong. There're lots of things to be afraid of, but the only one that counts is losin' the two of you. That..." She kicked at the floor. "That I wouldn't come back from."

Cullen stood, moving over to her left as Lucas went to her right. "Then, you really don't have anything to fear because Lucas and I aren't going anywhere." He brushed his thumb over her chin then along her cheek. "Between our natural abilities and your skill with a scalpel, thinkin' we're in for a long life ahead of us." He cupped her jaw. "And you're more than strong enough, but we'd sure like it if you'd let us show off, just a bit. Soothe the bear side of us by battlin' those ghosts for you. We'll let you fight our fears, in return."

Love gleamed in her eyes before she closed them against a wash of tears. She took a few more deep breaths then opened her eyes, smiling at them. "Are you two always going to say the right thing? Because it's going to get mighty annoying."

She reached for Lucas when she stopped suddenly, pain shaping her features a moment before she bent over, leaning against the wall as she grabbed her stomach.

He braced her shoulders, balancing her weight. "Darlin'? What's wrong?" He cursed as he felt a shadowed stab of pain through his core. "Where does it hurt?"

She breathed out a few times, grimacing as she straightened a bit. "I'm fine. Just a cramp. It'll pass."

"That sounds as if you've had more of these." He grunted at her guarded nod. "When did they start?"

"I'm fine, Lucas, really. Just give me a second."

Cullen growled. "Answer Lucas. When. Did. They. Start?"

She sighed, groaning as her eyelids fluttered for a second. "Yesterday. After you two left. But they go away."

The man cursed under his breath. "It's a side effect of mating. We've neglected your needs."

"What I *need* is for you to not have any gaping wounds on your shoulder. To not have your blood on my hands. This..." She waved at her stomach. "This is nothing but an annoyance."

Lucas tsked. "Hollis. Mates have been known to die if they're separated for too long before their bodies have adjusted to being bound. You being fully human... I can't imagine what you're going through."

She chuckled. "So, you're telling me I could die from lack of sex? Which is ironic, seeing as I hadn't had any before last night."

Lucas clenched his jaw as his bear paced back and forth in his head. Hearing her remind them that they'd be her only lovers made the animal acutely aware of her scent. Of how it mixed with Cullen's. Of all the ways he still needed to mark his mates before he'd consider their bond truly sealed.

He took a deep breath, ignoring how his canines lengthened slightly, pressing against his upper lip. "While

I'd gladly spend the next week naked with you two, discovering every inch of you and Cullen, it's not about the sex. It's about the connection. The intimacy. About showing you how much we love you. That our pleasure depends on yours."

"See? Charming and annoying." She focused on Cullen. "Are you sure you're okay?"

Cullen took one of her hands and placed it on his forehead. "Am I running a fever?"

She frowned. "No. It seems Lucas was right, and it was a byproduct of the chloroform hinderin' your connection with your bear."

He nodded then moved her hand to his shoulder. "Does my wound feel as if it isn't healing?"

"It feels and looks good. Better than good, but Lucas didn't have so much as a scratch—"

"That's because I was able to shift almost immediately." Lucas sighed. "Cullen waited, which means it'll just take a bit longer. But he's a far sight better off than you, right now. Those cramps... They'll only get worse until you'll pass out from the pain."

She looked between them, her gaze falling to Cullen's crotch then back before groaning as she bent over, again.

Cullen leaned over. "Sweetheart."

"It's not that I don't want you two—I do. God, do I want you. It's just..." She bit at her bottom lip, worrying it for a while before letting it slide free. "I don't want to be the reason you don't recover because you pushed yourself too far. Too fast."

"Thinkin' my shoulder can stand up to a round or two of loving my mates. Besides, you promised I wouldn't be the only one naked once I woke up."

She smiled. "I did promise, didn't I? And I hate breakin' a promise."

Cullen smiled. "Then, let's get you more comfortable."

Lucas smoothed his hands along her hips, turning her until her back pressed tight to his chest. She moved with him, holding her breath as he drew gentle circles across her abdomen, easing the tight muscles. Cullen went to one knee, removing her boots and pants. It took a few minutes before she relaxed, letting her head fall into the crook of Lucas' shoulder.

He nuzzled her neck, kissing the soft spot behind her ear. "Better?"

"I guess that depends on your definition. The pain's gone, but the burning desire that took its place isn't much better."

He smiled against her skin, inhaling the sweet scent of her. "We'll take care of that, too. Love you as many times as you need."

She reached for Cullen, thumbing his jaw then sliding her hand around to the back of his neck, drawing him in close as she threaded her other fingers in Lucas' hair. "I need a lifetime's worth. So, don't you boys ever scare me, again."

Cullen cupped her chin, brushing his thumb across her cheek. "We'll do our best, sweetheart. Though, I'm not sure a lifetime will be enough for us. But it's a good place to start."

CHAPTER NINETEEN

Hollis leaned into Cullen, slowly sliding her lips over his, enjoying the way their mouths molded together before she sighed and opened for him. He growled, delving his tongue inside, tugging her closer to deepen the kiss. She moaned, scratching his scalp as she anchored her fingers in his hair, preventing him from easing away. Instead, he stepped into her, pushing her tight against Lucas, using his mate's shoulder to tip her head back.

Hollis blinked open her eyes once Cullen finally released her, gazing up at him and Lucas. She still couldn't believe this wasn't a dream, though the longing clenching her abdomen seemed determined to prove it was all very real. She smiled then focused on Lucas, mentally telling Cullen to kiss the other man.

Cullen chuckled. "And you questioned whether you were truly our mate. Just over twenty-four hours and you're already talking inside our heads."

"Can't let you boys have the upper hand. Not when I'm already outnumbered two to one."

"I'll gladly side with you where Lucas is concerned."

Lucas cupped the back of Cullen's head, pulling him forward until their lips were a breath apart. "I believe it's my turn to help her pin you to the bed. Or maybe the wall. So, don't get any ideas about being in control. Your ass is mine."

He yanked Cullen the last inch separating them, taking his mouth in a brutal kiss. Cullen responded in kind, crushing their lips together when Lucas went to pull away. Heat prickled along Hollis' skin as images of the men loving each other flickered through her mind—Cullen's muscular form moving behind Lucas, his skin gleaming with a hint of sweat, Cullen's mouth locked on Lucas' shoulder.

Lucas hummed. "I like where your thoughts are driftin', Cullen. But like I just said, after the effort I put in to drag your ass back here, thinkin' it's mine, first."

Hollis huffed. "I'm the one who removed the bullets and stitched him up. Thinkin' I should have some say in who gets to fuck who first."

Cullen moaned at her words. "Damn, sweetheart."

Lucas chuckled. "Language, darlin'. But you have a point. So, how about a compromise? I'll help you bring our mate to the edge, then he can paint his release all over your skin while I empty inside him."

Hollis pursed her lips as she pushed air slowly out through her nose. She forced herself to swallow as heat flamed up her neck and into her cheeks.

Cullen tsked, glancing at Lucas then back to her. "How about a new plan? We get you the rest of the way naked, and you grind your pussy on my face until you come, then

Lucas and I can play. Because, sweetheart, you smell positively desperate."

A shiver shook through her, and she had to clench her thighs together to stem the ache throbbing deep in her core.

Lucas nodded. "That's a great counter-offer. And I know exactly how I want to help."

She glanced down at Cullen's groin, moistening her lips as she stared at his shaft. He didn't make a move to hide how hard he was. Or how a line of fluid leaked from the tip as he shifted back, leaving a wet smear across his abdomen. Desire burned along her flesh, and she reached for him, drawing her fingers along the length of his erection.

She met his heated gaze. "Are you sure you don't want me to help you out with that first? Be a shame to waste it."

"Don't worry. You'll get a taste. But first...I want you to flood me with your release."

She released a harsh breath. Christ, if they kept talking like that, none of them would get a chance to play. She'd climax simply standing there. "Not. Helping."

"Then, let's get you naked, and on top of me."

"But your shoulder—"

Lucas silenced her with a light kiss. "The only 'but' here is yours and what we plan to do with it." He leaned in. "Remember what it felt like to have my finger inside you? Have you wondered if it would make you come even harder?"

"You know I have. Ever since you touched me..." She locked her gaze on Cullen. "I can't stop thinkin' about all three of us. Together."

"We'll save that for round two. For now..." He tugged on her shirt. "This has got to go."

Hollis lifted her arms, helping them remove her shirt and camisole. Then, she turned, tsking Lucas until he allowed her to undress him. She didn't miss the way Cullen watched them interact, smiling as she ran her fingers over every inch of Lucas, tracing the bands along his chest and stomach until she fisted his cock. She stroked her closed hand down his shaft, humming when a drop of fluid beaded along the slit.

"Like I told Cullen. I'd be happy to help both of you out, first."

Lucas glanced at the bed then back at her. "Why limit yourself to just one form of pleasure? Cullen..."

Cullen grinned, holding out his hand and leading her the few short steps to the bed. He climbed on, lying across the mattress with his head nearly tipping off the other side. Then, he beckoned her to him, laughing when Lucas simply lifted her up and straddled her across Cullen's chest.

She inhaled, looking back at Lucas across her shoulder. "You want me to sit on his face?"

"I believe he used the word 'grind', but sit works." Lucas moved around to the other side of the bed, his cock dangerously within reach. "And it makes it a lot easier for you to indulge in your other desires."

Hollis snagged her bottom lip, worrying it as she glanced from Cullen over to Lucas then back. Cullen grinned then wrapped one hand around Lucas, stroking the man's erection. She watched as his fingers moved along Lucas' length, Cullen's thumb spreading the slippery fluid around the head before fisting down to the base. Her breath caught in her chest as her lip slipped free from between her teeth around a luscious moan. She shook her head then reached for Lucas, gently placing her hand above Cullen's. She moved with him, inhaling as more fluid covered the thick head, making Lucas' skin look shiny in the wavering lamplight.

Cullen stopped for a moment, allowing her to lower her grip until it had replaced his. She stared at her fist, noting how her fingers barely made it around the width of Lucas' cock. The man was large, in every sense of the word, and she smiled at the thought that she was his— that both men belonged to her as much as she did to them.

"Guess feeling possessive isn't just a shifter thing." Cullen laughed when she stuck her tongue out at him. Then, he nudged her thighs, shaking his head in mock frustration. "Now, now, sweetheart. Play fair and scoot up here."

She glanced back to Lucas, already imagining how good he'd taste, when Cullen dug his fingers into her ass. She snapped her head down, her gaze clashing with his.

He arched a brow. "Can't lick you from there. Put your knees beside my shoulders."

She paused, still unsure about the position he wanted before shaking her head. When it came to them, she'd discovered she was powerless to deny them anything, especially if it involved their hands or tongues on her body. Hollis leaned forward, allowing Cullen to help position her until her cleft was level with his face. He hummed his approval, taking the opportunity to draw his tongue along the length of her. She moaned his name, pushing her hips forward more. Any reservations she might have had vanished with the slow glide of his flesh across hers.

Cullen sucked on her clit then eased back, looking up at her. "I suggest you distract yourself with Lucas, or this is going to be over in thirty seconds."

She glared at the smug tilt of his lips, wondering if she should shift away, when he licked her slit. Pleasure scorched the nerves along her cleft, and she had to close her eyes to keep the sensation from dragging her under.

Cullen chuckled, the vibrations sending another flash of heat across her skin. She opened her eyes and focused on Lucas, determined to take the man over before Cullen made her shout out her release. She bent forward, touching her lips to the tip of his cock. Spicy musk filled her senses as she lapped at his skin, rubbing her tongue around the head before slowly sinking down his length.

Lucas moaned, gathering her hair as she bobbed along his cock, each upward stroke exposing the hard shaft covered in her saliva. Cullen stopped licking her for a moment, lifting one hand to run it along Lucas' cock. She glanced down at the man, half-considering shuffling off so she could offer him a taste of their mate, only to curse under her breath when he winked at her then buried his face between her thighs, again.

"Christ, Hollis. I can sense how close you are, already." Lucas grinned. "Perhaps I should join Cullen—"

His voice cut off as she leaned forward and took him deep. She'd be damned if they'd get a chance to gloat over how easy she was to please. How they'd made her come before she'd gotten Lucas remotely close to pumping his release down her throat. She could be just as determined.

Lucas flexed his fingers in her hair, drawing a muffled gasp from her. "It's not a competition, darlin'."

She thought about answering but decided to increase her pace, instead. Competition or not, she didn't like to lose.

Lucas laughed, again. "I don't see how flooding Cullen's tongue is a loss, but then, you are stubborn."

Hollis glanced up at Lucas, watching his response as she paused with him deep in her throat, doing her best to swallow before easing him out. The man's eyes squeezed shut as the lines in his neck corded. She smiled, taking a moment to bob between his legs and lick his sac. A hushed, "Yes," sounded around them, his fingers flexing in her hair, again. She made another pass, nipping at his flesh then laving it. Every flick of her tongue made his muscles twitch, and she knew he was getting close.

Cullen hummed, fingering her clit as he dropped a kiss on her inner thigh. She cursed, locking her legs around his shoulders as she tensed her muscles in the hope of staving off her release. One more pass, and she might explode.

"You're not the only one, *mate.*" Lucas met her gaze, his jaw clenched. He motioned to Cullen. "Cullen. I suggest you up the stakes a bit. Give our girl the push she needs."

Hollis scoffed. "I don't need more of a push. I'm barely hangin' on as it is, and we only just started."

Lucas grinned. "Just the start of tonight, darlin'. And I believe you wanted to feel us play with your ass, again."

The thought made her moan as she tensed even more around Cullen's shoulders. He returned to her cleft, licking at her folds as he pushed inside her, pumping her sex a few times before easing free. He ignored her huff of frustration as he traced her crease, finally teasing the tight opening. She inhaled, holding her breath as he swirled the slick fluid around before slowly pressing forward until his palm cupped her flesh.

She stiffened, clenching around his intrusion. While she wanted nothing more than to keep sucking Lucas—taste his release warm and salty on her tongue—simply not flying apart took all her strength. She sighed, conceding defeat as she slipped off her mate's length, bracing one hand on the bed as she kept the other wrapped around Lucas' shaft. Even if she didn't have the ability to finish him, she couldn't quite bring herself to let go—wanting that intimate connection with him as Cullen took her over.

Cullen lapped at her sex, sucking at her skin as he set up a steady rhythm with his hand, fucking her ass then retreating. She pushed into every stroke, tilting her hips as she pressed herself harder against his mouth. He growled his approval, attacking her clit as he moved his other hand back, sinking two fingers inside her pussy.

She shouted his name, the telltale quivering inside her sex foreshadowing her impending climax. He didn't stop, alternating his thrusts, pushing her higher until she thought she'd shatter.

Lucas leaned in close, his lips feather soft across her ear. "Come for him, Hollis. I want to smell your release on his face. Taste it on his tongue when I claim his mouth."

His voice curled around her, sending her over the edge. She tensed for a few ragged breaths then broke, flooding Cullen's tongue as her body contracted around him. He kept moving, drawing the orgasm out until she sagged against him. Lucas shouldered her weight, easing her off Cullen and into his arms.

Hollis huddled within his embrace, listening to the steady beat of his heart as he smoothed his hand along her back, gently bringing her back down. The bed dipped a moment before Cullen joined them, brushing away her hair as he dropped a kiss on the curve of her neck. She sighed, content to stay wrapped in their arms, when more images flashed inside her head—the men entwined, Cullen's head tilted back as Lucas claimed him from behind. She opened her eyes, wondering which one of them had pictured the scene when Lucas inhaled.

His eyes gleamed red as he threaded his fingers in Cullen's hair, pulling his mate in for a thorough kiss. Her stomach fluttered at the sight, the empty ache in her groin intensifying. She smiled when Lucas finally released his mate, lifting his hand to trace the corner of Cullen's mouth.

"I knew you'd taste like her. God, so sweet." He glanced at her then back to Cullen. "I think it's about time we finally silenced those doubts still chattin' away inside your head."

"They're not doubts." Cullen huffed at Lucas' smug grin. "But I'll gladly show you how I've wanted to claim you all this time."

He rolled onto his hands and knees, but Lucas shook his head. He dropped a kiss on Hollis' mouth, smiling when she focused on Cullen.

Lucas laughed. "I feel exactly the same, darlin'. Our mate looks good enough to eat."

Hollis moistened her lips, crawling off Lucas' lap. She met Cullen head-on, taking his mouth in a desperate kiss.

Cullen let her lead, seemingly aware that she needed to expend some of the energy straining her muscles. Despite the release she'd had, she still felt raw.

She broke the kiss, palming his chest before moving along the dips and planes. "Christ, you boys are large. In every respect. Don't think I'll ever grow tired of simply touching you."

Cullen smiled, gently holding her wrists. "Then, it's a good thing we've got a lifetime ahead of us."

She frowned. "Still might not be enough. But like you said...it's a start. Now, I believe you said you and Lucas could play once you'd taken care of my needs."

"Haven't come close to that, sweetheart." He tsked. "Please, still part bear. And you smell even more desperate than before. I reckon you won't be truly sated until we've fulfilled that vision you've been having." He leaned in close. "Have both of us love you at once."

She arched a brow, avoiding his attempt at a kiss. "And I believe you said that was for round two. Which means it's time for round one."

"Wasn't that when you came all over my face?"

"That was just the warm up. The main event involves you coming all over me while Lucas finally gets your ass. So, I suggest you get comfortable."

CHAPTER TWENTY

Cullen clenched his jaw, glancing over his shoulder as Lucas retrieved a flask of oil from one of the saddlebags he'd brought in from the horses, before moving back to the bed. Though Cullen had pictured this moment a thousand times, it didn't compare to now. To seeing his mate's muscles flex and ripple, his body a lean reflection of his bear. Or how long and hard Lucas' shaft was as it bounced between his legs, the head nearly purple with need.

More fluid gathered along the slit, tempting Cullen to simply turn and suck the man off. Taste his release as he had Hollis'. Prove to his bear that neither of his mates would ever leave.

Lucas shook his head. "You need more than that to silence your Kodiak. Trust me. I know. So, give our girl what she wants while I take care of you. Then, you can return the favor while we make Hollis' other desires a reality. Because if I don't soothe my bear soon, and fully claim you..."

Cullen's bear roared in his head, daring him to take control. Lucas answered with an audible growl, a hint of white showing beneath his upper lip.

The man arched a brow. "Do we really need to go a few rounds to decide who's more alpha? Because I will, if that's what it'll take. And don't think just because you're bigger than me, you'll win. But..." He smoothed his hand along Cullen's back to his hip. "I'm pretty damn sure your bear wants me in control as much as mine does. Especially when it knows you get me, next."

Lucas moved in close, tugging Cullen's back against his chest. The man's breath feathered across Cullen's flesh, making it bead. Lucas licked at the patch of skin just above Cullen's collarbone. "Mine."

He struck, sinking his teeth into Cullen's flesh, nearly taking him over from that act, alone. Any thoughts of reversing their positions faded with the feel of Lucas' mouth on his shoulder—his body hot and hard against Cullen.

His mate hummed as he eased away. "I thought you might see it my way. Now, give Hollis a kiss while I get us ready."

Cullen focused on Hollis, smiling at the flush staining her neck and cheeks. Her eyes still looked lust-dazed, her chest rising and falling nearly as fast as his. He crooked his finger, beckoning her to him. A stunning smile lit up her face as she glanced over his shoulder, pursing her lips at whatever Lucas was doing.

Lucas chuckled. "I can hear your thoughts, darlin' and I'm pretty sure we already said you'd be part of this." He moved his hand back to Cullen's body, the slick glide of them across Cullen's skin making his heart race. "Would you like to help before I make him cover your skin with his release?"

Her eyes dilated, eclipsing the blue. "God, yes."

Cullen snagged her as she tried to crawl past him. "That can wait until after I kiss you."

Hollis melted into his arms, all but wrapping herself around him as he ran one hand down her back, tugging her closer. She ate at his mouth, the scent of her need drowning out his senses. If he'd thought she'd been desperate before, it didn't compare to the way she all but climbed inside his skin.

Her breath feathered across his neck when he finally eased back, keeping her close. She thumbed his jaw, looking at him as if she was trying to memorize every detail of his face. "Tell me, is it always going to be like this? Feel as if my skin's on fire until you both love it away?"

Cullen dropped a kiss on her nose. "You're not the only one on fire, sweetheart. But if we can just claw our way through the next few weeks—get this damn spur finished—we'll take some time for us. See if we can lessen the need, even if just for the winter."

"I like the sound of that. But until then, I'll take tonight and go from there."

Cullen smiled, releasing her on a sigh. She didn't move far, using one hand to trace the muscles in his shoulders and arms. He twitched at the gentle contact, determined to kiss her, again, when Lucas' hand skimmed along his back, dipping down his crease to circle his ass. Cullen stilled. Though he'd pictured Lucas touching him, it hadn't come close to actually feeling the man caress his body—the slow glide of his fingertips as he teased the opening, slipping his finger inside Cullen.

Dark, burning desire followed Lucas' progression, Cullen's muscles clenching around the intrusion. Lucas paused with his finger completely inside before easing it free, adding more oil then repeating the motion. Each new thrust eased the pinching sensation until nothing remained but Cullen's need to have the man fuck him. Finally end the lingering doubts that Lucas was his. In every way.

Lucas pressed against him, nipping at Cullen's shoulder. "I've been yours since the first day we met. But I agree. This is long overdue."

He eased away, adding a second finger. Cullen let his head bow forward, praying he'd hold off long enough for Lucas to get inside when Hollis' breath hitched. Cullen managed to open his eyes as her gaze settled behind him, no doubt watching Lucas as he claimed Cullen's ass.

"Christ, Lucas. That's the hottest thing I've ever seen." She glanced at Cullen then focused on Lucas, again. "What does it feel like?"

Lucas paused, two fingers lodged deep inside Cullen. "Would you like to see for yourself?"

Hollis' eyes dilated as the flush on her skin darkened. "You asked that as if I might say no."

She held out one hand, moistening her lips as Lucas drizzled some oil along her fingers, swirling it around with his thumb before nodding at Cullen. She moved beyond Cullen's peripheral vision, just her toes wiggling amidst the blankets as her hand smoothed along his buttocks, two fingers pushing through his tight ring of muscles before plunging deep.

"God. I never dreamed it'd feel so good. So intoxicating. I could do this for hours."

Fire shot along Cullen's nerves straight to his cock, threatening to empty it across the bed.

Lucas chuckled. "Based on Cullen's reaction, I'd say you only have a few minutes before he covers the sheets instead of your chest. So, if you want to taste him, first, you'd best get in position because that time is going to quickly diminish once I get my cock inside him."

Cullen cursed at his mate's words, knowing he'd be hard pressed not to shoot his release down Hollis' throat if she put her mouth on him. Not if Lucas held true to his claim and sank inside him.

Lucas slapped his ass. "Do you really think I'm teasing?"

Cullen twisted to glare at his mate when Hollis scooted in front of him. He hooked her elbows, stopping her from lying on the bed. "If you want to put that pretty mouth on me, then you'll have to do it my way—facing me, on your hands and knees, with your ass up high so I can touch you, too."

She moaned at his words, snagging her lip before crawling into position. He hummed, running his hand along her spine—tracing each vertebra as he drew patterns on her skin until he reached her crease. As much as he needed Lucas to claim him—to take the other man in the same fashion—his bear also needed to finish their possession of Hollis. To watch her writhe between him and Lucas as they took her as one, knowing that final act would seal away any doubts that they'd spend the rest of their lives together.

The flask of oil appeared at his side as Lucas' voice

echoed inside his head, telling Cullen to ease some of his bear's uncertainty by touching her the way he'd imagined. He smiled, holding out his fingers to his mate. Lucas covered two with a layer of oil, helping spread it around before easing back. He paused in his own possession of Cullen, allowing Cullen to focus on Hollis for a moment. He leaned over her, skimming his fingers along her flesh until he reached the tight furl. He circled the opening, slicking her skin with oil before slowly pressing inside her.

Hot, crushing pressure encased his fingers, nearly taking him over. "So damn tight, sweetheart. I can't wait to feel you squeeze my cock like this."

She didn't answer, choosing that moment to wrap her lips around his shaft and take him deep to the back of her throat. Pleasure shot out from his sac, burning along his cock as he gritted his teeth, physically holding off his release. He paused with his fingers lodged inside her, doing his best to focus on how firmly she gripped him rather than the warm, wet glide of her mouth along his length. She must have hollowed her checks as the suction along his shaft increased, dimming the edges of his vision.

He let his head bow forward, managing a few more passes of his fingers, as she continued to bob between his legs. "Just remember. You're next, sweetheart."

She popped off him, nipping at the crown. "All the more reason to taste you this go 'round."

He shook his head, despite the fact he knew she was watching him. "I need—"

"I know what you need, and you'll get it. But I plan on getting what I need, too. And right now, I need you to come in my mouth and all over my chest."

Cullen growled, the animal side of him wanting to stake his claim other ways, when Lucas smacked his ass, reminding Cullen the other man hadn't come close to finishing what he'd started. Cullen glanced over his shoulder, noting the feral look in his mate's eyes as he slathered his cock with oil, smoothing more around Cullen's hole before locking their gazes together.

Lucas tsked. "Did you really think I'd be that patient? Allow you to change the course of events? It's time for me to finally take what's mine." He wrapped one arm around Cullen's torso, yanking him back against his chest. "And you are mine, mate."

He scraped his teeth along Cullen's shoulder, sending a rash of bumps cascading along his arms. Cullen closed his eyes, focusing on the way Lucas eased his cheeks apart with his other hand, brushing the head of his cock across Cullen's ass. His mate pressed against the opening, pushing steadily forward as Cullen's body resisted the intrusion. There were a few moments of burning pressure before his muscles relaxed, allowing Lucas to thrust inside him, slowly inching forward until his mate's sac slapped against Cullen's flesh.

The hand on his chest flexed, Lucas' nails scratching at Cullen's skin. "Damn. I never expected…"

He didn't finish as he stopped with his cock fully inside Cullen before dragging it back, pausing with just the head rimming the hole. Cullen clenched his jaw, still adjusting to the sensation when Lucas slammed back in, making Cullen's body shudder from the impact.

His mate's head fell to Cullen's shoulder, Lucas' breath hot against his flesh. "Christ, Cullen. So tight. So fucking good." He drew a few gasping breaths before kissing him. "Are you okay? Is this too much?"

Cullen growled, palming his hand over Lucas' hold on his chest. He didn't know if the sensation was too much or not enough. All he knew was that he'd lose his sanity if Lucas didn't fuck him.

He pressed into Lucas' groin, keeping them locked together. "Stop worrying about if you're hurting me and claim me, already." Cullen moaned, shaking within the other man's embrace. "Lucas, please…"

Lucas growled, scraping his teeth along Cullen's shoulder, again, before pulling back then driving forward. The hard penetration gave way to scorching need, each stroke echoed by an answering grunt from his bear. Cullen dug his fingers into the back of Lucas' hand, anchoring himself as his mate pounded into him, his pace increasing. Cullen fought the release burning along his spine, trying to distract himself with the intricacies of the upcoming bridge crossing, when Hollis' mouth returned to his cock.

He opened his eyes, snapping his head down to gaze at her as she moved along his length, her skin gleaming beneath him. Christ, he'd left her hanging as soon as Lucas had pushed inside him.

Hollis made a few more passes then eased free, glancing up at him. "I'd be more concerned if Lucas didn't have all of your attention. Having tasted just a hint of what you're experiencing…" She shivered, the sweet essence of her arousal thickening around them. "I've never seen anything so arousing as him claiming you. Besides, if you really want to please me, you'll stop fighting and give me what I want."

She returned to his shaft, licking at the fluid that

covered the head before sinking down the length. Each bob of her head seemed at odds with the biting penetration of Lucas' thrusts, and Cullen knew he wouldn't last long. After months of resisting their connection, he was just too far gone.

Hollis moved along his cock, hollowing her cheeks, nearly pushing him over before popping free and dipping down to nuzzle his sac. One hand held his shaft, pumping it as best she could while the other slid behind his balls to vee around Lucas' shaft—preceding every firm stroke forward. Every retreat. He clenched his jaw, trying to hold on, but aware he'd already lost the fight.

He gathered her hair in his hands, tugging on it until she finally looked up at him. He moaned at the next sharp thrust, trying not to pull the strands too much. "I know you want to taste me, Hollis, but...I need to see my release painted across your chest. Another visible mark that you're mine."

She glanced at his cock, licking her lips as if she planned on continuing before sighing. Instead, she pushed onto her knees, taking his mouth in a desperate kiss. Cullen used his other hand to drag her closer, moaning when she arched into him, letting him have complete control as he plundered her mouth, holding on until his lungs burned before releasing her and resting his forehead on hers. His rough breath fluttered the hair around her face. She dropped another kiss on his chin then went to her elbows again, taking his straining cock in her mouth.

"Hollis."

She eased free for a moment. "I promise some of your release will make it onto my skin, but...I need this. Need you."

How could he deny her? He sighed. "I won't last another minute with both of you loving me."

"Then, don't."

He clenched his jaw then tipped back his head, hitting Lucas' shoulder as the man increased his pace, shimmying the bed against the wall with every thrust of his hips. Cullen held on tight, losing himself in the feel of his mates wrapped around him before grunting in defeat. Having Lucas fuck him was so much more than he'd anticipated, and he knew he'd never look at either of them the same way, again. He only hoped he measured up.

Lucas licked his shoulder. "You're fucking incredible. Come for me."

His mate struck, sinking his teeth into the muscle as the man's cock swelled inside Cullen. He shouted Lucas' name, praying he wasn't yanking Hollis' hair, as he gave into the rush of heat up his shaft. His cock flared then he was coming, his first spurt coating Hollis' tongue. She hummed in seeming victory, swallowing the next pulse before pulling free and holding the tip against her chest. He emptied onto her flesh, each splash like a brand upon her skin.

Cullen closed his eyes, content to ride out the rest of his orgasm as Lucas growled against his shoulder, the man's shaft jerking inside Cullen as his mate climaxed— his teeth still locked in Cullen's muscle. A sense of peace washed over him, his bear snorting his approval, despite the fact the damn thing already wanted to claim Lucas in the same fashion—filling Cullen's head with images of their positions reversed. He mentally told the creature to back off, when Lucas chuckled against his skin, finally releasing him. A flick of the man's tongue sent another rush of heat along Cullen's veins, and for a moment, the thought he might finish, again.

Lucas released a contented sigh, dropping a kiss on Cullen's spine. "Not even a minute, and already your bear is pouting. Guess Kodiaks really are more highly strung than other grizzlies."

Cullen glanced back as his mate, noting the smug tilt to the man's lips. "I'm sure your bear would be equally insistent if I'd claimed you, first. But...my animal can wait a few more minutes. Let me enjoy the simple pleasure of having you both surrounding me."

Lucas leaned forward, cupping Cullen's chin as he drew him close enough to mold their lips together. Lucas' scent filled Cullen's senses, the essence tempered by a hint of his aroma. Cullen held the man's gaze for a few more moments after Lucas eased back then turned to focus on Hollis. She'd relaxed onto her elbows, his seed splashed across her flesh. A wicked grin captured her lips as she looked back and forth between them.

Lucas grunted behind Cullen, gently easing free before crawling onto the bed. Red flashed in the blue depths as his focus centered on Hollis' chest. "Fuck, Hollis."

He reached for her, yanking her against them as his mouth came down hard on hers. She moaned into the kiss, blinking open her eyes once Lucas released her.

He placed his hand on her chest, using one finger to spread Cullen's seed across her skin. "I knew you'd have to taste him. But you're not the only one."

Lucas lowered his head, sinking his teeth into her flesh. Hollis gasped, her eyes rolling shut as her back arched, her hair pooling on the blankets behind her. Cullen moved in beside her, staring at the spot Lucas had marked after his mate had eased back, stumbling off the bed.

Cullen inhaled, smiling at the combined aromas of his mates. "Do you know what it does to me to smell my release mixed in with yours and Lucas' scents? What it does to my bear?"

She arched a brow. "I hope it makes you want to love Lucas in return. You could mark me in the same way once he's emptied on my chest."

"Oh, sweetheart. While I love the thought of that, I can also smell how desperate you are."

"True. But I'm more desperate to have you touch Lucas. I can wait."

Cullen chuckled. "Based on the fact you're drippin' down your thighs, I'm thinkin' you can't." His eyes narrowed. "Are we scaring you? Imagining us both taking you and actually having it happen are distinctly different. If you need more time—"

"I'm not scared, Cullen. Promise. There isn't a way either of you could touch or love me that doesn't excite me. But I can also sense how much you need to finish your bond with Lucas. The same way he just did with you. I'm yours. Surely, your bears know that. But I sense your Kodiak isn't quite as convinced where he's concerned."

Cullen turned to glance at Lucas. His mate winked at him as he cleaned himself off, wetting a cloth before returning to the bed and rubbing a damp material along Cullen's ass. Cullen clenched his teeth, his muscles tensing from the simple contact. God, just a touch and he wanted more. Wanted to feel Lucas give beneath him. Know the man belonged to him.

Hollis sighed. "See? You must be desperate if I can

hear you screaming Lucas' name inside my head. You two can have me as soon as we recover. Promise. But for now, I want to watch you make love to him."

Cullen twisted back to face her. "I have every intention of claiming Lucas, but make no mistake. The only place he's finishin' is inside you." He released one of her arms, massaging some of his seed into her skin before gathering more on his finger then sliding it along her cleft. "After we eat our fill."

She gasped as he shoved her thighs apart, making room for Lucas when the man shuffled in beside him. They each grabbed a leg and settled it over their shoulder, spreading her wide. Cullen let Lucas lead, licking a path along her folds then nipping at her clit. Hollis cried out, sinking her fingers into their hair as if needing the anchor to keep her from flying apart. Lucas made another pass, pausing to look over at Cullen. Moisture glistened on Lucas' lips, begging to be tasted.

"Damn good idea." Cullen leaned into Lucas, taking his mouth in a hard blending of teeth and lips.

Hollis' sweet arousal burst along his tongue, mixed in with traces of spicy male. Cullen hummed, refusing to retreat until his lungs burned in need. He gasped in a breath, smiling at Lucas before focusing on Hollis. More arousal dampened her flesh, and Cullen bent forward— licking a path from her cleft to her clit. Her moan sounded through the room, another wash of arousal coating his tongue.

He sank his finger inside her, watching as Lucas followed suit in her ass. The double penetration had her chanting their names as her head thrashed across the bed. Cullen repeated his thrust, inhaling sharply when he felt

Lucas push into her ass, the ghosted feel spiking Cullen's cock against his stomach. Despite the fact he'd just climaxed, his bear obviously wanted more.

Cullen growled against her cleft, loving the way it made her tense in response. "Hell, yeah, sweetheart. I want you to come all over us."

Hollis fisted the sheets—muscles quivering, her eyes squeezed shut. She seemed determined to hold on until Lucas kissed his way along her torso, sipping one distended nipple into his mouth.

She broke, her strangled cry filling the room. Tremors shook through her body as her skin flushed a deep shade of pink. Lucas ran his hands along her torso, finally bringing her back down. She gasped in a few rough breaths, blinking until she managed to open her eyes fully, focusing on Lucas as he hovered above her.

A knowing smile curved the man's lips as he gave her body a long sweep. "God, you're beautiful when you orgasm. Thinkin' we might need another change of plans. Watch you do that over and over and over."

She arched a brow, hissing out her next breath when Cullen eased his fingers free of her body. He raised them to his mouth, holding her gaze as he sucked off her release, knowing it wouldn't be enough. That he'd never get enough of her. Of Lucas.

Lucas snaked his arm around Cullen's back, dragging him in for a harsh kiss—much like Cullen had done to him. His mate's tongue swept into his mouth, tangling with his before retreating. Lucas hummed as he pulled back, brushing his thumb over the corner of Cullen's mouth. "God, you two taste good together. I think..." He paused, glancing down at Hollis when she whimpered. He studied her, then cursed. "You need more, don't you?" He shushed her with a gentle kiss. "So do we. Are you comfortable?"

She nodded, brow slightly creased, when Lucas shifted his position, settling between her thighs. Cullen knew the moment his mate had thrust inside. Hollis' head tilted back as her hands flexed against Lucas' back, leaving tiny scratches across his skin. Lucas seemed equally affected, gathering her in his arms, claiming her mouth as he pumped his hips. Each stroke shook the bed, the steady creak of the springs spurring Cullen into action.

He eased off the bed, retrieving the flask of oil Lucas had set on the small table next to them. Cullen drizzled a line along his cock, smoothing it around before setting the flask aside. His bear roared, eager to finally rid itself of any lingering doubts. Of finally knowing Lucas was his —completely.

Lucas paused, his groin crushed against Hollis' as he glanced at Cullen over his shoulder. His gaze fell to his shaft then tracked back to his face. "Like I said before, I've been yours since the day we met, but I'm all for making it official."

Cullen crawled in behind him. "Good. Then, you won't mind shuffling back. Can't claim your ass this far away, mate."

Lucas chuckled, cupping Hollis' hips as Cullen helped drag them backwards until Lucas' knees were near the edge. Cullen skimmed his hands along Lucas' back, tracing the line of muscles as they twitched beneath his touch. The man was strong and lean, and just knowing he belonged to Cullen...

Lucas chuckled, again. "Feeling a bit possessive?"

Cullen smacked the man's ass, moaning at the way he flexed from the simple contact. "Your bear's no different, as proof from the marks on my shoulder."

"Then, stop wasting time and fuck me, already. Silence that voice inside your head."

Cullen smiled. Seemed his Kodiak wasn't the only one on the edge. "It's more of a constant growl, but you're right. It's time."

He smoothed his fingers along Lucas' crease, spreading the oil across his skin before pausing at the puckered opening. He touched the furl of skin, giving Lucas a moment to anticipate his next move before slowly sinking his finger inside. Cullen moaned at the firm pressure along his finger, pushing all the way in before easing back out. He repeated the process, adding a second digit once Lucas' muscles had relaxed.

He leaned over his mate, nipping at the man's shoulder. "Mine, Lucas. You, Hollis, your bear. All of you belong to me. Mine to love. Mine to protect." He eased back, pressing the head of his cock against the tight ring of muscles. "You'd both best remember that."

He pushed forward, keeping the pressure constant until the tip slipped inside. Hot, slippery flesh wrapped around Cullen's shaft, and he couldn't stop from thrusting forward, hilting himself inside Lucas. His mate clenched around him, Lucas' head bowing toward his chest.

Hollis slid her hands along Lucas' back, massaging the man's skin, until some of the tension eased. Then, she threaded one hand through his hair, drawing him down to her and slanting her lips over his. The position raised Lucas' hips slightly, giving Cullen the perfect opportunity to start up a steady rhythm.

He drew back, grunting at the loss of contact before sinking back inside—reclaiming the lost inches. He pressed his groin into Lucas' backside, enjoying the slap of the other man's sac against his before repeating the thrust, this time with a bit more force. Lucas met his stroke with a tilt of his hips, angling Cullen even deeper.

Cullen cursed, tightening his grip on Lucas' hips as he thrust, again, harder, faster. After fighting their attraction for so long, Cullen wanted to make this moment last. Draw it out until he'd had a chance to memorize every detail. The way Lucas' body gave around him. The firm press of his muscles beneath Cullen's hands. The contrast between Lucas' skin and Hollis' as their mate writhed beneath them, her soft cries adding to the heady atmosphere. Once wouldn't come close to being enough, and Cullen was quickly losing the fragile hold he had over his control.

Lucas growled, glancing back at him across his shoulder. "This is just the beginning, Cullen. We have a lifetime of nights ahead of us. So, stop worryin' about holding on and stake your damn claim."

Cullen closed his eyes, knowing he couldn't hold off any longer. Not with Lucas clamping around his cock while Hollis chanted their names, her sweet scent heavy in the air.

Cullen clenched his jaw, shifting enough he could wrap one of Hollis' legs around his hip. He needed to feel her skin against him. Feel her connection as he pounded into Lucas, all semblance of gentleness gone. Lucas grunted, meeting each punishing stroke while still thrusting into Hollis.

The bed creaked, banging against the wall with every

hard stroke. Cullen focused on the rhythm. On the slick glide of his shaft. On the breathy whimpers Hollis made as Lucas pushed her higher. Their combined scent flooded his senses, and he knew he wouldn't last much longer.

Hollis gasped, yanking Lucas down to her. She glanced at Cullen over the other man's shoulder then licked the patch of skin near the base of Lucas' neck. "Mine."

"Yes."

Lucas rasped the single word then levered against where her mouth clamped around his flesh. She held firm, maintaining her hold until she gasped in a rough breath, collapsing back on the mattress. Her entire body shook, the flush creeping up her neck marking her climax. Lucas moaned, his hips jerking erratically before he grunted, stiffening beneath Cullen's hold. The man's muscles clenched tight, the droop of his shoulders signaling his surrender.

Cullen closed his eyes as his own release burned a path along his shaft. He didn't want it to end. Despite the fact he knew it was just the beginning, he wanted it to last longer. Keep his mates wrapped in his arms, content that they were safe. But even as he tried to push the sensation away, it gathered strength, overriding his control and taking him headlong into release.

He sighed in defeat, slipping one arm under Lucas' chest and pulling him flush against his chest. He grinned at the fading marks Hollis had left, settling him mouth beside them. Lucas' skin prickled beneath his lips a moment before Cullen exploded inside the other man, sinking his teeth into Lucas' muscle as Cullen's cock emptied in a series of spurts.

The room dimmed, closing in until it was nothing

more than the three of them entwined on the bed, their joint heartbeats echoing in Cullen's head. He held on, savoring the moment, bleeding all he could out of it before finally easing back. He licked at the divots he'd left on his mate as his bear snorted then settled, any lingering doubts fading into the steady rasp of his mates as they breathed through the last remnants of their releases.

Cullen's muscles relaxed, and he found himself curled over Lucas, hoping they didn't fall and squish Hollis into the bed. He thought about moving but decided to wrap his arms around them, instead, holding Lucas tight against him as Cullen wove his and Hollis' fingers together.

Their mate sighed, moving her other hand to Lucas' shoulder, smoothing it where she'd branded him. "I wish these would last longer. That I could mark you both the way you mark me."

Cullen squeezed her hand, dropping a kiss on Lucas' spine. "You've already marked us, sweetheart. In a way far more powerful than some scars on your shoulder. You're ours. Period."

Tears pooled in her eyes, a few slipping down her cheek. Cullen reluctantly eased free, knowing Hollis needed more than her mates hovering above her. She needed to be held. Cherished. And damn if he didn't want to give her all of that and more.

Lucas glanced back at him, his gaze confirming he'd heard Cullen's thoughts. He shifted to the left, allowing Cullen to curl in on the other side—once again wrap them both in his embrace.

Cullen traced a finger along Hollis' chin, humbled by

the moisture clinging to her skin. "Not sure what we did to deserve you, but we'll take it. Now, how about a bath?"

She laughed. "There's no tub. I checked. And even I wouldn't chance that river at night."

"There's a full rain barrel outside. It won't be warm, but it'll do in a pinch. And there's nothing Lucas and I would like more than to spend the rest of the night warming you up."

"Why is it always my ass that has to freeze?"

"We'll take turns, just to be fair." He smiled. "Besides, we have plans for that ass, and we all need to clean up if we're going to make them a reality."

Her breathing caught as she glanced between them, the flush on her cheeks returning. "You keep talking like that, and no amount of rinsin' will keep me clean."

Cullen growled, scooping his arms underneath her then lifting her off the bed.

"Wait. Your shoulder."

"Is fine. Feels better than ever now that my bear is... less ornery. Which means we can spend the night lickin' you if our little water venture doesn't cool your desire. There's nothing we'd rather do than watch you come over and over. But you definitely won't get any rest with my release dryin' on your skin and Lucas' dripping down your thighs."

She winked at him. "It's not the only thing dripping down my thighs, Cullen."

He grunted, tripping a step before catching his balance. "You're determined to have us claim you, again, right now, aren't you?" He shushed her when she went to answer. "We'll be quick. Then, we'll do whatever you need to keep you comfortable. Deal?"

"I've discovered you two are hard to deny. Fine, freeze me—just as long as you hold true to your promise and warm me back up. And I have my own plans, so you're both going in, too."

"Always a counter-offer. But you've got a deal, Doc."

She wrapped her arms around his neck. "Then, I'm yours."

CHAPTER TWENTY-ONE

"Lucas."

Lucas groaned, blinking several times in an effort to clear his vision, before the wooden ceiling finally came into focus. Just a hint of light brightened the dull gray beyond the window, a chorus of birds breaking up the silence. He turned his head, smiling at Hollis as she stared at him, her weight braced on one elbow. Her hair sat in a tousled mess about her head, the light blush on her cheeks still evident from last night.

He hummed, lifting one hand and trailing it along her shoulder. He circled the marks they'd left behind, faint but there. She'd done more than simply bring him and Cullen together. She'd made them whole. Given them a reason to get up in the morning besides laying down miles of iron rails. And he knew he'd never tire of seeing her like this—wrapped between them, an easy smile curving her lips. His bear snorted, reminding him they still needed to love her together before it would truly settle. Have no doubts that she was, and always would be, theirs.

He mentally told the animal to bugger off. They had a lifetime of loving ahead of them, and he, for one, didn't have any doubts. "Hey, darlin'. Everything okay?" He winked at her. "Hungry?"

She swatted his chest in feigned annoyance, though he didn't miss the way her eyes darkened, or her breathy inhale. "That's a constant state where you two are concerned, and I'm not talking about food. But I need to use the outhouse. And after the way you boys reacted last time, I thought it might be best to wake you, first." She arched a brow. "In case you think I need protectin'."

"Wench."

She batted her eyes at him. "Wouldn't want your bears to think I'm ditchin' you. In case they're still...concerned."

He cursed under his breath. "Seems our connection is even stronger if you picked up on my bear's thoughts."

She shrugged.

He reached for her, thumbing her cheek as he cupped her jaw. "Remember what I said about them actin' on instincts? I'm not sure why they need to love you that way before they'll be completely satisfied, but I can assure you their other halves don't harbor any doubts. Not after all you've done to prove your love. Thinkin' we're the ones who haven't shown you enough what you mean to us."

Her expression softened. "Cullen was willin' to die to prove your boys' faith in me as a doctor. I don't have any doubts, Lucas. Or regrets. And just in case your bears are listening, I'm yours. For always. Now...about that quick trip outside."

"Your wish, darlin'." He swung his legs over the edge then pushed to his feet, offering her his hand. "We could all use a trip." He tugged her against his chest, smoothing his hand along her back. Soft skin caressed his palm before he dug his fingers into her ass. "Thank you."

Her lips quirked as she leaned against him, gently grazing his jaw. "For what?"

He snorted. "Everything. For not runnin' when you had the chance. For going against your natural instincts and wakin' me up when you could have just scooted out. I know how hard it is for you to push aside those tendencies. And both sides of me appreciate your efforts. I promise we'll work at being less paranoid." He nuzzled her nose. "But mostly, for saying yes."

She dropped a kiss on his chin. "Then, you're going to be thankin' me, again, because I'm definitely saying yes to what your bear has in mind."

"Tease. That's not helping me get you out the door." He glanced over her shoulder. "Especially with Cullen lookin' at us the way he is."

She twisted, smiling when the man crawled across the bed, stepping out behind them. Lucas released her enough that she could spin as Cullen bent to capture her lips in his. Lucas moaned at the raspy hum that vibrated through her chest and into his—as if she couldn't get enough of them.

Hollis winked at him once they'd parted, then drew her fingers across Cullen's shoulders. "The swelling's gone down, and most of the bruising has faded. I should remove those stitches as soon as we get back so your bear can finish the job."

Cullen placed his hand over hers, holding it firm against his skin. "Thinkin' you're equally responsible for my healing, but I won't say no to you removing them. They itch far more than I thought they would."

"Itching's a good thing. It means you're healing." She glanced at Lucas. "Can I visit the outhouse, now, or are you boys going to need to do another perimeter check, first?"

Lucas tsked her. "You can tease us all you want, because caring about your safety is worth it. Though, I'm sure we'll be fine just standing watch."

She looked as if she was going to roll her eyes before shaking her head, instead. She accepted the shirt he gave her, slipping her arms through then buttoning it up. He smiled at the warm feeling burning in his chest as he quickly yanked on his pants then waved at the door. Hollis followed him through to the other room, stopping long enough to grab one of her pistols as he tossed Cullen his breeches.

Cullen grinned, leaning in and whispering something that sounded like, "That's my girl," before strapping on his own weapons then handing Lucas his.

Lucas nodded his thanks, listening at the door for a few moments before swinging it open. Though he didn't expect to encounter any issues like they had last night, he wasn't going to take any chances. The branches in the trees off to his left shook as a gathering of birds took flight, squawking all the way to another roosting site. He let his grizzly surge forward, hoping his increased senses would pick up on any unwanted visitors. His bear grunted, focusing on the sweet scent standing next to him, and the way his and Cullen's essence wove through it.

"Great, all my damn grizzly can sense is how good you

both smell." He glared at Cullen when his mate laughed. "I doubt your Kodiak is much better."

"It's not. But I can't really argue with how focused it is on the two of you."

Lucas chuckled, heading toward the small shack hidden amidst the trees. He waved Hollis in, venturing farther into the surrounding forest while Cullen stayed close. Though Lucas couldn't quite pinpoint it, something felt off. He stopped to check a set of prints in the mud, jumping when a hand landed on his shoulder.

He muttered under his breath, looking up at Cullen. "Must you scare another ten years off my life?"

"Thought you heard that twig snap." He nodded at the prints. "Everything okay? I sensed something was bothering you."

He stood then waved at the marks. "Wolves."

"They're common around here."

"I know. But I can't shake the feeling that we're being watched."

"Probably because we are."

Cullen pointed toward a small clearing in the direction of the proposed line. Just a hint of yellow brightened the patch as the sun threatened to peek above the distant horizon.

"I saw a couple take off. Bettin' they can smell us, too." He cupped Lucas' shoulder. "I'm sure it's leftover adrenaline from last night."

Lucas stared at where his mate had seen the animals. "Probably."

Cullen sighed, pulling Lucas' back against his chest as he wrapped one arm around his waist. "Speakin' of

298 | KRIS NORRIS

which... I'm not sure I thanked you for all you did. I know what it cost you to kill those men—"

"No thanks required. No one hurts my mates. Period."

"Still." Cullen dropped a kiss on his neck. "Thank you. Now, how about we get back to our mate. The girl has needs we should fulfill before we finish surveying that line. I'd like to make it back to town today. Just to be safe."

Lucas nodded, glancing one more time around the area. At least the prickly feeling between his shoulder blades was gone. He sighed. Cullen was right. Lucas was still on-edge from the ambush. But he'd eliminated the threat.

His grizzly snorted its approval as he returned to the outhouse, quickly relieving himself before following his mates inside the cabin. They rinsed off their hands then tended to the fire, hoping to stave off the chill still hanging in the air. Hollis motioned to Cullen, making him sit still as she checked his wounds, gently cutting the stitches free. She mumbled something about having only just put them in last night, but it got lost to the pulse of need through Lucas' core. Seeing the black thread reminded him of all he could have lost. How much they owed their mate.

He moved in behind Hollis, curling his arms around her as he breathed in her scent. The usual aromas filled his senses, accompanied by a touch of wood smoke. She hummed, letting him bridge some of her weight— seemingly content to stay wrapped in his embrace.

He kissed her neck, enjoying the shiver that wove through her. "You must be exhausted, darlin'. We've been negligent in that area, too."

"I can sleep later. Once I've gotten my fill of you two."

He chuckled. "Not sure that's going to happen anytime soon."

"Then, I suppose I'll just have to drink more coffee. Which you can make *after* you've silenced those doubts your bears have."

He smiled against her neck. "Are you sure you're ready?"

She glanced back at him, arching a brow. "If the slick feeling between my legs is any indication, I'm more than ready."

A dull roar sounded inside his head as his bear growled its approval. Cullen appeared in front of her, tangling his fingers in her hair and drawing her mouth to his. Lucas felt a ghosted caress against his lips, their joint pleasure burning beneath his flesh. He waited until Cullen eased back before scooping her up in his arms, loving the way she laughed then rested her head on his shoulder. He kissed her forehead, walking into the other room.

Cullen darted in front, climbing onto the bed and scooting back, giving Lucas enough room to place Hollis on the edge. She smiled up at him, dragging him to her for another soul-searing kiss before turning to gaze at Cullen. She wet her lips, crawling toward him, licking and sucking at his cock as it bobbed against his stomach.

Lucas retrieved the oil, again, watching Hollis' ass sway as she devoured their mate, taking him quickly to the brink. Cullen reached for her, sinking his fingers in her hair. He gave her a few more passes along his shaft before guiding her up his chest, swallowing her protest with a firm kiss.

Cullen cupped her jaw once he'd finally released her, helping her straddle him. "God, you're beautiful."

She paused, glancing back at Lucas, her eyes glassy, her chin quivering, before she turned to Cullen, stealing another kiss then letting her forehead rest on his. She didn't speak, just sat there, seemingly lost in the moment. Cullen rubbed his hands along her back, finally tangling his fingers in her hair, again. She moaned when he yanked her head to one side, baring her neck.

"Ours, Hollis. For always."

He licked her flesh then closed his mouth over her muscle. Lucas felt the sudden rush of pleasure, the distinct increased clarity between them as his mate reasserted their claim.

He loosened the top on the flask, moving onto the bed then drizzling some along her crease. Her muscles flexed at the sudden contact, a rash of goosebumps cascading along her skin. She glanced at him over her shoulder, Cullen's fingers still locked around her hair, before closing her eyes on a hum as Lucas swirled his finger around her opening then slowly sank inside.

"God, Hollis. So tight. And the way you clamp down on me..." He leaned forward, nipping at her flesh. "We're going to make you come so hard."

He eased back, gathered more oil on his fingertip then pushed back in. Her muscles clenched around his intrusion, holding him tight before finally easing. He added a second finger, scissoring them apart as he moved faster—adding a bit of force to each plunge. Hollis lowered onto Cullen's chest, using the position to tilt into every thrust, her rough gasps sounding around him. He kept stretching her, using his other hand to grasp

Cullen's shaft between her legs. His mate grunted, arching into Lucas' hand as he fisted it down to the base then back up.

Cullen glanced at him over Hollis' shoulder, his canines showing beneath his upper lip. Lucas answered the man's challenge, dipping under Hollis enough he could lick the slick fluid off of Cullen's shaft before taking his mate deep to the back of his throat.

"Damn, Lucas." Cullen pushed out a few rough breaths. "I need more than your mouth."

Lucas took him deep, again, before nipping at the thick head then straightening. He swirled the tip around Hollis' cleft, soaking Cullen's skin with her arousal before positioning it at her sex. Cullen didn't wait for Lucas to drag Hollis onto his cock, claiming her sheath with a firm thrust.

Hollis arched, her head tilting back as Cullen maintained his hold in her hair. Her body shimmied with each forceful stroke, Cullen's pace obviously driving her to the edge. Lucas eased his fingers free, smiling at her anguished cry. He poured more of the oil along his shaft, waiting until Cullen finally paused before palming her skin. Hollis inhaled, glancing at him as he pressed against her ass, careful not to push forward until the tight ring of muscles gave beneath the pressure, and he slipped inside. Her head bowed toward her chest, a shiver working down her spine.

Lucas curled over her, nuzzling her neck. "Breathe, darlin'. We'll wait until you're accustomed to having us both inside you. But once you're ready..." He nipped at her skin. "Going to make you see stars."

She drew in a series of gasping pants, finally moaning

in seeming need. "By all that's holy, move. Lucas. Cullen. I need…"

"We'll give you all of that and more."

Lucas dropped a kiss on her sweat-damp flesh then eased back, slowly withdrawing until only the head stayed locked inside her. He paused, giving her ass a light smack before thrusting back in, reclaiming the lost inches. Cullen countered his movement, pulling out once Lucas' sac had slapped against his then pressing in, again. They kept their pace slow, wanting to build her up gently. Keep her poised on the edge until she had no choice but to fall.

"Now." Her voice rasped around them, the gravelly tone calling to his bear. "Harder. Just…give me more."

Lucas lowered his head at her plea, his bear rising closer to the surface. It roared its agreement, filling his head with images of her climaxing around them. He gritted his teeth, managing one more slow drag of his cock before he relinquished control.

"Yes!"

The single word hissed free as she pushed onto her hands, her nails biting into Cullen's shoulders. He palmed her ribs, holding her steady, still thrusting into her from below. Hollis chanted their names, rolling her head from side to side until her breath stalled and she arched. Lucas froze, on the verge of spilling into her, when she shouted her release, the steady contractions along his cock sending him over.

He lowered his head, thrusting into her quivering channel until the world dimmed around him, and he came, emptying hot and wet inside her. He felt Cullen push into her several more times before his mate shouted her name, levering up until she was trapped between them. He mouthed one side, mentally telling Lucas to mark the other. Twin heartbeats pulsed in his head as he settled his lips against her skin, tasting her flesh as he sank into her shoulder.

His grizzly snorted, pacing a few times then easing, finally content both its mates were just as committed. Lucas mentally told the animal he'd known that already, but it merely grunted, allowing him to focus on Hollis and Cullen. Cullen had his arms wrapped around both of them, his chin resting on Hollis' shoulder. She felt boneless between them, the steady rustle of breath suggesting she'd passed out.

Lucas managed to raise his head, despite the desire to simply fall onto the bed, still entwined. "Cullen."

The man scrunched his nose, finally peering at Lucas through one eye. "I know, but…stay here. With us. Just for a while longer. Then, we'll clean up our girl and tuck her into bed for an hour. After that, we'll insist she eat something before we survey the last of the line. But for the next five minutes, don't move. Don't think. Just hold us and breathe."

Lucas smiled, once again relaxing against Hollis. Hell, he'd give them as much time as they needed—stay wrapped in their embrace for hours. Then, he'd watch Cullen's back before seeing them all safely home to Devil's Gate. But Lucas wasn't going to stay for long. He was done waiting for Buford to make a move. Once this trip was over, Lucas was taking the battle to him. It was time the bastard met Lucas' other half. And his grizzly wasn't in the mood for talking.

CHAPTER TWENTY-TWO

"You're back."

Hollis jumped, placing her hand on her chest as she glanced up from capping the last of her salves, looking at the man standing in the doorway. Her heart thrashed against her palm, and she had to crush the curse threatening to burst free. "Joseph."

The reverend stared at her, hat clenched in his hands, eyes dark. He took a single step inside the clinic, the door still open behind him. "I wasn't sure if you'd stay out another night."

"Cullen wanted to inventory the bridge supplies. He thinks some of the trestlework might need to be reinforced."

He nodded at the jars in front of her. "I assume your trip was a success."

"Yes. I just finished making the last of the liniments. I should have enough to get through the winter, now. And most of my other supplies arrived on the train an hour ago. I've been busy putting everything away. Which reminds me, I didn't have a chance to thank you for watching over the clinic for me."

He shrugged one shoulder. "It was quiet. Caleb closed the saloon early, so the men didn't get too violent. Guess he was worried Sheriff Quinn wouldn't be pleased if you came back to a room full of patients." His lips quirked. "Quinn seems to be very concerned about your...well-being. As does James."

She didn't miss the veiled undertone. "They're simply worried about completing the spur before the snows set in. Fewer healthy men means the railroad might not get finished."

Joseph snorted. "Right, it's all about finishin' the line."

Hollis frowned. "Are you okay? You seem...upset."

He flashed her a forced smile. "Perfectly well." He backed up, shoving his hat into place. "I just wanted to make sure you were here before I headed up the line to gather a few of my own supplies."

He nodded then left, his footfalls quickly fading. She stared at the closed door, wondering if she'd imagined the entire conversation, only to push the thoughts aside. It was mostly likely just fatigue—seeing a reaction when there hadn't been one. All she needed to do was get more sleep.

She laughed at the thought. There was little chance of catching up on sleep before the railroad was finished. Not with the endless string of patients, and her seemingly endless desire to touch and taste her mates. Even now, her body ached for them, a few sporadic cramps tensing her abdomen.

Hollis groaned inwardly, raking her hand through her hair as she leaned against the counter. Now wasn't the time to be thinking about loving Cullen and Lucas. Running her fingers and tongue all over their plated muscles—taking their shafts deep to the back of her throat. She needed to be ready if a patient walked through the door, not oblivious to everything except the heat slowly coiling in her abdomen.

As if on cue, the door opened, swirling cold air through the room. The temperature had dropped significantly after the storm, and it smelled as if the first snowfall was on its way. Hollis twisted, mentally preparing herself for whatever injury awaited her, only to inhale roughly when Lucas stepped into the clinic, closing the door firmly behind him.

She grinned, not giving him a chance to say anything before covering the short distance between them and taking his mouth with hers. He stiffened in surprise then chuckled into the kiss, instantly taking control as he smoothed one hand down to rest on her ass, tugging her even closer. She moved with him when he tilted her head back, deepening the kiss before easing away and nipping a line along her neck. Burning need followed each brush of his lips and teeth, simmering beneath the marks he'd left on her shoulder.

Lucas hummed, biting at the muscle through her shirt. "God, darlin'. I'm not sure what motivated you to launch into my arms, but I approve of your tactics. So much so, I'll be expecting that kind of welcome every time I come through the door from now on." He nuzzled her neck. "What I wouldn't give to reassert my claim. Right here. Right now."

She couldn't quite crush the moan that rumbled

through her chest as her nipples beaded into achingly hard points beneath her camisole. "Lucas."

He chuckled, again. "I should probably be worried about how much power you have over me with nothing more than my name. Cullen never affected me quite this much."

"Thinkin' that's all changed now that you two have finally fully bonded."

"Wench. Must you always be right?"

"I have to be when it's two against one."

"Just me here, darlin'. And I believe we already promised to take turns siding with you." He smiled then frowned as he inhaled. His gaze swept down her body, then back up. "Hollis? Are you okay?"

Her muscles cramped, again, at his words. "Fine."

He tsked, releasing one hand to tap his forehead. "Mated. And the connection has only grown stronger since this morning. That means I know when you're lyin' to me. You're in pain, again, aren't you?"

She sighed, trusting him to bridge her weight as she relaxed in his arms. "It's not bad. Just the odd cramp."

"What I sense is more than a cramp." He glanced around the clinic, focusing on the adjoining bedroom. "Does that door lock?"

"I think so..."

Her voice trailed into a gasp as he lifted her up and quickly walked across the room, closing the bedroom door behind them. He reached for the bolt, sliding it over before turning and pressing her against the wall. He didn't talk, capturing her lips in a brutal kiss as he removed her belt, laying it on a small table off to her right before working on the buttons of her pants. She moaned when they hit the floor, the cool air beading her flesh with goosebumps.

He growled, skimming his fingertips up her thighs, making small circles over her hips. "You need to come to us before the pain starts."

She moistened her lips, still trying to play catch up. "Then, I'd never leave your bed because the ache returns the moment you both leave."

Lucas pursed his lips, leaning in to rest his forehead on hers. "The burning need should eventually ease."

"I thought this morning was supposed to speed that along."

He paused, catching her gaze. Red flashed in his eyes then darkened into a deep blue. "Once wasn't nearly enough."

He nipped at her neck, unbuttoning her shirt enough to expose her shoulder. He latched onto her muscle, sucking at her skin as he dropped his pants, nudging her sex with his shaft. She rasped his name, moving her thigh to his hip when he palmed her flesh. The position sank the first inch of his cock inside her pussy. She squeezed her internal muscles, trying to draw him farther inside her, when he growled and punched his hips forward, burying himself balls deep.

Hollis latched onto his shoulder, muffling her cries as he pounded into her, no semblance of control evident in the way he knocked her against the rough wood with every stroke. Fire burned beneath her flesh, dimming her vision at the edges. She held on, doing her best to meet each punishing stroke as the urgent feeling in her stomach expanded, threatening to pull her under. She managed to hold her release at bay for a few more minutes before his next deep thrust shattered her defenses, and she broke, flooding his cock with her climax.

"Fuck, yes, Hollis."

Lucas dropped his mouth to her shoulder, again, sinking his teeth into her muscle as he jerked against her, emptying in a series of spurts. She crested, again, barely crushing her scream against his clothing as the room dissolved, his harsh breathing the only sound registering around her. She tightened her hold, wanting to stay wrapped in his arms until Cullen returned and they could do it all over again, only together.

Lucas lifted his head, softly taking her lips in his. The gentle contact clenched her chest, and she knew she'd never be the same. Never see her life, her future, without them in it. That they'd somehow broken her down, and the only way to rebuild herself was with them.

Tears stung her eyes as she held Lucas close, content just to breathe him in. She'd never felt so raw. As if they'd striped her bare and exposed far more than just skin. That they'd revealed the heart she thought she'd buried with her mother. A riot of emotions roiled through her, all culminating into a singular thought...

Mine.

Lucas sighed, dropping a kiss on her forehead then easing back. He tilted his head down, waiting until she made eye contact before giving her a brilliant smile. "Always. And you're ours. Until our dyin' breath, though I have a feeling even that won't be enough to drag us away. I'm afraid you're good and rightly stuck with us."

She tiptoed up, planting a soft peck on his nose. "Wouldn't have it any other way." She thumbed his jaw. "You know I love you and Cullen, right? That nothing and no one could ever change how I feel. I realize I'm a bit late to the game compared to you two, but—"

He captured her mouth, swallowing her last few words. He traced every inch, delving in for another round before seemingly being satisfied. His breath caressed her jaw as he stayed dangerously close. "Despite the fact I feel your love for us inside my chest, I don't think I'll ever get tired of hearing you say the words. What it does to me..." He grinned. "And I can assure you, Cullen's even more worked up over it." He shrugged. "It's his Kodiak. It tends to get dramatic."

"Then, I'll have to make a point of saying it more often." She swatted his shoulder at his smug smile. "But don't think I'll be wallowin' in this sappy stuff long."

"I'm sure you'll be back to threatening to shoot our asses quicker than we'd like. Though seeing you tied in knots is pretty damn intoxicating."

"Wasn't me who pinned me to the wall."

He laughed. "Guilty as charged. And now that I've taken the edge off..." He signaled her to wait for a moment as he darted over to the pitcher and basin by her bed. He poured some water in the bowl, rinsing himself off then wetting a cloth for her. While she realized he was just trying to clean her, she couldn't deny that every swirl of his hand over her flesh made the temperature rise around her.

Lucas tsked, tossing the cloth onto the small table. "Now, darlin'. You keep reacting like that, and I'll have to clean you, again."

She stuck her tongue out at him. "I've pretty much resigned myself to the fact I won't be dry before you two finish this spur, but I suppose I can dream. Though simply lookin' at you…"

Lucas groaned, once again trapping her against the wall. "Have mercy. Do you know how difficult it is to walk around when I'm so hard I can barely think straight?" He shook his head. "Besides, you need to rest." He held up his finger, silencing her protest. "Even for just an hour or two while there's nobody knocking on your door. You've barely slept since you got here. And Cullen and I have only added to you fatigue, even if it was for the best possible reasons."

"I wouldn't say having to stitch him up was all that great, but what came after was definitely worth losing sleep over."

"Which is why you're going to get some, now." He nudged her. "Please."

She glanced at the closed door.

He grabbed her hands, leading her to the bed. "I'll personally stand guard, and I promise to wake you if you're needed. But until then…" He kissed her forehead after he'd removed her boots and tucked her under a blanket. "With any luck, I'll send Cullen in to get you. Perhaps you two can find a way to get dirty, again, before we draw you a proper bath."

"And give up dunkin' in a rain barrel in the middle of the night?"

"Wench. Sleep. I'll be close. Promise."

She nodded, half convinced she wouldn't do more than stare at the ceiling, only to rouse a bit later as voices sounded in the other room. She listened for a moment, still sleep-dazed when she heard Cullen's name. The room tilted a bit as she swung her legs over the edge, the cold floor chasing away some of her grogginess. It took a couple of tries to tug on her boots before she made her way to the door.

Fatigue burned along her muscles. She never should have agreed to nap. It had only made her feel worse— tease her body with a hint of what it needed. Though since getting several hours of sleep in a row seemed unlikely, she'd just have to adapt.

She sighed as she entered the main area, frowning as Lucas paced the length of the room, hands fisted at his sides. Reverend Miller stood near the entrance, hat clenched in his grasp. The man seemed more than a bit nervous, his gaze darting between Lucas and the slightly open door to his left. Lucas must have sensed her presence. He glanced over at her, stopping mid-stride. Love lit up his eyes, followed closely by concern.

Hollis joined them in the main room, nodding at Joseph. "What's wrong?"

Lucas steeled his expression. "What makes you think something is wrong?"

She merely hitched out her hip as she arched a brow.

"The crew's in trouble." Joseph stomped forward. "But Quinn isn't sure if he should ride out there or not."

Hollis swung her gaze to Lucas.

He huffed out a rough breath. "Reverend Miller says he saw several men ride past him towards where Cullen is working, while he was gathering some wood to carve crosses out of. But he never actually saw them attack the crew or heard any gunfire."

"I know Buford's gang when I see them, Quinn. We both know they weren't heading that way to talk."

"All I'm saying is that I only have a fraction of

information to go on." He held up his hand. "And before anyone says anything, I'd like to point out that it's not a simple dilemma."

"If Cullen's in danger..." She stepped closer to him. "There's only one answer."

"That's not what I mean." He raked a hand through his hair. "Set aside the fact I'm not sensing anything that suggests he's in danger—"

"You're not what?" Joseph arched a brow. "How would you know if he's in danger when he's miles away?"

"That's not the point." Lucas stared at her. "Cullen's not the only one I feel the need to protect."

Her chest tightened at the pained look in his face. "I'm fine."

"And it's my job to ensure you stay that way—along with the rest of the camp. Weren't you the one who said you couldn't treat people if you were the patient?"

"You would pick now to toss that back at me. But sunset's still a few hours off. And I promise I'll stay inside the clinic."

"Right. The same place I allowed a man to attack you. I feel so much better knowing that."

"Lucas. I didn't suddenly lose my ability to fight and shoot because some cowboy got in a lucky punch. If there's even a remote chance Cullen and the crew are under attack, at least one of us should go."

Lucas clenched his jaw, making the muscle jump as he glanced at the ceiling, softly counting to ten. "Since I know this isn't an argument I'll win, and because I'd never forgive myself if the reverend did, in fact, unwittingly see an impendin' attack...I'll go check it out. But you have to promise me you'll stay put. No matter what. If someone needs your help, they can come to you."

"I'll keep watch." Joseph motioned to a gun on his hip —one Hollis had never seen him wear before and definitely hadn't been holstered around his waist earlier when he'd stopped by. "Give her a hand if necessary."

Lucas' eyes narrowed before he discreetly scented the air. Color rose on his cheeks as he fisted his hands for a few moments before cursing under his breath. "See that she doesn't take any unnecessary risks." He turned to her.

She motioned to the door. "I'll be here, waitin'. I expect you both to make it back in one piece."

Lucas gave her a curt nod, looking as if he was going to give her a kiss before glancing at Miller. Her mate sighed then turned, marching out the door and down the steps. She darted to the doorway, watching mud splatter across the road as Lucas jogged to his office. He disappeared inside for a few moments, reappearing with a rifle and an extra saddlebag. He secured both on his horse then mounted, glancing back at her one more time. Hollis smiled, fighting the urge to follow when he nudged his horse into a canter. The echo of hooves died, his silhouette finally fading from sight.

A strange hollow feeling settled in her chest as she closed the door. While she had complete faith in both his and Cullen's abilities, it didn't quiet the nervous roil in her stomach. Especially knowing they wouldn't be able to access their other halves if things went sideways. Not with the crew looking on. A hand landed on her shoulder and she spun. She'd forgotten Joseph was still in the room.

She sighed, absently walking over to the window and

gazing out. "So, that's where you were heading earlier? To gather some wood?"

The floor creaked as he took a few steps toward her. "I find carvin' settles my mind. Allows me to see the bigger picture when I'm stuck on a problem."

She merely nodded. "Since when do you wear a pistol around your hips?" She glanced at him over her shoulder. "Do you even know how to use it?"

A light blush brightened his cheeks before he attempted to draw himself up. "Just because I'm a man of the cloth doesn't mean I'm any less of a man."

"I never said you were. I asked if you knew how to shoot that gun. Because you're just as likely to injure yourself as anyone else if you start challenging folks without having the skill to back it up."

"I know enough." He motioned to the window. "Is Quinn gone?"

She frowned. "You saw him ride out of town."

"Just checkin' that he didn't double back before I did this."

Joseph drew his weapon, pointing the muzzle at her. The gun shook in his grasp, but there was no mistaking the feral look in his eyes.

Hollis turned. "What the Hell do you think you're doing? Put that away before you hurt yourself."

"Sorry, Hollis, but this is for your own good. You need help seeing the bigger picture."

She arched a brow. "Did you hit your head? Eat some kind of mushroom? Because you're not making any sense." She huffed when he stood there. "And put the damn gun away. I'd rather not get shot."

"I don't want to hurt you. But I need to make sure

you'll come quietly. I promise this is for the best. Once we're settled some place new, you'll see. Quinn and James aren't good for you. They can't offer you what I can, so... move over to the door. I've got a wagon waitin'."

She glanced out the window, pieces starting to click together. "You never saw a gang, did you? You lied to get Lucas to leave."

"They're just using you."

She tamped down her anger, though half of it was directed at herself. She hadn't taken the time to put her holster back on after her romp with Lucas. A mistake she greatly regretted.

Hollis forced herself to take a slow breath. "Joseph—"

"I mean it."

He shook the weapon, backing up in what looked like an attempt to get a better angle, only to bump into a small table covered in instruments. He lost his balance, dropping the pistol as he grabbed for the surface. The gun hit the floor, discharging on impact. Pain seared along her arm, the distinctive ping of the bullet sounding behind her.

She reacted, retrieving his revolver before he had a chance to do more than stare at the increasing red patch on her sleeve. Then, she opened the chamber and dumped out the remaining bullets, glaring at the man. She didn't speak as she darted into her room and secured her holster, leaving his pistol on her table before making her way to the counter by the sink.

Joseph seemed frozen to the spot, his eyes mostly white, his hands shaking. She resisted the urge to knock him over the head, grabbing one of her blades. Her arm throbbed in response as she gently cut off the sleeve, letting the blood-soaked fabric fall to the floor. A long gash marred her biceps, dripping blood slowly down her skin.

A gasp sounded behind her before the preacher moved off to her left. "Hollis—"

"Don't!" She glared at him, noting the way he took a few quick steps back. "Of all the foolish..." She dapped some alcohol on the wound, hissing out her next breath. "If I'd had my damn pistols, you'd be full of holes, right now. What on Earth possessed you to draw on me?"

She shut down any response with another firm glare. "I suggest you get your belongings and leave. If Cullen or Lucas find you here..."

He swallowed then shook his head. "You have to come with me. Please. I'll make it up to you. I promise. We can move—"

"I don't love you, Joseph." She released a weary breath. "I didn't want to come right out and say it. Didn't want to hurt your feelings, but that's a bit of a moot point, now. So, please...leave before the men get back. Because I'm finding it hard to think up a single reason why I shouldn't simply shoot you, myself, let alone stop one of them."

Disappointment shadowed his face before he turned and stumbled to the door. It creaked as he opened it then glanced back at her before heading out. Pain clouded her vision, and she closed her eyes against the bitter sting of tears. She should have trusted her instincts. There was a reason she'd noticed his gun.

Hollis pushed the nagging thoughts aside, smearing a layer of liniment across the open sore. Another rush of pain seared across her flesh, and she cursed as she wrapped a layer of gauze around her arm, tying it as tight as she could without restricting blood flow. She'd have the change the bandages fairly regularly until the bleeding stopped. Which meant the pain wasn't going to ebb any time soon.

She glanced at the whiskey bottle tucked at the back of her supplies, cursing, again, when she realized there wasn't enough for a decent shot. Now, she'd have to go to the saloon. Irritation bunched her shoulders as she headed for the door, stopping when the thunder of hooves echoed through the wooden slab. The floorboards beneath her feet shook, making her instruments rattle across the table. She frowned. Not enough time has elapsed for Lucas to have made it all the way up the line and back. So, unless Cullen had already been on his way home...

She darted to the window, looking out as gunshots lit the air. A dozen men were gathered in the street between the clinic and the sheriff's office, each holding a weapon. One of the men urged his mount forward, doing a complete circle as he eyed anyone gathered on the street.

The guy raised his hand, waving his gun. "Rumor has it you have a doctor in your midst. I'm giving you all one minute to bring him to me before I start making patients."

Hollis cursed, glancing around the street as best she could through the glass. With most of the crew working, the majority of people left in the camp were support workers. Even Marla was caught off to one side, a box of vegetables in her arms.

The guy fired a shot into the sky, drawing a few startled screams. "Thirty seconds, Doc. Or I start shootin' at more than clouds."

Calm settled over Hollis as she checked her pistols then headed for the door. She'd spent years dealing with men like this while traveling with her father. A skill she knew she hadn't lost. The cowboys turned to stare at her as she stepped out of the clinic to stand on the porch, arms at her sides, her twin Colts visible on her hips. She didn't speak, choosing to wait until they addressed her.

The man glanced back at his companions then dismounted, letting the reins drop as he strode toward her, his gun still palmed in his hand. He nodded at her, a cruel smile twisting his lips. "Afraid we don't need a whore, right now. Though, if you give us a few minutes, that might change."

Hollis cocked her head to the side, mentally cataloging her best line of defense, as she stared at the man. "I believe you were bellowin' for the doctor?" She made a point of looking at each of his men. "Though, I don't see anyone in need of my services."

"You're the camp doctor? You?" The man laughed. "You're a woman."

"That's mighty astute of you to notice. Now, is one of your men bleedin' or not? Because I have other patients to attend to."

"If you're the doctor, how come you're bleedin'? And you're armed?"

"I'm armed because I try not to bleed. Doesn't always work out in my favor. If you're done wasting my time, Mr. ..."

"The name's Buford. Thomas Buford. And you are?"

"Dr. Chambers."

"Well, Dr. Chambers, it seems a couple of gentlemen from here got on the wrong side of a fight last night. Killed all but one of my men. Thankfully, my younger brother managed to escape, but he's not fairing so well, and I'm thinkin' he'll die if he doesn't get some kind of medical care."

She looked at his crew, again. "I don't see anyone here fitting that description."

"Poor lad wasn't strong enough to ride. Which means you need to come with me."

"And you thought you'd be able to plead your case by stormin' in here and shootin' at people?"

"You're talking to me, aren't ya?"

"Where are you keeping him?"

Buford laughed. "Do I look like a fool? We'll escort you."

"I never said I'd go."

"Suit yourself." He climbed the few short steps to the landing, stopping a couple of feet away from her. "We can shoot everyone in town, instead, if you'd like."

Hollis studied the man. If she'd learned anything from her father, it was how to judge whether a threat was real or not. And based on the look in his eyes and the cocky smile on his face, Thomas wasn't bluffing. She surveyed the crowd, again, trying to determine if any of the men or women would back her up, when a gun cocked off to her right. She glanced sideways, inwardly cursing as Joseph stood at the side of the clinic, a rifle in his hands.

He motioned to Buford. "Put the gun down and step back from the lady."

Thomas arched a brow, his lips quirking as he made a show of holstering his weapon. Then, he pulled a cigarette from his pocket and lit it, tossing the match on the ground. "So, even the preachers in this camp are armed. No wonder we haven't had much luck robbin' its supplies, other than out on the line." He took a long draw, blowing the smoke out in a ring. "I sure hope you know how to use that, or you'll be meeting your maker far sooner than you'd planned."

Joseph looked her way just as one of Buford's men moved. Hollis drew, hitting the outlaw in the arm, knocking him back in his saddle, as she cocked her other pistol, leveling it Buford's head. She held firm, ignoring the hushed murmurs, her entire focus on the men gathered before her.

Buford's smile faded as he glanced at his companion then back at her. "Mighty nice shot. Something tells me you weren't always a doctor. But you're outnumbered."

"Doesn't mean I won't take you and three or four of your men with me to the grave. Is the preacher really worth dyin' over? Besides, you kill me and your brother's a dead man." She held his gaze, knowing she really didn't have a choice. "So, which is it going to be? My help or a pine box?"

He didn't respond for several seconds before laughing. He motioned to his men to stand down then crossed his arms over his chest. "Feisty. I like it. Fine. We'll leave just as peacefully as we came as long as you come quietly."

"It'll take me a few minutes to gather my supplies."

"No. Hollis, you can't." Joseph took a step toward her then stopped. "They'll kill you."

"You let me worry about that, Reverend. You just keep the rest of these folks safe."

Buford rolled his eyes then motioned her inside. He didn't speak as he leaned against the wall, watching her put additional supplies in her bag. Her arm protested each movement, the raw wound burning beneath the gauze.

She took the time to change the dressing then dropped the bloody bandages in a bowl in the sink.

Buford glanced at the remnants of her sleeve on the floor by his feet then lifted it up. He inhaled, a feral smile curving his lips before he tossed the ripped fabric beside the bandages. "Wouldn't want the local wildlife to get attracted by all that blood, now would we?"

"I suppose not." She met his gaze. "You never know what might show up."

He grinned, leaning in close as he inhaled a second time, a flash of red showing in his eyes. "You mean like maybe a bear?"

Her breath hitched as she watched the red slowly fade into brown, a set of canines puffing out his upper lip.

He chuckled. "Did you think your friend was the only one?"

"How…"

"My brother saw the guy shift before he escaped. Not to mention the fact you reek of a scent that's clearly not yours. The kind a mate leaves behind." His mouth lifted into a smug grin. "Who'd have thought I'd find the answer to two prayers in this bloody camp town."

She did her best to school her features, praying he couldn't tell about Cullen, too. "If you know what he is to me, aren't you worried he might follow?"

"Actually, I'm counting on it. You ready?"

"If you're a shifter, then why does your brother even need help? Isn't he like you?"

"Doesn't always work that way. So, you'd best hope you can save him."

She turned, stopping when he grasped her elbow.

He leaned in close, a hint of wild animal swirling

around them. "If you're smart, you won't try anything, because I promise you, my other half isn't nearly as nice as the man."

Buford released her arm, following her out. He held her reins as she tied on her bag then mounted the closest horse. His gaze dropped to her weapons, but he didn't seem all that concerned.

The outlaw strode back to his gelding, looking more than calm when the thing reared before settling. He drew it around in a circle, glaring at the townsfolk. "If I think any of you are followin' me, I'll kill her." He nodded at his men, smiling when several of them turned and galloped off. "Stay close, Doc. We don't want you to get lost."

The horse snorted when Buford nudged it into a trot then followed after the other men. He kept his mount next to hers, seemingly indifferent to the way she glanced up the line. His words replayed in her head, but she wasn't sure what scared her more—that Lucas would follow or that Buford wanted him to.

The man waited until they'd cleared the town before looking over at her. Red flashed his eyes, again, as he nodded. "And just so you know, if George dies, so do you."

CHAPTER TWENTY-THREE

"Get more ties. I want another three hundred yards laid before we head back." Cullen moved along the line, directing the next section into place. "Weather's changing, gentlemen. We need to reach that bridge in ten days' time or we'll never beat the snow."

The men nodded, the clang of the sledgehammers on the spikes echoing around them. Cullen looked up the line. Just a few more days, and they'd reach the narrowest section, with cliffs rising on either side. Any gunman with an ounce of skill would be able to pick them off. And even though Lucas had made plans to supplement the security, Cullen couldn't shake the feeling that Buford would do everything he could to capitalize on their obvious vulnerability. Especially after what had happened the other night. Cullen had a bad feeling the situation had escalated beyond supplies and money the outlaws could steal from the line—that he and Lucas had made it personal.

Cullen ignored the way his stomach clenched at the

thought. He should have listened to Lucas and gotten a posse together to hunt the outlaw, and his men, down. Instead, Cullen felt as if he was chasing the bastard's shadow at every turn.

"Hey, boss!"

Cullen turned to acknowledge Frank.

The man pointed behind them. "Looks like Quinn's got something important to tell you."

Cullen shifted his gaze, locking it on Lucas as his mate barreled toward them, mud flying in every direction. The inklings of fear tightened Cullen's gut as he made his way toward the sheriff. It didn't take his increased connection to sense Lucas' concern or notice the firm press of his lips as he reined in his horse, sliding off the saddle before the animal had fully stopped.

Lucas tossed the reins to one of the crew, marching quickly toward Cullen. "Where are they?"

"Where's who?"

Lucas darted past him, scanning the area before glancing back. Lines creased his forehead, his increased breath misting in the cool air. "Buford's gang."

Cullen surveyed the woods encroaching on each side of the railroad. "Am I supposed to know the answer to that question?"

Lucas huffed, marching over to him. A pink flush stained his cheeks, the hard line of his mouth pinching tighter. "Reverend Miller said he saw Buford's gang ride past him on their way here. Claimed you and the crew were in danger."

"Not sure what to tell you, Lucas, but we haven't seen anyone. And I'm not sensing any danger."

"Damn it!" Lucas kicked at the mud, fisting his hands

at his side. "I knew the bastard was lyin'. He didn't smell right."

"But that doesn't make any sense. Why would he lie about an attack? It's not as if you wouldn't discover the truth once you got here."

"Like I fucking know. The guy's been actin' weird since we informed him we were taking Hollis..." The color drained from his face as he looked back the way he'd ridden. "Shit!"

Cullen snagged his arm. "Easy, mate. Talk to me."

"Isn't it obvious? He wanted me gone so he could do something to Hollis." Lucas slapped his leg as he headed back to his horse. "I wondered why the idiot was wearing a pistol."

Cullen jogged up beside him, palming Lucas' thigh after he'd climbed on his horse. "Look, I know we don't like the man, but he's a preacher. I don't think he'd hurt Hollis."

"Hurt, no. Threaten? That's completely different. Especially if he thought he was—how did he put it—saving her immortal soul. I noticed a wagon parked at the side of the clinic. Didn't think much about it, until now. Something tells me it's his, and he has no intentions of leaving alone."

"A wagon?" Cullen let the growl burning in his chest rumble free, yelling out instructions to the crew before heading for his horse. "Over my fucking dead body."

Lucas didn't answer, choosing to nudge his horse forward. He kept the animal at the fast walk until Cullen joined him, finally urging his mount into a full gallop. Cullen followed suit, riding in silence as they wound their way back. The wind chilled his face, but all he felt was the burning need beneath his skin. The way his bear clawed at his control, threatening to take over with every ragged breath.

He did his best to mollify the creature, picturing Hollis in his arms, Lucas snugged in behind her. Both their scents surrounding him. But Cullen knew he'd likely lose his fragile hold on his animal and finally show the camp who—what—he really was, if Joseph had harmed her in any way.

Lucas grunted beside him, sliding a glance his way. "You're supposed to be the calm one, remember?"

"Since when has my Kodiak ever been calmer than your grizzly?"

"I can dream, mate. But it's important we keep it together. We can't help Hollis if we're wearing fur. At least, not initially. Once we know she's safe, however..."

Cullen sighed. Whether Lucas intended it or not, he always had a way of talking Cullen down. Easing the tight feeling that lingered beneath his skin. Though it probably had something to do with the guy always being right. They needed to remain calm. Besides, all they had were suspicions. Until they knew if there was even a true threat, getting worked up was a waste of energy.

His bear snorted but settled, pulling back as they rode into the camp. They reined in their horses, jumping down amidst a spray of mud. They ignored the people gathered on the street, vaulting up the steps and into the clinic.

"Hollis!"

Cullen sighed at the fear in Lucas' voice as their mate's name seemed to echo through the empty space. The man stormed into the adjoining room, reappearing with a shake of his head. Cullen inhaled, stopping cold as her scent filled his head. Only it wasn't the usual sweet essence that wrapped around his chest, making it hard to breathe. This aroma was earthy. Metallic.

He turned, beating Lucas to the sink by a few steps. A loud roar pounded through Cullen's head as he stared at the blood-soaked bandages, some tattered fabric layered on top. The room dimmed at the edges, a warm feeling billowing up from his legs, when Lucas grabbed his shoulder.

"Breathe, Cullen."

Cullen frowned, nothing really making sense, until his mate growled, pressing his body tight to Cullen's.

"I'm scared, too, but you need to breathe, or you'll pass out on me. And I can't do this alone, mate. Just thinkin' she might... I can't."

Lucas shook him this time, breaking through the daze. Cullen gasped in a few breaths, doing his best not to throw up when the iron-tinted odor burst along his tongue. He palmed the counter, waiting for the sensation to pass before closing his eyes. Anger slowly bled through the pain, his bear surging forward.

Cullen straightened, finally looking at Lucas.

Lucas leaned in. "You back in control?"

"I wouldn't go that far, but...I'm better." He picked up the piece of her sleeve, doing his best to sift through the different aromas. "It's hard to tell for sure, because there's so much of her blood on it, but I can definitely identify two other scents. One is Miller's. The other...could be a patient's, I suppose. But it smells...odd."

Lucas took the fabric then inhaled, color flushing his cheeks as his lips pinched tight. "It's vaguely familiar—

like I've encountered a version of it before. And I smell gun powder."

"I was hoping I'd imagined that. If Miller did this, I'll kill him."

Lucas arched a brow. "Only if you beat me to him. Can you sense her? All I can tell is that she's alive."

"Same here. Our connection's getting stronger, but with her not being a shifter... It's not nearly as developed as my link to you. But I have no doubts my bear can track her."

"Mine, too. Would have been nice, though, to have had a bit more of a sense of what we'll be facing. If it's one man or ten." He swallowed with obvious effort. "How badly she's hurt."

The floor creaked behind. "It was only a graze."

They turned, staring at Joseph as he stood in the open doorway, jaw set, hands clenched around his rifle as he pointed the barrel at them.

Cullen growled. "You had better have a really good explanation for what happened here, Preacher, or I'm going to tear you apart."

"I'm the one with the rifle, James. I doubt you can draw before I fire."

"Based on the way it's shakin', you'll be lucky to hit me, even this close. The chances of you killing both of us..."

Joseph swallowed with effort, worrying his lip before shaking his head. "I just want some answers."

"So do we. Where's Hollis?"

His chin quivered for a moment as his expression fell. He motioned to the door. "Buford took her. The man came riding in here with about a dozen men. Shootin'. Yellin' for the doctor to come out or he'd kill everyone. I tried to help her, but..." He glared at them. "He said someone from town killed his men and injured his brother. That was one of you, wasn't it?"

"Buford?" Cullen glanced at Lucas. "You're sure?"

"I was standing right there when he said his name. Now, answer the question. Did you kill his men?"

Lucas inched forward, hand hovering beside the hilt of his pistol. "I did. And I won't apologize for it. They were threatening Cullen. Would have eventually killed Hollis, too, if I hadn't stopped them."

"Then, this is your fault." Joseph narrowed his eyes, sweeping his gaze the length of Lucas' body. "What's a shifter?"

Lucas blinked, inhaling roughly before wetting his lips. "A what?"

"Don't play stupid with me, Quinn. I was worried Buford would hurt her when he followed her into the clinic to get her bag, so I slowly moved over to the doorway. I heard them talking. Buford said his brother saw a man shift and that Hollis smelled funny. A scent that wasn't hers because she'd *fucked* her mate recently." He snorted. "Normally, I would have thought he was talking about Cullen, since James used that same term yesterday, but it's you, isn't it?" He glanced between them. "Or are you just taking turns? Wouldn't surprise me. And here I thought I could save her..."

Cullen moved, ducking low then lunging forward. He caught the reverend around the waist, knocking his arms up as they all stumbled backwards into the wall. The rifle fired when his hands impacted the hard surface, blowing chunks of wood down on their heads as Cullen fisted Joseph's jacket, pinning him against the wood.

"I believe I already warned you about calling our mate a whore." He leaned in close. "The only reason you're still breathing is because I want answers. Where did they take her?"

Joseph glared at him. "I don't know. They rode off. Headed northwest. He said he'd kill her if anyone followed." He looked over at Lucas as the man crowded in beside Cullen. "Except you. He wanted you to follow. Said he wanted to settle the score."

Lucas smirked. "The bastard isn't the only one out to settle a score. Did he say anything else about shifters?"

Joseph glanced between them, more white coloring his eyes. "Hollis said something about Buford being one and wondering why his brother needed a doctor. But I couldn't hear what he told her. Then, they walked outside and left."

Lucas growled then pounded his fist against the wall. "Damn it. We have to leave. Now."

"Wait. What's a shifter? I've heard of legends and folklore, but—"

"It's nothing. The man's insane. He's talking gibberish."

"Then, why would Hollis say it?"

"Because she's trying to stay alive. She knows better than to anger a madman by tell him he's imagining things." Lucas bent close. "Was Buford the one who shot her?"

Joseph looked away as his shoulders hunched. "I told you. I was trying to save her. It was an accident. I just grazed her arm."

Cullen hovered an inch from Joseph's face. "I'm only going to say this once, so you'd best listen carefully. You're going to go back to your church, pack up, and leave. And if anyone ever comes snoopin' around here because of our unconventional relationship, I will hunt you down and kill you. Is that clear?"

"You're condemning her soul to Hell. You know that, right?"

"You shot an innocent woman you'd planned on kidnappin'. If loving us is a sin, then you'll be there long before anyone else." He eased back, finally releasing the man before bending over and picking up the rifle. He opened the loading gate, collecting the rest of the bullets in his hand before shoving the empty gun at the preacher. "I meant what I said."

Joseph glanced at Lucas then turned to the door.

"And, Preacher?" Cullen motioned to the rifle. "I'd think twice about aiming that at anyone else. Your next target might not be so generous in letting you live. I know I won't if I see it pointing my way, again."

Lucas moved over to Cullen once the reverend's footsteps had faded. "That scent on her shirt? Now, I know why it's familiar. I smelled it this morning where I saw those tracks."

Cullen groaned. Fuck, he should have sensed it. Recognized the hint of human in the wild aroma. Realized that a pack of wolves hadn't just happened by.

Lucas slapped him in the shoulder. "It's not your fault. I was there, too, and I didn't catch it, either. Too damn focused on you and Hollis." He arched his brow. "But I bet I can fucking follow it, now. Pick it out of every other odor we encounter."

Cullen nodded. "From what the reverend said, it sounds as if he only thinks Hollis has one mate."

Lucas' shoulders drooped. "It was a rash decision. But she was having more of those cramps and just smelling her all wet and wanting... I'd planned on letting her sleep until you got back then having you wake her up the same way." His eyes widened then narrowed. "Shit! That must be why Joseph got the jump on her. I removed her holster, and she wasn't wearing it when I left. Damn it!"

"Easy. This wasn't your fault. And blaming ourselves isn't going to help get her back. Are her guns still in her room?"

Lucas frowned, walking into the other area then reappearing. He held up a pistol. "Hers are gone. I assume this one was Joseph's. She must have grabbed it after and clipped her belt on."

"The fact Buford let her leave with them..."

Lucas nodded. "He doesn't really see her as much of a threat. Which means at least half of his remaining men must be shifters, too. Explains why they smell similar if they're living as a pack."

"Pack or not, they aren't expectin' two men to come lookin'. We can use that to our advantage."

"I might let you take on a couple, if I feel like sharing."

"Lucas..."

"Let's go. Every moment we spend here is another she's with them. Alone."

The man didn't wait for Cullen to answer him, choosing to spin on his heel and head out the door. Cullen took one last look around, praying it wasn't the last time he'd be standing in the small room, imagining Hollis treating patients. But if they weren't successful—if anything happened to her—there was little chance they'd be back. At least, not as men.

He huffed then followed Lucas out. They didn't speak, climbing onto their horses then racing out of town. They headed northwest, clearing the camp before reining in their mounts. Lucas jumped down, slowly walking across the ground until something must have caught his attention.

He knelt, running his fingers across the soft mud. "There's a drop of Hollis' blood here. Her arm must still be oozing. And there's a cigarette butt. The thing stinks the same as the scent that was on her shirt."

"Buford."

Lucas nodded. "Looks like they're heading into the foothills. There's a stream that runs along the south ridge. Bet my ass their camp is somewhere along it."

"You got their scent memorized?"

His mate turned, eyes red, teeth showing beneath his upper lip. "Couldn't forget it if I tried."

"Then, lead the way. Hopefully, our connection will kick in more once we get close enough."

Lucas glanced at his horse then in the direction they were traveling.

Cullen sighed. "I know what you're thinkin', but... We can't risk shifting until we know what we're up against. We need to ensure she's safe, first. And as much as our bears want to save her, they also want to rip those men apart. Might be best if they didn't face them to start off."

"If anything happens to her...or you..."

"Nothing is going to happen to any of us. You heard Joseph. They need her. To treat his brother. And we can't be that far behind. We'll get her back."

Lucas released a weary breath. "Guess we're going to be taking turns talking the other back from the edge. All right. Let's ride."

They struck off, following the trail, stopping only when the scent got muddied. The sun dipped low on the horizon by the time they finally reined in their mounts at the edge of a river.

Cullen inhaled, bombarded with a multitude of aromas, all similar to the one they'd been tracking. He nudged Lucas when his mate moved in beside him. "Thinkin' we're getting close. There are way more crisscrossing scents."

"Probably be best if we left the horses here. Go in on foot the rest of the way. They only think I'm coming. It'd be a shame to lose that element of surprise by riding in there."

"Just, don't go bargin' in without a plan."

Lucas smiled. "Me? Act rash? Isn't that your forte?"

"Jackass. Fine. We'll both keep it together until we have some sort of strategy."

"Agreed." Lucas grabbed his elbow. "Unless it looks like she's in danger. If that happens…"

Cullen nodded, looping his reins around a tree. "Ready?"

His mate took off, darting amidst the brush as he followed the river. Cullen trailed behind him, constantly telling his grizzly to be patient. Regardless of what they faced, they'd end this tonight.

CHAPTER TWENTY-FOUR

"Here we are, Doc."

Hollis glanced at Buford, sliding down from her horse as the man grabbed her reins. She surveyed their camp. Several tents were scattered around a small clearing, a blazing fire flickering in the center. He had a few more men walking around the perimeter, the red flash in their eyes when their gazes clashed impossible to miss.

Buford hooked her elbow. "Feel free to leave your weapons here."

She arched a brow. "You boys really that afraid of a couple of guns? Thought you'd be stronger than that."

He snorted. "Shootin' us will only make us angry. But then, you probably know all about our kind, don't ya?" He trailed his fingers through the ends of her hair. "Does your bear mate have a name?"

"I never confirmed he was my mate."

"You don't have to. His scent says it all. Though, I'll admit you have more of those on you than most people. Guess that goes along with treating people. They all rub off on you. Makes it hard to pinpoint any particular one—except his. Like I said, fucking the man definitely imprinted it on your skin. And it won't fade like the others are starting to do."

Hollis clenched her jaw. If Buford wasn't lying, it was only a matter of time before he realized Cullen's wasn't fading, either. A fact she definitely wanted kept secret. Especially when she knew her mates would do exactly what Buford had hoped and come for her. Not that she expected any less. She'd track them to Hell and back if someone had taken them. But having both of them show up when Buford and his men were only expecting one might be the advantage they needed. While she didn't doubt how strong her mates were, going up against a gang of shifters was risky, at best. And if she wasn't armed...

Dread settled in her gut as she unclipped her belt and laid it across her saddle. She had no qualms about throwing a few punches, but this wasn't a saloon with a couple of drunken cowboys. And she knew firsthand that their strength would vastly outweigh hers.

"Easy, Doc. Don't get hysterical on us, yet. You still have a job to do."

She glared at him as she untied her bag. "That's what you think this is?" She squared her shoulders. "Where's my patient?"

"This way. And yeah. If you could have seen your face when I told you to leave your pistols here..."

She ignored the jibe, striking off toward the tents as Buford led the way. His men watched her walk across their camp, lips curled into mocking grins. She kept her expression neutral as she scanned her surroundings, mentally mapping out the area. She needed to get a gist of the layout before the sun sank completely below the horizon, or she'd likely trip later when she found an opportunity to escape. While she didn't normally run from a possible fight, she wasn't stupid. And slipping away was a far better plan than taking on a bunch of...

Damn, she didn't even know what kind of animals they were. Though, the fact they seemed to co-exist suggested they shared the same species—one that was accustomed to living in packs. Canine, maybe. Unless all shifters co-existed without bloodshed.

She groaned inwardly. She should have questioned the boys more about their kind, instead of blindly accepting what they were. Now that she thought about it, she really didn't know that much about shifters—bears included—other than they had increased senses and accelerated healing. Which meant there could be several different animal spirits hiding beneath his men's tanned skin.

Buford stopped at the tent in front of him, glancing back at her. "George is in here."

She nodded, pushing back the flap then stopping cold. "Christ." She moved quickly over to the cot, thankful the tent was tall enough she didn't have to bend over. She placed her fingers on his neck, cursing at the weak thrum beneath the tips. "How long has he been like this?"

"He managed to ride home last night. Been in here ever since."

"And you didn't think to try to get a doctor sooner? I'm actually amazed he's still alive. The amount of blood loss alone." She peeled back the thin blanket they'd tossed over him, staring at the blood-soaked cloths covering his skin. "Multiple bullet wounds."

"Three, to be exact. Leg, upper chest and his side."

She lifted one of the cloths, holding back another curse. "They're deep."

"Which is why we brought you."

"You should have gotten someone the moment he staggered into camp. This..." She shook her head. "I'm not sure how much I can help him."

Buford moved in behind her, his breath hot against her neck. "You'd best hope you can save him or it's not going to end well for either of you."

She glanced back at him. "Threatening me won't change the outcome. I can either save him or I can't. Most of that depends on how strong he is. If he can survive me treating him. Based on the fact there's no blood seeping out from beneath him, the bullets all likely still inside."

"Again, that's why you're here. Even I could stitch up a few holes. But they seem to be making him sick."

"Lead doesn't mix well with the human body. Any kind of body, really." She sighed, placing her bag on a small table beside the cot. "I need a few bowls of water and more cloths. And a bottle of whiskey. Strongest you have. I'll also need someone who's willing to help out. Hold a few items for me while I try to remove the fragments."

"I'll send someone to get you the supplies. I'll hold whatever you need."

She arched a brow. "As long as you keep your mouth shut. I can't work if you're constantly reminding me I'll die if he does."

"What's the matter, Doc? You don't like my kind of motivation?"

"You're nothing more than a bully. And despite how it

might look, cuttin' into a man's flesh isn't easy. So, either stand there quietly or get me someone who will."

Buford stared at her, his gaze traveling the length of her body before he looked over her shoulder as the tent flaps rustled behind her. "Mac. Get the lady a couple of bowls of water, some clean cloths and that whiskey from my tent."

"I believe the years of training and practicin' medicine has earned me the title of doctor. Just as your endeavors have earned you the labeling as an outlaw." She motioned to his brother. "Please stand up by his head."

"A might touchy, aren't we?"

"Perhaps I'm just tired of being judged by my gender instead of my skills. I assure you...you shouldn't underestimate either."

"You mean the way you were able to clip my man without killin' him from a good ways off?" He leaned toward her once he'd moved to the head of the cot. "Something tells me you might have earned the title of outlaw, yourself."

She probed George's injuries, deciding to tackle his upper chest, first. "The term outlaw implies you've been caught. Or at least discovered." She glanced up at him. "So, no, Mr. Buford, I was never an outlaw."

He shrugged. "Outlaw. Gunslinger. Mercenary. It's all the same to me. And there's no way you learned to shoot like that by chance."

"Guess we all have some mysteries about us." She removed her chloroform, pouring some over a piece of gauze. "Please hold this lightly over his mouth and nose until we're done."

Buford twisted his head. "That reeks."

"Would you prefer I cut into him without making sure he's asleep?"

The man glared at her, the tips of his canines peeking out beneath his lip. He did as she said, though he clearly wasn't amused by her comment. He glanced behind her, again, nodding to someone before focusing on her. "Where would you like your supplies?"

"Up here beside my instruments."

A bowl clattered off to her right as she tested George's responsiveness then turned to thank the other man, only to freeze as her gaze locked on his. Gray hair highlighted a mass of messy brown locks, more coloring his beard. Deep lines crinkled his blue eyes and the corners of his mouth, but there was no mistaking the shape of his face. The firm line of his jaw—the same one she'd stared at for sixteen years. The man narrowed his eyes, giving her the once over before taking a step back. His mouth quirked as he stood there, staring at her.

Buford cleared his throat. "Something wrong, Doc? You look paler than George."

She forced herself to swallow, nearly choking on the lump clogging her throat before shaking her head. She grabbed one of the cloths, wetting it down then twisting back to her patient. "I'm fine."

"You sure about that?"

She huffed, steadying her hands then cleaning away the blood and dirt from George's skin. "You mean besides being forced to come here and treat a man who clearly needed a doctor twelve hours ago? Or the fact you keep threatening to kill me if I don't save him? Yes, I'm sure. Hold that cloth steady. Wouldn't want your brother to wake up in the middle of me diggin' out this slug."

Hollis focused on George's wound, all too aware of the man still standing silently beside her. Years without knowing if he was alive or dead, and now, he was no more than four feet away. Though, it might as well have been a hundred for all it mattered. She'd ceased being a part of his life long before he'd left, and she doubted anything would change that, now.

She worked slowly, doing her best to minimize the blood loss as she opened up George's wound enough to remove the misshapen bullet, along with bits of his shirt and a few pieces of lead. She flushed the hole with more whiskey then stitched it closed, layering one of her salves over the incision followed by more gauze—tying it in place.

Then, she repeated the procedure with his leg, thankful that one had merely gotten stuck just beneath his skin. It wasn't until she moved to the last wound that she spared Buford a quick glance. The man's gaze clashed with hers, no hint of compassion in his eyes.

Hollis straightened, gently dabbing at the hole in George's side before using her tweezers to judge how deep the bullet had penetrated. "Slug's really deep and angling in toward his stomach. Might be best if we left this one for now. See how he does. Let him get some strength back before I do more damage than good."

Buford grabbed her wrist, clenching to the point of pain. "I know as well as the next person that he'll die of infection if you leave that in there."

"He'll likely die by my hands if I open him up enough to dig that hunk of metal out." She grunted. "Breakin' my wrist won't improve the situation any."

He growled, the sound not quite as deep as Cullen or

Lucas, but with the same gravelly tone that most likely mimicked his inner animal, then released her. He motioned to his brother. "Take it out."

She rolled her shoulders, shaking out her hand. "I really think it would be better if I left—"

"I said take it out!"

His voice resonated around them, the dark undertone coloring each word. She glanced at her patient. The man's skin was deathly white, with beads of sweat lining his brow. Chances were he already had an infection—one the whiskey and salves might not counteract.

She nodded, giving Buford a new chloroform-soaked gauze to hold over his brother's face. The last thing she needed was to have the effects wear off while she was still digging around. She reached for one of the cloths, washing the area, again, then pouring on more alcohol. George's legs twitched as she opened the wound slightly, trying to do the least amount of damage possible.

Buford grunted. "Why is he moving?"

She didn't look at the guy, focusing on her task. "Chloroform has that effect, sometimes, especially when he's been breathing it in this long. It's nothing. He's still asleep."

"You sure?"

"I've had to hold people down before from the tremors, despite the fact they weren't conscious, so, yes. I'm sure. Now, are you going to shut up and let me work, or should I just stop with your brother's guts hangin' out while you question my every move?"

He answered with a snarl but remained silent as she carefully cut her way to the bullet.

She sighed, placing the mangled slug in a bowl. "Damn

thing hit a rib. Shattered everywhere. I'll get as many pieces as I can."

She dug around, searching for the small pieces of metal and cloth before finally retreating. Despite her efforts, the wound looked even worse than before, more blood oozing down his skin.

Hollis looked over at Buford. "I need a bullet."

The man frowned. "You need what?"

"A bullet. He's bleedin' more than simply stichin' will solve. So, I need to cauterize the wound. A bullet, please."

Buford muttered under his breath but handed her the bullet. She used a small knife to separate the head, pouring the black powder into George's wound. The powder ignited with a flash when she placed a match against it, the scent of burnt flesh wafting around them.

"Bloody Hell." Buford covered his mouth. "Are you crazy?"

She leveled a glare at the man. "Do you want him to have a chance at survivin' or not?" She readied a needle. "I'll clear off some of the damaged skin and stitch the rest closed."

He watched her work, still cursing under his breath. Tension hunched her shoulders as she smeared on a couple of her salves, hoping the combined effort might increase his chances, then covered the wound with more gauze.

"You can remove that cloth, now." She stepped back, finally looking at Buford. "He needs to rest and have those bandages changed regularly. He also needs to be kept cool. A steady supply of clean water will help with that. I have some medicine I can give him once he wakes up. To help with the pain. But other than that..."

"So, he's gonna live?"

She met his questioning gaze. "I don't know. If he makes it through the night, his chances go up slightly. It all depends on whether the infection spreads or if I managed to drain it."

He snorted. "Is that your way of saying I should keep you alive? So, you can keep tendin' to his needs?"

"It's my way of saying he isn't anywhere close to walking out of here anytime soon. You might want to keep that in mind the next time you get into a shootout. Bullets have a way of killin' regular folk." She rinsed off her hands and instruments then packed up her bag, leaving a vile of clear liquid out. "You can give him a few drops of this every few hours once he wakes. Now, if you think you and your men can watch over him, I'll be on my way."

He laughed, snagging her wrist, again. "Do you really think you're walking out of here? It's not just your skills as a doctor I wanted. You're bait."

"You asked me to treat your brother, and I've done all I can. I suggest you let me ride out of here before this whole thing erupts into a bloody battle. Because it will if I'm still here when *he* shows up."

His smug smile made her clench her fists to stop from punching him. "Do you really think I'm afraid of one bear? I have ten other shifters to back me up. And in case you didn't know, a bear's one true enemy is a pack of wolves. So, don't get any romantic notions that he'll be saving you. He's coming here to die."

Fear settled hard in her gut. Eleven wolves. Even with Cullen's help, she wasn't sure if they could take on that many. She needed to get ahold of a pistol. Anything to help out.

The tent flap fluttered behind them as one of his men poked his head in. "There's a guy walking up the path. Isn't even trying to hide. Same scent as what's all over her."

Buford's smile widened. "Perfect. Let him come all the way into camp." He jerked her against him, pulling a knife from his belt as he spun her around.

Mac glared at Buford, stepping in front of him. "Thomas. What have I told you about hurting ladies? Your score is with the man outside, isn't it? You'd be wise to let her go."

"Not now, McCalister. Go join the rest of the men. We might need your marksmanship, yet." He shoved her forward with him, still holding her firmly against his chest —the blade brushing her neck. "I suggest you stay very still. Now...let's go say hello to your man."

CHAPTER TWENTY-FIVE

Lucas stopped at the edge of the clearing, sensing Buford's men flanking him—no doubt hoping to close in behind him. He estimated the outlaw had about fifteen others in the small camp, at least half of which were shifters if the strength of their scent was any indication. Not that it mattered. They were just an inconvenience he'd have to face in order to get to Hollis. One he'd deal with as soon as he knew she was all right.

He braced his feet apart, waiting for Buford to walk out. It only took a minute before the man appeared on the other side of the open space, Hollis braced against his chest—a knife poised at her throat. Lucas' grizzly roared at the sight, surging forward just enough he felt the animal's strength tense his muscles—a line of sorts. It would let him lead as long as Hollis remained unharmed. If that changed...

Not that Lucas would fight his other half. He'd already made peace with the fact he wasn't leaving there without shifting. It only came down to a matter of when.

Buford chuckled, dragging Hollis harder against him as a few of his men lined up in a lopsided arc around him. "Mr. Quinn, right? The sheriff? I should have guessed you were the man beneath the fur and claws. Why that stupid little camp has been so hard to dispense of. If I'd known you were a shifter, I would have challenged your other half months ago."

Lucas focused on Hollis, mentally telling her everything was going to be okay. He snorted when she arched a brow, silently telling him she didn't need to be coddled, she simply needed a distraction to break free. Not that he'd expected any less.

He crossed his arms over his chest, dragging his gaze to Buford. "Robbin' the company is par for the course. Raidin' the town—not gentleman-like, but nothing I didn't expect. Taking my mate against her will—holding a knife to her throat—that won't go unchallenged. Let her go, and we can settle this like men."

"Men? Is that what you told my crew last night? My brother? That you'd settle it like men?"

"They attacked us. I was only defending myself."

"Since when is killin' nearly a dozen men merely self-defense? From what George told me, you hunted the last few down while they tried to escape."

Lucas shrugged. "My mate was nearby. I couldn't chance they'd come back and harm her, now could I? You shouldn't start a fight you're not prepared to see through to the end."

"Your mate shot one of my men in the arm from twenty-five yards out without blinkin' an eye. Something tells me she's not helpless."

He grinned. "The lady has many skills. One of which I assume just saved your brother's life."

Buford sneered, yanking her against him, nicking her skin. Blood welled up along the thin line, making her wince. "That remains to be seen."

"It's a far sight better than any of you deserve. You want me..." Lucas waved his arms wide. "Standin' right here. Fur. Skin. I don't care how you want this to go down. But there's no reason to hurt her when I'm the one who shot your brother. Who killed your men."

"All the more reason to take what matters most to you."

Lucas fisted his hands, the tingling along his spine foreshadowing his impending shift. He glanced at Hollis, giving her a small nod, praying Cullen was in position, when a gun cocked behind Buford. He stared over Buford's shoulder, focusing on the older man pointing his weapon at Buford's back, the man's mouth pressed into a thin line.

The guy narrowed his eyes. "That's enough, Thomas. Even gunslingers have a code. We don't kill women or children. So, for the last time, let the lady go, then you can settle your differences with the sheriff."

Buford growled, twisting slightly to look at the guy. "Damn it, McCalister. I knew letting you tag along was a bad idea."

Lucas stilled. Had he heard Buford right? He studied the guy, noting the similar jaw line, the same blue eyes. He just didn't know if Brett McCalister recognized Hollis.

McCalister sneered at Buford. "As I recall, you came lookin' for me. And I've held my tongue while you and your brother made fools of yourselves. But I won't stand here while you use a woman as a shield. The same one who just dug three slugs out of your brother in an attempt to save his life. Ain't no honor in that." He arched his eyebrow. "I'm not going to repeat myself, again. Let her go."

"You're surrounded by almost a dozen men. Do you really think you'll still be breathin' if you pull that trigger?"

"Son, I've been doing this since long before you were born. Most men in my profession don't live long enough to forget what it was like to be young. Cocky. So, I reckon I've had my run. But if the sheriff, here, really is the man responsible for all the trouble you've been having, having me kill just a few of your defenses might tip the scales."

Buford laughed. "Well, I'll be damned. Never thought I'd live to see Brett McCalister go soft. And this from a man who's killed more than his fair share of men."

"Men, yes. You want to kill Quinn? Go right ahead. But you'll let Hollis go."

Buford stilled, glancing at Hollis then back to Brett. "I see. Well, here's the thing, Mac, I don't recall her telling us her first name. Though, that explains where she learned to shoot."

"No!"

Hollis screamed as Buford drew, stomping on his foot then knocking his elbow when he fired. Brett got off a few rounds, hitting men on either side of Buford then catching the man in the arm before falling backwards, blood blossoming on his shoulder. Lucas lunged, giving his bear full control as his paws hit the dirt, tearing through his clothes with little effort. He kicked free of his boots, charging at Buford as Hollis dropped her weight, breaking free of his hold with another slice of the knife across her shoulder. Blood soaked through her shirt, the red color sending a blaze of heat through Lucas' gut.

He calmed his mind, quickly eating up the distance between them. Shots rang out around him, a jolt of pain searing across his side. He ignored the telltale burn of the bullet, determined to get between Hollis and Buford's men. Hollis managed to gain her feet as he stopped in front of her, his fur raised along his back. He turned to roar at the outlaws gathered around him. Four were motionless on the ground, blood pooling beneath their bodies. The rest held their ground, guns drawn but standing there as if waiting for a signal.

Buford stepped in front of the others, a cruel smile twisting his lips. "You're big, I'll give you that. But let's see how you fair against a pack of wolves."

He leapt forward, shifting mid-air as his men followed suit. Lucas focused on Buford, countering the man's attack when his wolf lunged at him. Lucas rose onto his hind legs, batting at another animal when it jumped toward him, scratching a line down his chest. He landed a strike, sending the canine tumbling across the dirt.

The rest of the pack howled, moving toward him as a unified front, when another roar sounded behind them— Cullen charging into the clearing at a full run. His Kodiak joined the fight, his large size making Lucas look small in comparison. He barreled through the gathering of shifters, tearing at them with claws and teeth, seemingly indifferent to any hits they landed.

Hollis cursed behind Lucas then sprinted off toward where Brett had fallen. Lucas grunted, clamping his jaws around one of the wolves then tossing it aside before following after his mate. She skidded to a halt beside the older man, falling to her knees and grabbing one of his pistols.

She turned, smoothly cocking the gun then firing at the canines attacking Cullen, using her other hand to reset the hammer after every shot. She emptied the chamber then reached for Brett's belt, emptying a bunch of bullets onto the ground then reloading almost as fast. One of Buford's men raced toward her as she was slipping in the last bullet, teeth flashing white in the flickering firelight.

Lucas roared, catching the wolf before it reached her, knocking it sideways. It rolled then righted itself, attacking, again, when two more flanked on either side. Lucas' grizzly held its ground, countering the strikes until a howl sounded behind him. He swung around as Buford jumped onto his back, claws digging into his hide, canines locked around his shoulder.

Lucas reared, hoping to topple the wolf off him, but barely maintained his balance when the other wolves lunged at his legs, their teeth sinking through his flesh. Hollis shouted his name, a shot buzzing past him as she fired more rounds at the wolves, before a menacing growl echoed through the air. Then, Cullen was on top of them, tearing Buford off Lucas and throwing him to the ground. He downed two others then focused on Buford, baring his teeth as he stalked toward the man's wolf.

Buford snarled, backing up. The animal glanced to its left then charged, running at Hollis as she bent to reload, again. Cullen turned, muscles already tensing, when a shot rang out behind them. Buford's head snapped back, and he dropped into the mud several feet in front of

Hollis. She froze and gazed over her shoulder, eyes wide, her face bleached white. Lucas stared at her father. He'd pushed onto one elbow, his back braced against a stump as smoke curled up from another gun. Brett grunted, relaxing back as his eyes faded closed.

Lucas scanned the area, looking for the next strike, but any survivors had taken off. He took a few staggering steps forward, scenting the air—determined not to get caught by surprise—when Hollis appeared in front of him. She wrapped her arms around his neck, burying her face in his fur. She mumbled something he couldn't make out, her grip tightening before she finally pulled back.

Tears pooled in her eyes then fell, leaving dirt-smeared lines on her face as she cupped his jaw, gazing the length of his body. "Christ, you're a mess. If this is too much for your bear, you need to shift so I can treat those wounds." She chocked back a sob, grazing her fingers above some of the marks. "God, Lucas."

He nudged her with his head, trying to assess how much damage the wolves had done, when the world tilted. He blinked then realized he'd fallen onto his side, the scenery washing in and out of focus. His bear sighed, relinquishing control. He shuddered then changed, the cool feel of mud against his skin rousing him slightly.

"Lucas!" Hollis cradled his head, eyes wide, mouth pinched tight. "Cullen! I need you."

Footsteps sounded close by, then Cullen popped behind Hollis' shoulder, mud and blood caked on his skin. He reached for Lucas, arching his brow as he swept his gaze the length of Lucas' body.

Hollis clenched her jaw. "You're both crazy, you know that? Taking on a dozen shifters!" She gave Lucas a tight smile then glanced at Cullen, the smile quickly fading. "Damn it, you're not in much better shape." Indecision creased her brow as she waved at them. "Is this something your bears can fix or..."

Cullen wrapped his arm around her then frowned, drawing his hand back. "Fuck, Hollis, you're bleedin'."

She snorted. "Trust me, it's nothing compared to the two of you. Now, can his bear fix him or not?"

Lucas chuckled. "Still conscious, darlin'. And, yeah, I'll be fine. Though, I wouldn't say no to some help from my favorite doctor."

"Do you really think you can charm my anger away? You nearly died..." She closed her eyes as more tears washed down her face before looking at him, again. "We should move you to one of the tents. I can clean up your wounds—see which ones might benefit from my kind of help. You, too, Cullen."

Cullen winked at her. "Mine aren't that bad. Honestly. I'll help Lucas in, and once you're convinced he's okay, I'll shift, again. Be good as new in no time."

She didn't speak as she stood, turning to look behind her. Lucas accepted Cullen's help, leaning most of his weight against his mate, as he glanced over his shoulder. He inhaled, nudging Cullen then motioning toward where McCalister still leaned against a stump.

Hollis gave them a quick glance then walked over to the man, kneeling beside him. He opened his eyes as Lucas and Cullen stopped behind their mate, Brett's mouth turning up into a smirk.

He laughed, coughing when the simple action must have hurt. "Don't think I'll ever get used to that whole shifting thing, no matter how many times I see it.

Though, I see the advantages of being far more than just a man—even if the naked part is a draw back." He glanced at Buford's limp body. "If I'd known what Thomas was from the start..."

Hollis clenched her jaw then reached for his shirt, batting away his hands when he tried to stop her. "Just sit still, and let me have a look." She exposed his chest then tsked. "You're lucky. It hit high and went straight through. Some stitches, liniment and a few bandages, and you should be fine. You'll have to be diligent about keeping the wound clean, though."

He snagged her hand before she could pull back. "You haven't lost your touch. As quick as ever with that gun."

"You're just lucky I remember how to use a single-action. Why you're still carrying around that Colt Peacemarker I'll never know."

"I like the familiarity of it."

She nodded, helping him up. "Let's just get everyone patched up."

Cullen all but carried Lucas to the closest tent as she followed in behind them, shouldering some of her father's weight. She placed him on one of the cots then darted off, returning with her bag and a pitcher of water. She pressed a cloth against her father's wound, instructing him to hold it tight before moving over to Lucas. She hushed his every attempt to tell her he'd be fine, meticulously cleaning each cut and scrape. She smeared ointment on most of them, checking the more serious wounds for any shrapnel—removing a few pieces embedded just beneath the surface. It wasn't until she'd gone over every inch of his skin she seemed willing to ease back.

"Are you sure you can heal those gunshot wounds? The bites? I can't begin to tell you how bad they look."

Lucas smiled. "I'll be fine. Just...need to shift, again, once my bear's ready. Then rest."

"No wandering off. You and your bear will stay where I can see you, understand?"

"Yes, Doc."

She shook her finger at him, tending to Cullen, next—giving him the same thorough once over. Then, she moved back to her father. She seemed strangely detached as she cleaned, stitched then bandaged the wound, her gaze never quite meeting the other man's.

Brett glanced at the strip of white around his shoulder then up to her. "Thank you."

Her lips quirked. "Least I can do after..."

"Thomas Buford was a mean bastard. Deserved far worse than what he got."

"Then, why were you workin' with him?"

Brett shrugged. "He wasn't that crazy when he first asked me to help him and his brother out on a few train robberies. I guess I'd just gotten comfortable. But I was fixing to leave, anyway." His gaze slide to Lucas. "If that's an option."

Lucas glanced at Hollis. "I reckon your help is worth a pass—this time."

"Understood." Brett stood, slipping on his shirt. "What about George?"

Hollis looked away. "I checked on him when I got my bag. I'm afraid he's already passed on."

Brett nodded. "You did warn Thomas diggin' that last slug out wasn't a good idea. Though, that boy was dead long before you got here. His body just hadn't caught up with that fact, yet." He grabbed his hat, tipping it at them. "It was nice seeing you again, Hollis. I'm glad you've made a life for yourself."

"Not the one you'd thought I'd have."

"Nope. Better."

She held out his pistol as he walked past her. "You'll need this."

He glanced at the gun, a smile spreading across his face. "You keep it. It might not look like much, but that gun has never let me down. About time I passed it on."

He walked out, his silhouette quickly fading into the darkness.

Cullen wrapped his arms around Hollis, gently pulling her tight. "You okay, sweetheart?"

She sighed, leaning her head against his chest. "Not sure. But I'll feel a lot better when you're both not bleedin'. So...fix yourselves."

"We're not the only ones still hurt. You have a few cuts you need to treat."

She glanced at the slashes across her skin, and the wound on her arm. "I'll make you boys a deal. That cabin isn't too far from here. If you think you can ride all that way before needing to shift, I'll take a dunk in that rain barrel then see to these injuries while you both rest by the fire. Thinkin' your bears would enjoy the warmth. That way, I can keep an eye on both of you—in case your other halves get stubborn."

Lucas shuffled onto his feet, swaying a bit before gaining his balance. "Only if you agree to rest naked by the fire with us."

She laughed. "I like the way you negotiate, Sheriff.

You've got yourself a deal. Though, no crying foul when I pounce the moment you both shift back."

"Wouldn't expect any less." He welcomed her into his arms as Cullen moved in from behind, holding them both tight. "Guess we'll need to find some clothes if we're keeping skin for a while."

"I'm sure there's lots around." She cupped both of their hands, threading her fingers through theirs. "I haven't thanked you both, yet, for coming."

Cullen tucked some hair behind her ear. "Was there ever any doubt?"

"No. Doesn't mean I shouldn't thank you, though. What you did..."

Cullen glanced at Lucas, motioning him in closer until the man could wrap them both in his embrace. "Nothing we wouldn't do for you, sweetheart. Though we wouldn't argue if you managed to stay out of trouble for more than a day at a time. First, Joseph. Then, Buford. You've been busy."

He laughed when she stuck her tongue out at him, dipping down to brush his lips over hers. "Love you." He twisted to Lucas. "You, too, mate."

Hollis smiled. "I love you boys, too."

Lucas nuzzled her nose. "Good, because you're stuck with us." He gave Cullen a playful shove. "Good thing I love you two. Though, I'd rather show you both—once we're no longer bleedin'."

Cullen gave him a mock shove. "Thinkin' I get first dibs, seeing as you got to play with Hollis in the clinic while I was working."

Lucas waved his comment off. "That quick tryst

against the door gave us the upper hand. Pretty much saved our asses"

"Which is why yours is mine, first."

"That doesn't even make any sense." Lucas chuckled. "Fine. You find us some clothes, and you can do whatever you want to my ass once we're healed."

Hollis tsked, handing them each an outfit. "Guess this means your asses are mine, first."

Lucas shook his head. "Cullen. Did that sound like a challenge to you?"

Cullen tugged on the pants. "I reckon it did, mate. One that can't go unanswered."

"My thoughts exactly." He smiled at Hollis, accepting the shoulder she offered in order to help him make his way to the horses. "You'd best get some rest when you can because I have a feeling it's going to be a long night."

EPILOGUE

"Go on, Boss. Only seems right you drive in the last spike. Damn line never would have gotten finished without you."

Cullen glanced at the crew standing around him, smiling at Frank when the man offered him his sledgehammer. He grabbed the handle, enjoying the comforting weight of it. How it fit perfectly in his hand. While he'd cursed this project more than a few times, standing at the end—knowing what they'd accomplished —put it all in perspective.

He looked down the line, admiring the way the rails glinted in the setting sun. Another few days and they would have run out of time, the year's first snowfall already covering the ground. Even now, the wind whipped through the valley, swirling the top dusting of snow into the air. He exhaled, focusing on the shiny silver head half buried in the gravel.

Cullen swung the hammer, hitting the spike square on the head, sinking it into the ground. A metallic clang echoed around them, finally fading into the rumble of the train as it rolled slowly up the tracks, stopping at the waiting platform. The machine hissed as steam bellowed around the wheels, a shrill from the whistle marking their success.

The crowd cheered, clapping their hands as the first passengers exited the cars. Voices rose above the hum of the engine, another round of applause filling the air.

Cullen placed the hammer on the ground, resting against the long handle as he watched the crew interact. They hardly resembled the men who had been determined to kill each other over a poker game the previous night. Though, he hoped finishing the line would ease the tension over the next couple of days as they dismantled the camp and headed home.

Home.

He still wasn't sure what happened next. Though he'd tried to broach the subject a few times with Lucas and Hollis, they'd both just shrugged and told him they'd know what to do when the time came. While he loved their easy-going natures, he couldn't help but worry they wouldn't find a solution that met all of their needs.

"James!"

Cullen looked up, scanning the crowd until he settled on a single face. He picked up the hammer, carrying it over one shoulder as he headed for the platform, taking the stairs two at a time. He headed straight for the man, accepting the hand stretched toward him.

Mr. Gilmore beamed, shaking Cullen's hand. "Damn fine job, James. Damn fine." He shook his head. "I'll be honest. With all the problems we had on this line, I wasn't convinced even you could pull it off. Glad you proved me wrong."

"Thanks, but I'm just a part of the reason we were able to finish the spur."

Gilmore's smile widened. "Yes, I heard Quinn was quite instrumental in maintaining order and keeping the crew safe, as best he could—despite a few individuals who seemed determined to derail this operation."

A hand landed on Cullen's shoulder, a familiar scent curling around him.

Lucas stepped in beside him, leaving his hand cupped on Cullen's shoulder. "Just doing my job. Though I'd be lyin' if I didn't say I'll be happy for a reprieve from having to babysit the likes of this crew for a while."

"Well, whatever it is you did, I approve." Gilmore took a step closer. "Tell me, how did Dr. Chambers work out? With the amount of supplies you kept ordering, I half wondered if she was shootin' the men in order to make more work for herself."

Warmth spread through Cullen's chest at the mention of her name. "She's the only reason we had enough men still fit to push this railroad through. The woman deserves a medal—or at least a bonus."

"That so?" Gilmore tapped his chin. "Does that mean you two don't mind having a lady doctor in your ranks? Because I have another project I wanted to discuss with the both of you, but I hadn't secured a doctor, yet. If you'd be willin' to work with Dr. Chambers, again, that would solve my problem. If she was willin' to sign back up." He glanced around the platform. "Not sure she'll want to work in these conditions, again."

"I think you'll discover that she's far tougher than she

appears. And we wouldn't have it any other way. She's part of the team."

Gilmore arched his brow. "I see. Then, I suppose I'll have to have a chat with her. See where she was planning on heading to, next."

Cullen hooked the man's elbow when he went to turn. "Why don't we discuss the logistics on the ride home? Then, we can ask Dr. Chambers if she'd be interested."

"Very well." He took a few steps toward the railcar then looked back. "Out of curiosity...if she's *not* interested?"

"Then, you'll have to find replacements for us, as well. Like I said, she's part of the team." Cullen moved in beside him, motioning to the train. "But let's not jump the gun."

Gilmore nodded, walking with them. They spent the ride discussing another line planned for the southeastern side of the state—one he thought they'd be perfect for. Cullen shook the man's hand, again, once they'd pulled into Devil's Gate, suggesting they meet for a drink in an hour.

Lucas fell in beside him as he headed for the clinic. "So...you sure you're up for another line? This one damn near killed us."

"Next one can't nearly be as bad, not when we won't have to spend half the time fightin' our attraction, then the rest trying to convince Hollis she belongs with us."

"True, but there'll always be another Buford. Men like Joseph who don't approve of our...pairing."

Cullen paused at the bottom of the steps. "Not sure a place exists that's free from both of those threats. But at least in a camp, we'll have more control. Haven't had any issues with where we all sleep since we sent the good reverend packin'. We'll just have to be more vigilant. Encourage anyone like him to move on before it goes that far." He grinned. "My bear has a way of convincin' folks to listen to me."

Lucas laughed. "Hate to break it to you, Cullen, but it's not your bear people are afraid of." He made his way up the steps. "You think Hollis will go for it?"

"Go for what?"

Cullen jumped at the sound of her voice, tripping to a halt on the landing outside the doorway. He sighed. "Do you make a habit of eavesdroppin'?"

"Do you make a habit of talking about me behind my back?"

He smiled. "It's the only way Lucas and I ever win a discussion. We have to plan ahead."

"Then, you should have your facts straight for this one. Go for what?"

He motioned her inside, scanning the room to ensure they were alone before looping his arm around her waist and tugging her against him. Lucas moved in behind her, effectively trapping her between them.

Hollis laughed. "Must be pretty important if you're gangin' up on me like this before you've said a word. Let me guess... Mr. Gilmore offered you another job, and you're wonderin' if I'm up for the challenge?"

Cullen gawked at her. "How..." He groaned. "Have you been using your connection to spy on our thoughts?"

Her smile was the only answer he needed.

He feigned annoyance. "Dangerous, mate. Not sure we can let that one go unchallenged."

"Please, you two know damn well everything I'm

thinkin' before I think it. Besides, the not knowing was killin' me." She arched a brow. "So? Was I right?"

Lucas tsked her. "You already know you are. But the question is...do you want to spend another year in a camp like this one? I reckon the caliber of patients isn't going to change."

Hollis pursed her lips, slipping free of their embrace before pacing to the other side of the room. She looked out the window, staring at something in the street before sighing and turning to face them. "Do you know why I haven't said much about where we go next?"

Lucas glanced at Cullen, then shook his head. "Not really."

"When I walked into your office that first day, I hadn't had a home in nearly twelve years. And I sure didn't expect to find one here. But what I got—what you two gave me—was far more than that."

She pushed off the wall, slowly moving toward them. "Saying I love you... It doesn't begin to express how I feel. What you both mean to me. I don't care where we live, or if my patients are an endless string of drunken cowboys fightin' over a hidden ace of spades. As long as I get to have you—be a doctor—I'll be happy anywhere. So, if building railroads is what makes you boys feel even half as good as what being a doctor does for me, I'll spend the next fifty years following you around on these iron rails."

She paused, holding up one finger. "We do get to be together, right? No more Josephs trying to save my soul."

Cullen chuckled, pulling her into his arms, again, then tugging Lucas in behind. "We'll do our best. And of course, we'll be together. We're mates. You're stuck with us."

"I'll take my chances." She motioned to the door. "Do you two have any more supervising to do?"

"Crew has the night off. We'll start tearing everything down tomorrow. Though we are supposed to meet Mr. Gilmore in an hour."

"An hour? Guess that'll have to do." She wiggled free, walking to the door then locking it behind her.

Lucas grinned, sidling up next to Cullen. "Do we want to know why you just locked the door?"

Her smile dimmed the room. "I just figured if we were all going to get naked, might be best if no one could walk in on us. Not with what I plan to do to the two of you. Now, do me a favor, and give each other a kiss."

McKenna Buchanan stood in the middle of the street, buckskin hat tilted low over her face, oilskin jacket billowing in the strong breeze blowing eddies of dirt along the barren road. Sweat beaded her skin, the unrelenting sun glaring overhead. She blinked back the salty drops that stung her eyes, hands poised by her hips, fingers grazing the handles of her revolvers. The long shadow from the clock tower stretched out across the parched surface, the pointed roofline nearly reaching her boots. The bell rang, the mournful tone shattering the silence as people gathered along the covered walkways, gazes focused on the man who moved out from the crowd, each step kicking up more dust. He stopped several yards away from her, his mouth lifting into an arrogant smile. He glanced back at the clock then turned to her as he dragged the cigarette from between his lips, a smoky trail lingering in the air.

Noon.

He nodded at her, brushing one side of his coat back,

exposing the white handle of his gun. It gleamed in the light, the polished surface bright against the black fabric of his pants. He tossed the cigarette on the ground, crushing it beneath his boot as he readied his stance, his gaze centering on her.

He openly assessed her, shaking his head as he arched his brow. "You sure you're up for this, darlin'? Seems a shame to have to kill you, especially when I'm sure we could come to some other kind of...agreement."

"Your inability to keep your hands to yourself and your pants buckled is why we're here. All we need is someone to count to three for us."

"Have it your way, though, I'm not the kind of man who kills a defenseless woman."

"No. You'd much rather rape them and leave them for dead." She lowered one hand, palming her gun. "And I'm not defenseless."

The cowboy glared at her. "Fine. The West doesn't have room for bitches like you, anyway." He pointed to one of the men in the crowd. "Mayor. You do the honors."

The gray-haired gentleman shuffled onto the edge of the street, hat clenched between his fingers as he held it at his waist. He looked at each of them, the white in his eyes more prominent than before. "You know Ralston doesn't condone gunfights—"

"Just count to three, old man, or I'll shoot you, first."

The mayor pursed his lips, glancing at McKenna. She gave him a curt nod, shifting her focus completely to her opponent. The murmur of the crowd faded away, the bastard's presence occupying her attention. The oily hair poking out from under his hat. The shadow of stubble shading his jaw. The way his hand twitched against his gun as he snarled at her, crooked teeth beneath thin lips.

"Very well." The mayor's voice strained against the sudden howl of the wind. "One. Two. Three."

She drew, the smooth glide of the wooden handle along her palm grounding her. The weapon slipped free of the holster, a puff of smoke following the pop of the round as she fired, her hand recoiling slightly from the force. The man jolted backwards, his eyes widening in surprise as he managed to fire once before crumpling in a billow of dust. Pain flared along her arm as his bullet grazed her skin, tearing a path through her clothes. She clenched her jaw, biting back the scream that welled in her throat as she paced over to his limp body, kicking his torso—judging his response.

The mayor scurried across the road, kneeling down beside the man before turning him over. Blood darkened the caked ground, the gunman's shirt stained red. McKenna sighed, then turned, heading for her horse.

The mayor yelled after her, his footsteps sounding behind her before he fell into step with her. "That was some piece of shootin'. Never thought I'd see Will Tanner go down like that. Man must have killed a dozen or more cowboys in gunfights just like that one." He snagged her wrist, pulling her to a halt. "Where'd you learn to shoot like that?"

She glanced at her arm, waiting until the man let go before striking off again. "The West is a dangerous place—"

"Taylor. John Taylor."

She sighed. "No names, Mayor. And it only makes sense to learn how to protect yourself." She stopped at the side of her horse, checking the saddle before reaching into her pocket and handing the man some coins. "That should clean up the mess I made. I'd appreciate it if you'd see to it that Mr. Tanner gets a proper burial."

"The man was an outlaw. Might be a nice reward for killin' him if you'd be willin' to stick around."

She looked at the older man over her shoulder. "Not interested. In being a sheriff, either. I just settled a score. Besides, I thought your fine town was getting itself a Marshal."

"There's been talk, but we're still waitin'. The Marshal over in Bisbee drops in every week or so, but we could use someone like you. To keep the peace."

"Not much peace to be had these days. Men like Tanner own these parts. Think they can take whatever they want because no one's willin' to stand up to them. I suggest you use that reward money to secure yourself a sheriff worth having."

ABOUT THE AUTHOR

Author, single mother, slave to chaos—she's a jack-of-all-trades who's constantly looking for her ever elusive clone.

And don't forget to subscribe to her newsletter to get the latest scoop on new and upcoming releases as well as exclusive free reads.

https://www.subscribepage.com/krisnorris

Kris loves connecting with fellow book enthusiasts. You can find her on these social media platforms...

krisnorris.ca
contactme@krisnorris.ca

f facebook.com/kris.norris.731

twitter.com/kris_norris

instagram.com/girlnovelist

a amazon.com/author/krisnorris